FLASHBYTE
Cat Connor

For information regarding permission email the publisher at 9mmPressNZ@gmail.com, subject line: Permission.

Formatting: 9mm Press
Publisher: 9mm Press, New Zealand

First published by Rebel ePublishers, South Africa
2012
Edited by Jayne Southern

For Caleb

Memory believes before knowing re-members. Believes longer than recollects, longer than knowing even wonders.

William Faulkner (Light in August, 1932.)

Chapter One
Gotta Get Away

"You're a smarmy piece of shit," I murmured under my breath. My mouth was dry. I could barely swallow. Every nerve in my body was on edge.

I took a swig of water from my canteen. The cool liquid fought my tight dry throat until it won and forced its way down my esophagus.

"Demelza, my dear, you spoke?" Ameer's voice oozed artificial sweetness as his head turned toward me.

I shook my head and bit my tongue.

What was keeping Dion? It was supposed to be as a short recon trip. He was late and it was driving me to distraction. It wouldn't have been so bad but I was stuck with Ameer, and the greasy sonofabitch turned my gut. He expressed his views on female operatives working inside Iraq with open derision, with no regard for my position or training. It was not possible to like him less.

My eyes refocused taking my brain with them.

Heat rose from the shimmering sand. From where I stood within the thick-walled building the outside looked bright and hot.

Dion emerged from the glare as a dark silhouette against tawny-beige. My ears filled with pleas and shouting. A chill raced up my spine sending cold barbs into my bones. Wind blew grit across the open landscape. Dion blurred.

It was all wrong. Beads of icy sweat trickled down my face.

Panic rose on a tidal wave of adrenaline.

With a jolt I was awake. My damp hair coiled around my neck like a noose. It wasn't the first time I'd woken like that. I doubted it would be the last. My dreams were trying to kill me. The Freddy Kruger aspect made my skin crawl. A cell phone buzzed, loud and insistent. The display flashed, illuminating the clock on the screen.

"It's zero-four-thirty. This better be good." I shook off the remnants of the nightmarish reenactment of a past life.

"A woman was found strangled in a parking lot an hour ago." Lee paused as if collecting his thoughts.

I waited.

"She was carrying identification," he said. His voice sounded a little stressed for so early in the morning.

"Good, that will make it easier for police," I said, sitting up and turning on the bedside lamp. "I'm awake. I'll play your silly game ... who is she?"

"You," he replied.

"Nope. Don't think I've been strangled tonight. Try again."

How life mocks my waking state.

Death by dreaming.

Glad I don't live on Elm Street.

"I saw her ID. I saw what she was wearing. Her name is Gabrielle Conway. She's five foot nine inches tall, blue eyes, long blonde hair, and slim. Ellie – she's you."

"You didn't really think …" I didn't finish my sentence. A car door closed on the street outside. I scrambled out of bed and hurried down the stairs. "You're here?"

Oh my, he wasn't sure. How much like me was the other Gabrielle Conway?

"I'm here. She looks *just* like you." His footsteps crunched over the gravel. "Let me in Ellie – I have coffee."

"I'm already at the door." I closed my phone. Sliding back the security bolt and releasing the dead bolt lock were the easy bits. I grasped the door handle, lifted as I turned and pulled. The top of the door moved half an inch.

Doors that fight back are no fun.

I could have fixed the door that's annoyed me so much over the years but instead I was building a new house.

I gave the handle another twist and yanked it hard. The wood creaked and door stuck fast.

To an outsider that may seem a little extreme. Trust me, it's not. I was counting the days until Carla and I moved into our new home. Our new home was off the grid. There was no paper or internet trail leading to it. Everything had been withheld from public record. Too many bad things have happened in this house, not sure why it took me so long to move on. Maybe because it was my home with Mac. Whatever the reason, I was looking forward to a safer home and no more surprises. And a freaking front door that opened without fuss.

"Going to be long?" Lee asked from the front porch.

"Almost got it," I replied, wrenching the handle and lifting again. "Give it a little low kick, will ya?"

As his foot connected with the wood the door swung inward.

Lee wore a grim expression and held two coffee cups. The presence of two cups was an encouraging sign, indicating he thought I was okay and not dead in a parking lot.

Good to know.

"Come on in," I said. "I'll be right back." I bounded up the stairs and exchanged my pajamas for jeans. Somehow, bright orange pants emblazoned with fuchsia bunnies seemed inappropriate when discussing my death. I ditched Mac's comfortable old tee shirt for a warm sweater, pulled on a pair of socks and my sneakers. I wasn't quite awake enough for my usual cowboy boots.

Lee was sitting on the living room sofa when I emerged. I took the coffee he pushed across the table toward me.

"I'm dead?"

"Sure seemed like it," he replied. The stress in his voice suggested he'd had a rough start to the day and was pleased I was still breathing.

"Interesting," I said. "Show me the ID."

Lee passed me his phone. "In the photo folder."

"Yep, looks kinda like me."

He smiled. "That's what I thought. Now look at the pictures I took of her at the crime scene."

I scrolled through. It was uncanny how much we

looked alike. "Who'd have thought there would be two of us?"

"Obviously that was one too many for the universe," Lee said.

I chuckled. "Yep, looks like the universe is cleaning house."

Lee began to relax.

"You should've known it wasn't me. You think I'd die and not tell you?"

I couldn't see myself going quietly. Mac might have been haunting me, but I was going to spread it around and haunt the hell out of everyone in Delta A when I went. It was a pretty safe bet that I wasn't going to live to a ripe ol' age and rock out my days on a porch.

"In reality? No. I don't."

I checked my watch. "Can we get to the crime scene and back before Carla wakes up? I want to see the woman."

"If we go right now."

I scrawled a note on a piece of paper and stuck it on Carla's door. Just in case she woke up while we were gone. It said I was at a crime scene and would be back before breakfast.

"Come on," I said, taking my coffee with me.

He followed, closing the door and checking it had locked. As I hurried to his car I saw a black SUV parked behind him. It was definitely one of ours.

"Who is that?" I said, as Lee pressed a button on the key chain in his hand; the car lights flashed once and the doors unlocked.

"Christian from Delta B," he replied, opening the passenger door for me.

"And Christian is here, why?" I waved at him as I climbed into Lee's car. A hand waved back.

"I figured you'd want to go. The victim looks like you. He's here to watch over the house and Carla."

Always thinking.

"Thanks, Lee."

Twenty minutes later we were dodging police and reporters to reach the body of the woman in the parking lot. I ducked under crime scene tape which Lee lifted for me and strode across the blacktop toward a gathering of police.

"Agent Conway?"

Flicking my eyes left, I saw a police officer, his jaw drooping at the sight of me.

"Surprise! Seems I'm alive." Another cop turned around and stepped back, almost tripping when he realized who I was. "Careful," I said with a small smile. His fumbled step allowed me to get closer to the body. "What do we have?"

A detective turned to look at me, astonishment etched in lines across his face. I almost didn't recognize him. Then his face returned to normal. Detective Dave Dixon.

"You," he said with a quick smile. "Take a look, Agent Conway."

"Thanks, Dave. Don't mind if I do."

The woman lay sprawled on her back, her face turned

to the left. Long blonde hair, disheveled. She wore dark blue jeans, a long-sleeved black shirt, and cowboy boots. It's hard to tell how tall someone is when they're dead on the ground. I looked at the soles of her cowboy boots. And saw a faint number in the arch. Eight. Same size as I wore. I guesstimated we were about the same height, and that the information on her ID was accurate. She had something around her neck. A pendant maybe.

"May I?" I said.

Detective Dixon nodded. I took gloves from my jacket pocket and put them on.

Kneeling by the body, I loosened a tangled silver chain around her neck and lifted up the pendant so I could see it. A heart-shaped locket. An inch long and an inch wide at the widest point. Inside were two photographs. One was the victim with a man in jeans and a casual shirt, the other of an older man in naval uniform.

"Seen this?" I said.

Dave leaned in to look, he shook his head. "We'll look into it."

"Thanks." I listened to the body of the woman for a few minutes as Lee talked with the police. A cold shiver ran up my spine. Someone thought she was me. I looked at the photograph again. To me it looked like her and her husband; the lone man in naval whites was perhaps her father.

We had more in common than just looks.

I stood up.

"I'm done. It's pretty obvious that I am alive."

"We'll keep you posted." Dave looked at me for a beat then said, "The resemblance is uncanny. Be vigilant, Agent Conway."

I smiled. "Thanks for the concern."

I turned to walk away and then stopped. From the edge of the parking lot came a voice yelling, "Agent Ellie! Agent Ellie!" Lee tapped my arm and pointed to two police officers attempting to stop a big man from barging into the crime scene. He was hollering my name.

What the hell?

Lee and I ran toward the officers just as they took the man to the ground. As I neared I recognized him. It was Tyrone, otherwise known as Caps.

"Let him up," I said to the officer who had his knee planted in between Cap's shoulder blades. "Now."

The officer stood. "He was trying to get inside the cordon."

"I know," I replied. "We saw." Caps dusted himself off in full theatrical mode. Then he and Lee did some fandangle handshake.

"Good to see you, man," Lee said. "What's happening here?"

A cop started to talk, I silenced him. "We're talking to Tyrone. Thank you, Officer."

Both officers backed away a few feet.

Caps grinned at me. "Good ta see y'all."

"What's going on?" I said. "Walk with me." Lee and I steered Caps away from the police and the cordon.

"I heard y'all waz dead, waz comin' ta see fo' myself,"

Caps said.

He'd heard already? I glanced back at the crime scene. Media crawled like vermin spreading their plague. Some held cameras over their heads trying to get a better shot of the body.

But he'd heard already?

"Where'd you hear?"

"Five-Oh scanner, yo. Then we's heard uh breaking news report, ya' know what I'm sayin'?"

"My death was exaggerated."

"Y'all need mah help? Me an' da boys haz got y'alls back."

"It's just some shit, everything's cool. But I appreciate the offer." I shook his hand. "Someone screwed up somewhere along the line."

"Fo' shizzle my nizzle," Caps replied, nodding with wisdom that came from life on the streets.

I grinned. "You know I don't get the shizzle-frizzle-frazzle-whatever-speak, Tyrone."

He laughed and nodded and the real Tyrone emerged. "I heard you were dead."

"Yeah, me too."

"I wanted to see."

"Yeah, snap."

"You need anything, anytime, Agent Ellie, you know where we are."

"Thank you." I meant it. He'd given me shelter before and I knew, without a shadow of doubt, he'd do it again. It occurred to me then that I couldn't see Tats anywhere.

I was certain those two operated as a single unit. "Where's Tats?"

"In the car." Tyrone's mouth hardened. "He didn't want to see your body."

"Where's the car?"

Tyrone pointed down the street.

"Go tell him I'm okay," I said. "If you hear anything ... you know where I am, right?"

Tyrone was Caps again. "Meh haz y'alls number."

"Say hello to your aunt for me. She's well?"

"She's well." Caps walked away and blended into the deep pre-dawn shadows.

Dawn was fast approaching as we headed home.

A silent drive.

Once back at home I dismissed Christian and hurried inside. Carla was still asleep.

"Now you can see I'm alive, can I go back to bed?" I said to Lee, wrinkling my nose at the rapid approach of morning. Sun crept under the curtains, long spindles of light reached out across the carpet like a piano player's fingers, or knives.

"If you want. I'll just sit here and wait for the next news broadcast," he said, picking up the television remote and pressing the power button. The television sprang to life, filling the room with unreasonable bright light and horrendously cheerful chatter.

"Do we have to have that on?"

"Uh huh," he replied.

"I'm guessing there is a reason?"

"You'll see," he said. "Did you miss the hordes of journalists at that crime scene?"

No, I did not. I shrugged. They're everywhere all the time. Like a plague of rats. This morning was no different.

"Move over then ..." I told him, kicking his foot. I couldn't see the television without craning my neck from my chair so sat myself onto the couch next to Lee.

"You might want to go get your phone," Lee said.

I took my cell from my pocket and set it on the table. "Have it already."

"I meant the landline."

"It's all the way out in the hall," I replied. "Everyone knows better than to call me before my morning coffee."

The news came on. I listened as the anchorman announced the lead story. His somber voice filled my living room. "Early this morning the body of a woman was discovered in an inner-city parking lot."

Lee turned up the volume. "Prepare to answer the phone," he said. "The little journalist prick who arrived at the scene when I was there earlier refused to hand over the photographs he took and ... you'll see ..."

They went live to a reporter in DC. "Breaking news this morning is the discovery of a body believed to be that of Supervisory Special Agent Gabrielle Conway. FBI has not yet confirmed the identity. It's believed Agent Conway was strangled."

"Hang on – were we not just at the crime scene? Am I a fuc'n ghost?"

"One Mississippi, two Mississippi, three Mississippi," Lee counted aloud. As his mouth wrapped around the fourth Mississippi my phone rang, his phone rang, and the phone in the hallway rang. He grinned knowingly. I heard him tell whoever it was on his phone that I was alive and well.

The display on my cell phone told me it was Dad calling.

"I'm not dead," I said.

"I know that, kid. SAC Caine Grafton would be bashing down my door if you were. Every news service in the metropolitan area is carrying this story. I'll get Bob and we'll get onto some serious damage control over at the Foundation."

"Thanks, Dad – can you let Aidan know?"

I didn't want my brother freaking out. He now accepted my job but I knew if I told him about this situation, he'd remember all the reasons why he's always hated me being a fed. The conversation would not end well for Aidan.

"Of course. We'll need his help as a moderator anyway."

"Thanks, keep me posted. Tell the Foundation kids I'll tweet later, we'll do a video chat when I get the time and they can see for themselves that I'm alive and well."

"All right." Dad hung up.

Lee handed me the phone from the hallway. "It's Gerrard."

"Noel. Good of you to call. I'm okay, alive even," I said.

I just brim with charm.

"Oh, I know. Just seeing if you need coffee."

"Lee's already taken care of it, thanks."

"I'll catch up with you later – lunch. My treat."

"Sounds good." I hung up and leaned back into the cushions and waited for the next call. I didn't have long to wait. My cell phone buzzed and flashed. Does no one sleep past six in the freaking morning?

I answered my phone. Part of me was amused by people calling the dead. But how did Rowan hear about it? He shouldn't even be awake. "Rowan – I'm okay. It wasn't me."

His voice bundled incredulity with relief. "There are two Special Agent Gabrielle Conways?"

"No, just one. But there is, or was, another Gabrielle Conway."

"I don't need to come home early and prepare for a funeral?"

"Nope," I said as I searched my brain, trying to recall the conversation about Rowan going away and to determine where he was. It was hard for me to keep track of his tours, gigs, publicity appearances, not to mention when he was in the studio recording with his band. Such a busy life when you're a mega rock star. For someone I considered to be an important part of my life, I sucked at knowing where he was and what he was doing. I justified that by reminding myself I'm his girlfriend, not his stalker.

Another phone rang.

"I'll see you guys in a few days. Tell Carla I got her message and I'll bring her something from Japan."

Ah, Japan. That's right, some talk show to promote the new album and other promotional appearances and interviews. The new album contained a few songs Rowan and I wrote together. We'd decided not to announce my involvement with the song writing on the album; if anyone read the track information from the CD insert, they'd see my name alongside Rowan's on a few of the songs. Considering how protective and overbearing some of his fans were, it seemed like a smart move to not mention my involvement out loud. I enjoyed enough attention due to the Butterfly Foundation. It was hard enough doing my job some days and growing harder all the time. Just having Rowan around made it difficult – publicity-wise. What I needed in my life was more unwanted attention? Yeah, not so much.

"We'll see you when you get home. Have fun." I tried to recall the entire conversation about Japan and remember who was going. I thought it was Rowan, Tony, and their bitch publicist who behaved as if I were poison, or the devil incarnate. Right or not, Rowan showed no signs of listening.

Rowan said goodbye and hung up.

Lee was holding the other phone away from his ear and trying to explain to my ex-mother-in-law that I was very much alive and that she didn't need to talk to my father about planning my funeral. He motioned for me to take the phone. I leaned right back into the sofa shaking my head. It wasn't going to happen. Lee thrust it toward me. Beatrice's voice bellowed from the small white receiver. I cringed and shook my head. I'd enjoyed not having her in my life and I wasn't prepared to open that door again now.

Another news report began. This time the reporter spent time extolling my virtues as an FBI agent and a poet, then highlighting my more philanthropic ventures. They were promising an in-depth look at the Butterfly Foundation in a later broadcast. I looked at Lee and ran my thumb under my chin. He escaped the phone call from my ex-mother-in-law.

"Which station started this crap?"

Lee smiled and flipped channels. "This one," he said, stopping and putting down the remote.

I called directory assistance and they put me through to the television station. A receptionist answered.

"Yeah, this is Supervisory Special Agent Conway – put me through to your news desk."

She started to argue.

"Okay, then put me through to whoever the hell is in charge of that station. Your CEO will do," I demanded. My tone conveyed an unwillingness to listen to arguments.

"Putting you through now, ma'am."

"Gee, thanks," I said as the phone rang in my ear briefly then stopped short as a male voice spoke.

"This is Colin Scott, how may I help?"

"This is S.S.A. Conway. You can stop reporting my

death and offer a public apology to my family and colleagues."

"We report what we know, ma'am."

"Your reporters are embellishing." I signaled Lee and he started making calls. "My body was not publicly identified in that parking lot. Your reporter is an idiot."

I had a feeling it wasn't just Caps who listened in on police channels.

"That's as may be, but no one denied the identity of the woman."

"And no one noticed me talking to detectives and viewing the body half an hour ago? Amazing."

"I don't know who you are."

"I'm not discussing this any further with you. The reporter in question has caused considerable difficulty this morning by jumping to conclusions and not waiting for formal identification. Cease and desist reporting the death of Agent Conway, immediately."

"I don't know who you are ..." The insincere sleaze in his voice pissed me off. I wanted to reach down the phone and shove my badge down his throat; maybe knock out some teeth on the way.

"Have it your way," I said. "In about four minutes a bunch of federal agencies are going to be crawling all over your station. It's going to look like alphabet soup down there." I paused, letting my words sink in. "They will have the District Attorney with them. You have any idea how pissed she's going to be at being hauled out of bed because *you* can't get your facts straight?"

"Do what you have to do, Agent."

I sensed some of his smugness withering. "I shall."

I hung up and looked at Lee. "Green-light the teams. That bastard thinks he's a law unto himself. Let's introduce him to some of our friends; make sure IRS is read in." There was a smile on my face, I couldn't help it. "Ask the DA about obstruction charges, and making false declarations." I picked up my coffee. "I want everything we have on this dead woman; she has a family, and they need to know."

Lee smiled. He called our SAC, and let him give the news to the teams standing by. "Caine wants to know if you want SWAT."

I grinned. "Don't toy with me like that!"

Over the phone, Caine's laughter bounced into my ear. I would have loved SWAT, but I'd already employed overkill involving as many agencies as I could.

Reporters piss me off. I called our new media liaison, Special Agent Sandra Sinclair. She'd already heard and was heading into the office. She also gave me some information. The television station in question and the reporter who did the live feed from the crime scene, was the same one who had been harassing Carla about a month earlier. He'd followed her to school and lurked around the grounds. He'd even followed her home once or twice. Another reason we were going off the radar with our new home.

I checked my watch.

"I need to talk to Carla before she hears this."

Lee checked his watch then looked toward the hallway. "She'll be up soon to get ready for school."

We both heard an alarm clock ring.

"Speak of the devil," I commented. "I'll go start breakfast – pancakes?"

"Sounds good."

His words were laden with suspicion. It wasn't that long ago that I was renowned for my inability to make anything more than coffee. As Bob Dylan sang, 'The Times They Are A-changin.' I had a feeling that I was going to need to swim to stop myself sinking. Drowning felt like a very real possibility. Nothing I could put my finger on, just a feeling that life was more fluid than usual. Dory from *Finding Nemo* swam into view. Dammit. Not that annoying fish. I watched her innocently swim up to Bruce the shark and introduce herself. Some days it would be great to be Dory: To have a short memory and trust everyone. Ha!

I knocked on Carla's door. "Good morning. I'm making pancakes!"

She called back, "Okay, won't be long."

As I entered the kitchen, I heard Carla turn on the shower. We had a pretty good routine going, she and I. We'd settled into life as a family. Being a mom didn't come naturally to me, but Carla didn't seem to mind. My saving grace was my father. He was my catcher. His signals, combined with his ability to block my wild pitches, saved the game time and time again. Dad was only too happy to play grandpa. The times when I was called away, he moved in, so Carla had continuity of care. I'd enrolled Carla at Oakton High. Her old school was too far from home and this way my dad was handy should anything go wrong.

I scooped flour from the flour bin and beat it into the egg mixture alternately with milk. The fry pan heated. Butter sizzled.

Lee poked his head in. "Can I help?"

"Set the table," I suggested.

He also poured orange juice and located the maple syrup. Bacon cooking filled the room with the best smell ever. Carla appeared towel-drying her hair. She hugged Lee. He kissed her with affection on the top of her head. She slipped an arm around me and snagged a piece of bacon.

"Morning, sweetheart," I said, stealing back half the bacon piece and shoving it in my mouth.

She smiled and sat at the table. Sun streamed in the window, painting the scene normal.

I set plates piled with pancakes in front of Lee and Carla, then fetched mine.

Lee nudged Carla. "Ellie always cook like this?"

"Yes," she replied, drowning her pancakes in syrup.

We did breakfast. I couldn't guarantee I'd be around for dinner, so we did breakfast.

"Did you teach her?" he asked, cutting pancakes with his fork.

"Nope."

Skeptical, he looked at the forkful of pancakes. "Is it

okay to eat?"

Carla squawked with indignation, "Uncle Lee, Mom is an excellent cook!"

"The child has spoken," I added with a smirk.

"How come you're here so early?" she said, ignoring his feigned wounding.

"We have a case."

"Is it interesting?"

The phones rang.

"Yep," Lee replied, pretending he couldn't hear the persistent ringing.

I put down my fork. "The media have been reporting my death since six this morning."

"Why?"

"Because someone who looks like me, with the same name, was strangled in Washington early this morning."

Carla nodded. Her fortitude was legendary. "I'm glad you told me. It's obviously untrue." With a cheeky smile she said, "Can I have the day off to grieve?"

"Nice try, kiddo. As you can see there is no grieving required, although I'm a little hurt that you'd be over me in a single day." I smirked as I shoveled another forkful of pancakes into my mouth. "We'll drop you at school on our way into the office."

"Rats!"

"You might want to tell Joey before he hears the news. These media people are tedious and don't let up."

"There's heaps of time. He gets up ten minutes before school starts."

Lee shrugged. "He's a guy, and last time I saw him, doesn't exactly need to shave every day."

I laughed. That was true. Once a week might be pushing it.

"That's kinda mean, Uncle Lee," Carla said.

"Says the kid who called me a dork. My point is he's a guy – he'll pick up the nearest almost-clean tee shirt and jeans, shower and leave."

"And unload an entire bottle of Axe body spray," I added. "Must he marinate in the stuff?"

"I think what you're referring to, Ellie, is the smell of teen spirit."

And with that I heard Nirvana playing. I glanced around the room. The radio wasn't on. Guess they were playing just for me. 'Smells Like Teen Spirit.'

"Are you two finished being mean-spirited about my best friend?" Carla asked between syrupy mouthfuls.

"I wasn't being mean. It was a simple observation."

Carla rolled her eyes at me.

I laughed. "Anyway I happen to like Joey," I said.

"Imagine if she didn't like him," Lee added.

The phones rang again.

"Mom, *are* you going to answer that?"

"I don't think so." I ate some more, accompanied by ringing phones.

"Why are the phones all ringing like this?"

"Because everyone wants to talk to the dead," Lee replied.

"I'm super popular in death. Who knew?"

The ringing started to bug me. The house phone was flicking to the answering machine all the time. The sound of well-meaning messages irritated me even more than the phones ringing.

Chapter Two
Real Men

There were several surprised faces when I dropped Carla at school. News of my death had spread like wildfire, not so the retraction ordered by the judge. There was an incident a few Christmas's ago when a judge was abducted. Long story short, I got her back in time for Christmas and they all lived happily ever after. Except, of course, for the stinky troll who abducted the judge. He's still serving time in a Federal prison. I knew the judge – her husband is a colleague of mine. So when the DA couldn't get the television station to silence their reporter, I called my friend Judge Hartwell. Proving once again it's not what you know, so much as who you are and who you know.

I figured Carla could handle the extra attention my death brought. "I'll see you tonight. Gramps will be there after school."

She smiled. "Cool, he makes the best snacks."

"Be good," I cautioned with a smile.

"Always," Carla replied giving me a quick hug.

Carla started to walk away as words tumbled out of my mouth, fueled by the death of Gabrielle Conway and concern at how ugly things could turn.

"Honey, walk home with Joey after school. Please."

She stopped and turned back.

"Is this about you being dead?"

"Mom is paranoid. Today, please humor me."

She flashed me a quick smile. "Sure, Mom. I'll walk with Joey."

A girl called out to her as I walked back to the car; I could see them chatting their way into the school building.

The office was bubbling and seething with talk of reporters being strung up, and comeuppance for the fourth estate, when Lee and I arrived. My extreme reaction to my own death met with approval.

I live to please.

A familiar silhouette sat in a chair in front of my desk. My heart thumped with an unnatural and disturbing rhythm, fusing with the butterflies fluttering in my stomach. Special Agent Noel Gerrard was waiting in my office.

Lee went looking for Sam, Kurt – Doc as he was usually known, Sandra, and Caine. Knowing I'd want reports and a briefing.

Noel's head swiveled as I walked into the room; cool blue eyes watched me pass and sit behind my desk.

"Noel," I said. "Slow day at NCIS?"

The hint of a crooked smile lit his eyes. "No ... just not as entertaining as your day."

Two coffee cups sat on my desk. Noel never visited without coffee.

"You heard anything?"

"Yes, I have. The dead woman is the wife of a navy lawyer."

"So she married a Conway?" That made it less creepy and more like bad luck. Two navy connections in her life then. Not like me at all. I had just one, my retired naval father.

He nodded. "He was reported UA yesterday."

"Think her death is related to his disappearance?"

"We don't know yet. My people are working on it."

His response didn't surprise me. "Navy lawyer and he disappeared."

"Yes, it appears so."

"Where was he stationed?"

"Headquarters of the Judge Advocate General, Washington Navy Yard."

NCIS had their office in the Washington Navy Yard too. Busy place.

"Do we have this information?"

"Yes. The media do not."

"Good luck with that."

Noel's eyes sparkled. He was enjoying the situation way too much. "As long as they're chasing you all over the city claiming you're dead, they're leaving the real death alone."

"Awesome!"

I drank half the coffee. It was no longer scalding and cool enough to drink without burning.

"We'll hand this over to NCIS and go on with our business. I've got a few cases waiting." I tapped a pile of manila folders on my desk. "Might even get through some of these."

I stood up and followed Gerrard to my closed office door. His hand rested on the door handle as he turned to me. "You free for dinner?"

Thought we had lunch plans.

"Not lunch then?"

"This case is going to keep me busy – I can get away for dinner though."

"My place. Come have dinner with Carla and me. She'll enjoy that."

He leaned so close I could smell his cologne and feel the heat rise from his skin. "What about her mom, will she enjoy it?"

"We'll see."

He tossed me a smile and left. Lee straightaway filled the void left in the room.

"This isn't our case, is it?" He lowered himself into the empty chair.

"Nope. NCIS."

"Good. Want the briefing on the television station?"

"Sure, fill me in."

I sat back behind my desk, Lee perched on his, making the wood creak and started talking. "They kicked and screamed a lot about freedom of speech. The DA waded in with facts. You're not dead. They lied. We also hit the station with a harassment notice. Fairfax Police Department came through with files showing Carla was harassed. The DA and Judge Hartwell insisted that the reporting of your unverified death was an escalation of the harassment."

"Nice."

"Looks like they all had some fun making the station

apologize."

"Great. Now these ..." I said, tapping the pile of files next to me. "We have work to do."

I thumbed through the first folder and didn't quite understand how it came to be on my desk. I showed it to Lee. "Seen this?"

He had a look, shaking his head. "We investigate car theft now?"

"Looks that way." I flipped through a few other files. "We also have a string of bank robberies, a murder, possible abduction, and someone selling the Jefferson Monument. He's sold it four times so far this year."

"Enterprising of him," Lee said.

I spread the file across my desk. "Call Sam and Kurt in here."

Lee stuck his head out the door and whistled. Moments later Sam ambled in. No Kurt.

"Where's Doc?"

Sam shrugged his broad shoulders. "Think he was called out."

"Okay, just us then." I waved my hand over the fanned-out pile of manila files. "Today's selection – we're picking blind."

Chapter Three
Bank Robber

I have this knack for picking interesting cases, even blind. It makes up for my knack in picking the slowest checkout at every store I've ever been in.

What thrilled me the most about the case I pulled was that the last bank hold-up was about ten minutes away from my brand new, almost-finished house. Traffic was minimal so I figured a quick stop to see the progress wouldn't hurt.

Later.

Work first.

I pulled into a parking lot outside the bank and took a moment to read the file I had with me. The robbery was the latest in a string of bank robberies across Northern Virginia. What was intriguing was the small amount of cash that was actually stolen at each bank. The main safes were on time locks and could not be opened. I had a feeling the robbers knew that.

Seven banks robbed and only one hundred thousand dollars taken, give or take some change. Why didn't they go after the safe contents? Why settle for a pittance when a fortune was waiting? The file contained nothing that helped me understand the robberies. Guess that's why it landed on my desk. All the robberies took place after three in the afternoon. Perhaps they weren't morning people.

I pulled my laptop from its bag on the passenger seat and fired it up. It took just a few seconds for me to open a map program I liked to use. I plotted the list of bank robberies and times on the map. A pretty pattern emerged. I saved the map, shut down the laptop, and put it back into the carry case.

Something niggled at me. I called the office.

"Can you pull up the case work on the current bank robberies?" I waited.

"Got it," Sandra replied.

"Did we get all the call data from the bank phones, incoming and outgoing?"

"Yes and no. All but the most recent bank."

"Grab that for me. While you're at it, put a trace on all phone activity to and from the manager's office. Include her cell phone." The niggle continued. "I want you to look for the same phone number appearing prior to all the bank robberies."

"You sure?"

"Humor me."

I straightened my shirt, adjusted my jacket, and checked my makeup in the mirror. Acceptable. Once inside the bank I located the manager.

"SSA Conway, ma'am. I'd like to ask you some questions regarding yesterday's bank robbery." I extended my hand.

"Madeline White. Come into my office," she said with a sharp glance at the teller nearest her.

I don't know what the young woman did wrong but

that was stinkeye if ever I've seen it. I followed the manager through a door that locked behind us. The corridor was wide with off-white painted walls, which made it light, but it was unnerving knowing the door had locked behind me. I followed the woman up a flight of stairs. She held open a glass door and ushered me in. I could see out into the bank through a large window.

"Have a seat, Agent Conway."

I smiled and sat.

"Were you here yesterday?" I said.

My phone rang. I flew an apologetic smile and answered the call. "Conway."

"Mom, you got a parcel."

"Carla, school?"

"Half day."

"I'm working, honey. I'll be home later. Grandpa can take care of it."

"Whoops, sorry," she said. The smile I loved so much was evident in her voice. "See you later."

The line went dead. I pocketed my phone.

"Sorry. Teenager."

Madeline smiled and nodded. She spun a picture on her desk to face me. Her and two girls; they looked about Carla's age. Fourteen.

"Twins? Brave woman," I commented. "It must be expensive with twin girls. Goodness. One is bad enough."

"Very. It seems nothing lasts these days and they *need* everything." She put the photo back where it was before. "And yes, I was here yesterday during the robbery. I called the police."

"Could you have opened the safe?"

"Yes, I can override the time lock. In fact, I am the only one who can."

"Who knows that?"

"All my staff."

"Is it the same in most banks?"

"I couldn't say. It's how I run this branch. There have been times when being able to override the time lock is a good thing. Sometimes a special customer requires more cash than we have available on the floor."

"Can you give me your version of yesterday's events?"

She nodded and picked up the telephone receiver on her desk. "Could we have coffee, please?"

I couldn't hear the reply and she hung up. My head filled with The Clash singing 'Bank Robber.'

"We might need refreshments. It was quite a day."

Moments later there was a knock on the glass door and a man appeared carrying a laden tray. He set it upon Madeline's desk then left. She poured the coffee then began the tale of woe.

"We'd had a quiet morning. Typical Tuesday really. Nothing exceptional at all. One of the tellers went home mid-morning with a migraine."

"May I have the teller's name please?"

"I can do better than that," she said. From a file drawer beside her desk she took an employee file and handed it to me. "This is Marjorie's file. You'll see she has suffered from migraines for as long as she's been employed by us."

"Twenty-one years. That's impressive." I read the file. There was nothing exceptional about Marjorie Smith at all, except she'd lost a sister six months earlier in a drowning. Marjorie had taken a few weeks bereavement leave during which time she moved house. I found her sister's address in the file and saw that Marjorie had moved into her sister's house after her death. I jotted a few notes into my notebook. People have a way of surprising me. I'm not much of a one for surprises.

The parcel. I hadn't ordered anything and I had long given up on the parcel I'd sent to Carla from New Zealand, months ago.

I flipped back to the task at hand and returned the file to Madeline.

"So after Marjorie went home?"

"Business as usual. I took my lunch break at two, was back here by two-thirty. It was just after three-thirty when the robbery took place."

"Did you go down to the bank floor?"

"Yes. I most certainly did. I pressed the panic button up here then went down. They're my people and I am responsible for their wellbeing."

"How many men were there?"

"Three."

I said men and she didn't dispute it, or correct me. As far as we know there were three people wearing bulky jackets, sex undetermined.

"Had you seen any of them before?"

"No. They wore ski masks and padded, big jackets."

"You are quite sure? None of them had been into the bank – say late last week, or even today?"

"I went over old surveillance tapes last night. I couldn't see anyone who looked like any of them. But all I had to go on were eyes and height."

"Do we have copies of those tapes?"

"Yes. I gave the police copies right away."

I liked her. She was smart. She was brave. She was super helpful and nice. She was in on the robbery. My brain wriggled about in my skull trying to figure out where that came from. I could hear the music again, only it wasn't The Clash. It was 'Cold as Ice' by Bobby Ray. If I needed further confirmation, then this song was it. They were together like glue. They got together with a crew. An overriding feeling emerged, pushed forward by Bobby Ray's lyrics. It was a mom-and-pop operation. Crapola.

"Did you manage to get any dye packs into the money?"

She shook her head. "No, they were too quick. We didn't have time. They shoved bags at one teller at a time, two men watched everyone else, and one watched the teller filling the bag."

"I see. Where was your guard?"

"He wasn't on the floor. He was found later in the bathroom. A door had jammed."

"That was unfortunate."

"Yes. Yes, it was."

Bobby Ray rapped with ever-increasing volume. I too had the impression she was as cold as ice.

"I'm sure you are aware that yours was the seventh bank robbery in as many weeks?" She nodded. "The robbers themselves aren't very smart. None of the robberies have netted large cash amounts."

"They haven't been caught. I would imagine that makes them quite clever," she replied. A small smirk turned her lips upward then faded.

"I suppose taking smaller amounts and spending short amounts of time in each bank, means there is less likelihood of tracking devices being attached to the money or dye packs."

She nodded her approval. "And I believe no one has been injured."

My phone buzzed. An incoming text. I glanced at the screen and saw it was from Sandra. She confirmed phone calls made to Madeline White prior to each robbery from a disposable cell phone. Interesting. My attention reverted to Madeline and her last comment.

"Yes, that's right. But it's only a matter of time before someone is shot and killed. These things have a way of escalating."

She fidgeted.

"I've seen it before. People running about with guns demanding money. Sooner or later it ends in death and a very, very long prison sentence." I leaned back.

The Clash came back overpowering Bobby Ray, the volume intensifying.

"It'd be much better to resolve this now before more lives are ruined." I leveled my eyes at hers. Making damn sure she knew I knew. "Don't you think?"

"I can see how that would be best."

The songs switched back and forth from The Clash's 'Bank Robber' to Bobby Ray's 'Cold as Ice' until I wanted to scream, then as if they realized, it suddenly all stopped. Slowly, quietly, in the background The Clash insisted daddy was a bank robber.

"Your husband? Is he in banking?"

"No." She shook her head. "He's a teacher."

The map unfolded in my mind allowing me to track back from all the banks to one common point. A high school. I wrote a few notes in my notebook. Then with the utmost confidence I said, "When did you decide to start robbing banks?"

She blinked. Her mouth opened. Closed. Opened. No words came out.

In the end she said, "I. Don't. Rob. Banks." That's right she doesn't. She has minions. A crew.

"Sorry, my mistake." I wrote more notes and without looking up, I asked, "When did you start planning robberies for your husband?" My eyes jumped from the page to her face, catching a telltale flicker of guilt.

"I don't know what you are talking about."

"I think you do." I watched her desperate attempt to remain poised. "I'm going to give you a minute to think things over."

I stood up, leaving my pen on the chair, out of sight to Madeline behind her expansive desk. I stepped out of the office pulling the door shut behind me. I sent a text to

Sandra telling her to activate the trace and that there was a bug in the room. I dialed the pen's number. Feeling every bit like James Bond. Then hit record on my phone. The number Madeline called popped onto my screen. I sent it to Sandra. She confirmed it as the pre-paid cell phone she'd discovered.

I listened to Madeline's conversation, delighting in the joy of super technology that meant I could hear her husband too. Not as clear as Madeline, but loud enough that I could understand every word.

To the assistant sitting behind her desk beyond another glass door, it looked like I was on the phone. Not that she cared. She never once looked up.

"The FBI is here. They know. I don't know how," Madeline rasped into the phone.

"Frank and Julio, one of them talked?" her husband suggested. Fear trickled through his voice.

"I've never met them. Did you tell them about me?" Panic edged in and made me smile.

"No." He sounded sure. "The FBI doesn't really know."

"You're not here. This agent knows."

I held my breath waiting for one of them to mention the bank jobs. If it was a movie, they'd be that stupid. I needed life to imitate art. I use the term art loosely.

"What does the agent know?"

Bingo. Oh, please be that stupid. Please.

"She asked me outright if I was planning robberies for you."

Silence.

"Just don't tell her anything. They'll never get anything to stick. Suspicion is one thing, proving it is another."

My breath caught in my throat. I feared the moment was lost.

"We did too many banks. The risk goes up with each robbery."

I swallowed and controlled the growing smile on my face.

"All right we'll stop. We'll pull next week's job this afternoon. They won't expect that. We'll hit University Drive today."

"We're going to jail, Howard. Who will take care of the children?"

"You knew the risk." His voice sharpened. "You knew."

She hung up.

I called Sandra. I didn't care who heard me.

"How many banks are on University Drive, Fairfax?"

"One second ..." I could hear Sandra's fingers on her keyboard. "Checking a list of banks and looking for those that have brick and mortar branches on University Drive." She cleared her throat. "Four. Continental Federal Savings Bank, Provident Bank of Maryland, SunTrust, and United Bank."

The names rolled around in my skull. One by one they came forward and faded away. I was left with just one. SunTrust.

"How spread out are the banks?"

"Three are close; SunTrust and Continental are in the same building with other businesses. Provident is nearby,

United is in the only one apart; it's at 4400."

It would make sense for it to be the bank that was furthest from the others yet I felt very strongly that it wasn't that bank.

"SunTrust. Get agents inside now, have them pose as customers. I want SWAT on site, standing by. Get agents in Continental too. If they're in the same building they could hit both at once. Also, notify the other banks on University Drive and get police and agents into all of them. Go."

Just in case.

I walked back into Madeline's office and sat down while palming the pen. I switched off and pocketed the pen without her noticing. A small smile crossed my lips. She was nervous.

"I hope this string of robberies ceases," I said.

"So do I, Agent Conway." Her poise returned. "Wasn't it you I saw on the news this morning? The report of your death appears to have been exaggerated."

"Reporters and hyperbole go hand in hand I'm afraid. They can really ruin a person's day."

"Do you have more questions?"

"No. I thought we'd just wait together."

"Wait?" She glanced at her watch.

"Do you have somewhere to be?"

She shook her head. "No, that's fine. What are we waiting for?"

I shrugged. I was happy to provide her with an alibi while her husband robbed another bank.

"Does your husband ever visit you at work?"

"He has once or twice. It's not the norm."

"So staff wouldn't recognize him?"

"Probably not."

I added today's bank job to the list of the other robbed banks. Once finished I passed her my notebook.

"Any of your employees ever work in these banks?"

I watched her eyes move down the list. Her head shook until she reached the last bank. Color faded from her face.

"That bank hasn't been robbed," she said as her voice crumbled.

I checked my watch which caused a map to unfurl in my mind. All the robberies happened in the afternoon. Flags on the map indicated banks that had already been robbed. Times appeared on the map. I calculated the likely starting point from the times and, if I was right, then I had an approximate time for the next robbery. Flags, strings, times, and pins; my mind map was crowded.

"Yes, I know, but in ten minutes it will be."

She moved to grab her phone. I intercepted and proceeded to remove the desk top phone and her cell phone.

"I can't have you sending some pre-arranged signal and risking lives."

She slumped in her chair.

The wait for the confirmation phone call was almost unbearable. The Clash launched into 'Bank Robber' all over again. Used to be a song I liked.

My cell phone rang, disrupting the outer silence and

piercing the inner concert with a violent clattering.

"Conway."

"Sandra here. We have just arrested Howard White and two high school students."

"Thank you."

I hung up, stood up, and took my handcuffs from my belt.

"Madeline White, you are under arrest for your part in planning eight bank robberies and the corruption of minors."

She stood.

I searched her for weapons and handcuffed her before leading her from the room and building.

The drive to the office was delightful in its silence. No inner concerts. No talking.

It took two hours to get Madeline's written statement, and another hour to write up my notes and hand over the case to the legal department for prosecution.

Carla called me.

"Mom, are you done?"

"Yep. Just coming. Do you want to go see the house tonight?"

She squealed. "Yes!"

Before I left I remembered I hadn't tweeted all day. It's not an addiction. It's a tool. I took my phone and sent a tweet.

EllieConwaySA: *Wrapping up a long day. Text from Super Girl says I have mail. #wheresmymail*

Within seconds I had a reply from another Twitter

friend.

JoanneJ: *@EllieConwaySA Amazing. Do you think that could be the missing package? #wheresmymail*

I replied: *@joanneJ I doubt it. But that sure would be nice! Going home now #wheresmymail*

JoanneJ said: *@EllieConwaySA Have a good night. Hope it is the missing package. #wheresmymail*

I scrolled through any *@mentions* looking for any that needed a response. There were a few from Foundation kids. I replied to those. Then sent a general tweet saying reports of my death were greatly embellished then called it a night, before I found myself replying to tweets all night and never made it home.

Chapter Four
Return To Sender

Elvis gyrated across the stage that was once my mind. I enjoyed his song choice for about five minutes. When 'Return to Sender' started again, I began to feel uneasy. Carla hadn't mentioned the parcel when she called back. During the drive from the city I had almost forgotten about it. My memory was jogged by an Elvis interlude and that didn't feel like a happy coincidence. As much as I enjoyed Elvis, his appearances inside my skull were often omens. Not good ones either.

I pulled into the 7-Eleven knowing we'd need milk, bananas, peanut butter, and bread. It was an attempt at an everyday task to bring my focus back to now and it didn't hurt that Elvis helped me remember what we were short of at home.

A sharp crack from behind sent glass raining down on me. Little shiny pieces of the back windshield fell into my hair and dropped into my lap. It took a moment to register what had happened. There was no jolt, no other car hit me. Traffic noise from the nearby streets made it hard to hear what was going on around me. I took a breath and filtered out all distractions. Another more familiar noise followed, and more glass. There were two holes in the front windshield. Cracks radiated outward, causing the windshield to resemble crazy paving. I shrank down in the seat and released my Glock from its holster. Peering between the front seats, I saw remnants of the back windshield hanging in the frame. I grabbed the radio and opened a channel.

"Break-Break. This is SSA Conway. Shots fired. Officer needs backup. 7-Eleven 9511 Blake Lane. Over."

"Go for Conway. This is Officer Konstram, I'm two minutes away. Over."

As I depressed the button to reply, another shot rang out. The passenger side-window blew all over the car interior.

I dropped the radio and opened my door. Josh Konstram's voice followed me as I slipped out the car, "Agent under fire. All cars. Agent under fire."

I could hear the radio going nuts. I wasn't going back in to answer it. I was much safer outside using the car body as a shield. I yelled into the store. "Get down, there's a gunman!" People who had been standing there, bewildered, dove for cover.

My phone rang. I scanned for the shooter. Another car near me was hit with several rounds. A bullet lodged in the front of the building; moments later one of the plate-glass windows shattered and fell inward. I had no target and it was frustrating not being able to shoot back.

My phone was still ringing.

I saw police lights.

It seemed that my phone wasn't going to stop. I ducked lower, crouching as close to the ground as I could, by the hood of my car and hit the speaker button.

"Conway?" Kurt said.

"Doc, where are you?"

"Coming around the back of the building by the dumpster."

"I think the shooter is in the parking lot across the road, maybe in a car." I said and disconnected.

Sirens screamed, bouncing off the building and deafening me. Lights flashed, police cars converged on the area. I wanted to move. I heard a whistle from behind me. When I glanced back I saw Doc peering around the corner of the building.

Another shower of glass rained down upon me. A bullet went flying through what was left of my front windshield and into another of the store windows behind me. Time to move. People inside were strewn with glass fragments. I scrambled up and ran to Doc. He grabbed my arm and pulled me behind him. I leaned on the wall and holstered my gun.

"You hurt?" he said.

I shook my head, sending fragments of safety glass scattering from my hair. Not hurt but having a bit of trouble dealing with the excessive adrenaline. Jacked. Jazzed. Bit shaky. Blood rushed through my body at an alarming rate. I wasn't sure if being so close to Kurt was helping or not.

As we listened we heard gunfire, return volleys, and finally a police officer called out, "We got him."

Kurt and I headed across the street. There was no traffic. I looked down the street to the intersection and saw police blocking Lee Highway from a hundred yards in either direction. Blake Lane was also blocked by police cars, about a hundred yards up from the 7-Eleven. Police had secured the gas station next door. Officers ran past us into the store to check on patrons.

"Shouldn't you go do your doctor thing?" I said to Kurt.

"I will in a minute," he replied.

Josh Konstram stepped into my path. "You okay?"

"Yep, thank you," I said, shaking his hand.

"Drinks on you?"

"Hell, yes. Where is he?"

"Found him in the trunk of that brown Chevy Caprice. He went all Beltway Sniper ... must've fancied himself as a white John Allen Muhammad."

"Alive?"

"No."

"Damn, would've been nice to know if it was me he was shooting at, or if this was a random act of crazy."

"Sorry, Ellie," Josh said. "Glad you're okay."

Guess a gunman in Northern Virginia opening fire on a store parking lot elicited a certain predetermined response level, and rightly so too. No one wanted history to repeat itself and I didn't want anyone to tell my daughter I was shot when buying peanut butter.

Doc and I had a look in the trunk of the Chevy. The shooter was well set up; he'd been shooting from within the trunk, just like the Beltway Snipers. The Bushmaster he'd been firing was on the ground. I looked at the lid of the trunk, where there was a hole. From the positioning of the gun on the ground, it appeared as though he'd had part of the barrel poking out of the hole when the police opened the trunk.

"Same gun as the Beltway Snipers used," I said. "No wonder my car looks like Swiss cheese."

Doc inspected the wounds in the sniper's head and the brain matter dripping all over the trunk interior.

"There are some good shooters in Fairfax PD," he said.

Luckily.

"How could he see to shoot?"

Doc looked at me then at the trunk. "Let's find out." From his pocket he pulled two pairs of latex gloves. We put them on and began a thorough inspection of the trunk. A messy business.

"Look," I said, wiping blood off a five-inch rectangular piece of plastic, about a half inch thick. Velcro on it matched a Velcro rectangle on the inside of the trunk lid. I turned the black plastic over in my hand. It was a screen. "There must be a wireless camera."

Doc was already inspecting the outside of the car.

"Reversing camera here in the bumper. He just had to line up the car and wait."

I turned it over in my hand. "So he had a movable GPS unit that doubled as a reversing camera. That's somewhat more advanced than the Beltway Sniper set up."

"Yes," Doc said, pulling off his gloves.

"Hey, Josh – check this out and bring an evidence bag," I called out to Josh Konstram who was talking to several officers. He hurried over to his car then ran to us.

"You might be able to retrace his movements through this GPS," I said, showing him the screen in my hand. "We're lucky it wasn't hit by any bullets."

"That's a GPS?"

"Yep, and a screen for the reversing camera in his bumper, and if it's the model I think it is, that camera also has night vision."

"Good stuff," Josh replied opening the bag for me to slide the screen inside. "I'll hand it over to our lab and see what data can be pulled from it."

"Excellent." I pulled off my gloves and looked at Doc. "We done?"

Doc nodded and took the gloves from my hand and pulled off his, over them, creating a tight ball of soiled gloves. "Let's go find out where that blood on your sleeve is coming from."

"Do what?" I replied as he took my left arm and turned me back toward the road. Ambulances had rolled in; paramedics were treating people from the store. I imagined there were a few nasty cuts.

"I'll be in touch, Ellie, when we find out why this guy was shooting," Josh called. "Murphy's next weekend. You're paying."

I grinned. "You're on."

Doc came to a standstill by the open rear doors of an ambulance. "Up you go," he said.

"No need," I said. "I'm okay."

He smiled. It was more an indulgent here-we-go-again smile than a real one. "You're okay, but I still need to look at your arm."

That was the first time I thought I should see what he was talking about. I looked at my right arm, it was fine. Doc was still holding my left arm and kinda tight at that, I looked at his hand and saw blood oozing through his fingers. Oh.

"All right then," I said, climbing into the ambulance with him. Doc dropped the ball of gloves into the biohazard trash.

A paramedic spoke, "Fresh gloves are right beside you."

"Don't need them, but I do need water and then antiseptic hand cleanser."

She passed Doc a bottle of water. He jumped out of the ambulance and washed his hands by pouring water all over them. Little rivers of red ran from his fingers.

When he climbed back in she took the bottle from him and pointed to a dispenser. Doc squirted a big glob onto his hands and worked it all over with care. I watched with fascination.

The paramedic donned gloves. "I'll assist."

Doc smiled; it was so fast I almost missed it. "Excellent. Scissors."

She handed him scissors. Doc cut away my sleeve revealing a small gash in my upper arm. It wasn't more than an inch long. Nothing to worry about at all. He poked and prodded for a bit and declared it free of glass. I just sat there watching, pretending it didn't hurt, as he poked at the open wound.

Doc asked the paramedic for local anesthetic.

"Can't you glue it?" I asked, not relishing the prospect of stitches.

"No, it's too big," Doc replied and pulled the cap off a syringe with his teeth.

I took a breath and thought about happy things while he stuck the needle in my arm and around the cut. It stung. While Doc stitched, the paramedic combed glass from my hair and checked for any hidden cuts.

Twenty minutes later I had ten neat stitches in my arm and a waterproof dressing over the top.

"Can we get my stuff out of my car now?" I said. Going home with a mangled shirt was not an option.

"Yes. Your arm feel okay?"

"Yes, thank you."

I thanked the paramedic who assisted us. We took everything of mine from my car. I stood behind Doc and changed into a clean shirt from my go-bag before anyone noticed what I was doing, then followed him down past the building to his car on a neighboring street.

"I'll take you home."

"Let's not mention this to Carla," I said.

"I won't."

I flipped on the radio; listening to music helped me think, and listening to music we could both hear made me feel less like a freak.

My thoughts didn't go far past Doc riding to my rescue. I stole a glance at him. He was tapping his right hand on the steering wheel in time to the song on the radio.

His left elbow rested on the windowsill, his hand rested on the wheel. Relaxed.

No one had been shooting at him. The windows of his car didn't implode while he was sitting in it. My heart raced. I felt jittery, like my insides were liquefying.

He looked over and smiled. "All right?"

"I think so."

"Jacked?"

I looked at my hands. They were shaking.

"Little bit."

Doc grinned. "Deep slow breaths. Concentrate on now."

"I know what to do," I snapped and instantly regretted my impatient tone. "Sorry, didn't mean to sound so—"

"It's okay. Don't think about it, just breathe."

Ten minutes later Doc parked in my driveway behind Mac's truck. The driveway ran up the side of the house from the road and my front door overlooked the drive rather than the street.

My driveway was once intended to be a cul-de-sac, but Mac had bought up the parcels of land behind ours and on the other side of the driveway. That put an end to the developer's smart idea of building townhouses close to us, and the cul-de-sac plan. We left the land we'd purchased in its natural wooded state.

"You use the truck?" Doc asked.

"Sometimes." I intended to clean it, which is why it was sitting on the driveway and not in the garage.

I glanced at the front porch. No parcel. We both sat for

a second. My brain expected more gun shots. When none came I figured it was safe enough to go inside.

The living room curtain twitched and Carla's smiling face appeared. She waved. I waved back and climbed out of the car, taking all my stuff with me and said goodbye to Doc. He backed out of the driveway while I walked to the front door. I gave the door a kick as I twisted the handle and pushed. I slid my bag to the ground and tried again, the door popped open. Every time I had to wrestle the front door, I thought about the joy of moving to our new home with non-sticky doors. Before I shut out the world, something beyond the driveway caught my eye. My eyes traveled over the grass and into the scraggly dogwoods that grew at the edge of the woods. A red deer grazed among the dogwood and young oaks. Carla bounced toward me from inside the house.

"Mom! How was your day?"

The deer looked up and disappeared. I closed the door and gathered my stuff.

"Pretty good, Carla. How was yours?" Her arm linked mine, as we walked down the hall to the kitchen.

"Everyone was asking if I was okay." She rolled her eyes and sighed. "I spent all morning explaining it wasn't you who was dead."

"Sorry." I dropped my bag and everything else on the counter and poured a drink of water. "We'll get over to the house; I just need to grab a sandwich. You hungry?" I took a slice of bread from the bag on the counter and spread it thick with butter. Carla watched as I took a bite.

"Are you hungry?" I said between mouthfuls.

Carla shook her head. Impatience was written all over her face.

"She's always hungry," Dad replied.

I took another bite and turned to see my father enter the room. I chewed fast.

"Where were you?"

"Putting away laundry," Dad said. His kiss prickled my cheek.

"Thank you. Do you want to come over to the house with us? We could get pizza afterwards."

"You girls go on. I'm going to your brother's this evening." Dad smiled. "I noticed when I was putting away your laundry that you still have Mac's clothes in the closet."

"Never seems to be the time to sort his things," I hedged, hoping to duck the subject. I could tell by the look on his face it wasn't working. "I'll get round to it."

"Are you taking all Mac's clothes to the new house?"

Of course I'm taking them.

"Never thought about it."

Liar, liar, pants on fire.

"This would be the ideal time for a fresh start."

"Maybe."

Mac laughed at me and whispered, "Maybe's ass."

"Leave the ghosts behind Ellie. Start new."

"I don't want to have this conversation right now, Dad."

"I know. I think you should go through Mac's closets

and drawers before the movers get here next week."

Maybe.

"Sure, I can do that."

Not.

Dad smiled. "I know you can." He changed the subject. "The package that so excited your daughter is in your office."

Carla tugged at my arm. "Mom, you *need* to open it."

"No, baby, I *need* to eat, it's been a long day."

"Mom!"

"I'll open it later," I said with a wink at dad.

Carla squealed, "No! Now. It's been there all afternoon."

I shrugged. "Well, it won't hurt it to wait until after the house visit and pizza."

"You *have* to open it!" She bounced around the kitchen, pulling me along with her. "You *have* to!"

"Let's have a look and see who it's from," I said. "Lead me to this mystery package."

She didn't need to be told twice. Carla bustled me into my office and pointed at a largish box on my desk wrapped in brown paper. It was about twenty-four inches long by sixteen wide, and I guesstimated twelve inches high. I looked at the postmarks, international postage stickers and the customs declaration. It weighed ten kilos. The postmark said New Zealand. That would explain the weight in kilos.

"New Zealand," I muttered. "New Zealand."

While I had been in New Zealand six months earlier on

a case, I'd sent a parcel home for Carla, but it never arrived. It wasn't as big as the one in front of me.

I checked the return address and name. Not my writing. Not someone I knew and not an address I recognized. Okay, so, I'd only recognize the address to the hotel I stayed in, and maybe the police station in Christchurch.

"Did you order something?" Carla said her voice rife with expectation. Elvis started up again.

"Nope."

I picked out a craft knife from a drawer in my desk and slit the tape holding the paper on the box. When I spoke to Carla I realized I'd been holding my breath during the tape-cutting exercise.

"Carla, can you please get me a pair of latex gloves?"

She nodded and ran off to the kitchen reappearing a few seconds later with the gloves.

"Why?" she asked, passing them to me.

"I'm not sure. But something feels hinky." My intuition was on a roll today. I was not prepared to discount Elvis and his singing, not after The Clash's earlier performance. Maybe if I'd never come across a bomb, I wouldn't be so nervous about parcels from strangers.

Mac's voice rang out. "Maybe's ass." He was so loud to me. Sometimes it was hard to believe no one else could hear him.

Dad hooked his arm through Carla's and edged her closer to the door. His eyes danced the same mix of curiosity and trepidation as mine.

The box itself was a standard post box. It didn't need to be wrapped. But was. Under the wrapper on the top of the box were numbers, written in what looked like black sharpie. 65039, 02410, 35918, 27099, 77553, and 18266.

I eased the brown paper out of the way and slipped the knife under the brown plastic tape that sealed the box. Three sides were taped, one was hinged. My fingers pried open the lid just a smidge. I took a flashlight from the shelf above the desk and shone it into the small gap I'd created.

So trusting.

No wires. No ticking. No electronics. Nothing stuck anywhere it shouldn't be. Even so, my breath caught in my throat as I opened the lid wide to reveal a black plastic bag. I don't know if it was trepidation or caution that wheeled through me as I felt the bag and determined there were several smaller items within it. Dad and Carla watched. Nervous energy flowed from my father, mixing with Carla's curiosity. I ignored the buzz happening in the doorway. There was no obvious way into the cold black bag. I took the knife, held my breath, and cut a slit, revealing several smaller see-through Ziplock bags.

I looked at Dad. He spoke first. "Come on Carla, let's go order that pizza."

"But I ..." she argued, "... but Mom."

"I want you to go with Gramps, now."

Her shoulders drooped as she was led away. Her head swiveled to look at me. "The new house?"

"Soon."

I pulled my phone and called Kurt.

"Got something that might interest you," I said as soon as he answered.

"I was about to call you. A possible case, I might need your help."

"Okay, but me first – because this is going to stink soon."

Silence.

More silence.

Then a long sigh.

"Conway, I don't even want to ask why. Where are you?"

"At home." I sighed. "Where else do really bad things happen? I'll call Sam and Lee."

"It's *that* bad?"

"Afraid so."

The call to Lee and Sam was quick. I let them know there was something sinister going on and hung up. I fished my camera from the drawer. From a small box hanging from my key ring I took a fresh memory card and inserted it into the camera. I photographed the box, the paper, and then took judicious pictures of the contents. From another drawer I took a large plastic bag and spread it on the floor. Package by package I unloaded the box, making sure the individual packages were not touching. I photographed them all. There were six. Six packets of what looked like meat. I didn't for one second think it was animal.

My gut feel was that it was the other, *other,* white meat.

I've never been a fan of Austin Powers and now all I could hear was Fat Bastard going on about how he ate a baby and how it was the other, other white meat. Bile foamed in my gullet. I shoved Fat Bastard and the hideous Austin Powers aside so I could concentrate. I really hoped it wasn't the other, other white meat, but if it was I hoped it was adult.

Interesting that the box passed through customs and into the country. Or did it? Things often aren't what they seem. I had doubts it was even mailed. Seemed odd that a parcel I sent never showed up but a box of meat did. I picked up one bag and turned it over in my hands. It felt like a piece of rump roast, right up until I saw the other side.

A four-inch black and gray panther tattoo. I dropped it. Blood splattered against the inside of the bag.

Elvis started up again. I would love to return it to the sender.

Someone sent me people parts.

So not cool. Swallowing hard, and breathing through my nose, prevented my last coffee spraying forth and contaminating the evidence.

I turned another bag over.

A silvery tiger tattoo.

Then another.

An emerald green snake, coiled around a skeleton with roses for eyes.

Photographing and not thinking helped contain my nausea. By the time I'd taken pictures of all the tattooed hunks of flesh I felt so sick I doubted I could stand. Crawling seemed smart. I crawled out into the hallway and leaned on the wall.

I could hear the television in the living room. Carla was watching MTV. Her laughter bounced off the walls. Then she called out. "Mom, Rowan's on TV."

"Good, watch it for me," I called back.

Dad's head poked out from the kitchen. He missed me the first time and looked again. "What are you doing down there?"

"Sitting."

"I can see that," he said.

"Waiting for the team. We got trouble."

Dad nodded. He never exhibited surprise at such statements from me. "I'll take Carla to see the house and then with me to Aidan's. I've ordered the pizza. Should be enough for the team."

"Thanks, Dad."

I didn't ask how he knew. It was the look I gave him when I opened the box.

"We'll get going once she's finished watching Rowan on TV."

A smile played on my lips. "I'll go watch with her." I tested my legs as I stood. I was aware of a distinct unwillingness to leap to my feet like normal. A more cautious approach was needed.

One that involved holding the wall and not looking into my office. Someone sent me pieces of people. My joy in solving the bank robbery case was long gone.

The house phone rang. I heard Dad answer it. My legs worked. They carried me to the living room.

"Hey, Ellie, Noel for you," Dad called hurrying up behind me.

Then I remembered. Dinner. Shit.

"El, dinner?" Noel said. His voice flowed softer over the phone than in person.

"I'm so sorry. I forgot. Dad's ordered pizza, come on over. We've had a slight change of plans though."

"Slight?"

"Okay, not slight. Delta is on its way."

I heard the quiet hiss as he forced air out through closed teeth. "I'm coming. I wanted to fill you in on your untimely death – plus pizza sounds good. Also heard there was a shooting on Blake Lane today, someone said you were there."

"Yeah, I was. See you soon."

I handed the phone back to Dad. He looked at me with interest.

"What?"

"You could do worse than Noel Gerrard," he said.

"I'm sure I could. You should get together with Sam and Lee. They like to discuss potential suitors too. Right now, I like the place I'm at with Rowan." My fingers crossed all by themselves. "Can I please choose my own boyfriend?"

Dad grinned. "Sure you can, kid."

"Rowan is one hell of a guy. Ever think that maybe I quite like him?"

"We love you, kid. That's all."

I didn't reply. Carla moved her feet off the couch so I could sit next to her.

"Rowan looks different on stage," she said.

I laughed. "Well, he's vertical for starters. Guess that's different from lying on the sofa."

Carla giggled. "What's it like to see him live?"

I could see where we were heading.

"It's something you'll find out when you're older," I replied giving her a hug.

"But some kids in my class have seen them ..."

"Carla, we've talked about this."

"I know," she huffed. "It's just that *everyone* else has seen him."

"And you just get to see him lie on the couch, or get to whip his ass at guitar hero ... and watch movies with him."

She smiled and leaned on me. "You're saying I'm lucky, huh?"

"I'm just saying that you get to know the man behind the microphone and that is worth so much more than a concert ticket."

We watched Grange perform their latest single and then the interview with Rowan, Gracey, Martin, Tony, and Derek, the people who made up Grange the band. Carla squealed as Rowan said, "Bringing you home a present, Carla." And winked at the camera. I nudged her. And she grinned. "You're right, Mom."

Within seconds her cell phone was buzzing. Guess half

the school was watching Grange on MTV. Rowan was great. He adored Carla and coped well with my job as long as I didn't talk about work.

I learned that lesson early on. He's not one of us. He's not a law enforcement officer. He's not a LEO. He doesn't appreciate the finer details involved in my daily round with the worst of humanity. His enthusiasm for life adds balance to mine and tempers my views. I don't understand his world any more than he understands mine, but at least in his no one shoots at him, and things don't explode. I do know that his manager and publicist would love nothing better than to break us up. They don't like my job and deem it detrimental to Grange. Cracked album that they were, they had valid concerns, but Rowan refused point blank to listen to them regarding me. I expected that sooner or later he'd be forced to listen and he would disappear from our lives. I wasn't sure how that knowledge made me feel.

"What was in the package?" Carla asked as the television show ended. She turned off the TV.

"Just some stuff that wasn't for me," I said, staring at the blank screen.

"Just stuff?" she repeated. "How come Grandpa and I are going to see the house without you then?"

I sighed. "You're going to Uncle Aidan's for dinner. I'll pick you up later. We'll stay in a hotel tonight."

Her eyes lit up. "A hotel. Cool." Before the words were even cold in the air she was already texting her friends. Her thumb froze mid-text. Her eyes met mine. "What about Shrek?"

"Take him to Aidan's with you," I suggested.

She nodded with approval. "Shrek likes it at Uncle Aidan's." The texting resumed. I took the opportunity to seek out my father and have a word. He was in the laundry taking down the cat carrier from a shelf. He passed it to me.

"Shrek was in your office standing over the box," he said. "He might still be there."

I went and had a look. He was. His big, gray fluffy self was patting at the bagged lumps of meat with a fat furry paw. Gross. I scooped him up and pushed him into the carrier.

"You can go with Carla to Uncle Aidan's. Now I remember why I like dogs. They're less likely to eat you if you die at home," I whispered to the cat. He purred at me. I knew given half a chance the cat would eat our warm dead bodies and enjoy the meal.

Dad stood in the doorway. "Have you warned your brother?"

"Not yet."

I sent a quick text asking that he watch Shrek for a few days. His reply was instant and affirmative. There were two reasons why I had the cat: It belonged to my deceased husband, and Carla loved Shrek. While I had the poor animal on my own, he didn't have a name because I couldn't remember if Mac had ever named him, and I was forever running out of cat food. Carla named him Shrek, and reminded me to buy him food. Shrek slept on Carla's bed.

I packed Dad, Shrek, and Carla out the door. I didn't want Carla around when Delta arrived to deal with the box.

Hell, I didn't want to be around either, but it was a bit harder for me to run away; being the SSA of Delta required me to suck it up and deal. Thus far, I'd managed to suck it up and ignore. That was as close to dealing as I was going to get.

The smell of coffee wafted from the kitchen. Dad had made us fresh coffee before leaving. The man had no end to his parental ways. I set out mugs on the counter and waited for the inevitable.

Chapter Five
If I Could Turn Back Time

A knock at the front door was followed by a curse and a creak, as the door attempted to repel entry in time-honored fashion.

"We're here," Lee called. "You ever going to fix the door?"

I poked my head out and viewed the four men standing in the hallway. Lucky I have such a big hallway. It was now full to overflowing, and no one in it was shorter than six feet tall.

"So I see, and no." I smiled. "Coffee's made."

"Pour it," Noel said, sniffing the air. "That's Simon's coffee, isn't it?"

I nodded. My father's coffee was legendary.

"I'll pour. Go into my office. You'll see the issue." I ducked back into the kitchen. The herd passed the doorway. I waited. About ten seconds later, there was a collective hissing from the office. I guessed they'd seen the box.

I waited.

One by one three men came into the kitchen.

Sam looked a little ill. "Chicky Babe, you get some interesting mail."

"Don't I though? I doubt this was delivered by a regular mail carrier. I'm thinking a box of meat wouldn't get through customs. Despite the stickers all over it, I suspect someone dropped it off at the door. Courier maybe, or some people-chopping freak."

"Good point," Lee said. "I'd like to think this wasn't mailed."

Noel remained quiet.

"Why the New Zealand customs declaration and overseas postage?" Sam said.

I shrugged. "I don't fuc'n know. What's with the six numbers on the box lid? Why send it to me?"

"Someone thinks you're a cannibal?" Lee offered. "Disturbing how they look like rump roast."

Saliva built in my mouth, thoughts of beef rump roasts were replaced by pork. It'd been years since I'd eaten Boston butt and suddenly I craved it. Roasted, or smoked, or barbequed Boston butt. My stomach growled. Why call it butt when the meat comes from a shoulder?

Sam frowned. Mr. T and LL Cool J meet Klingon. Not a good look. "The numbers must be relevant. I'll exercise the gray matter over those for a bit."

Kurt appeared in the doorway. "Nice parcel." He removed latex gloves and dropped them into the trash under the counter. "I'll take it into the lab. Those tattoos are distinctive and might help with getting IDs on the bodies. Could be the same artist, which would give us something to work with."

"Bodies?" Sam asked.

"Yeah. Six, I think."

"Not all one person then?"

"Nope. Not unless the person had some kind of bizarre skin condition that turned him or her into patchwork."

There was a smirk edging in. A people-patchwork quilt. Pretty, with all the tattoos, but not something I fancied cuddling under. Weird that I hadn't noticed the variation in skin color, or maybe it was more tone. Why didn't I notice? Jiminy Cricket hopped onto Doc's head, rearranged his hair, and settled in.

But Doc was a real boy already.

"So the tattooed lumps all came from men," I said. Jiminy nodded his head and beamed a happy smile.

"Could be men," Doc replied. "Is there something I should know?"

"Possibly."

"Share?"

"Jiminy Cricket is sitting on your head. Seems to think the victims are all men."

"Real boys."

"Yeah."

Well, they're not donkeys. My sense of the absurd kicked in. I wondered if Jiminy was telling me they were asses.

"Asinus to be precise," Jiminy said with a nod.

"Does that mean someone's nose will grow if they tell a lie?" Doc said, running one hand through his hair. The action dislodged Jiminy who tumbled backwards. He grabbed at a lone hair strand and hauled himself back up.

"Maybe." I shrugged. "Maybe it will." That'd make it so much easier to interview suspects. Or it would if we had any. Jiminy settled into Doc's hair again. He looked shaken after his near miss.

I thought about the box and its gruesome contents for a few minutes. Doc tapped me on the arm.

"Sorry, what do you need?" I said, dragging my eyes off the top of his head and refocusing.

"You to be present for a few minutes. Can you do that?" he replied, peering into my eyes in a medical way.

"I'm not un-present. I was thinking. I do that from time to time."

"Nothing else going on?"

Jiminy jumped to his feet, bowed, and disappeared. Worry wart.

"Nope, a box of body parts is enough for one evening." I smiled. "What do you need me to be present for?"

"There are six numbers in the box lid, and I suspect six different bodies."

Sam moved one step closer.

"They could be some kind of identity number," I surmised. "Now that's interesting."

Sam and Doc nodded. Lee and Noel stopped talking by the door and looked over. It didn't take them long to catch up.

"I'll Google the numbers and see if anything jumps out," Sam said.

"Smacks of a long shot. If it's that easy, we'll have this case solved in less than a day. That'd be a new record for what appears to be a multiple murder," I said. "Unless of course they weren't murdered ... bodies stolen from a morgue, maybe?"

"I'll look into morgue disappearances," Lee said.

"Statewide, and check out hospital morgues as well as city and county." I took a breath. "If you get nothing, widen the search to include the entire east coast."

"How about New Zealand?" Lee said.

"I'll call Detective Faye Smith and see if she can offer any insight. I still don't see this parcel coming by mail."

The customs declaration and stamps concerned me. The whole package disturbed the hell out of me. My first priority was to make sure Carla was not in the DC area. Freaks can't be trusted to keep their freakishness away from children. I was pretty sure we wouldn't have this solved within a day. Sure miracles happen, but I'm not holding my breath waiting for one.

"Run the pictures of the tattoos through our new biometric software, if any of these people were ever arrested we'll be able to match our pictures with their identity."

It sounded like another long shot. Having them in the biometric database would be almost too easy.

Sam agreed with a nod. "Another resource to consider – Cyber is monitoring social network sites and compiling a database of tattoos and distinguishing marks."

"That sounds like a class action lawsuit in the making," I said.

"I don't think they're mining data to that degree, I heard they were monitoring people who bragged about crimes, or who were known associates of criminals. I'll ask if they can give us a hand trying to identify our victims."

"I take it this is a need-to-know kinda thing?"

"I'd say so, I sure haven't heard anything about it out in the world," said Sam.

It's not something we'd want to be talking about in public. People might stop posting their awesome new tattoo pictures if they thought we were copying them to our databases, along with their names, location, the contents of their friends list, ISP address, and anything else that might help us solve a crime or two.

My phone rang, damn near giving me a heart attack. I answered it to find Sandra on the other end of the line.

"Ellie, we have a problem."

No kidding?

"A new one?"

"Nope – continuation of an earlier situation. You're dead again." She blew out a sigh. "Any idea where the team is?"

"Here with me, so is Noel. Do you need him?"

"Nope, this isn't navy. This time it's a Greer Conway in Alexandria."

"Description?" My heart was pounding. Two dead Conways didn't sit well with my already unbalanced equilibrium. I wanted to shove my head between my knees to counteract the dizziness and encroaching gray, but didn't want to draw attention to my ridiculous reaction.

"Brown hair, blue eyes, five foot nine, slim."

A little bit of relief wriggled in at the brown hair. Not another clone of me then. It also opened up the possibility of it being unrelated. Different name. Not me. Weaseling its way to front and center in my mind was the shooting at the 7-Eleven. What if he was after me?

"Cause of death?"

"Strangulation."

The same as the other Conway woman.

"Whose case?"

"So far, Alexandria PD."

"Keep us posted."

I closed my phone and looked up at the settling cloud of doom as it drifted down from the ceiling. Below the cloud were the expectant eyes of Delta A. Sam raised an eyebrow, his signal that he was waiting.

I cleared my throat.

"A woman by the name of Greer Conway was strangled in Alexandria this evening."

The silence that reverberated around me was not good, but I used it to my advantage. "I need a few minutes to think." I slipped out of the kitchen and headed for the living room, closing the door behind me.

Chapter Six
Blood On Blood

Two dead Conway women is so not a coincidence. Twenty minutes of thinking about the safest place for Carla led me in a circle and landed back with Rowan.

Who'd have thought the safest place for an impressionable teenager was with the lead singer of a rock band?

Safer than with me.

Safer than with my family.

I rock this parent thing.

Noel knocked on the living room door. "Everything shipshape in here?"

"Sure." My cell phone was cradled in my hand. "Maybe it's time to cut the pretense and paint a big fuc'n target on my back and stick a flare on the roof."

He wasn't smiling, but I glimpsed a spark in his eyes that suggested he was amused by my target idea.

"You do attract aberrations."

"More than most?"

"Nah, yours are just louder that's all."

I nodded. "I need to make a call. Gimme a few?"

"I'll go on a coffee run."

I must have looked confused, because he grinned and pointed toward the kitchen. Noel pulled the door closed as he left.

My fingers scrolled past Galileo in my phone directory

and clicked on Grange. It rang and rang. I waited and counted each ring. Rowan answered right before the phone went to voicemail.

"Hi, Ellie."

"Hey, how's Japan?"

"Haven't seen anything apart from the airport, television studios, and the hotel." He sounded tired.

"What time is it there?" I glanced down at my watch. It was just after seven on Wednesday night.

"Nine, Thursday morning."

"Shit that's freaky, you're in the future."

"You didn't call me to ask about the time. What's wrong?"

"Nothing," I replied, crossing my fingers.

"I'm not buying."

Big surprise: the men in my life never do.

"When will you be home?"

"Leaving here Friday, I'll be home tomorrow night – time zones make things confusing. What's the matter?"

I sighed, I had to tell him. "I am once again the plaything for a fucktarded freak."

"And this is nothing wrong?"

I ignored him, shrugged my shoulders, and said, "How good is your bodyguard?"

"Don't you shrug your shoulders at me."

How could he possibly know that?

"I didn't." I crossed my fingers. "How good is your body guard?"

"Uncross your fingers," Rowan replied. "The answer is

'very.'"

Damn, he knows me better than I thought.

"Credentials?"

"Ex-SWAT."

Okay.

"Are you going to be busy when you get home?"

"Are you done with the light interrogation?"

"For now."

"What do you need?"

"A safe place for Carla."

"I'll pick her up. Country or city?"

"Country."

"All right. I'll take her to my country house." A no-nonsense business tone edged into his voice. "This must be serious."

"I could be overreacting."

He laughed. "You know, I can't recall you ever doing so."

"There is always a first time." Any minute now I might start acting like a girly girl and cry over a broken nail.

"Where is she now?"

"With Dad and Aidan."

I could hear his thoughts before he spoke them. But I listened without interrupting.

"This is so bad your ex-navy father can't keep her safe and your first thought is me – the one man in your life who is not armed."

Put it like that, it sounded nuts.

"My brother isn't armed."

"Ellie."

"Yes. It has the potential to be that bad."

"Do you want me on an earlier flight?"

"No."

I could hear him tapping on the keys of his laptop. I knew what he was doing. Telling his manager and publicist he wanted an earlier flight. Moments later, I heard the phone ring in his hotel room.

"Be right back," Rowan said and answered the other phone.

I could hear his side of the conversation. Listening to his tone gave me a clue how much resistance was thrown up by the other party. Quite a bit. He remained calm but firm.

Then he was back. "Sweetheart, I can be home by lunchtime tomorrow." He cleared his throat. "We're done here."

"You're done? You've been there two days."

"We're done. I'm cooling my heels waiting for the flight home. Four interviews, one live TV appearance. A few crazed public appearances. I'm done."

I knew the irritated tone in his voice. He hated sitting in hotel rooms waiting. It wasn't as if he could go sightseeing or do anything like a regular tourist.

"Your publicist is going to hate me even more now."

A smile crept into his voice. "That isn't possible." More tapping. "I'll be there tomorrow afternoon. Flying into Dulles. I've emailed you the flight information."

"Thank you."

"If it's not safe for Carla to be at home, it's not safe for you either."

"Rowan."

"Just sayin'."

"I heard. See you tomorrow."

I hung up. I did hear. Long ago I perfected the art of hearing without listening.

Noel knocked as he opened the door. "Coffee?"

"Pizza? I'm starving."

"Both," he said. He held a plate in one hand and two coffees in the other. Talented man.

I took the plate and a large bite from the end of a cheesy piece of pizza. Lee and Sam wandered in with a pizza box each.

"Pepperoni?" Sam said, dropping the box he carried on the coffee table.

"Thank you," I muttered between mouthfuls.

Doc came in and dropped another pizza box. It was a regular pizza party.

"I've had the package picked up by the lab. Didn't think you'd want to spend the night with it."

"Thanks," I said, and shoved another chunk of pizza in my mouth.

I had this theory that if I just kept eating I wouldn't throw up every time I thought about the box's contents. There were so many things wrong with the current situation that my mind wanted to shut down. I searched it for any hint of a migraine or other such trouble on my immediate horizon. Nothing lurking.

When I looked up, I found Doc watching me stuff pizza in my mouth. My eyebrows rose, questioning his interest. He grinned.

"Just amazed at how much you actually eat," he commented as I reached for a third slice.

I couldn't answer: It's rude to talk while feeding one's face. My cell phone rang. I knew the song. It was Carla. She'd been playing with my phone and added a special ring tone just for her calls. 'Don't Worry Be Happy' rang out across the room.

I answered before Lee could start singing. Carla needed her laptop and some clothes. I promised to pack them. I told I'd pick her up later. The hotel was still on.

She hung up and I put my phone back on the coffee table.

Noel slouched on the couch. "Where's what's-his-name, the singer?" He sat forward and peered under the couch.

"Yeah, that's right, I hide him under the furniture."

"Closet?"

"If he comes out of the closet, there might well be tears."

Noel smiled. "Now that would be something new."

"Idiot."

"Where is he?"

Damn nosy.

"Japan."

"Does he know about this?" His arm waved toward my office down the hall.

"No. I've asked him to take Carla for a few days though. She needs to be somewhere safe."

Noel's cup slipped from his hand, bounced off the edge of the coffee table. Everything became slow motion as he reached for the flying cup. His fingertips just grazed the cup's surface before it collided with Lee's knee. Lee rubbed his knee and retrieved the cup from the floor.

"No harm done. It was empty," he said, passing it back to Noel.

A sheepish Noel nodded then looked at me with surprise. "The safest place for your daughter is with a singer in a rock band?"

"Yes."

"I could've ..." He let the words trail off.

"I know. I want her out of the DC area. Safe, secure, comfortable." I held up my hand as he tried to find the words to countermand my decision. "It's not a debate."

"Can I talk to you, alone?" Noel's voice was quieter than usual.

My radar was tingling up a storm. Something was up with Agent Gerrard.

"Sure. In the hall?"

He led the way. Sam, Lee, and Doc all pretended they were clueless and launched into an energetic discussion about the package contents and their theoretical origins.

Noel closed the door. We were alone and, for the first time, being alone with him caused a sinking feeling in my stomach.

I headed him off. "How's the dead navy wife and missing husband case coming?"

"Starting to look as though she was kidnapped and her body dumped. Large amount of money missing from his account and he took out an impressive personal loan before he went UA." He shrugged. "Maybe it wasn't enough."

"Or it's not about the money and she was dead from the get go."

"My people are working on it."

"Good. Let me know when you figure it out."

He paced a few steps away then turned to look at me. I swear I felt the air pressure change.

"What's going on?"

"My gut tells me the second Conway woman makes the first one no coincidence," I said with care.

"Mine too. But neither of us have jurisdiction."

"If this is a serial killer we can." Someone who kills Conways. I really hoped the target on my back wasn't glow-in-the-dark paint.

"I'll look into it. There is someone I can talk to over at Alexandria PD."

"Thank you."

"Are you sure about sending Carla away with the rock star?"

Bam. That was what he wanted.

"Yes."

"I just don't see how she'd be safer with him."

I blinked twice as I tried to figure out how it was any of his business. There was something else going on. There had to be. I chose to ignore the possibility of underlying issues. "I don't want her in Virginia."

"You don't trust any of us to help take care of her?"

Whoa! Where did that come from?

"Excuse me? This isn't about who I trust. It's about getting Carla out of the state. About knowing no one will find her or send her packages." It's about her not being killed because she bore my surname. "There is a possibility that the name Conway is some kind of killer trigger. We don't know yet if the deaths are related. I don't want to find out by finding my kid dead, or have her find me dead."

His face clouded with many emotions, even a few I didn't recognize. I wasn't comfortable with any of them.

"She's safe here. We can all be there ..."

I know he heard the words he splattered across the hallway, and I know he remembered just how safe she was six months ago in FBI care. The stuff nightmares were made of punched through into my consciousness: I heard my daughter shriek as she struggled against tape that bound her to a headstone. Terrifying didn't come close to describing how I'd felt seeing and hearing that. I'd had Sam, Lee, and Doc with me. Misha and Joey had been behind us at a safe distance. The fucktard who had abducted Carla had shoved an explosive barrette in her jeans' pocket when she'd refused to wear it in her hair.

Being in protective custody and having a team of FBI agents taking care of her had not prevented her abduction. She's not a toy. There are no second chances with

79

her life. I took a breath and tried to decontaminate my psyche. The feelings of terror that had haunted me from that day had more arms than an octopus and were just as hard to escape.

"El, we can all be there ..." Noel was still trying.

Trying my patience.

"Yeah, well, it didn't work so great last time, remember?"

A smile flickered in his eyes. He conceded. "Agreed." His posture changed, any anger dissipated. "Perhaps the rock star has a use after all."

"Maybe," I replied. "He has a name. It's Rowan."

"I know, El." He took my hands. "Just be careful, he's not one of us."

I nodded. "That's a big part of his charm."

His shoulders shrugged as his head nodded. It was almost imperceptible. "You can do so much better."

"Better? He's a good person." Momentary confusion over his statement cleared to reveal his actual thoughts. "You? You and me?"

A weak smile and quiet confirmation.

And there it was, out there for us both to cower from. The loudest neon flashing *yes,* ever. Doomed from the initial utterance to haunt us for all time. The very notion of *us* was ludicrous.

"You sound like my father," I said, blocking all the other words that wanted to jump out. All the times I'd looked at Noel and wondered what was going on behind his blue eyes ran through my mind. Sometimes late at night I'd wake up thinking I could smell coffee, expecting to see him. It was fantasy, and that's where it belonged.

My internal voice whispered, Forward momentum, Ellie; you made a decision – no more Special Agents. Have you forgotten how it ended last time? I shook my head. It's not something I will ever forget.

"You okay, El?"

"Sure."

A loud thud vibrated through the floor. My hand closed around the grip on my Glock. Noel pushed me against the wall. His body shielded me from the unknown.

Someone outside had dropped something heavy.

My mind played evil tricks as it enjoyed the closeness of Noel's body and the comforting musky spice of his cologne. Concentrate. He smelled good. Concentrate. No more LEOs.

My eyes focused on the front door. I willed them to look beyond the solid wood.

The living room door opened a crack. Then swung wider.

Lee stepped out. "Someone's out there," he whispered. "You okay?"

"We're fine." I ducked out from under Noel. "What'd you see?"

"A figure standing by the front door. Think it's a male. About six foot, rangy bordering on scrawny."

Sam's deep voice flowed from the living room, coating the carpet and rising up the walls.

"Chicky, a male, got him on the front surveillance camera."

He'd tapped into my security system. Nice.

"Okay. If it's a clear enough picture for an ID, try running it through the system," I replied, watching my words travel back along the path his made. Cool.

Noel grabbed my arm, I yelped. His hand dropped. "Are you injured?"

"I'm okay, it's nothing."

"El!"

"The Blake Lane shooting. I got cut. It's nothing."

He shook his head. With a crooked smile he whispered pointy sharp words in my ear, "Think about it – we'd be good."

My shoulder twitched upward, as if to stop the serrated assault on my ear drum.

Chapter Seven
We Rule The Night

I motioned to Lee. Employing stealth mode, we moved in silence down the hall to the laundry room, which opened to the left about three quarters of the way down the hallway.

The back door to my house was a side door, accessed from the laundry room. I needed to turn off the external motion-sensitive security lighting. My fingers ran along the wall in the dark laundry room until they found the switches and flipped them down. At the outside door, I pointed two fingers at Lee's eyes then back at mine. Eyes on me.

My left hand twisted the door knob. One click. Two clicks. Pull.

The door released and sprang inward. I darted outside staying close to the house. Rather than stepping away from the security provided by my house and using the path, I opted for walking in what was left of the side garden. The weeds wouldn't mind.

We crept along the side toward the driveway. Darkness all around me softened as I moved, enabling my eyes to adjust. Ahead and to the right the outline of the garage created a deep, sharp line in the night. The weeds and grass underfoot deadened our approach to the front of the house.

A faint glow emanated from the windows, sneaking out

through gaps in the drawn curtains. Low noise. Television. An attempt at normal life sounds. So no one knew there were three armed men inside, ready to burst through the front door on my signal. The fingers of my right hand flexed one by one, then re-gripped the Glock I held.

With a nod at Lee, I slid down the wall into a couched position and peered around the corner. The suspect was still by the front door. I stood up. Lee angled in closer, but still a good two feet away.

I looked at him and mouthed the words, "On two." Then counted, "One. Two." I stepped out of the shadows with my gun trained at the lone male.

In a clear voice I called, "FBI! Get on the ground."

Lee moved beside me. The suspect stood still.

"FBI! On the ground!" Lee ordered, approaching the man, with his gun pointed at his head. Lee reached out one hand and grabbed the man's right arm. Within a blurred second he was lying face down on the ground with Lee's knee in the middle of his back. His face registered surprise, then confusion.

"And you are?" I said. His eyes were dull. He looked vacant.

Light flooded out as the front door opened, illuminating the area in front of the door and spilling onto the path from the driveway.

He didn't reply.

"Conway, more mail?" Kurt asked as he stepped over the box toward the prone male. "Name?" he said, giving the man a poke in the ribs with his shoe.

No comment.

"Search him, Lee," I said.

Sam hollered out the door. "We got him in the system. Jonah Powell."

Jonah groaned. Lee holstered his weapon, handcuffed Jonah and searched him. He pulled a wallet from his back pocket and threw it to me. I opened it. Driver's license. He was an organ donor. Six hundred dollars in cash. Two credit cards, neither of them bore *his* name. And a small plastic bag, containing small white crystals at the very bottom. I waved it in his face.

"Meth?"

He closed his eyes.

"You deliver a package to me tonight for meth or for cash?"

He smiled and revealed decaying teeth; they matched his scabby face. The overall image combined to scream 'addict.' Get an addict to act as courier. They'll do anything for cash or their drug of choice. Only this one got so wasted first he didn't know he should drop the parcel then leave.

"Doc, can you get anything out of him?"

"Doubtful. But I'll try. Maybe detox will make him talk."

"Rehab is for pussies," Jonah muttered, then giggled.

"You're not going to rehab, buddy. You're going into a cell. We'll do this the fast and hard way," Doc said. "You'll wish you could go to rehab by the time we're an hour in."

85

Lee pulled him to his feet.

"Transport?" I enquired, looking at Doc. A conversation from earlier popped up and waved a flag. "Didn't you want to talk to me tonight?"

"Hold that thought, Conway," he said with a lopsided grin. "It can wait until morning. I'll deal with Jonah Powell, courier to madmen, first."

A smile worked its way to my mouth. The edges turned up without the official nod from me.

"Are you taking him in your car or would you like me to get someone to come pick him up?"

"Can we have him picked up, please? Tell them to bring a van, one that can be hosed out."

Lee was on his cell phone already. He spoke to Sandra, relaying instructions.

I hollered into the house, "Hey Sam, will you watch Jonah here while we check out this box?"

Sam appeared. He excused himself as he passed Noel in the doorway. Sam took Jonah by the arm and pulled him out of the glare of the lights.

Doc, Lee and I crouched by the large package. Again it wore a customs declaration and international airmail stickers. The stamps were from New Zealand. Noel hurried into the house then returned with latex gloves, flashlight, and a craft knife. A quick game of Rock-Paper-Scissors, determined that Lee would open the box.

Part of me wanted to go stand by Sam, out of harm's way.

I stayed put.

No one breathed.

Moving with slow precision Lee cut the tape securing the lid, slipped the knife inside the front edge and ran it along the very front of the parcel. With care he lifted the lid an inch and shone the flashlight beam inside. "Don't think it'll go bang," Lee said on an outward breath. Cautiously he folded the lid right back to the ground.

Inside was a large black bag. Lee grasped a loose bit of plastic and lifted it as high as was possible, and then slit the bag open. As the cut edges fell apart they revealed more clear plastic bags. Doc counted the bags.

"Six."

I stared at the contents. It didn't look like anything much – just lumps of meat in a butcher's shop window. Doc picked up one bag and turned it over in his hands a few times.

"What is it?" I asked.

"Could be more rump pieces," Doc replied.

"Rump ... you mean more hunks of ass?"

"Yeah, it's another box of ass."

A smirk lurked close to the surface. My internal struggle began. I could hear the voice that instructed me not to laugh. The death of innocent people is not funny.

But a box of ass?

Dammit!

I felt it as a lump in my sternum, bubbling, pushing and pushing, until it exploded from my mouth in a raucous laugh. Free, the laugh bounced off the porch and sailed back toward the driveway and the road. The still night was broken wide open.

There were no take backs.

Lee chuckled. Sam snorted. Doc cracked a smile that edged ever closer to all-out laughter. Even Noel grinned. Jonah stared vacuously.

His blank stare served to heighten my lack of self-control. "If you lay off the chicken feed you might get your sense of humor back."

He had no comment.

Doc nudged me. "You talked too fast for him. He's fried."

"That's a medical term?"

"Yes, yes it is."

"Good to know."

With a crash we all returned to work mode. A hush enveloped us as we stared at the bags of rump.

"Are they from the same bodies?" I asked Doc. "Best guess. I understand that even you can't possibly know for sure."

Just because he acted a little like a superhero at times didn't mean he was one.

"Nope. Look at this." He picked up one of the clear packages and turned it over, skin side up. "These are all darker skin tones, deep olive, brown, and black. The first lot ranged though hues of white to pale tan."

"This is interesting." We have an equal opportunity killer on the loose. Or should that be 'a politically correct killer?'

From behind me I heard a thud. I spun around. Jonah

was sprawled on the ground. My eyes scanned for Sam and found him crouched by a small shrub.

He called out, "Gun!"

Ah crap!

Noel hit the light switch inside the front door plunging the area into darkness. Something whizzed by my head. I ducked and ran back around the corner. The sound of bullets hitting the house followed me.

Dammit, I've already done being shot at today.

Footsteps thumped down the interior hallway.

Lee exited the laundry door and came up behind me, whispering my name. Guess he didn't want a bullet in the head.

"Noel and Doc?" I peered around the corner, trying to ascertain the direction of the shooter.

"Noel was calling it in. Doc grabbed the package and is finishing off his examination inside."

I saw Sam move. He dropped to his belly and dragged himself forward using his arms. Hiding his profile from the shooter. Smart man. My father would put it differently. Up here for thinking, down there for dancing.

"Lee – garage! Sam needs cover." I prepared to cover Lee's movement. He hunched over and ran, sliding down by the front wheel of the truck. I could just make out his crouched shape.

Pfft. Wood splintered. *Pfft.* A house window shattered.

My phone vibrated in my pocket.

I tugged it free and answered.

"Night scope and rifle?" Lee asked.

Why hadn't I thought of that? Brain freeze maybe. "Gun case under the back seat of Mac's truck. Go in through the back passenger door. One sec."

I shoved the phone back in my pocket, felt for my key and activated the beeper. Three buttons. One to open the doors. One to lock the doors. One for the alarm.

Pfft.

I heard glass shower down in my living room as I pushed the button to unlock the car.

Pfft.

Shit: The interior light. Lee opened the door. The interior of the truck lit up like sunshine. Followed closely by *tink-tink*, as bullets punched through the side windows. Lee slithered into the back seat. Pulling the door shut. The light faded.

Bullets through the back window of the truck gave me an idea of direction. He was in a good position. The shooter wasn't an idiot.

A harsh click came from inside the Tacoma. Lee must've lifted the seats to access the gun case. More *tink-tinks* as bullets hit metal. The shooter seemed determined to ruin the Tacoma, which did nothing for my mood.

Set back about ten feet from the edge of the driveway were several large trees with younger smaller trees grouped close by, almost a thicket but not quite; beyond them about twenty feet of lush green grass where I'd seen the red deer earlier; beyond that woods. I surmised the person was not on the grassy area but farther back in the actual woods.

The passenger door nearest me opened. I wanted to fire into the woods. But I couldn't see anything to fire at, plus I had a handgun and that wasn't going to do a damn thing. Lee leaped out cradling the rifle in his arms and dashed across the driveway then slid into to the shadows next to me.

I holstered my Glock and took the rifle. It took a moment to adjust to the weight. He'd changed the scope from the one I'd used at the range to the night vision scope. I looked down the scope, moving the weapon through the darkness in front of me in a slow and even sweeping motion. The cross hairs fell on trees and bushes.

"Move, you moron."

Sirens pierced the cool air. I watched, not breathing. My finger played on and off the trigger. I searched low then heightened the search in twelve-inch increments as nothing showed in my scope.

Another shot.

I spotted the muzzle flash.

"One o'clock," I hissed at Lee. He called Sam with a position.

Then he moved. I watched. Another movement. The shooter was lying prone beyond the grass just inside the wooded tree line

I had the shot but wanted him alive. Dead people don't talk much. I wanted answers, not more dead ends or another dead ass.

"Lee, I'll pin him from the left. You and Sam move in

from the right for the arrest."

"On it."

Aiming two feet to the left, I fired one shot. Moments later I fired twelve inches to his left. He returned fire. My next round lodged in a tree just above his head. He returned fire again. A bullet lodged in the downpipe twenty-four inches from my head. I'd rattled him and had his attention.

Another two shots from me and then Sam hollered. I used my scope to find him. He stood over the shooter, the shooter's rifle in his hands, pointing at the shooter's head.

Police cars screeched to a halt on the street.

I called out to the team, "Police."

With much care, I placed my rifle on the ground by my feet and grabbed my badge. I didn't want to be confused with the shooter. With my arm outstretched and my badge clasped in my fingers I walked toward the police cars. Drawn by the flashing red and blues, like a moth to a flame. I'm a sucker for rolling lights and men in uniform. No wonder everyone thinks Rowan isn't the one for me. The doors were open. Officers crouched behind them ready to fire.

I announced myself, "Supervisory Special Agent Ellie Conway. The shooter has been detained."

A familiar voice called back. "Hey, Ellie. Where's the shooter at?"

It was good to hear a friendly voice, although I could've done without it twice in one day. "Lee and Sam are bringing him in from the woods, Josh."

"Just one?"

"Just one. Used a high-powered rifle and night scope, from what I could tell from here. We'll know more when they get back."

"Everyone else okay?" He came out from behind the car door and walked toward me.

"One dead delivery boy. Lots of broken windows."

I can imagine how pleased my insurance company will be with that. I'm never going to get a no claims bonus.

"Twice in one day, Ellie? Don't think that's a coincidence do you?"

"I doubt it, Josh. Still, how the hell would anyone know I was stopping for milk on my way home?"

"Same way someone knew where you lived," he replied.

"Let me know how you get on with that GPS unit." I smiled, ending the conversation. "See you next weekend at Murphy's."

Chapter Eight
Pop Rocks And Coke

Pulling into Dad's garage felt a bit peculiar, driving Mac's Toyota Tacoma truck and not heading out to Quantico felt even more weird. The only time I ever drove his truck was to go out there. It bothered me that someone found my home.

Okay, to be honest, it bothered me that someone found my home *again*. The sooner we moved to our new secure address the better. I was troubled. My address wasn't in the book. I didn't go around shouting it from roof tops. How is it people keep finding it? Which led me to another thought: I didn't want that same fucktard finding my Dad.

How did someone know I'd stop at the 7-Eleven today? Being shot at ruins my usually sunny disposition. Being shot at twice in one day downright pisses me off.

Lee and Sam waited on the street in a black Ford Expedition. About as invisible as anyone can be in a car wearing federal tags. I gave a quick wave as I zapped the garage door with the remote on the wall. The door hesitated for a moment then fired into action and began to close.

From the living area of the house, I heard the television and Carla's voice.

Dad looked up as I walked into the kitchen from the laundry room. "Car in the garage?"

I nodded and stole a cupcake from the counter. "These are good," I muttered after swallowing a mouthful of cake and frosting.

"Everything okay?"

"Sure. Carla's going to go stay at Rowan's country place for a few days. He'll pick her up tomorrow. How was Aidan? You remember to leave the cat?"

"Not okay then," Dad said. "You think there would be enough room for her old Gramps at that fancy-sounding country house? Aidan was fine and so is the cat."

I smiled. "You wanna go too, huh?"

I know I did.

"Sounds fun."

"I'm sure Rowan wouldn't mind," I said taking another cupcake.

"Didn't you eat tonight?"

"Yeah, I did, but it got a bit interesting after that. Guess I burned it all off."

"Will you stay here tonight?"

"No. We'll stay at the Marriott. Got another package tonight and another Conway was killed."

Dad paused; he leaned on the counter. "Another Conway?" he whispered. "Male or female?"

"Female."

"Is this a coincidence?"

Our eyes met. Neither of us believed in coincidence.

"I don't know what this is, but I don't like it. You and Aidan need to be extra careful."

He nodded. "Go get Carla. I'll box up some cupcakes

for you girls to take."

I kissed Dad's cheek and hurried down to the living room. Carla was on the phone. I checked the time on my watch, tapped it and made eye contact in an enquiring way.

She smiled and said hurried goodbyes.

"Late for phone calls."

"Joey."

"I know, but it's still late."

"Summer holidays and you know his parents are ... neglectful."

I knew that too. That's one of the reasons why Joey spent so much time at our place, where at least he was supervised, fed and cared for.

"Let's get going. We have a reservation. Tomorrow night you'll be in New Jersey with Rowan."

She squealed and leaped to her feet. "Me?"

"Yes."

"Oh my gosh. They will die!"

"Who will die?"

There's been enough death for one night.

"Just everyone at my school!"

Good, the entire student body from Oakton High School will drop dead upon hearing this news from my daughter. I couldn't be more proud.

I smiled, shook my head and suggested she get her shoes on so we could leave.

Carla stopped just inside the garage.

"Why are you driving Mac's truck?"

"My car is with the mechanic," I replied, crossing my fingers behind my back. "It needs some work." It may have even been written off by the insurance assessor due to the multitude of large bullet holes and expense of all new panels.

My car was Swiss cheese.

She looked at me for a beat then smiled, "That's right, Kurt brought you home tonight."

"Yeah." I tempered the sigh of relief that threatened and opened the passenger door for her, hoping she wouldn't notice the bullet holes. The sooner we were out of the brightly-lit garage the better.

"Mom, there's glass on the seat."

Shit. Must've missed some of it.

"Sorry, sweetheart, brush it off. It's windshield glass it won't cut you."

She screwed her head around and looked out the back. Then looked at me as I climbed into the driver's seat.

"Where from?"

"A stone went through the window." I shrugged. "That's why I was so late – had to get the Apex windshield guy out."

That part was true at least. I was just glad the weather was good and they'd fixed the windows right there and then. They couldn't however do a damn thing about the bullet holes in the panels.

It was late. By the time we reached the hotel, Carla was fast asleep with her head resting on the car window. I felt mean waking her.

We checked in without a hitch. Memories surged forth and squeezed themselves into my consciousness despite my best efforts to lock them out. We stepped into the elevator behind the porter with our luggage. The impossibility of holding back the memories of a night best forgotten became apparent.

I remembered every second of our life together. Every second. It didn't take much to bring the more vivid moments back. Like the night someone ran a knife across my throat, leaving me with a thin scar. That was the night Mac and I ended up staying in the Marriott at Metro. I was bootless, bloodied, and lacking in luggage when we checked in. He was an amazing mixture of amused, concerned, and tired.

The memory faded before it became unmanageable.

I checked I had boots on my feet as my fingers sought the faded scar around my throat.

"Mom, why did you do that?" Carla asked, watching me with sleepy eyes.

"What, sweetie?"

"Touch your throat like that."

I smiled. The elevator pinged. "This is our floor."

She hurried to catch up as I strode along behind the porter. Carla grabbed my hand.

"What was it, Mom?"

"Nothing, sweetheart. Just a memory."

"Of this hotel?" she whispered.

"Yes."

The porter disappeared through a doorway. We caught

up. I took the key card and tipped him for his help.

Sometimes I dreaded the way Carla's inquisitive mind worked, and the thought of her drilling me about the past didn't thrill me. Turned out I didn't need to worry. By the time I'd closed and locked the door behind the porter she was almost asleep in the bed nearest the window. Midnight faded into the past as I checked email then surfed TV channels.

Chapter Nine
Hello, I Love You

Morning slammed into me at high volume. I pulled a pillow over my head and pressed down.

It didn't help. The noise pounded against my hands as they held the pillow. I peeled back a corner and growled, "Turn it down!"

The volume dropped significantly.

I wasn't done yet, "We're in a hotel. Have some consideration for other guests."

"Sorry," Carla muttered. "Why are you so cranky?"

"Tired."

She bounced on my bed. "Do you have to work today?"

Gee, let me see. Two boxes of meat landed on my doorstep yesterday. They're people meat but not my case; they're just my problem. A heap of case files sitting on my desk waiting for me. Then there are the two Conways dead in mysterious circumstances. Again, not my case, but the potential is there for it to be my problem. And the little matter of the Blake Lane shooting. Did I have to work?

"Yes, but I'd sooner hang with you," I said.

"I could stay here. You can go to the office."

"Ah, no, not by yourself."

"It's a hotel, what could happen? I'm fourteen!"

"Exactly – you're fourteen!"

"Mom!"

"Don't start with me; I haven't even had coffee yet." I rolled over and tried to smother myself again. Music started up. I looked at Carla. It wasn't her. I was hearing 'Rockin' Robin' and I had no clue why.

"I'll get the coffee," Carla said.

I suspected she was trying a different tactic to allow me to let her stay in the hotel by herself. Good luck with that.

Before I could come up with a reason for the new song she was on the phone ordering room service. Listening to her breakfast order cemented my earlier thoughts. She would not be staying in the hotel by herself.

Carla hung up.

It seemed like a good idea to repeat her breakfast instructions back to her, "Coffee, pancakes, bacon, French toast, orange juice, chocolate croissants, and a banana smoothie ... did I get that right?"

Carla grinned. "Yes."

"I'll stay here until Rowan picks you up."

It'd take us until lunch time to get through the mountain of food. I threw back the covers and crawled out of bed. Time to locate clothing and hit the shower in the hope the water would wash away the song. Trying to figure out what it had to do with the night's events was set to do my head in.

I'd envisaged a quick shower. The steaming hot water and high pressure showerhead seduced me into a record-breaking long shower. I emerged prune-like and lobster red. Boiled clean.

Clean is good.

The song was gone.

Breakfast was waiting for me. Carla was eating. True to her teenage years, she piled her plate high and was making short work of it. It astounded me how much food the child could put away. She remained lean and willowy no matter how much she ate. She was a credit to her good genes and love of sports. I watched her fork reach out for another pancake. It occurred to me I needed to get in quick before there was nothing left.

My phone rang.

With one eye on the diminishing pile of French toast and pancakes and one on my phone, I chose pancakes and French toast. Voicemail could get the call.

Breakfast was good. It was obvious to me that maple syrup was the nectar of the gods, not ambrosia.

Abandoning my sticky plate I crawled over my bed and grabbed my phone from the nightstand as it buzzed again. Four new voice messages and a bunch of new *@replies* on Twitter. I pulled my pen and notebook from my bag and started with the oldest message. It must've been left while I was in the shower.

First message: Caine offering to watch Carla if I needed to go into the office.

Second message: Sam would be late in.

Third message: Doc remembered he needed help with something.

The fourth message was interesting. My pen scribbled the number on my notebook. I scrambled back over the bed and hooked up the room phone. Reading the number out loud, I dialed. The phone rang twice before it was answered with so much excitement that it disguised the voice I expected to hear.

"Gracey, is that you?"

"Yes," she replied, her breathing ragged. "Ellie?"

"Yep, I got your message but don't understand the problem. Can you tell me again?"

She started firing words at me so fast they blurred. "I didn't know who to call. It's gross. Why would anyone do that? It's just horrible. Then I remembered you were FBI. You don't mind do you? I mean, this is just horrendous."

"Stop!" I found myself taking a deep breath. "Breathe. Again, this time slow down. What's horrendous?"

"The doorman brought up a package for me," she said with much more control, but the squeaky echoes of fear still lurked as her voice raised a few octaves in the telling. "I'm a vegetarian! It's meat! Someone sent me MEAT. Did I mention I'm a vegetarian? This is crazy shit!"

Any other day sending meat to a vegetarian would just be rude. Today it spelled trouble spreading. I wanted it to be some fan who got it wrong, or even an incorrectly addressed package meant for someone else entirely. The cold, clawing dread in my gut said otherwise.

"Where is it now?"

"In the lounge on the coffee table. I don't even know anyone in New Zealand. I've never even been there."

Oh good grief. More meat from overseas. "New Zealand?"

"The doorman was all thrilled about the box having come from New Zealand."

"Were you in New Zealand with Grange?"

Seemed like a weird question coming from me. You'd think I'd know which members of my boyfriend's band were on that tour. It was horrific and very traumatic for me and Rowan.

"No, I went home from Australia. I was sick. I didn't do New Zealand."

"You need to give me your address. I'll have someone collect the box and talk to the doorman."

"Not you?"

I looked at Carla who was watching cartoons and picking at the few remaining pancakes.

"I'm busy this morning. I'll have someone pick it up. Someone from my team."

She sighed. "All right," Gracey replied then gave me her address. Color me surprised.

"You're in Virginia? I thought you all lived in New York."

"Tony is in Maryland and Derek lives in New Jersey. Martin lives in Connecticut. We all have New York apartments. Guess you know where Rowan lives."

I didn't know Grange was so spread about the eastern seaboard.

"You're fairly close to at least two members of my team in Merrifield. Have you met Lee?"

"No, I don't think so."

"You'd remember – he looks like Tony."

The longer you look at him the worse it gets.

She laughed. "I heard stories from New Zealand about Lee. Is he going to come get this box?"

"He will. He'll be there within the hour."

I hung up and called Lee. I gave him Gracey's address and a quick rundown on the box.

He wasn't impressed either.

And the song was back. 'Rockin' Robin' was playing so loud I started tapping the beat with my foot. I closed my eyes and listened to the song. It was something. My laptop sat on the small desk in the room. I clambered over the bed and sat at the desk. I typed Jaybird Street, Robin Conway. There was no Jaybird Street in Washington DC but there was Jay Street and a Conway family lived there. I called the office.

"Sandra – get someone to Jay Street Northeast. A Robin Conway lives there. Check she's still alive."

"Sure," she replied and hung up. I loved that she didn't question why or how I knew, just that it had to be done.

I took a few minutes to check Twitter. Ah, the joy of surfing the internet on cell phones. I could tweet from anywhere. I didn't even have to sign into Twitter to tweet. I could text tweet. Today I used the Twitter application on my phone. That way I could see all the tweets in my timeline. The hash tags I'd been using were still going strong which meant there was still a lot of undelivered mail out there. How bizarre, real mail doesn't get through but boxes of ass have no trouble being delivered. Maybe the ass bandit should set up a rival postal company.

Several people on my 'friends' list were tweeting about current events. It was interesting. I joined in for a moment or two. A loud knock came from the door. Carla bounded from her bed and rushed for the door. Was I that bad?

Noel's voice drifted toward me with the smell of excellent coffee.

"Mom, Special Agent Gerrard is here to see you," Carla announced and bounced back across the room to her bed and the television.

Noel poked his head around the wall. "Hey, El, okay for a guest?"

"Sure," I replied putting my phone down. "Have a seat."

Noel sat on the end of the bed and grinned at me. "Nice room." He bounced a few times. I heard the coffee slosh in the polystyrene takeout cups. "Comfy." He passed me a cup.

"Thank you. And you found me how?"

"Caine. Have a few things you might be interested in."

I sipped the coffee and nodded. "And they are?"

"Do you know Ameer Reza Sedghian?"

My coffee forced its way back up my gullet bringing pancakes with it.

***

He smirked. Had my life not depended on him I would've slapped him, good and hard. I had requested another liaison but no one wanted this job and now I was stuck with Ameer Reza Sedghian – the one person who had volunteered. I conjured a mental image of my finger marks glowing in red welts on his face. The picture in my mind soothed the annoyance that had wormed into my consciousness, building during the morning, as time ticked by. The waiting grew unbearable.

"Well?"

Fake charm oozed as he spoke, "Of course, my dear. My sources are good. I am very thorough."

I muttered under my breath, "I just bet you are."

"Please repeat, I did not hear."

A cold smile crossed my lips. "It was nothing."

The steady thud of running footsteps halted our conversation. Ameer held his finger to his lips. I tensed.

***

I swallowed hard.

"No."

"You sure about that?" His blue eyes searched mine, as if he expected another answer.

"Yes."

He was a dead man walking and now he walks nowhere. It was a long time ago. I thought the packages from New Zealand stirred some memories but not anything like the torrent stirred up by Noel. It'd been a long time since I'd heard Ameer's name.

"Then I don't suppose you can help me."

I took another drink from the coffee cup and hoped I wasn't as pale as I felt. "Don't suppose I can."

"You ever heard of Habib Faisal Arbab?"

"No."

I felt a cold chill slice through my bones.

***

I pulled my phone from my pocket, took his picture, and sent it to Jonathon. Long silent minutes passed before I received a text response.

"Ah, your name is Habib Faisal Arbab. Does daddy know you are mixing with such dangerous company?"

Habib didn't react.

"Your father Sheik Arbab is an old friend of ours. I do not think he will be pleased with his son and only heir."

Habib remained stone-faced and unaffected. I flicked open my phone and dialed the office, "Jonathon can you get the Sheik on the line? Let him know we have his son."

Habib threw himself to the floor, "Please, no!"

Saleh dragged Habib to his feet. Ameer snorted in disgust at Habib's behavior.

"Never mind," I said, and hung up on Jonathon.

"So you speak English and are willing to have a conversation?" I said to the shaken young man.

"Yes."

I shook my head at Ameer. "You chose badly, if this is the caliber of your little play group, you won't be much of a threat."

"Stupid American girl," he hissed half under his breath.

Saleh grimaced. I knew he was suppressing the urge to

smack Ameer around the head.

"Ameer! Pay attention!" I said, rapping him on top of his head with my knuckles. "How many in this organization?"

He sneered but didn't answer.

"How many?" I repeated.

"There are four I know of." Habib paused as if unsure if he should continue. "And a fifth who gives Ameer his orders."

"All Saudi?"

"Yes, I think so."

"Your first lie."

***

"El?" Noel spoke, forcing the unwelcome memory aside. "Where did you go?"

"Nowhere; I'm right here."

"Uh huh, and you don't know Habib Faisal Arbab?"

"Nope."

"And yet I get the feeling that's not entirely true, El."

I tested my smile. "Really? Sorry I couldn't help." It occurred to me that someone who didn't know who Sedghian and Arbab were, might have some questions. From the depths I dragged up an innocent voice. "Who are these men?"

"A dead man and someone the system says was involved with him, prior to his death."

"And this concerns me how?"

"Habib Faisal Arbab is a person of interest in the missing JAG lawyer case. We found laptops belonging to both Mr. and Mrs. Conway. His contained emails from someone calling himself Habib Faisal Arbab. Arbab said he had kidnapped his wife and wanted hundreds of thousands of dollars in return for the woman."

"Why?"

"He believed Gabrielle Conway was someone he used to know, a woman called Demelza."

"Just Demelza, no surname?"

He shook his head. "He only referred to her as Demelza."

My insides were like jelly being whipped into a maelstrom. The more he talked the more memories surfaced and the sicker I felt. I finished the coffee and threw the cup into the trash. My fingers massaged my temples hoping to stem the brewing headache. It'd been a long time since I'd heard that name. That name hung on the desperate voice of a colleague and warped with memories of Ameer Reza Sedghian.

***

I started to relax when I recognized Dion's voice. He was back. I peered out the small window nearest me. He stood in the middle of the courtyard, sweat running from his brow, created shiny rivers in the dusty dirt that clung to his skin.

Ameer's hand grasped the thick fabric of my camouflage jacket; his fingers blending into the desert colors. His head shook. "No." His voice was a harsh whisper in my ear.

"It's Dion," I replied, thrusting his hand off my sleeve.

"No, wait."

I watched from the window as Dion doubled over, hands on hips. Deep breaths shuddered through his body. He'd been running. His pack and sidearm were gone.

With great effort, he called my name again, "Demelza!" then dropped to his knees.

Ameer's hands clamped down on my shoulders. The force stopped me from moving toward the door. "No," he growled. "See?"

I felt my eyes widen as if to take in as much of the scene in front of me as possible. I looked from Ameer to Dion. At first, I could see nothing and then noticed his jacket pockets appeared bulky.

"Oh my God."

"He found them," he said with a sigh. "He has a message."

"What?" My gaze remained fixed on Dion.

"He is a dead man."

"No!" Determination resounded in my voice. It was just wrong. "No! We help him!"

"Woman – he will have a camera on him – he is wired. They are watching, waiting for the target to approach him. Then *ka-boom*!"

***

"You okay?" Noel asked. He missed nothing.

I knew my head was shaking no. "I'm okay." I lied. It certainly wasn't the first time I'd done so. With my job it was a necessity. But it was the first time I'd done it so badly.

"El?"

"Stay with Carla for a few minutes. I need to do something." I grabbed my cell phone and the key card and left the room.

I paced. Of all the fucktards in all the world, I had to be the biggest. If I hadn't channeled so much righteous indignation and dropped so many agents on the television channel, Habib would be thinking he'd killed the right Gabrielle Conway. Or at least would have more trouble locating the one he wanted. Me.

I paced back to the door. It wasn't helping. Dammit.

From a window I could see the sky. A cloud bumped into another cloud. For a moment it looked like a butterfly. My eyes closed for a second. When they opened Mac's face looked down at me. I blinked and the clouds drifted apart. Mac was gone.

I paced again. Wearing a track in the recently vacuumed carpeting. I thought if I worried the carpet long enough Mac might join me. He didn't.

From memory I punched in a phone number. I never believed I'd be calling it again. The wait for the automated system to answer seemed interminable.

"You have reached the Shangri La Laundry. Press one for business hours. Press two for accounts. Press three for —"

I cut off the robotic voice and pressed three. More waiting. Seconds seemed like minutes.

Finally I heard a woman's voice.

"Shangri La special services."

"I have a bird problem."

"Can you be more specific?" she replied.

"I keep chickens."

There was a click and then silence. Two breaths and then another voice.

"It's been a long time, Demelza."

My words felt sticky in my throat. "Yes, yes it has."

"Do you need to come in?"

"No, Jonathon, I need to know why Habib Faisal Arbab is in the country."

"How did you come by this information?"

"He thought he killed me yesterday morning. I'm betting he knows now he didn't. He also knows my name."

"That is not possible."

"No, it should not be possible. But. It. Is."

"He cannot enter America without alerting every agency known to man. He's on the watch list. He's also on the no-fly list. Are you sure it's Habib?" There wasn't a trace of sarcasm in his voice.

"I have not seen him and would prefer to keep it that way."

"Is your source reliable?"

"Very."

"I will look into it myself."

The burning question in my mind was identity. To my

knowledge, there were two people who were in the room *before* the blast in New Zealand ten years previously. Habib and an agent named Tim Cosgrove. They survived because I sent them away before the explosion. Tim did not know who I was.

"How would he find out who I am?"

"We'll look into it, Demelza."

"It had to come from inside. How would anyone recognize me after all this time?"

I hung up and paced some more.

Sure, I had a moderate-to-high profile, what with the Butterfly Foundation and the poetry book Mac and I wrote. But not high enough that a terrorist would come looking for me after ten years. I wasn't a green-eyed redhead. I was my regular natural blonde blue-eyed self. There is nothing in my FBI records that suggested I was ever deep-cover with the CIA. According to my files, ten years earlier I had been working an undercover FBI operation in Florida. I hadn't been chasing all over Iraq, or in New Zealand attempting to bring back the terrorist we believed had killed a CIA operative.

I wasn't there. It didn't happen. I searched my brain for anything anyone knew about Operation Kiwi. The director knew I'd been seconded to the CIA, it was her idea. She thought I would benefit from the experience.

I wasn't pacing anymore; I was sitting on the floor with my back pressed against the wall. Sitting in hallways was becoming a habit, much like long-sleeved tee shirts and baseball caps.

My fingers extended beyond my sleeve. I tapped my nails together which called my attention to their uneven length. Four longish on one hand, three on the other. One recently broken but showing growth.

Good, Ellie, think about how much you need a manicure, never mind that a terrorist knows who you are and wants you dead. Nothing new there. But how could he know? Not even Dion Edwards knew who I was. America's most wanted rotated past me on a carousel. I had an overwhelming urge to scream, "Sit on that and spin!"

Think Ellie! Doc knew something. He'd seen my medical records. He knew I'd been in New Zealand and injured in an explosion. No details as to how it came to be. Just the resulting shoulder reconstruction and the air lift to a U.S. naval vessel.

I was no closer to any answers.

Suddenly the boxes of meat seemed almost irrelevant. I rubbed my face.

I knew Noel was standing there, just outside the door to my room. Watching. Trying to decipher my facial expressions.

Carla would still be on her bed, lying on her stomach and oblivious to the drama around her. Between bouts of texting her besties and cartoon heaven, there was little room for mundane adult goings-on. Her focus was on staying at Rowan's and how excited her friends were; it was more than enough for my fourteen-year-old daughter.

Footsteps.

The vibration closed in.

I recognized Noel's footfalls. He crouched in front of me. Eye contact. Direct and unwavering.

"El, do you need to tell me something?"

Yes, I do.

"No." I smiled. "It's all good."

"So this JAG lawyer and his wife *were* the intended targets of some random Arab terrorist?"

"It didn't sound random. I'm sure you'll get to the bottom of it. He must've had some involvement with Habib what's-his-name."

"If he does I'll find it. Alexandria PD has copied me in on the other Conway murder. Seems Conways are the target of the moment and as a living Conway you might take a few extra precautions."

"I'm in a hotel – that's about as extra as it will get," I replied and watched a shadow butterfly dance above his head on the wall.

"When is Rowan picking up Carla?"

"About lunchtime."

"Want me to hang around?"

"Not necessary. Doc will be over soon. He's wants me to look over a case with him," I said.

"Not working the boxes of meat thing then?"

"I'm a recipient." I shrugged. We both knew that meant I was out as lead investigator. Then Gracey came into view. "But not the only one."

"There's nothing you need to tell me regarding Arbab?"

"Nope."

"You're sure about that?"

"Yep. I'm going to hang around the hotel until Rowan picks up Carla. Then I'll head into the office."

"You have nothing to tell me?"

"Nope, not a thing."

Noel leaned in and pecked me on the cheek then stood up. He walked away leaving my face burning under his kiss.

"Call me if you think of anything."

"I will." Not.

Noel walked down the hall to the elevator and waved over his shoulder. A few more minutes of sitting followed. One of the maids, pushing a laden trolley, rumbled up the hallway. I slipped back into our room. Carla was still alternating between texting and television.

"Are you packed, Carla?"

"Yes, Mom."

"Any calls?"

"Uncle Lee and Uncle Sam."

"Messages?"

"They're in Merrifield."

"Thanks."

I texted Doc and let him know he should drop by to discuss his case, then I lay on my bed and stared at the ceiling. Life was messy again. It didn't used to matter much before Carla. Now messy meant danger for her and extra worry for me. Not good.

My eyes closed.

A hot wind stirred sand, blowing it over the boxes of meat, semi-obscuring the chunks of flesh with gritty gold. I could hear Dion calling me. His voice filled with fear as it wavered from the courtyard. There he stood, pretending he'd been captured, trying to lure me out. Working with Ameer the whole time. His cunning plan to have me report his death.

People don't look for dead men.

The scene shimmered. We leaped forward eight weeks to New Zealand and Ameer's re-entry to the west. I flew over to bring him back; he had a date with Gitmo. Then the last thing I saw before the world exploded – the thing it took me six months to remember – Dion Edwards alive and well. Calling the shots, running the terror cell. He watched me die in that explosion. Demelza was dead. Everyone but Tim and Habib were dead. He couldn't know who I was. My cover was a CIA legend; it was excellent; there were no seams or cracks.

I was Demelza.

And then she died.

Chapter Ten
It's Now Or Never

"Mom!"

Half asleep, my hand reached for the Glock on the nightstand. Carla called out again, this time more panicked.

"MOM!"

I rolled off the bed as my eyes searched the room. That was when I realized it was the very same room I'd stayed in before.

"MOM!"

My index finger moved back and forth along the side of the barrel. "Where are you?"

"Here," she said with a sob.

Bathroom.

I opened the door with my left hand, holding the gun in my right. Carla was in front of the mirror. I saw his reflection immediately and looked back toward the bath tub. I holstered my gun. It would do no good.

"It's okay Carla, go into the other room," I instructed. I don't know where the calm came from but I sure hoped it would last, at least until she was out of the room.

She passed me, watching the mirror with a mix of confusion and terror. "How?" she whispered.

"I don't know."

"Have you seen him before?" She was behind me and feeling braver.

There's a time for truth. Simple truth.

"Yes."

I couldn't feel her against me anymore and figured she'd gone back to the relative safety of her bed and the television, or maybe her laptop. I shut the door.

Mac nodded.

"This is new. Tired of Messenger?"

"Trying something else," he replied and stepped out of the tub onto the thick bath mat.

"Scaring my child half to death by appearing in the mirror – not smart."

"Didn't expect her to be here."

"That makes two of you. What is it you want?" I could see my reflection and his. Why wasn't I freaking out? This isn't a Messenger window. This isn't an hallucination brought on by a migraine or head injury. Carla saw him.

He didn't look incorporeal. In fact, apart from being a little thinner than last time I saw him in person, he looked pretty good, even for a dead man. Obviously not a zombie: no hunks of putrid flesh hung off his bones and he wasn't trying to bite me.

"You know what room this is?"

"Yup."

Oh, so it was a haunting of familiar places.

I wanted to reach out and touch him but half of me was scared my hand would go right through him and the other half was scared it wouldn't. He looked so alive.

I see dead people. Carla sees dead people. Strange and yet normal at the same time.

"Why are you here?"

"Because you kept secrets and someone knows," he said, adjusting the red baseball cap on his head. Red cap. He hadn't worn that last time. Guess you can wear what you like on the other side.

"Yeah? So did you. I met someone in New Zealand who met you. Said you were FBI and working out of the embassy six, maybe seven, years ago."

I picked up my hair brush and gave the impression I was brushing my hair. My heart wasn't in it. I heard the door handle outside click and turn. Carla.

"What are you doing?" I called.

"Letting Doc in," she called back.

Twenty seconds later Doc knocked on the door. "Conway, problem?"

Mac stepped back into the tub. I looked from him to the door and then replied. "No."

"Mac, why were you in New Zealand?"

He started to fade. "Faye got the time wrong. It was ten years ..." His face blurred and shimmered becoming one with the wet wall. "Always and forever."

Doc knocked again. "Open up."

I splashed water on my face, dried off, took a breath, and opened the door. I saw the gun in Doc's hand. Doc moved in, he swept the room, checked the shower, and pulled the curtain back on the tub.

"Expecting someone?" I said, as he holstered his Glock.

"Carla said there was a man in the bathroom."

I smiled. "A freaky mother-daughter moment is all."

I made my way over to the bed and gave Carla a hug. "You okay?"

"Uh huh," she whispered. "I knew him, didn't I?"

"Yeah, you knew him. It was Mac."

"But he's—"

"I know. Just not sure he does, baby."

Doc interrupted. "You got time for this case of mine?"

"Sure," I replied and hugged Carla again. "You going to be okay?"

She nodded.

"We'll be right here, talking shop. Headphones?"

She pulled her headphones from her bag and plugged them into her laptop. I watched in silence as she chose music and turned up the volume.

"You wanna tell me what happened in there?" He indicated the bathroom with his hand.

"I see dead people," I replied with a small grimace.

"Shared hallucination? I don't think so." He smiled. "I'm a doctor. Hence I have seen plenty of dead people – none of them have ever talked. And I heard talking."

He heard talking.

"You heard me talking to myself."

"No, Conway, I heard a male voice answer you."

Holy freaking shit.

"Can we not do this, please?"

"Shall I call a priest? I'm pretty sure you both didn't share an illusion, and I sure as hell know I wasn't part of it."

I laughed it off, despite the worrying fact that Kurt heard a male voice. "We're good. It was nothing."

"Nothing?"

"Nothing. We're good. Tell me about your case?"

He didn't look as though he believed me but moved on anyway.

"A friend called. He's a doctor in a small town. Specialized in emergency medicine and went back to his home town to take over the ER there."

"Tremendous. And the problem?"

"Inexplicable deaths. Over and above what would be considered normal."

"There's a level of normal for death within a hospital?"

He shrugged. "People die."

"Imagine that? But do they stay dead? Because in my experience they freaking don't."

"You're special."

"So – someone's running around a hospital killing people?"

"He thinks so."

Air escaped through my teeth. "Have you seen the files?"

"Some. He forwarded me copies of five recent deaths. I think he's right."

"How?"

"This is the bit that sounds a little bizarre." Doc grinned. "Which makes me think I've come to the right place ..."

"Smartass. Spill it!"

"They died of various things, but all were recovering well, then without warning died. An asthmatic about to be sent home. A flu case, about to be sent home. A migraine sufferer, about to be sent home. A moderate concussion under observation ..."

"About to be sent home? I'm sensing a theme."

I'm pretty quick like that.

"Ditto. The patients are well enough for discharge yet die hours before their release." He relayed the information with clinical precision yet consternation lurked in his eyes.

"Spending time in hospital is detrimental to one's health. It's as I have always maintained – hospitals are for dead people."

"We may have a medical professional killing within a hospital."

"I concur."

"Good. I want you to come with me on this."

"Come with you?"

"I told Grant I'd be coming home and bringing my wife."

"Doc, you don't ... oh crap!"

He grinned. "You might want to practice calling me 'Kurt' not 'Doc', Mrs. Henderson."

And I thought having Arbab after me made for a bad day. Whoa! Back up. Home?

"Home? This is your home town?"

"Yes."

"Suppose you were in the same class at school too?"

"Yes."

"Okay, so two small-town boys from the same class became doctors. Anyone else get a look in or did you two steal the glory for the entire town?"

"I'm sure other people did well."

I had the impression Kurt didn't go home very often. Probably had never been to a reunion (nor had I) and hadn't kept in touch with many of the people from his youth. It's a familiar theme within our circle.

"Local boy makes it big and goes home to save the town folk from serious accident and illness ... nice." I piled up pillows and leaned back on them. "Back home, who knows you are FBI?"

"Grant."

"Your parents?"

"It was easier to just let them think I was a doctor."

We all have secrets.

"Was?"

"My parents both passed away in the last five years."

That makes it easier. That's two people fewer to break the cover story.

"I'm sorry. Any siblings?"

"No. I was a late addition to their lives."

Good to know.

"I can think of things I'd rather be doing, that don't involve being your wife ... but I'm in. Carla is going away for a few days slash weeks. Until the boxes of meat thing is resolved."

And the terrorist out to get me is caught, but that's an

aside, I don't want to make a fuss about it.

Small town America sounds awesome. I do small town America. Sometimes I miss Mauryville and country living. Not so much the way it all came crashing down around me. But some days, part of me wants to go country again.

A smile crept across my face.

"This might be fun. Where are we going?"

"Lexington."

Nope, didn't hear that. Try again.

"Pardon?"

"Lexington," he repeated, louder.

"Oh jeez. So the hospital we're talking about is Stonewall Jackson?"

I could feel the world spinning out of control. So not good! Lexington, Virginia. Stonewall Jackson Hospital. I saw Mac studying my face with his hazel eyes, telling me I'd been unconscious for some hours, had a skull fracture and a broken arm. Not my finest moment. The best thing about it all, I couldn't remember how it happened. I was stunned to find myself in hospital and with such injuries. I recalled that Mac was less than delighted to know I could remember nothing. In all fairness we did find out that I'd been drugged with Ketamine and that didn't help the memory situation.

My life is an endless parade of bizarre moments held together in a twisted framework of fragile memories.

"Hey, Conway, what's going on?" Doc tapped my arm.

The stupid thing was I knew it was him, but all I could

see was Mac.

"There's someone at the door," Doc said. "I'll get it. You just sit there and concentrate on speaking or breathing, or whatever it is you aren't, but should be doing."

My hand flipped out and smacked him as he moved.

"I'm right fuc'n here."

Processing this latest horror was not easy. Lexington blew my mind. I never thought I'd have to go back there. Once upon a time, it was the nearest big town to me and a favorite coffee destination. What fresh hell is this, that's making the past determined to shit with me in so many exciting new ways?

Doc and Rowan appeared before me. Doc's expression was one of bemusement. Rowan's was one of concern. Poles apart.

Carla threw her headphones onto the bed and bounded across the room to hug Rowan.

Chapter Eleven
All These Things That I've Done

I left Doc in the room and walked with Carla and Rowan down to his waiting car. A well-dressed, well-toned, and muscular man opened the door for her. I watched Carla scramble in, leaving her bags on the sidewalk. She fastened her seat belt and sat grinning at me through the open window.

I eyed the man as he placed bags in the trunk. He wore a sidearm.

Moments later he was introduced to me.

"Ellie, this is Jed – he's my bodyguard. He'll be accompanying us today."

I shook his hand. Ex-SWAT. Then I saw something else. It wasn't SWAT, it was navy. A hint of navy.

"SEAL?"

He nodded.

"Little Creek?"

"Virginia Beach," he said.

DEVGRU. "Who's the driver?"

"One of my men," Jed replied. "Fully qualified, been with me for about four years now. Also former SEAL."

I nodded.

"Have a safe trip."

"Yes, ma'am."

He climbed into the front passenger seat, closed the door and left me alone with Rowan in front of the Marriott. Sideways looks from passersby gave hints that perhaps Rowan may be famous. The holster I wore on my hip probably deterred the usual autograph seekers. The last two days had spun me in freaking circles and I really didn't care what anyone on the street thought as I stepped into his arms. I wanted to jump in the car and go with them. The idea of sinking into oblivion protected by two former navy SEALs felt good. It was a special level of safety and security. One my child needed.

"You okay?" he whispered into my hair.

"Sure. I'm okay."

Maybe I was holding on a little tight.

"Darlin', this isn't okay. This isn't all right. I don't know what's going on—"

"It's work. Everything will be fine."

Arbab won't find me before Noel finds him. The boxed meat is some kind of sick joke. Mac will stay dead. The killer in Stonewall Jackson Hospital will be some statistical anomaly, not an actual killer. Silver linings all around.

"I'll take good care of Carla. Come join us when you can. We're playing a charity concert next week. Would be great if you could come."

"I'll do my best."

"Stay in touch."

"Count on it." I remembered the undercover operation. "You have my cell number. I will be undercover, just go with anything you hear and don't question it."

He nodded. I felt his chin rub the top of my head.

"Gracey called me."

I tried not to tense.

"Really?"

"She told me about the box of meat, Sam and Lee, calling you."

Good that he thinks meat, not hunks of assorted people. Damn that ass bandit.

"And?"

"Management decided to increase security for the entire band." There was a pause so laden with thoughts I could've cut them all free. "The FBI is involved – a favor? Or is this something serious?"

Don't want to go here. "It's part of an investigation," I said and added, "Not mine."

I didn't lie. It felt good. It's not my investigation.

"We'll get going."

"Yeah, you should. You look exhausted." Exhausted or not, his blue eyes still shone with a suppressed smile.

"Come for a few days, soon as you can." Rowan tipped my chin up with two fingers and kissed me, slowly. "Soon."

I could've stayed there forever.

"Definitely."

He let me go and opened the door.

Carla squealed, "Bye, Mom!"

"Bye, sweetheart, be good."

I closed the door while looking into Rowan's eyes and wished I were going too.

By the time I walked back up the hallway to my room I found a smile. Hell, I was dating Rowan Grange. The smile came from knowing at least twenty million women had died a little inside when that news hit the blogs and trashy magazines. Someone would've caught our kiss on camera and that too would make them die a little inside.

Doc lay on my bed. Feet crossed, hands behind his head, watching television.

"Comfy?"

"Yes. Everything good?"

"Absolutely."

"What's with the ..." He ran his finger over his own smile.

"Women worldwide hate me," I replied happily, while checking for anything Carla may have left behind.

"And that makes you smile?"

"Yeah. I'm a bad person."

I reached under the bed and pulled out a pair of socks and a tee shirt. The kid would lose her head if it wasn't screwed on. I dropped them into my open bag.

Lexington. I'm going back to Lexington. Yep, that killed the smile.

"Sandra called about Robin Conway."

"And?"

"Strangled in her bed."

"Fuck! I should've listened when I heard the damn song the first time."

"What song?"

"'Rockin' Robin.'"

"You hear any songs that mention my name you let me know A-sap," he said, switching off the television with the remote and standing up. His voice softened, all humor gone. "Sometimes a song is just a song. You're human. We don't always get things on the first go-round."

"That's another Conway. Another one. This is not good," I replied, resting against the counter edge.

"I think we should head down to Lexington this evening. Any preference on hotels or motels?"

"Not The Mountain Oasis," I said without looking at him. That really would be pushing my mental stability to the outer reaches.

Space: the final frontier. There was a weird buzz and *Star Trek* morphed into something new and I couldn't stop it. Nathan Fillion sauntered into view. Took me a second to catch up; I knew it wasn't Castle I was seeing but what was it? Firefly. I looked up at Mal Reynolds and realized I was on his ship. His eyes met mine and he said, "Here's how it is—"

"No, Mal, let me tell ya how it really is. I need to join your crew. God knows I'm interesting enough to fit in, and enough people want me dead to make it fun for you."

Half a smile twitched in the corner of his mouth. "Welcome aboard," he said and faded to gray just like his surroundings.

"See ya, Mal," I whispered hoping it wasn't audible.

"What was that?"

"Nothing."

I glanced around the room and zipped my bag closed.

"I'm packed."

Chapter Twelve
Living In Sin

"Do you need to go into the office?" Kurt asked as I completed the paperwork to check out of the hotel.

"Nope. Need to drop in at home though. Need some stuff." I put my credit card back in my purse, folded the paperwork with care, and then stuffed it into my bag. I am a mass of contradictions.

"Hope to see you again, ma'am," the receptionist crowed.

I nodded and moved away from the desk.

Kurt held the door for me. "It's a crime scene, complete with police cordon tape and guards."

I figured as much. I pictured a chalk outline around the tweaker's crumpled body – not crime scene procedure in reality. The thought brought a smile to my face. Now I'm living a B-grade movie, complete with chalk outline and crazed killers. Gotta love it.

"I still need to pick up some things," I replied, and tapped on the trunk, reminding him to open it for me. With my bags stowed I swung into the front passenger seat of Kurt's car.

"Hey, I drove here last night. I can't leave Ma ... my truck here indefinitely." A way out lurched into focus. "Maybe I should follow you."

Yeah. Then I'd have my own car and I could escape Lexington whenever I felt the urge. Or just never turn up.

That would work. Well, for about half an hour, before someone found me. A red Toyota Tacoma 4x4 double-cab, riddled with bullet holes, was going to stick out like a dog's you-know-what. Of course they could simply activate the GPS in the truck; it was installed so no matter which car I drove, I wasn't off the grid. The old double-edged sword dilemma. The GPS kept us safe and directed emergency services when everything turned to custard, but it also meant I couldn't run away. Some days I just wanted to run.

Eyes watched me. I glanced sideways. Kurt watched me, his hand still on the ignition key.

"Lee or Sam could pick up your car and take it back to the office," he said.

For a moment I wondered if my thoughts weren't thoughts but spoken words. I didn't want to ask and he was still looking at me as if I had two heads.

Opting for a de-escalation of the look I was getting, I pulled out my phone and called Sam. He was only too happy to pick up the truck.

Good. That was settled then.

"You're sure about home? Can't we buy whatever you need on the way?"

"It's easier if I stop in at home."

I can't go back to Lexington with blonde hair, looking so much like me. I lived in Rockbridge County, people know me down there. What's more they know I married Mac and that I'm FBI – hell, I think all of Mauryville came to our wedding and the launch of our bestselling poetry book – not necessarily in that order. The combination of the poetry book and Rockbridge County made me feel sick.

Visions of Abigail swinging from a nail on my back-door almost choked me. Poor Abigail, she was a good chicken.

Kurt started the car. "We'll go to your place."

A horrid ball of dread squished into my stomach. No amount of telling myself it would all be okay diminished the anxiety. An internal jitteriness translated into my hands shaking.

I checked my cell phone, in case I'd missed something important. An offer of coffee with my Dad or maybe a sale at Bed, Bath & Beyond; they would be important. Straws tumbled all over and I was left grasping the very last one.

When I turned it over in my hand it read '*screwed.*'

Kurt must've detected movement. "What you got there?"

My hands were empty and shaking. Imagine that?

"Nothing."

He sighed. It was quiet but it was a sigh. One of those don't-tell-me-it-was-nothing sighs. I looked out the window. All hope faded. I was going back to Lexington and nothing short of my death would stop that. There was an out. Maybe I could tell Doc I wasn't ready to go back; he was there, he'd understand.

Maybe's ass.

A sudden growl made me jump. My head spun. It

wasn't from Doc, or the vacant back seat. Was it from me?

Out the windshield, I could see home, or at least the trees that signposted my road. As we turned the corner I could see the street. It was a quiet street with wide grass verges. Not even a street really, but a cul-de-sac that appeared as though it had sprung from the woods surrounding it. Almost at the end was home. FBI and police tape waved gently in the breeze. Two police cars sat, one on each side of the street. Just sitting. Silent sentries.

Fluttering became pounding as Doc pulled into the driveway. My breathing quickened. Adrenaline? I almost jumped out of the car while it was still moving.

Tape was tied to the mailbox, strung across the lawn, and around the front door. I headed for the back door, not even bothering to acknowledge the officers. I knew Doc would badge them and follow me.

My heart pounded, leaping partway to my mouth as I opened the backdoor. My fingers tightened around the butt of my Glock. Jumpy much?

Doc coughed. Before I knew what had happened I'd spun on my heels and drawn on him.

"Conway!"

I looked from Doc to my Glock and back.

A smile and a quick apology wouldn't cover it. I slipped the Glock back into my holster and shrugged.

"Little jumpy, sorry."

"You're kidding?" He let his feigned astonishment rain down.

Instructions from the voice in my head poured forth. Ignore him. Do what you have to do. Go upstairs and don't be you anymore.

There was so much effort involved in not running up the stairs three at a time. Two at a time was plenty. My heart raced.

Doc was behind me. I kept telling myself he was there. Don't shoot Doc. I went into my bedroom and into the walk-in closet. The search through drawers began. Fifteen minutes later I stood in my bathroom with two packets of temporary hair dye and a dark-blonde wig. In front of me on the counter was a small box containing colored contact lenses. Brown.

Goodbye blue eyes? I heard The Who singing 'Behind Blue Eyes'. It took me a minute to realize it wasn't Limp Bizkit singing.

I looked deep into my dark blue eyes, trying to find something that suggested that going back to Lexington was the right thing to do. No matter how tentative the suggestion.

"Conway?" Doc's voice penetrated the closed bathroom door. "You all right?"

I looked at the time on my watch.

Staring at the mirror for ten minutes wasn't helping me make a decision. My brain kicked in. It had to be the dye.

"Yeah, I'm fine."

I opened the box and mixed the dye. With an old white towel wrapped around my shoulders I covered my hair, root to tips with the first pack of dye, then mixed the second lot and repeated. I hoped two packs of dye would allow good coverage. Nothing worse than a patchy home-dye job and I didn't have time to go to a salon.

The smell was almost overpowering. I went back out into my room. Doc was sitting on the sofa by the far wall, reading a book. He looked up.

"Thought I could smell dye. What color are you going?"

"A dark brown, I hope," I replied, catching sight of my darkening hair in the bedroom mirror. "Ten minutes and we'll know."

Just so long as it doesn't go green.

I used the time to pack some extra clothes. No telling how long we'd be gone. A nagging feeling of disquiet churned. I shoved some of my favorite clothes into the bag, including my academy sweats.

From my nightstand I took two spare Glock magazines, and a new box of nine millimeter bullets. I packed them into the same bag I'd shoved the extra clothes. I could've sat down and just chilled but I was scared Kurt would ask me questions and I might spill the truth. A great big cloud of dark hovered over my head.

The end of the world is nigh.

Best to keep busy.

Time spared me too much thought by moving faster than I expected.

"I'll wash this out," I said as I ducked into the bathroom, shut the door and turned the shower on. For three seconds I debated the pros and cons of sticking my head under the water streaming from the shower head or stripping off and having a shower. Two seconds later a pile of my clothes lay on the floor and I was washing out the dye. Rivers of dark brown poured over me and ran down the glass walls.

I finished rinsing and stepped out, dripping all over the bathmat. Wrapping the old white towel around my head I grabbed an extra towel and dried off. It wasn't long before I was dressed and standing in front of the steamed mirror, watching as a small clear patch appeared and spread.

I unwound the sodden towel from my head for the big reveal and let my hair fall down my back.

It was dark brown all right. No sign of green or any missed areas.

With the care that came from knowing I wouldn't be home for a while, I hung the towels and bathmat so they wouldn't go moldy. I did consider dumping the now blotchy old white towel straight in the trash. But there would be no one home to take the trash out. Moldy towel in the trash would smell as much as a moldy towel in the laundry hamper. There was a knock at the door. I reached over and opened it.

"What do you think?" I asked as Kurt surveyed me.

"I like it."

"Me too."

I ran a brush through my hair, pushing my bangs back off my forehead. My eyes fell upon the contact lens box. I didn't want to put them in.

"Brown?" I held the box up for Kurt to see.

"No."

That was quick.

"Okay."

His expression changed. "Go brown."

"Okay." What the hell? All of a sudden I was Miss Congeniality. Stop me before I agree again.

"You all right?"

"Of course," I replied. "Just getting ready to be your delightful wife."

"Blue, Conway. Keep your eyes blue."

Whatever. I dusted a light coating of mineral powder across my face, smudged a thin black line of kohl pencil close to my lashes, and added a swipe of mascara.

"Done." I tossed the mascara back into the vanity drawer. I kept a pre-packed makeup bag in my go-bag. So I already had everything a girl could require in a bathroom, in the car.

"If only all women could get ready as fast as you," he said, leaning on the wall. Our eyes met in the mirror. "Can I check your arm?"

Without arguing, I wriggled my left arm out of my long-sleeved tee shirt and showed him. Doc pulled the waterproof dressing off and inspected his handiwork.

"Looks good. Let's leave it without a dressing now."

"Okay."

There I go again, being agreeable. The end of the world really is nigh.

He dropped the bandage into the bathroom garbage bin. I shoved my arm back down my sleeve and hooked a couple of hair ties around my wrist for later.

"Let's do this."

A loud rumble shook the floor. I staggered and reached for the swaying wall. An explosion ripped through the house. Wood creaked and crumpled, walls buckled, the floor began to split. Another explosion.

Doc grabbed me as I fell back toward the mirror. With one hand on the wall and one grasping my arm, he pulled me closer.

"Okay?"

"Yep," I replied. We edged back into the bedroom. I snatched my bag from the bed, along with the holster from where I'd dropped it on the chair and snapped it to my belt. Smoke alarms beeped with ear piercing decibels from all over the house.

People were yelling.

Doc stood staring out the door.

"What do you think it was that exploded?" I asked, joining him.

"I don't know ... the stairs are falling."

I looked down the hallway and saw the banister hanging in midair. A smoky haze filled the air below us. As I watched, the insistent beeping from the smoke alarms poked little holes in the haze. I blinked; smoke was beginning to hurt my eyes.

"Follow me," I said, heading back into the bedroom. I swung open the balcony doors and stepped out. It felt solid. I dropped my bag to the ground below. Next to the balcony was a ladder. I reached out and grabbed hold of the top rungs. Cold steel felt good under my hands. Six feet away I saw a gaping hole that used to be the downstairs bathroom. Back in the other direction another large hole of splintered wood.

"It's stable," I said, clambering down as fast as possible. When my feet hit the ground, Kurt started his descent, semi-climbed, semi-slid, down the ladder, landing with a thump. I picked up my bag which was covered in dust. We headed toward the driveway, picking our way over splintered wood and broken glass. Another explosion shook the ground. I stumbled and ducked as a large hunk of wood slammed into the ground next to me.

Doc's hand grabbed mine. We emerged from the rubble- and debris-filled side of the house onto the driveway to find police in a panic.

"This is not good," I muttered, wiping dust from my face with an equally grimy shirt sleeve. Flames leaped from the roof. "Shit!"

"Hope you have everything you need," Doc said, as more flames joined a thick black curtain of smoke.

"I have what's important. Carla is at Rowan's and the cat is at my brother's. Nothing else matters a damn." I shucked the bag I'd been carrying from my shoulders and dropped it on the driveway. "Nothing else matters ..."

Apart from the flash drives in my desk drawer.

Shit!

I took off at a run, racing around the other side of the

house and slammed through the back door. Thick smoke billowed in the hallway. Smoke alarms were overshadowed by cracking wood and breaking glass. I pulled the neck of my tee shirt up over my mouth and nose, and charged into the office. My fingers scrabbled in the top drawer, before pulling out a bunch of keys and flash drives. I shoved them into my pocket and ran.

The hallway was now pitch dark. Smoke hurt my lungs and burned my eyes. I blinked hard and fast and dropped to my knees. It was easier to see on the ground, and a little easier to breathe.

Crawling fast, I found the laundry room, kicked the door shut as I entered, then jumped to my feet and flung open the back door. My lungs were gasping for air as I ran from the house. Doc grabbed me. His hands placed something over my mouth and nose. I felt cool grass and solid ground beneath me.

"Breathe."

I did. Clean fresh oxygen.

After a few cleansing breaths I lifted the mask. "I'm good, thank you."

"After that stunt, I sincerely hope you got what you needed!"

I patted my pocket. "I did."

"Hope it was worth it."

"It is."

Six flash drives that contained my life with Mac. Pictures, movies, poems, life. They hung on the keychain with the spare keys to his truck, and the keys to my former home in Mauryville. I'm not ready to let that all go.

Not yet. It was my life.

Flames leaped. Orange. Yellow. Acrid black smoke billowed. More flames curled from under the eaves. Popping sounds erupted from within the burning house.

"Ammunition?" he said, helping me to my feet.

"Yeah … we should get the hell away from here."

He hoisted the portable oxygen tank over his shoulder and we hurried to the driveway. I called out to the police officers standing around. "We have exploding ammunition, back up!" A coughing fit followed. Guess my lungs weren't quite as recovered as I thought.

Sirens screamed closer and closer.

Little burning balls fired from the house, looking like tracer fire. Several hit the garage, causing a nearby cop to yelp and hurry out of the way.

"How much ammo we talking about?" Doc said as he encouraged me to get in his car.

"Approximately six boxes of shotgun shells, twelve-gauge. About four boxes of nine millimeter rounds and I don't know how many .38 specials."

"The explosions are all coming from the back," he said as another firecracker noise erupted.

"Most of the ammo was in my office, at the back." I remembered the rifle. "There's a box of rounds for my M16 in the office too."

He grinned. Funny how my mentioning an M16 always drew grins from men.

"You don't have any grenades or Scud missiles in

there?"

The smile on his face faded when he thought I was thinking about my answer. I shook my head, dust fell. "Nope."

Fire engines pulled up. Flames and black smoke filled the sky, with the occasional tracer fire. The house where Mac lived was gone. The home he shared with me was gone. I twisted and wriggled in the seat and eventually pulled my cell phone from my pocket and called my father.

"Dad, get them to install sprinklers in the new house. Today."

"All right. What's up?"

"I'm homeless again. Carla's at Rowan's. I'm heading to Lexington on a case." I sensed the panic taking hold. "My fucking house just burst into flames!"

"You're okay?"

"Of course."

"That's all that matters. It's just stuff, Ellie. Stuff is replaceable."

"I know. It's just – twice? What are the odds?"

"I'll get your brother to do the insurance. Just go do your job. We'll take care of it."

"Thanks, Dad." Then I had another thought. "Can you cancel the moving company? There won't be anything left to pack."

That solved the problem of packing Mac's belongings.

"Sorry, kid. I'll get on to them."

I hung up to find a cop standing in front of the car, patiently waiting.

"Can I help you?"

"Craig, the officer over there, tells me your plumber came by this morning to fix the hot water cylinder."

The cop didn't seem sure that the cylinder needed fixing. And he was right. I didn't call a plumber because there was nothing wrong with my hot water.

"There was nothing wrong with it. You might want to check the cylinders, once the fire's out. There are two. I'd say that's the point of origin for the explosions."

"I hear you're away on a case. Who shall we contact regarding the house and fire?"

"My father." I wrote his phone number on the back of one of my cards and handed it to him. "Or you can contact my SAC, Caine Grafton."

"Thank you. I'm very sorry about your house."

He seemed very sorry, which made it all that much harder for me to bite back the tears I could feel prickling behind my eyes. I blinked hard and forced them away.

I closed the car door and fastened my seat belt while my house burned. It felt like I'd been here before and it was only going to get worse. I couldn't stop my mind going back to the last time my house exploded. All I could think was to be thankful there were no heads cooking under the hood of Doc's car.

I held my breath as he turned the key in the ignition. Just in case.

I could see it all so clearly: We were making our escape from my home in Mauryville. The car wouldn't start. Mac jumped out to look under the hood, expecting to employ his skills as MacGyver and fix the problem. Instead he discovered a severed head and everything got so much worse.

This time the car started without a hitch. Doc didn't notice I was holding my breath.

"Want to listen to some music?" he offered. He gave a couple of short blasts on the car horn as we left.

Chapter Thirteen
Turn It On

Doc filled me in on his buddy Doctor Grant Neal during the three hour plus drive. Every time I looked over at him I heard Kevin Costner singing. By the time we were half way to Lexington, I was well versed in Doc's years at medical school with Grant and well-practiced in calling and thinking of Doc as Kurt. I also knew all the words to every song on Costner's 'Turn It On' album. My phone went every twenty or so minutes throughout the drive, but oddly it didn't stop the music in my head.

Sam checked in; Lee checked in; Noel wanted to make sure there was nothing I could tell him about Arbab; Rowan called to say Carla was enjoying his swimming pool, they were going to have a barbecue for dinner, and the rest of the band was joining them.

I checked on Twitter. Lots more *@replies* and comments from people still waiting for mail. A bunch of comments from The Butterfly Foundation kids who were still discussing my non-death. I followed the tweets on the Foundation hash tag. It made it so much easier to track conversations. The Foundation used *#Butterflykids* as the hash tag. I sent one tweet.

EllieConwaySA: *Am away with work, kids. Don't believe everything you see on TV. #Butterflykids*

Police called to say they'd found another box at my house, left after the explosion. It was by what had been the mailbox, but no one saw who left it. I had them turn it over to Lee.

"Another box," I said to Kurt.

But no more dead Conways, which was a relief.

"Damn." He checked his rearview mirror. "There's a car, two cars back. A silver sedan of some kind. See if you can get a look at it in the wing mirror. We could have a tail."

So the 'damn' wasn't about the new box of ass then. I checked the mirror and caught a glimpse of the car in question.

"I'll try for tags," I said, watching as the car came into view again. Sometimes bends in roads are good things. I leaned forward and picked up the radio handset. "SSA Conway requesting QV."

"Go ahead SSA."

"Tango, Romeo, Alpha, five, five, five."

"A silver Mitsubishi Galant registered to a company in Fairfax. Central Holdings Limited."

"Owner?"

"Company is owned by Abbudin Nader, who lives in Fairfax."

Any other day the name would've meant nothing. The clawing dread and the sudden onset cold sweat, pointed to something. It coincided with Kevin Costner singing 'Turn It On' – it's good that *he's* not afraid of anything. It's beginning to look as though I should be.

"Thank you." I hung up as soon as the soothing voice in Comms said goodbye.

"What have we got?" Kurt asked, his eyes flashing to the rearview mirror again.

"A car registered to a Fairfax company, owned by one Abbudin Nader. Could be heading south for business."

"Could be."

The part of me that was shaking and feeling sick wanted to call Noel and tell him someone with an Arab name might, or might not be, following us. It sounded whacky. Not everyone with an Arab name is out to get me.

I started reciting the names of people I knew, people I worked with. People I'd helped. Anyone I could think of with an Arab-sounding name. Hoping it would calm me. I was just about calm when the car pulled out to overtake. One look at the passenger caused bile to rise so rapidly I threw up in my hands.

Habib Faisal Arbab.

Kurt pulled off the road and stopped. The silver car disappeared into the horizon. So it wasn't a tail? Kurt didn't say a word as he climbed out of the car and grabbed a bag from the trunk. He opened my door; I saw a bottle of water and a towel in his hands. I stuck my dripping hands out the open door; he poured water over them, and then thrust the towel into my right hand.

I felt awful. I couldn't tell if it was 'embarrassed awful' or I felt 'sick awful.'

"Do you need to change? Did you get puke on your jeans?"

I looked down. A few drops of bile and coffee melted into my jeans. I took the towel and wet it then rubbed at the dark patches. They spread. It wasn't going to work.

"I'll change."

My legs swung out of the car as if they intended to stand and walk me to the trunk. They sure tricked me. I stood. For a split freaking second.

"Okay, here we go. Up and at 'em, Conway." Kurt was in front of me. He placed his hands on the sides of my rib cage and lifted. Not letting go until I was leaning on the car door. "How're you feeling?"

"Stupid."

"You've been whacked out all day. Now this. Think a check-up wouldn't hurt."

"I'm okay. I promise. I just felt sick. Perfectly fine now." I lied through my teeth: I was clammy, shaky, and nauseous. My head had started to twinge. Traffic slowed as it passed us. Rubberneckers.

"I believe you. You must be fine. You can't even stand straight and you look like you've seen a ghost."

That'll be because I did.

"I'll change my jeans and then we can get going." I heard the words. Then I saw them. Words bouncing on the gravel like rubber balls. One started to roll away. It rolled then stuck fast in front of the back wheel. I tried again. "I'll change ..."

"You said that. Do you want help?"

"Would you hand me a pair of jeans?"

He smiled. Moments later he dropped a pair of jeans over the door. "This is how we're doing this. Unbutton and unzip your jeans, take them down far enough for you to sit and take out your legs."

There were so many smartassed comments brewing and I couldn't utter any of them. I just did as he suggested. Kurt pulled off my boots and then my jeans. He helped me put on the clean pair, then pushed my boots back onto my feet. Without making a single remark.

My sullied jeans were crammed into a plastic bag and tossed in the trunk. Our journey continued without incident, with the windows wide open to disperse the smell of vomit.

We checked into the hotel as Mr. and Mrs. Henderson, I listened as Kurt took care of the check in, making sure we had champagne, after all we were on honeymoon. That was either news to me, or I hadn't heard when he tossed that at me earlier.

The girl at the front desk watched us.

Honeymoon? That upped the level of intimacy involved. We were escorted to our suite. Kurt, ever attentive, walked with his hand resting in the small of my back. There was no running away now.

At the door he nuzzled my neck while the room was opened.

He broke away with reluctance to thank the young lady who'd shown us to the room, take the key and give her a hefty tip.

I wandered through the small living area and into the bedroom. Alone, I fell backwards onto the bed and closed my eyes. On the inside of my eyelids I saw flames licking the bookcases and photographs that once lined the walls of my home. I forced my eyes open; the flames disappeared. With some effort I convinced myself that a hotel under an assumed name equaled safe. Whoever blew up my house didn't know where I was.

I had no idea where the silver Galant went, but I knew it wasn't in this hotel parking lot and that's all I needed to know. My eyes closed, soothing the irritating beginnings of the headache I'd felt before. I readied an internal fire extinguisher in case the flames returned.

When my eyes opened again the light was dim and I could see Kurt though the door, which was ajar. He was talking on the telephone not his cell phone. I rolled over, propped myself up on my elbow and waited for him to finish.

As I lay there coffee wafted from the other room. I needed that coffee. Kurt was still talking. I figured I wasn't interrupting, seeing as we were married. I tiptoed past him. That was when I noticed I wasn't wearing boots.

Panicked, I looked down. I still had jeans on.

I heard him say, "She's just woken up. We'll be over in an hour or so."

I guessed it was buddy Grant as I poured a coffee and added a generous amount of sugar. I curled into an armchair with the cup of coffee. Kurt joined me.

"Have a nice nap?"

"I did. Must've been tired. I feel much better." That wasn't a total lie. I did feel better, just not as much as I implied.

"We're going to Grant and Kim's for drinks later. You up for that?"

I nodded. My head didn't explode or even hurt that much. It was all good.

"Sounds like fun."

"Remember, everyone thinks we're just married."

"I got that from the display at the front desk, thanks."

"Just a reminder."

"What? That we gotta play grab ass all night?"

He did a small shrug and grinned. "There are worse things."

"Good to know."

"You're comfortable with this?"

"Yeah, you're not repulsive," I replied, and moved on. "Grant called you about the deaths, yes?"

"Yes."

"So does he know I am FBI?"

"Nope. Figured it would be better if no one knew."

"Good. I can observe without anyone getting antsy." I sipped my coffee. It wasn't Columbian, nor was it made from one hundred percent Arabica beans. But it wasn't horrible, just close to it. "I'll finish this unusual tasting coffee then have a quick shower. Jeans okay? This is casual?"

"Jeans are fine." He smiled. We both knew he'd be wearing a very smart dark blue or maybe charcoal gray suit.

"Why not try the suit jacket over jeans?" It was a suggestion I'd been longing to make.

"You sure?"

"Yeah. Be a man on the edge. Throw caution to the wind."

Kurt's eye brows rose. "Man on the edge, huh?"

I shrugged. He went into the bedroom then came back wearing a gray suit jacket, a dark tee shirt, and light blue straight jeans.

Kevin Costner all the way. A song filled my being. 'Long Hot Night'. Oh man, that so isn't fair. My mind made a frantic attempt to shut down Kevin Costner and Modern West before it really was a long hot night. I swallowed my coffee before it choked me.

"That works."

"You're sure?"

"Uh huh."

I couldn't say anything else, I was afraid my voice would crumble. More important, I was afraid I would crumble. I crammed my mind full of images of Rowan to push the Kevin Costner thing away. Rowan Grange. Women hated me. Women hated me because I dated Rowan Grange.

Rowan wasn't like anyone I'd ever met. I concentrated on Rowan and how women worldwide hated me. It felt good.

I needed my phone. The internal jitteriness returned with a vengeance. I was still capable of doing math. Too much coffee, plus zero food since breakfast, plus stress equals I need to eat, and eat now. I cannot go out for drinks without eating. That was a recipe for disaster.

"Any clue where my phone is? And we should eat before we go out." I hoped that sounded as casual as it should. I didn't want him going all freaky on me.

He was still admiring himself in the mirror.

"We'll head down to the restaurant and have dinner. Your phone is on the nightstand, charging."

Wow.

"Thank you for doing that." I stood up, waited for the spinning to stop, then went to get my phone. I lay on the bed and called Rowan.

"Hey, how's it going?" He sounded happy. Upon reflection, I concluded that was how he almost always sounded unless he was dog tired.

"It's okay. We're down in Lexington, about to go have dinner. Miss you."

"I miss you too."

"How's Carla?"

"She's brilliant. Having a good time. Derek is teaching her to play drums."

That explained the noise. Great! That's just what I needed, a drum-playing teenager.

"You couldn't teach her guitar?"

Rowan laughed. "If she has her way, she'll learn to play every instrument known to man."

"Make sure she knows she is not getting a drum kit!"

"You sound better?"

I looked around. No Kurt. He must still be in the living area, admiring himself.

"Don't jinx it. I'm not feeling wonderful – think I've

picked up a bug."

"If you have, you're in good hands. You're with Doc right?"

"Yep. I better get going, just wanted to check in with you guys."

"Check up on me and make sure I'm not being a bad influence on Super Girl?"

"Not at all. You are great with her." I meant every word.

"Okay, darlin', I'll hear from you later?"

"You will, not sure when, but you will."

I pressed the end call button and set the phone back on the charger. The coffee I'd drunk sloshed around my stomach as I stood up. It took some effort to ignore it but I managed. After a brief search I found tidier jeans and a nice long-sleeved button-down black shirt. I carted my essentials – makeup, deodorant, shampoo, and so forth – into the bathroom.

"Doc, I'm having a shower," I called as I turned the shower on. I noticed a damp towel hanging on the rack. It reminded me of how carefully I'd hung up the towels at home, right before the house exploded. A long sigh escaped. I erased the burning house images and concentrated on the present. Kurt must've had a shower already. That explained why he was looking so fresh and why he smelled so good.

No ghosts emerged from the steam.

The shower helped more than the nap. I felt almost alive by the time I was dressed, made-up, and blasting my hair with the hotel hair dryer. I didn't smell like smoke anymore; going out to meet people smelling like a house fire wouldn't make the best impression, and I don't need the extra help to make a crappy first impression.

Doc appeared in the open bathroom doorway.

"You look nice," he commented, leaning on the door frame.

I unplugged the hair dryer and put it back in the drawer. Tossed my hair about a little bit then ran my fingers through it, smoothing out the fly-away strands. Raking my bangs with my fingers covered the scar on my forehead. I fastened the buttons on my cuffs. Hiding scars was what I did best.

"So do you." I gave him a quick once over. "Step over here."

He stood next to me. We both looked in the mirror.

"This works, we look like we belong," he said, smiling. "Let's do it, Conway."

"Just like that, huh?"

"Bite me."

"Oh, the temptation." I smiled. "You need to get used to calling me Ellie."

His eyes searched mine within the mirror.

"Gabrielle," he whispered.

A chill ran up my spine.

"Don't ..."

Chapter Fourteen
Superman Tonight

Red meat seemed to be the best option as I gazed at the menu in my hand. I'd noticed the three people in the restaurant, who all took too much interest in us as we'd entered.

Steak. Doc played the attentive new husband without fault. I opted for water over wine.

His hand reached across the table, fingers seeking mine.

"Can I call you by your middle name?" he said, his voice barely audible.

"How did you introduce me to Grant, in conversation?" I matched his tone.

"As Mrs. Henderson." He smiled. "It's an old joke. He used to say when I married I would have to call my wife 'Mrs. Henderson' because I wouldn't be able to remember her name."

"Forgetful?"

He grinned. "I had a lot of *friends* in college."

"Of the female persuasion?"

His grin widened. I took that as a 'yes.'

"Rylee—"

"Better than your first thought." I smiled. "You do know that my phone will ring at some stage, and I can't guarantee I won't answer it with either Ellie or Conway."

"Hence the newlywed status. People expect names to

get confused."

"Call me Rylee if you like. It's not so much different from Ellie that I won't know you mean me; I can fudge it and say anyone overhearing me say Ellie heard wrong."

Gabrielle Rylee Conway. Ellie Conway. Rylee Henderson. What a progression.

The steak was good. I think I finished it in record time. Hungrier than I thought, and I thought I was plenty hungry. A waitress approached our table.

"Would you like dessert, sweetheart?" Kurt leaned across the table and kissed me, his lips just brushing mine.

I held in the urge to laugh check and replied, "No, I'm good, thank you."

He pulled my chair out for me. Smiling, I slipped my hand in his and we sauntered out of the restaurant toward the hotel car lot. Unless we were in our hotel room alone, we were a couple. A newlywed couple.

Sometimes life is just meant to entertain. Sometimes you have to go with it.

Kurt drove. I enjoyed seeing familiar stores and places I used to visit. I couldn't help but cast a sidelong wary glance at the Interscape Café as we drove by. Kurt also looked over at the tree-lined parking lot, his face registering the resurgence of a memory.

We looked at each other and gave miniscule shrugs. We'd survived.

I remembered the day he told me in that parking lot that he didn't ever want to eat at my house. Funny how life changes. Not always funny ha ha though.

Kurt pulled the car into the driveway of a beautiful old house.

"We're here. You ready to do this?"

"Sure, Doc. Let's do it."

He leaned in and kissed me. Then paused to whisper in my ear. "The curtain moved, we're being watched."

With my lips close to his ear I whispered back, "We've been under the magnifying glass since we hit the Rockbridge County line, or hadn't you noticed?"

"I hadn't."

"The curtain twitched on the neighbor's windows too."

Kurt pulled back as we heard a door open. A male voice called out, "Hello!"

"We're up, Rylee. Don't forget to call me Kurt." Kurt said, plastering a big grin across his face.

"Here we go," I replied, following suit. I wanted to tell him to stick close as another wave of clammy queasiness hit, but didn't want him to think I was ill. So I said nothing and hoped I still looked okay.

Many questions occupied my thoughts, none of them good. Where did the Silver Galant go? Why was Arbab heading into Rockbridge? Should I call Jonathon with the information? Should I call Noel and tell him I do know Arbab, and I even saw him today? Should I mention any of this to Kurt?

All my thoughts lumped together and I shoved them, smoldering, under the car mat as my door opened and Kurt reached in for my hand. Ever the attentive husband.

As I stepped out of the car he pulled me to him, his lips brushed my ear long enough to say, "Smile, you look like you're trying to save the world." He turned to Grant. "Rylee, this is Grant Neal."

I extended my hand and smiled. "Good to meet you, Grant. I've heard a lot about you."

"Then you have me at a disadvantage because your husband kept very quiet about you," Grant replied shaking my hand. "You look a little familiar."

I extracted my hand from his grasp. He didn't look at all familiar, so I guessed he hadn't been a doctor at Stonewall Jackson when I was admitted.

Leon Kapowski's face drifted across the blank slate behind my eyes. He was the doctor I remembered from Stonewall, a neurosurgeon who now worked at Inova Fairfax Hospital, and was still my neuro guy. Lucky man.

Kurt whispered in my ear, "Lost you for a second there, all right?"

I smiled, hooked my arm through his, and gave him a quick kiss on the cheek to disguise my whispered answer, "Not even a little bit."

With a display fit for stage, Kurt twirled me into his arms and looked deep into my eyes.

"I'll stick close."

Grant laughed at Kurt's exhibition. "Come on you two lovebirds – Kim's waiting inside."

Kurt kept his arm around me as we followed Grant up the path, and into the delightful old house. Music was playing in the background. I listened and heard 'Superman Tonight' from *The Circle*, Bon Jovi's latest album.

Grant ushered us into a spacious living room where an attractive blonde-haired woman waited. The music was no louder in there. I wondered if only I could hear it, and if so, why that song?

Kurt greeted Kim with warmth and introduced us. It was obvious he knew her. My eyes searched for the stereo or something that would explain the music.

A stereo system sat idle. The television was off. There wasn't even an iPod playing. Guess the song was for me and only me. No doubt the reason would become apparent.

"Red or white or bubbles?" Grant asked, standing by an old oak sideboard.

Not bubbles. Bourbon would have been my first choice, but as it wasn't offered I went with the least of the three evils.

"White, please," I said before Kurt could answer for me.

Grant handed me a glass of Chardonnay. "White for Rylee, how about you Kim?"

"Bubbles for me."

Kurt did the sensible thing with a wave of his car keys. "Just juice for me, Grant."

Grant poured himself a glass of bubbly and sat next to his wife on one sofa. Kurt and I occupied the other sofa.

Small talk ensued for about half a glass of wine. The song kept coming back. Over and over again. The lyrics flashing on a screen in my head. Jon Bon Jovi was singing about how he didn't know a person but wanted to save her and how he didn't know what that meant. I edged ever closer to screaming, "Stop! I don't know you either and I don't know what that means!"

It was a fight to keep the smile on my face and stay up with the current conversation. I had the feeling I wasn't sparkling as I should. Although mentally there were plenty of sparks. I could ignite if I didn't watch out.

It was small talk. Catch-up crap. It didn't involve me. I wanted to get to the bit where people were dying but had an inkling that wasn't the point of the evening. Grant wanted to catch up with his buddy. I made an effort to listen and appear interested.

It transpired that Kim had once dated Kurt. Early on in their college days. But she'd married Grant by the time they graduated. I knew she was a nurse, but didn't work at the hospital. She worked in a private fertility clinic. Guess there are people out there who are desperate for children. I found that notion foreign. I had Carla; we'd chosen each other when she was almost fourteen. I'd never wanted babies. Mac had wanted babies. When I was a teenager I opted out of parenthood by birth, because my mother was fuc'n insane and I didn't want to be that woman. Mac's mother was just as crazy. Any children would've had a double whammy of nuts.

Everyone was looking at me.

I missed something.

"Sorry, daydreaming." I tried to look apologetic.

Kim laughed. "Grant was asking what it was like living

164

with a hero."

A hero?

I kept my mouth shut while I reassembled the missing conversational strands. Kurt's bemused expression was no help.

"He's my superman," I said. As the song's decibel count sky-rocketed I couldn't think anymore. Kurt's arm snaked around my shoulders and gave me an affectionate squeeze.

Grant seemed to like my answer. I needed to pay more attention to what was going on. The song blared. Without thinking my hands clapped over my ears, but that just locked it in, trapping the noise within my own head.

The volume escalated. It was as if I was wearing ear buds and someone was pumping the volume on my iPod. Louder and louder. Noise so loud it hurt. My ear drums were going to burst. Nothing else existed. There was no off switch. I expected blood to pour from my ears as the level increased again.

Then nothing.

Silence. My hands fell away. Silence. For a few beats I thought I was deaf. The music had deafened me.

I turned my head to find three people looking at me. There was no bemused expression on Kurt's face now. No smile. His brow furrowed and eyes darkened. Kim's face registered concern. Grant was leaning toward me.

I picked up my glass and took a sip. Kurt took the glass from me and switched it for his juice.

"Where were you?"

"Right here," I said.

"You couldn't hear me?"

"Did you talk?"

Grant and Kurt looked at each other. Kim kept her eyes on me.

"What happened?" Kurt asked, fully focused on me. I could see how he pulled so many girls in college. It was that intense Kevin Costner thing that lightened instantly with a smile. There was nothing little boy about him. He was all hero. He could be the one. His eyes held mine and didn't let up.

I didn't know what to say. How could I tell him the music in my head was so loud I couldn't hear anything else? Confess to having Bon Jovi in my head? Nope. Admit to thinking he was Kevin Costner? He should just know.

"Bit spacey. It's been a long day," I said, hoping he'd buy it. I couldn't very well remind him, in front of his friends, that my house exploded. Or about the boxes of ass. Or mention the terrorist thing he didn't know about. Or harp on about the shooters. I had a feeling it was some kind of weird-assed migraine or a stroke and was waiting for the pain to kick in.

"Sorry, I didn't mean to ruin your evening," I said to Kim and Grant.

"Don't be silly," Kim replied. "You should get a good night's sleep. We can catch up tomorrow."

"I think we will," Kurt said. "I'll come into the hospital and we can go over the files."

"We can use my office," Grant said.

"That's settled then." Kurt stood up, took my hand, and pulled me to my feet. His voice dipped until it was husky and laden with honeymoon intent, "Let's you get you to bed."

Twenty minutes later I was undergoing the Kurt Henderson version of the Spanish Inquisition in our hotel room. I peeled off my clothes and pulled on pajamas in the bathroom, Kurt waited outside the door, which was ajar. He'd forbidden me to lock it or even shut it. It'd taken a lot of discussion to get the door anything less than wide open.

Once in my pajamas he insisted I get into bed. I could see his black bag on the desk.

I attempted to talk my way out of any impending medical exam. "I'm fine, tired. It was a shitty day. I'm a bit stressed and the wine hit me."

He looked like he might buy it then changed his mind.

"And I think you experienced some kind of auditory episode."

Crap!

"I'm okay, Doc."

"You can't convince me, Conway."

"I don't have to convince you, Doc. I'll be fine, after a decent night's sleep." I picked up my charged phone. "Left it behind." I checked for missed messages.

Two I didn't expect.

I read them.

One from Kevin – no, not Costner – a cop I knew from

Mauryville. Someone had come in and asked for directions to my property. I still owned the land where my first home once stood. Never got around to selling it. I'd never got around to doing anything with it. What was left of the house was still there too. It hadn't quite burned to the ground, but it was beyond repair and needed bulldozing. Doing something with the Mauryville property was on my five-year-plan.

I called Kevin.

Twenty seconds later I was making a call to Jonathon Tierney and I didn't care that Kurt was sitting on the bed watching me as I went through the security process and talked of chickens. I just had to do it fast, before my brain froze up again.

Jonathon's tightly-wound voice almost echoed down the line, "Tierney."

"Habib Arbab is in the company of Abbudin Nader. Nader is driving a Silver Mitsubishi Galant, tag: Tango, Romeo, Alpha, five, five, five. The car was in Mauryville, Rockbridge County. This evening someone asked for directions to my old house. We're way beyond guessing how he knows who I am. We need to stop him now before he finds me."

"Demelza. I'll deploy a team."

"If he's gone to the old house, then he's following an old trail but that doesn't mean it's a cold one. Plenty of people know me in Mauryville. Someone could inadvertently give out information."

"Anything else?"

"I was shot at by a sniper. He was using some clever technology and may or may not have been after me. There was also another sniper at my home, but he may be related to another case." It was starting to sound pretty horrific. "Three women have been strangled, all were Conways."

"And?"

"My home in Oakton blew up. No clue if it's related."

"We shall work on the assumption it is."

"Yes, let's."

Let's work on the assumption that this whole goddamn mess is related.

"There is a unit on the way for the rendition."

A smile crossed my lips. "It's not a rendition: He's not in anyone's custody."

Then a barrel of clarity hit me. It *is* a rendition. They don't want him on American soil needing questions to be answered. They're going to render him to a black site. I guessed a Gulfstream IV, registered to a front company, would be at the closest military base.

"It's not just my life at stake here."

"Have faith, Demelza."

I hung up and checked the second message without looking at Kurt.

One deep breath later and I was making another phone call. "Mr. P. It's Ellie. Someone came round?"

"Ellie, girl! Didn't know if you'd get my message – my fat fingers don't take to this texting fad."

"I got it, sir." I could see him as clear as day, standing

on his front porch wearing those denim overalls trying to text by stabbing at the phone buttons with his oversized sausage fingers. He was Mauryville's answer to *Dukes of Hazzard's* Uncle Jesse. I was on dangerous mentally unstable ground, and needed to stem the impending *Dukes of Hazzard* interlude.

"Good. Some nasty looking men came sniffing around earlier this evening, saying they wanted to buy honey. They didn't want my honey. They kept asking who lived out here, did I know if anyone called Gabrielle lived this far out."

"Did you?"

"No, ma'am, I did not. I called ol' Kev, and did that texting palaver to you."

"Thank you Mr. P. I'll come out and visit soon. I promise."

"Not until these folk have gone off on their merry way, girlie. It's not safe."

"Not until then."

I hung up and flopped back on the bed. Waiting for the inquisition to resume with renewed vigor.

He started slow. "A lot of people care a great deal about keeping you safe ..." He crawled across the bed toward me. "... I am not the enemy." He was leaning over me. His face level with mine. "I am one of those people who care a great deal. I cannot help you if you don't tell me what the fuck is going on!"

I took a slow breath. "So now you know."

"Now I know I've brought you somewhere that has the

potential to be life threatening. If you'd told me earlier ..."

"We can't play the 'if only' game with this one. I had no idea Arbab would end up in Mauryville trying to find me. I don't have a crystal ball."

"What did you know before you agreed to accompany me as my wife?" He rolled over, propped himself up on an elbow facing me.

"That someone called Gabrielle Conway was murdered the day before yesterday in Washington, and there was some connection to Habib Arbab. And then another Conway woman was murdered in Alexandria, with no apparent connection to Arbab." Guess he had a phone book.

"And then another Conway in DC," he added. "You didn't find all this sudden interest in Conway women and a terrorist noteworthy?"

"Not especially."

"I do."

"You're not me," I countered.

"I think we can assume the sniper in Blake Lane wasn't a random shooter, can't we?"

"Never assume anything."

It makes an ass out of you and me.

"What does Arbab want with you?"

"He seems hell bent on my demise."

"Why?"

Oh, that's such a long boring irrelevant story.

"I don't think it matters why."

"He wants you dead and it doesn't matter?"

"The reasoning behind his behavior is not as important as his behavior."

"Ah, Conway, you've reached a new level in evasive bullshit." Kurt leaned closer and growled, "Talk."

I suppressed the brewing smirk and obliged. "A long time ago, I sent him home to his father. He was sure his father would have him put to death because of the company he was keeping. I hoped the same. Seems he is still alive and out for revenge, and as I said, the why is irrelevant."

"Is this a religious thing?"

"A jihad? Not that I am aware of. This is one man with an ax to grind."

"All you did was send him home?"

I embarrassed him in front of other men. He dropped to his knees in front of me, begged for his life, and was then sent home to his father in utter disgrace.

"Yep. In fact I saved his miserable fuc'n life by sending him away. If he'd stayed he would be dead like everyone else in that apartment."

Then I wouldn't have him as a problem now. Damn! I rolled my eyes. I'd brought it upon myself.

I watched Kurt's mind working. I love how men show all the workings on their faces. Saves all that guesswork. When it's blank there really is nothing going on, so don't bother asking. He wasn't blank. I waited for the next question.

"When did this happen?"

There it was.

"Ten years ago, give or take."

"Ten years and now he's coming to find you?"

"Yeah. Long memory."

When I piss off people, they stay pissed off. I could see his mind still ticking over.

"Why, Ellie? Why did he wait so long?"

"He thought I was dead. Everyone involved in the operation thought I was dead and anyway no one knew my true identity. Four people survived: Arbab; the officer I sent him away with, a guy named Tim Cosgrove; Dion Edwards, a former CIA operative turned terrorist; and me."

"So what happened to change his mind?"

"I don't know."

"Maybe we need to be figuring out that part while this special rendition unit flies in here and hopefully finds him."

"Once he's gone it won't matter." I was feeling quite glib.

"It will matter the next time someone comes for you."

"There is no one else to come for me."

"Dion Edwards? If I'm not mistaken he's on our Ten Most Wanted list."

"He thinks I am dead ..." and just like that I saw his point. "Oh, I see."

I yawned, managing to cover my mouth. Too late. It infected Kurt. He yawned, throwing it back at me.

"We're safe here, for now. I didn't use your name. Sleep. We'll add this to the list of puzzles for the morning," he said.

"I'm sorry. I didn't think Arbab would impact on your case. He was last seen in DC."

"It's not that Arbab is impacting on my case. It's that you shouldered this, all of it, and didn't give any of us a chance."

"Sometimes denial is the best way forward—"

"Not when it affects your health. Not when I'm right here, caught up in it."

"It'll work out, it always does."

"You're not dead yet, so I guess that's a start."

As my eyes closed, I heard Kurt check his weapon, put the security chain on the door, and felt the bed sink as he climbed under the covers bedside me.

I didn't argue about us sharing a bed. Not only did I not have the strength to go through the whole flipping-for-the-sofa lark, but the last thing we needed now was any suspicion cast upon us by hotel staff.

His breathing lulled me into a secure sleep.

Chapter Fifteen
No Apologies

Morning brought a waft of coffee and croissants, and then I heard someone leave our room. I lay there considering getting up when breakfast arrived on a tray and I didn't have to.

"This is nice," I commented as Kurt placed the tray on the bed beside me and slid out the newspaper he'd tucked under his arm. I was quick to see two coffee cups and enough croissants for us both. "Let me guess, honeymoon suite thing?"

"Yes. Figured we'd eat in here."

"I'm all in favor of breakfast in bed." I shuffled up until I was sitting, and didn't even rock the tray.

"You feeling better?" Kurt asked as he helped himself to food.

"I think so."

The croissants were delicious, melt-in-the-mouth good. The coffee was excellent. I could see sun peeking through the curtains. Glorious sun to follow marvelous coffee.

"You're smiling," Kurt said.

"Yeah, go figure."

"You slept the sleep of the dead, by the way. Twice I checked you were still breathing." He took another croissant. "See, sharing is good. Lighten the load, Conway. We can take it, you know."

"I know. It's me."

He laughed. "The old 'it's not you it's me' thing, right?"

"No. It really is me. I don't like making a fuss."

Yet falling over, vomiting, hearing things, seeing things, talking to dead people, all come so naturally?

"You don't like asking for help is more like."

That could be part of it.

He spread out the newspaper on the bed then reached for his coffee. We were done talking. I flipped on the television and surfed channels while drinking my coffee. Nothing held my attention. I didn't feel like cartoons and there were a lot of channels playing them. I searched for news and came across *Entertainment Today*. I could hear Mac's voice, so clear and so full of mockery. "*Entertainment Today* ain't news, babe."

I paused to agree before moving on. A picture of Rowan and Carla flashed up on the screen. I turned up the volume as Mary Hart said, "Yesterday evening Rowan Grange was seen in the company of a young woman, believed to be the daughter of his girlfriend, FBI Agent Ellie Conway." She paused. The picture changed to one of me and Rowan, I recognized the background. It was two weeks old and taken outside a restaurant. I never saw anyone with a camera, but the paparazzi don't have to be close to snap a picture with the gear they use. Hell, he could've been across town. Bastard. I focused on what was being said. "Sources say that Agent Conway is not with the pair. Earlier reports of her death were untrue. She's believed to be out of town."

I nudged Kurt. "You watching this?"

"Yes."

Another picture flashed up of Carla with Rowan, eating ice cream. I scanned the photo and saw Jed sitting at the next table. There was a small amount of reflection from the window; the photo appeared to have been taken at an angle to minimize the glare.

"It's long been known that Rowan is very fond of children," Mary Hart said her voice lousy with conspiracy. "Could this be a new phase in his relationship with the child's mother? Time will tell."

I turned off the television and sat staring at the blank black screen for a few seconds. My head moved from side to side. "What the fuck is wrong with these people?"

I reached for my phone and called Rowan.

"Good morning."

"You sound better," he said. "Carla's still sleeping. Had a late night."

"As long as she's not too much trouble and you're coping."

"All right, what is it?"

"*Entertainment Today* is spouting on about you and Carla, and how I'm out of town." That sort of thing was not new to Rowan. As much as he tried very hard to keep out of the limelight unless working, avoiding paparazzi and anyone with a camera phone wasn't possible. "You need to know something, and I would like you to let Jed know as well."

"This is bad?"

"This is manageable bad," I replied, crossing my fingers. "Seems someone is looking for me. If this person sees this trashy shit on television or online or in some magazine, then they'll know I have a daughter, and that she is with you."

"Seems, or someone is?"

Trust him to pick at my statement.

"Let's say the person in question *is* looking for me."

"Has this got anything to do with the box of meat Gracey received?"

"No, completely unrelated." I was quite sure about that. In fact that was all I was sure about.

He went quiet. I heard his television volume go up. "News, Ellie, check the news, channel six."

I turned the television back on and switched to six.

Images of my burned house. Fire engines. Police. FBI agents. Thankfully, no sign of me or Kurt. I didn't think there were any news crews there that fast.

"Yeah, about that. I had a bit of a problem at home yesterday," I said. "The house blew up."

I sensed pursed lips as his reply came, clipped and tight, "Bit. Of. A. Problem?"

"I can see how you would be a little upset by this. But *I* am fine." I watched the news broadcast and saw a still shot, from a camera phone maybe, of me and Kurt getting into his car. Artificial happiness forced itself into my voice. "See, there I am, safe, getting into Kurt's car. Gosh that's great."

"Your hair is a lot darker."

"Yeah. I'm sort of undercover. Except now, I'm not. Now every fuc'n person in Virginia knows I got into Kurt's car with dark hair." I took a breath. "This is just fan-fuc'n-tastic. When did this story break?"

I looked at Kurt, he was holding up the newspaper, opened out and in front of his face. I could see the inside spread. House explodes in Oakton. Colored photographs of the burned-out shell, the same picture of us getting into the car. I covered my phone with my shoulder and spoke to Kurt, "Tell me that is this morning's paper ..."

The paper shook 'no.'

"Fuck!"

With the phone back by my ear I could hear Rowan. "Ellie, I'll talk to Jed. I'll give him your number. You can explain to him better what you need to keep Carla safe."

"And you, Rowan. Both of you. Your management and publicist are going to tell you to break up with me, again."

"It's a daily occurrence," he said with a smile in his voice.

But this time they have a valid point. I'd break up with me if I could.

"Do what Jed says, call me if you need me. Keep my kid safe?"

"That goes without saying. Take care."

I hung up and stared at the television. Kurt said nothing. He folded the paper and took a deep breath.

"We need more coffee," I said. "You still wanna keep the charade up of us being married, or do you think enough people have now made the connection?"

"You are Rylee Henderson. Let's live in denial."

I smiled. If we don't admit it, then they can't know for sure. I liked it.

"Okay, let's ignore the photograph of Supervisory Special Agent Conway and Supervisory Special Agent Kurt Henderson getting into the car, and the caption in the newspaper."

Kurt dropped the newspaper to the floor, reached across and took the tray and my cup. With a grin he bounced to the end of the bed, reached under the blanket grabbed my feet and pulled. In one energetic move he pinned me under him. His body weight crushing me.

"You could at least take your weight on your elbows," I said, as the last of the air left my lungs.

He laughed, but did as I asked.

"Now we know why Arbab thinks you are alive. Paparazzi."

I closed my eyes to avoid his intense blue gaze.

"You met Rowan six months ago. How many times have you been photographed with him or linked to him?"

My eyes flicked open; his registered surprise. "Not often, until maybe a month ago when I accompanied him to an award ceremony."

Rowan led this fucktard to me? And his management were worried I would hurt his image. Idiots.

"I was ten years younger, a redhead with green eyes—"

"Facial recognition software has come a long way in recent times. It's possible that you seemed familiar enough for him to run a comparison."

I searched the inner workings of my mind, and old files I kept hidden there, for how would he get a picture of Demelza. "My ID or my passport: he would have had access to both while we were in the desert."

Kurt leaned closer. Playful. I lifted my legs and pushed him off me.

"Too bad, I was enjoying that," he said as he rolled away.

"Yeah, me too, but that's beside the point," I said with a swift smile. It was dangerous around Kurt. Feelings I kept well in check simmered close to the surface the longer we were together.

I swung my legs over the edge of the bed and stood up. Must've just been tired and stressed yesterday. Everything felt balanced again. Balanced is good. In fact it is more than I dared hope for.

I found clothes and managed to shower with the door shut, without incident. A light dusting of mineral powder, a little black eyeliner, and then I swiped some black mascara over my lashes. My bangs hung past my eyebrows almost in my eyes, causing me to flick my head. The hair slipped back, irritating me. Scissors would fix that.

My eyes watched my every move. It was odd. I was watching me watch myself. Flashes of my past scrolled across the mirror. The timeline began when I was twenty-one. It paused at the twenty-three mark and showed me pictures of heat rising and shimmering over gold sand. It was a pretty desert landscape but I knew it wouldn't last. I reached out with my index finger and swished the image, it rolled to the left revealing an old building that appeared to have risen from the sand. Dion stood, bent over, sweating in the courtyard. My open hand hit the window. The only solution to his plight was to shoot him, but Ameer convinced me he would do it.

Lying bastard.

Lesson: Trust no one. I swished another image, time flashed forward, about seven years. An image of a coffee bar froze on the screen. In a booth sat a dark-haired man with a map. Mac. He looked up and smiled at me. The mirror trembled and the picture dissolved.

Time to leave the bathroom before more weird shit happens.

Kurt had destroyed the bed and by the look of it, had fun doing so. Sheets and covers crumpled in a heap, trailing onto the ground at the end of the bed.

"Have fun?"

"They expect a certain amount of crumple," he replied and threw a pillow at me. I threw it back; he ducked, and the bedside lamp went flying and smashed onto the floor. Kurt fell off the bed laughing like a mad man. "How to destroy hotel room 101. Did you learn that from your rock star boyfriend?"

I laughed. "You signed the register and booked the room. This comes out of your pocket."

A pillow hit me on the side of the head.

Lesson: Don't start something you can't finish.

I scrambled onto the bed and snatched another pillow before Kurt could. He tried to sneak around the end of the bed, but I smacked him over the head. *Thump*. Kurt hit the ground. Laughter rose from under the pillow and then moved. Standing on the bed, ready with another pillow to pound him, I watched him trying to be stealthy. His head poked up. I hit him again. Moments later he waved the white sheet of surrender. He crawled up onto the bed and flopped down. I felt his hand tighten around my ankle but it was too late – unbalanced, I fell, and was again pinned under Kurt.

"This is getting to be a habit," I muttered, pushing him off.

"Objective achieved," Kurt replied, flat on his back next to me.

Of course. We were way too quiet for a honeymoon couple.

"Who knew you could be fun?" I said, rolling over him and off the bed. "I need to be armed today. How are we going to explain that?"

"Can you carry fully concealed?"

I gave it some thought. I could, if it was winter and I was wearing a jacket. But it was summer; my Glock 17 wasn't exactly invisible in its holster. Even wearing it in the small of my back wasn't going to make a difference under a tee shirt.

"I might have to carry it in my shoulder bag." The bag in question was hanging on the back of a chair across the room. My Glock was on the dresser, next to Kurt's. I slipped the bag strap over my head and put the Glock in it, complete with holster. The holster was not going to work. I dropped it on the dresser and put the gun into a smaller zipped compartment, leaving the zip open. This had to be short term. It was no way to treat the tool I needed to help me do my job. I could grab the gun easily enough from the compartment. Pulling it free of the actual bag wasn't as smooth as I'd hoped. If it came down to it, I'd shoot through the bag.

Problem solved.

"You're meeting Grant when?"

"At eleven. You're coming; I'm not leaving you alone."

"I'm fine here; bored, but fine."

"You're coming."

I was going and not unhappy about it. At least I'd be doing something. I hoped it would lead to something tangible in the hospital killings.

Chapter Sixteen
I Gotta Woman

Grant was waiting in his office when we arrived. Last night's newspaper folded on the corner of his desk, and the morning paper open in front of him. My heart sank. I had a feeling I was about to find out how observant Doctor Neal was.

He waved us in and pointed to chairs.

"It's not the world's biggest office, but we should have enough room." He folded up the newspaper and placed it upon the other paper. "I have the files here." His hand tapped a pile of folders. I could see color-coordinated tabs running down the open edges. Grant looked at me then addressed me, "Feeling better I see. Do you want to sit in on this or go shopping?"

Bless him for thinking I'd like to go shopping and not be troubled by the menfolk and work.

I smiled. "Much better, thank you. If you don't mind, I'll stay."

"We never did get around to talking properly. What is it you do?"

Kurt stood up and closed the door. He knew what was coming too.

"I'm in law enforcement," I said. No sense lying about that and being snapped. Law enforcement was such a broad term. I could be in a communications center somewhere, or a laboratory. Sure enough Grant's eyes drifted to the newspapers. He thought he recognized me from the pictures, I saw the look on his face.

"How long have you been married?"

Kurt answered, "Can we get on with this?"

"You're not, are you? You're the woman dating Rowan Grange?"

"Question or statement?" I parried.

Kurt leaned closer to Grant. "For our sake and the sake of this investigation, we are married and she is Rylee Henderson. No one is to know otherwise. End of story."

"You could've told me."

"No, I couldn't – you suck at acting." Kurt smiled. It disarmed Grant and all his doctor cool went out the window. Fascinating.

"Files?" I interrupted the bonding moment. "Walk me through the deaths."

Without warning Kurt grabbed my arm and excused us.

In the corridor outside Grant's office he pushed me against the wall. He leaned into me, one arm resting on the wall over my head. His mouth close to my ear.

"It was a failed rendition, wasn't it?"

I had nowhere to go and felt sudden panic and I couldn't breathe. Air would not fill my lungs no matter how hard I tried.

"Rylee – Ellie – it was, wasn't it? That's what went wrong in New Zealand?"

"Yeah."

"How the hell did you end up on a CIA rendition

team?"

"O'Hare had me seconded to a special joint operation. After some twisty turns I ended up 'deep cover' within the CIA and part of the operation."

That's enough now. No more.

He pulled back a little. I met with his most intense life-dissecting stare and it was uncomfortable as hell.

"Who knows?"

Very few people.

"You. O'Hare. My former handler Jonathon Tierney."

Footsteps approached us. Kurt lowered his mouth to mine. As the footsteps faded so did the kiss. "We're here to find a killer, not make out in the hallway," I whispered. "Now you know about me, let's get this case closed."

"If it is a case."

"You know it is," I said.

Kurt apologized to Grant for our leaving.

I picked up a file and fast realized I wasn't going to be a lot of help with the initial phase. So I settled back to listen to the two doctors discuss how patient A was due for discharge and died during the night. By the time they got to patient E, even a non-medical moron like me could see the pattern. Grant handed Kurt the file for patient F.

My phone rang, followed by Kurt's.

I answered my call. It was Sam and he wasn't happy.

"The medical examiner says the boxes of meat – five in total now, three left for you, one for Gracey, and one for a lady called Sarah Jane Franken – contain pieces of at least fifteen different people. We're trying to get somewhere with the first box and the tattoos, and the lab is working on DNA. There are no reports of so many people disappearing, or bodies turning up missing chunks of ass and thigh."

Fifteen. That is a lot of dead bodies. A lot of people to go missing at once. There have to be reports filed somewhere.

"They were all delivered the same way?"

"Yeah, someone is paid to deliver them. Regular courier companies. The lone oddball was the tweaker who delivered the second box to you."

"How are you getting on tracing them back to the courier companies?"

"Slow, Ellie. We do know they're not coming from overseas. Despite the customs declarations and stamps."

"Recipients. There has to be a link between us all. Something that is triggering this response."

"So far nothing."

"Dig deep. We've all got something in common: You need to find it. This is not random."

"I feel like I'm snooping on you."

"Sam, it's me. We've worked together for a few years now. We know each other pretty well. It's not snooping; it's doing your job."

"Why'd you get three boxes?"

"That, Sam, is something that may hold the key ... you'll figure it out."

"Take care out there, Ellie."

"You too."

I hung up. Kurt was still talking. I could tell by the tone of his voice it was Caine on the other end of the call.

I slipped the file for patient F off Kurt's lap and opened it up. Maybe what it needed was the eyes of a non-medical person. I read the file. It didn't make much sense. I skimmed all the others while Kurt talked to Caine.

"And by the way, Grant, I get how absorbing the medical aspects must be for two doctors, but there is a pattern here with these deaths. These people all died between two and six in the morning."

"That means they all died on the same shift," Grant replied. He tapped at his keyboard for a moment. "It's not that unusual. Look at this."

Grant showed me a study conducted in Brazil on hospital deaths, both ICU and non-ICU, where the objective was to demonstrate cardiovascular mortality follows a certain circadian rhythm. I looked at the percentages.

"They're saying thirty-eight percent of people not in the ICU die between six in the morning and noon, but the second highest percentage – twenty-five percent – die between midnight and six in the morning."

Grant nodded. "Our death times in these cases aren't so unusual."

"I think your percentages are higher. This study involved seven hundred deaths over four years. We're talking about a spike in deaths over a much shorter time frame. At the outside I'd say a twelve-month period. Do you have figures for the deaths that occurred in this hospital between six a.m. and say, noon, over the last year?"

He shook his head.

"We have a record of every death, but that sort of information has never been extrapolated."

"I'm picking the only increase is in the sudden deaths between two and six." I looked at Grant. "You've been a doctor for a number of years, what is your opinion regarding most frequent time of death?"

He tapped a finger on his desk. "In my experience it is between three and four in the morning."

"Interesting isn't it, this time of death thing?"

He nodded.

"See? I knew you were needed down here," Kurt said to me with a smile.

"How many beds do you have?" I said to Grant.

"Eighty."

Small hospital.

"Staff?"

"Approximately two hundred."

"Nurses on wards?"

"Sixty-two"

"How can I get information on who works what shifts? Do you have access to that?"

"The nurse manager does."

"I don't want to involve anyone else. Is there a roster anywhere?"

He nodded. Seconds later he pulled up the rosters for the previous four weeks.

Kurt attracted my attention. "Can I have a word outside?"

"Sure."

We excused ourselves. Kurt checked the corridor for lurkers. There was no one around.

I leaned on the wall and listened as he spoke.

"Regarding the three strangling cases earlier in the week. Another woman was killed early this morning. This time in Roanoke, and she was tortured."

"Same name?"

"She was a Conway."

That wasn't good.

"Christian name?"

"Gillian."

I moved on. Really: What else could I do? I'd never had a connection to Roanoke – the guy was now swinging blind.

"Thanks for the update."

"You're welcome," he replied, reaching past me and swinging Grant's office door open. "Back into it then."

Grant greeted us with a nod. I sat down and hoped there would be no more interruptions.

"Where were we?" I asked Kurt.

"Rosters."

Yeah, rosters. I focused on Grant.

"Grant, can you print the rosters and anything else relevant, we'll take them with us. Oh, anyone due for discharge tomorrow?"

The printer on his desk clunked, whirred, and buzzed, before firing out pages of information into the tray. He typed for a few minutes.

"No one's updated patient records since rounds this morning. Won't know until later who is being flagged for discharge. We have fifty-one patients at the moment. Five of those are in pediatrics and four are obstetrics."

"I would keep an eye on them all, but I don't know how you can do that – you can't tell staff to look out for someone killing patients, when it could well be a staff member. But you need to think about how." As an afterthought I added, "I suppose cameras in the rooms are a violation of privacy?"

"Yes."

Chapter Seventeen
Live Before You Die

It was pleasant in our hotel room. We had fresh coffee and peace. I could relax. No chance of recognition or sudden death.

Caine called me to let me know he was briefing NCIS Agent Noel Gerrard on the Roanoke murder, as his murder case was pertinent to the FBI investigation and vice versa. That in turn reminded me I never did tell Noel anything regarding Arbab.

"I want in," I said.

Kurt stared at me, his coffee cup frozen mid sip.

"That would be monumentally stupid," Caine replied. "Monumentally."

"Yeah, you said that already. Now we have two cases, both of which have something to do with me. The one that concerns me is someone murdering people with my name."

"Boxes of body parts don't concern you?"

"Nope. I'm sorry people are dying, but I don't feel like I'm about to be hacked up and stuffed into a box by whoever the hell is doing that."

The ass killer is not an imminent threat to my welfare, or Carla's.

"What about the investigation into the hospital deaths?"

"I don't think it's going to take that much investigating. Someone is killing people. Everyone is dying between two and six in the morning. People don't visit between two and six a.m. I think it's someone on the staff. That would make sense. I'm just not sure how the hospital can safeguard other patients until we find the culprit."

"Guess they can't use security cameras," Caine said. I heard the amusement in his voice. "No doubt you already went there."

"Yeah."

"All right, wrap up this hospital thing – then you can both join the investigation into the deaths of Conway women."

"Ballpark, how many statewide?"

"Ninety or so."

"Not good."

"This is anything but good."

"Killing fields spring to mind. You sure about this case? I reckon Kurt would be fine by himself," I ventured.

Kurt coughed. It was unnecessary, I knew he was there.

"Ellie—" Caine used a snarl to good effect.

"I'll stay and help. Just don't let anyone else die."

"We've got police all over the state chatting with any-one whose name is Conway, but more especially watching women between the ages of twenty-five and forty. We can't afford to panic the population, so we're asking about unusual phone calls and vehicles new to the areas," he said.

"You'll have to canvas immediate neighbors; otherwise

the Conways are going to smell a big, fat, panicky rat."

"We're stretching the local police pretty thin, but they're doing their best."

"What about media? How much has been released?" I said.

"Nothing has been released. But that won't stop them," Caine said.

He was right. "Unleashing hell doesn't do much to silence those bastards."

"Names are being withheld, as are descriptions of the victims. We don't need some dickhead of a journalist piecing things together."

"If someone let slip they were suicides and not murder, they'd back off? Don't they have some kind of code about reporting on suicides?" I was grasping at straws and I knew it.

"There is some sort of journalistic code when reporting suicide. But in this case we'd be opening ourselves up to accusations of a cover-up."

"Suppose that's a bad thing?"

"I can't see the director going for it," Caine said. "Our saving grace at the moment is that the deaths are spread out."

"Okay. We'll talk soon."

I dropped my phone onto the sofa. "People are dying all over," I muttered, picking up the cup of coffee from the end table. "If I was Arbab, and I knew who I was looking for, but didn't know where the person was ... I'd start killing and I'd keep killing until I drew the person out."

"You scare me."

I tapped my booted foot on the floor.

"He's going to create a pattern in the deaths, or a trail if you like, something that leads to him."

If the mountain won't go to Mohammed, then Mohammed must go to the mountain. Now he's found a way of moving the fuc'n mountain.

"You scare me."

"I scare myself."

"Let's go over this paperwork," Kurt replied, bringing over the stack of printouts. He dropped them on the sofa with two packets of highlighters. "The sooner we get this killer caught, the sooner we can join the manhunt."

We each took a sheet and highlighters. Matching deaths to nurses to corresponding wards didn't seem too difficult. It was a small hospital; I couldn't imagine it taking long to find the overlap. Except it did.

The deaths were spread throughout the hospital, not confined to particular wards. The common denominator was the patients all went through the emergency room prior to admittance. No surprise there.

"So is this the trigger? The emergency room?" I could understand it; hospitals weren't my favorite places by any means. Even so, it seemed a bit extreme to be killing. I spread files over the floor and started picking them up one by one, reading the notes from the emergency room.

Mostly boring stuff, regarding why they were in the ER, but I began to notice comments from nursing staff regarding each patient's behavior.

Holy crap.

Each and every one said the same thing. Uncooperative. Difficult. Demanding. I gave the comments some thought. Okay, so sick or injured people can be a bit cranky and snippy. I'm no picnic myself when sick or hurt, but I tend to take my annoyance out on those closest to me and it comes off as contrariness. Trust me, contrariness is an okay character trait compared with what I was reading in the files in front of me. I was getting a picture in my mind of some very difficult and downright mean patients.

"How unusual is it to see the sort of comments I'm seeing here?" I asked Kurt while showing him a few of the files with comments marked.

"Not usual at all."

"Every file has a comment regarding each patient's behavior in the emergency room. And they all behaved badly."

"We need to compare files of people who are still alive to see if this is relevant."

"Let's go."

Looked pretty relevant to me: Every file? Someone doesn't like the grumpy patients.

I gathered up the files and dumped them into my bag.

"Game face," Kurt whispered as we left the safety of our room.

I took his hand and grinned. "How's this?"

"You might ease up on the smile. The brief was honeymoon not loony tune. You look demented."

Chapter Eighteen
Living On A Prayer

Grant wasn't in his office when we arrived. Didn't take long to find him. He was in the ER doing what doctors do.

Chaos spun all around me. We stood aside, almost hugging the wall, while people moved with haste in all directions. Kurt craned his neck to see into the triage area. A sliding door next to the triage window opened and closed, letting gurneys and staff through.

"Wait here. Something's going on."

"Okay."

From where I stood I could see into the waiting room. It looked full. A quick head count put the number of occupants at twenty. Some looked quite ill, others injured, and the rest could've been support people.

Twenty.

That's a lot of people. Looking at the ill and wounded, I mentally cut out five of them. How could a roomful of people disappear?

I hooked my phone out of my bag. And called Sam.

"It's me," I said, leaning back on the wall.

"Chicky. Problem?"

"Fifteen is a lot of people to disappear all at once."

"It is."

"So maybe they didn't. Maybe whoever it is kills over time and keeps them on ice?"

"I don't want to find the meat locker," Sam said.

"Me neither. See if you can locate it before I'm done down here?"

Sam chuckled. "See what I can do, Chicky."

"Use your super meat-discovery powers."

I hung up.

Kurt hustled over. "I'm going to wade in here and help Grant. They've got a multi-vehicle crash coming in."

"Can you do that? Don't you need to hold a Virginia medical license?"

Kurt smiled. "I do. I'm an FBI asset and thanks to them I am licensed to practice in all fifty states and our territories."

Of course he is; that's why O'Hare wanted him to join Delta in the first place.

"What can I do?"

He pressed a key into my hand. "You have the key to Grant's office. I'll be by when I can."

"Awesome."

I'm useless because no one knows I'm FBI. So I can't go asking tons of questions of staff, or can I?

I headed back to Grant's office and let myself in.

How did they die?

Making myself comfortable in Grant's chair, I spread the files over the desk and took over the place. The hunt was on for the causes of death. All we had was unexpected death following illness. They had to have died of something. A complication? Another illness? Heart attack? Brain freaking fart? There had to be something.

The most recent of the deaths were still in the hospital morgue, the other bodies had gone to a county morgue for autopsy. There were no autopsy reports attached to the files. The notable missing item? A police report. It made me wonder if sudden death within a hospital had to be reported, or was that only if foul play was suggested? But Grant was suspicious. Why not involve local cops?

I picked up the phone and called my trusty old friend Kev out in Mauryville. A police perspective wouldn't hurt.

"Hey, Kev, it's—"

He laughed. "You think I don't know! How are ya, kid?"

"Good. Got a hypothetical for you."

"Shoot."

"Say a bunch of people died unexpectedly in a hospital over a period of three months, and a doctor suspected something wasn't right, in what circumstances would he fail to contact local police?"

I could hear Kevin muttering to himself before he answered. "Seems to me that a doc would have to have a very good reason to keep that out of local hands."

"Say what?"

"How hypothetical is this?"

"Let's just say I can't use any names and leave it at that."

"Six months ago, Mrs. Abernathy died in Stonewall Jackson Hospital. Her daughter told me she was due for discharge the next day."

"What'd she die of?" I scrabbled through files looking

for the Abernathy one. It wasn't there. But all the files I had were recent, within the last three months. Could this have gone on longer?

"She was an old duck, about eighty-four. They said heart failure. Funny thing is she wasn't in for her heart. She had asthma."

"Gimme a date of death," I said, picking up a pen. In the back of my mind I cottoned on to the eighty-four and had to accept it may have been heart failure and unrelated. He gave me the date, spelled out her name, and even supplied her date of birth. I wrote it all on a Post-it note and thanked the gods it was not blue or yellow. More people should use neon green. "I'll look into it."

"As to why someone wouldn't report it to local police? Could be the person they suspect has connections to the local police or could be that this is a small town and everyone knows everyone."

"Or?"

"Or, they don't want everyone knowing that people are dying. Think about it, how many people live in our little county?"

"About twenty thousand."

"Give or take, now; that hospital is vital. They fly patients out to Richmond if and when they have to, but if the brown stuff hits the spinning thing down here ... first port of call is the hospital," Kevin said.

"You think the hypothetical doctor is protecting the population by not letting this out?"

"No, I think he's protecting his own ass, but he's convinced himself he's protecting the population who need to use the hospital. People die – fact of life. People die needlessly and all of a sudden every death is under the microscope."

"Small town, everyone knows everyone ... then why haven't people started putting two and two together?"

"Because people die, Ellie. Because it all seems quite reasonable when it's explained by a doctor you trust."

"I'm going to go find out about Mrs. Abernathy. She was from Mauryville?" I stopped talking and let the images form. "Abernathys lived by you, Kev?"

"They did. Old man Abernathy still does. One of the kids came home, she's a nurse, and she takes care of him now. Real tragic type woman she is. Her only kid was killed by a drunk driver."

"When did she come back?"

"Maybe a year ago."

"You think she'd mind if I dropped by for a chat?"

"Sure she wouldn't."

"Okay, what's her name?"

I could hear Kev thinking. Then he resorted to flipping pages in his notebook. "I got it here somewhere; she came in to make a complaint against a young'un who's been tearing up and down the road out of town like a rally driver." More pages flipped. "Here we go – Dionne Bailey."

"Did she go to school in Lexington?"

"I don't know."

"I'll get on with this, um, hypothetical case here."

"Keep in touch."

I hung up. The files beckoned but so did coffee. I needed coffee. The coffee pot was empty. I grabbed the key and my wallet; time to find the hospital cafeteria. As I wandered through the building, hoping to smell coffee and be led by my nose, I wondered how good a place the cafeteria would be for gossip. Small hospital, small town, people like to talk.

Around the next corner I smelled the tell-tale aroma of fresh coffee and followed it to a small cafeteria. To get to the counter I walked past about twelve tables. Most of which were empty. But I noticed three nurses sitting in the far corner. There was a table in front of them, empty. I mentally marked it as mine. A few other tables were occupied by visitors or doctors. I bought a coffee and a muffin then sat near the nurses. I could hear their conversation. Small talk. A few comments on various patients, no names mentioned. Nothing untoward said. The comments were nice ones. The vibe wasn't one of a group of killers or even a single killer. They were colleagues. They cared about their patients and they were genuine in wanting to help. I downed my coffee and tossed the Styrofoam cup in the trash can on my way out.

As I glanced back over my shoulder I noticed a doctor watching me. It could've been an indication of recognition on her face. There was a definite hint of something.

There was a nurse in the corridor by Grant's office door. I stopped her.

"Where would I find my patient records?"

She smiled. "Records are kept in the basement, you can take the stairs." She pointed down the hall to a doorway. "We keep records for fifteen years; after that they're destroyed or removed by the patient, assuming they're no longer needed."

"Thanks."

I let myself into the office once she'd gone and took the piece of paper with the Abernathy woman's details on it. Something told me that her death was connected to the recent deaths.

It was a slow walk down the stairs, to the first basement level. Stairs carried on. I read the sign telling me the morgue was farther down.

A smiling man greeted me from behind a counter as I swung through the double doors into a well-lit, warm basement room. Beyond him rows of shelving stretched back toward the wall. The room was deep and long. Lots of files were crammed into the extensive shelves.

"Can I help?"

"I hope so," I replied. "My aunt died here six months ago and I was wondering if I could pick up her records?"

The lines around his eyes softened. "I'll see if the records are here."

I gave him her name, date of birth, and date of death. The man with the warm smile disappeared in between rows. He came back holding a thick file.

The file thumped onto the counter under its own weight.

"This is it. I can't release it without ID." He sounded

apologetic.

"I never thought of that," I said with a shrug. "I'm here with a friend. She had an accident. So while she is being taken care of in the emergency room, I thought I'd come down and get them. You know, to save my uncle the trip. It's quite a way from Mauryville."

"Sure."

I turned to leave. "That'll teach me for leaving my purse behind."

"Hang on, miss." With a glance over my shoulder I saw the file being held out. "Take it. Your aunt died, we don't need her file."

"Really?"

"What harm can it do?"

I smiled, thanked him, and hurried away with the bulky file under my arm.

An hour later I was convinced Mrs. Abernathy had been murdered by the person responsible for the more recent deaths. There was no autopsy. I knew we had to go back over rosters for the entire year. The whole thing became a mind-numbing exercise in following a paper trail made of breadcrumbs. Grant had a large whiteboard on the back wall of his office. I hunted through his drawers for pens. With his Post-it notes I labeled all the files in chronological order, by death date, earliest to latest. Writing the numbers on the board showed the emergence of a pattern. Deaths from six months to six days ago.

Six.

Every death occurred on a day with a six but one. The

one that wasn't a six was the sixth day of the week. I grabbed my phone from my bag and opened the calendar. Today was the sixteenth.

Go back a year.

I wrote notes on the board. With my phone open I started scrolling back, noting all the dates we had to check. Every Saturday; every sixth, sixteenth, twenty-sixth. My feeling was that tracing the deaths back would give us a starting point.

A trigger: Something so horrific that it caused this spate of deaths. The more I looked at the list the more I thought the event happened in the emergency room.

Armed with the list of dates to check for deaths, I hurried back to the ER to find Kurt. It'd been at least three hours. There were more people than ever in the waiting room. Triage was separated from the waiting room by a reception desk and that was where I went.

I introduced myself as Mrs. Henderson and asked if my husband was free. The best thing was I didn't even flinch. It was no different from convincing the records keeper that I was Mrs. Abernathy's niece. The receptionist introduced herself as Katrina. "I'll buzz you in; you can sit with me until he's free."

Anything was better than sitting in the waiting room with the sick and wounded. I'm not germ-phobic by any means, but no need to tempt fate.

Katrina buzzed me in through triage. She gave me a chair and a coffee, and settled in for some gossip.

Her phone rang. "Hello, this is Katrina speaking.

You've reached emergency. How may I help?"

Moments later she pressed a button and hung up only to have the phone ring again.

I was fascinated by her telephone voice. I'd heard that voice so many times from so many places. My mind began to wander off alone, accompanied by the lilting telephone voice of Katrina.

"Hello, this is Katrina speaking, how can I help?"

Was every receptionist I'd ever met called Katrina? Or did they all go to specialist reception school to learn to inflect their words like that? I listened as Katrina put the caller through to someone else then hung up.

A lull ensued followed by a question directed at me.

"You look just like that woman who is dating Rowan Grange. I saw them in a magazine the other day. He is so hot. Are you related?"

"To Grange? No."

"Silly, to that woman. She's an FBI agent or something. They said that on the television, that *Entertainment Today* program."

Ah, real news.

"Oh, her," I replied thanking the stars that acting was all in a day's work. "She looks nothing like me."

"She does, you could be twins." Katrina bowed her head close to mine. "You can tell me, are you sisters?"

"No, wish I was. Grange isn't bad on the eye, decent voice too. He'd be okay as a brother-in-law."

She considered my response. "Pity; free concert tickets would be okay. How long have you been married to

Kurt?"

Kurt? Time to take more notice. Katrina looked about Kurt's age.

How long had we been married, what had he told people? Crap.

"Not long, we're on our honeymoon." I rolled my eyes. "Never marry a doctor."

She smiled, batted her eye-lashes and replied, "He's quite a catch. We all knew, all of us, that he and Grant would go far."

Problem is he didn't go far enough, because he came back.

"We?"

"I was in their class at high school."

It has been my experience of high school that people from high school can turn out to be malicious killers later in life. Imagined wrongs. Misplaced devotion. I started to look at Katrina in a different light.

"Did you know Kurt well?"

She came over all wistful. "He was the best looking boy in my year." Then it all changed. "I didn't know him well at all."

Something in her voice gave me pause.

I knew of Kurt's many girlfriends in college, but suppose it started earlier than that? Nothing for it but to spring it on her.

"How long did you date?"

She shuffled papers, her cheeks flushed as she moved everything to one side then back again.

"Not long. A couple of months."

"What happened?"

"He went away to college and never came back." Her voice perked up. "I married Chuck Sackett. He's a plumber. He has his own plumbing business."

Plumbing.

The police said a plumber had been to my house the day it exploded, even though I hadn't called one. I made a mental note to investigate the plumber thing myself.

"Do you have children?"

She shook her head. "We have not been blessed that way. I'm hoping that this round of treatment will be successful."

"Fertility treatment?" I felt stupid as soon as the words left my mouth but I ploughed on. "Here in town?"

"Yes, at the clinic."

Such a small place, yet there is a fertility clinic. What was Grant's wife's name? Lisa? Kim? Candy?

Kim.

"Kim works there, Grant's wife," I said inclining my head a little.

Katrina smiled. "Yes, she does." Katrina dropped her voice to a whisper laden with intrigue, "It must be hell for her."

"Why is that?"

"She can't have children," she murmured, closing a file and sliding it into a tray on her desk.

"Maybe they don't want children," I offered. My comment met with a horrified glare.

"Of course they do, they're married. Everyone wants children. Why would you get married if not to have children?"

Wow. Such a strong reaction. I decided to keep my views on children to myself. Katrina wasn't the person with whom to discuss my decision not to procreate.

"I see your point."

I also had a feeling some kind of crazed religious belief system was about to crop up.

"Kurt always wanted lots of children ..." she added. There was a wistful quality to her voice.

"Really, even as a teenager?"

I could imagine him as a randy teen but not talking about future children. I doubted Katrina knew of his loose behavior at college.

"We talked about having children, at least four."

And yet I had the feeling he never did the deed with her. I'd have bet good money on her wearing a promise ring and being one hell of a tease. My mind was beginning to wander. I pulled it back.

"Four? That's a lot these days."

"I always knew he'd be a doctor or something, so four would be okay."

I was hearing something else in her voice. She felt cheated. I needed to get her off the subject of Kurt.

"So, Doctor Neal? He stayed here?"

She shook her head. A patient appeared in the window above the desk. Katrina answered the woman's query about waiting time as best she could. Once the woman shuffled back to the waiting room Katrina turned to me. "We dated you know ..."

Hang on. She dated both of them?

"At high school?"

"No, while he was at college; he came home for the holidays and we dated. We were together for a year, long distance."

"That must've been hard."

She shrugged. "Harder for him, men have *needs*."

Just men?

"When did you marry ..." I searched for his name. "Chuck?"

She smiled.

"Five years ago."

"That's great." From the corner of my eye, I saw Kurt wave me over. "Here's my husband. Thank you for keeping me company." I stood up and pushed the chair in.

"If you're at a loss while you're in town, just call me. We'll have coffee."

"Thank you."

I bolted.

Kurt escorted me out of the ER and back to Grant's office. I told him about Katrina. He grinned.

"She was very religious ... according to her parents."

"Oh really?"

"Uh huh. Church every Sunday; bible class every Wednesday night; promise ring."

"And the truth?"

"Skank."

I channeled my teenage daughter and said, "You didn't hit that?"

"Hell, no," he replied.

I smiled. Had that one figured already. Katrina wasn't just a skank though. She saw a way out of small town life by screwing boys with a future and it didn't work out. Now she was a receptionist married to a plumber she didn't like very much. Sucked to be her.

"There's something about Katrina, I can't put my finger on it but it's like I've seen her before. A long time ago though." There was a mental bookmark inserted before I could even react. I would check it out later. I felt it was important.

"You lived out in Mauryville. No doubt you've come across her at some stage. Small town."

"Maybe."

And there it was in my head. Mac's voice with a resounding, "Maybe's ass."

Kurt scanned the whiteboard and my scrawled notes. "You've been busy," he commented then turned to me.

"There is a pattern. Six is the trigger."

"Six," he repeated, his voice dull with tiredness.

"You've had a shit of a day. Let's get out of here." I picked up the whiteboard eraser and cleaned off all the scrawled writing. Just in case someone other than Grant saw it.

As an afterthought I picked up the black marker and drew a giant six in the middle of the whiteboard. There was a chance that it meant something and he just might know what.

Chapter Nineteen
Saturday Night

I saw the silver car a split second before I saw Arbab open the front passenger door. No hesitation. I reached inside my bag and pulled out my Glock. Kurt spun around. He must have detected my movement. Perhaps his superman terrorist alert tingled. A woman leveled with us, blocking my view, also unwittingly blocking me from being recognized. She looked at me and shrieked. Kurt lurched forward pushing me into the car. I scrambled into the seat as he swung the door shut. The woman stood in front of the door screaming, "It's ... it's ..."

There was no way for me to see where Arbab was or if he could see beyond her. She was three times my width and then some.

I craned my neck to see around her, to no avail. Kurt leaped in the driver's door and floored it. As we took off from the parking lot I saw Arbab watching the hysterical woman with disdain. He turned and headed into the hospital. She stood rooted to the spot, tears pouring down her face, pointing after us as Kurt drove away. I shoved my gun back into my bag and wished I was wearing a holster. Guns shouldn't be in bags.

Anxiety escalated into a clawing, vomit-inducing ball.

Arbab in Lexington. Why did he come back? Surely he would've moved on, after not finding me. Roanoke. He killed in Roanoke. It made no sense to go to Roanoke if he was tracking me. I needed to know more about the dead woman there. What the hell was that woman screaming about? Was it the gun? The screaming and the tears triggered a memory or four. I knew that scream. I'd heard that particular pitch before, usually from much younger women and usually when I was around Tony Sharron, Grange's lead guitarist. Or Lee when he was mistaken for Tony. It wasn't the sort of reaction I'd ever witnessed with Rowan. Fans tended to keep their distance when he and I were out and about.

"Was that him?"

"Uh huh."

"Do woman often shriek and cry around you?"

"Not so much. First I thought she was reacting to my gun ... but I think she recognized me as Rowan's girl-friend."

My phone rang and I considered letting it go to voice-mail but the tougher, more together, part of me reached into my pocket and answered the call.

"Chicky, I'm coming down to Lexington," Lee said without the need for pleasantries.

"Why?"

It seemed reasonable to ask, given that he and Sam were working on the case involving boxed meat in Washington.

"I started looking into the plumber who visited your house prior to the explosions. Also, the sniper at your place. I'm coming down. Will fill you in when I see you."

I told him which hotel we were in so he could book a

room in advance.

"Sam?"

"He's working up here in DC; he's roped in a few Delta B agents to lend a hand."

"Awesome."

"What name are you using there?"

I smiled. He was going to love it.

"Mrs. Rylee Henderson."

Lee's smooth laugh flowed into my ears.

"See you in a few hours, Mrs. Henderson."

I pocketed my phone and noticed we'd stopped. After a quick look around it was evident we were in the hotel parking lot. Kurt was sitting looking at me with a quizzical expression.

"Lee is coming down, something to do with the explosions. Seems he doesn't want to discuss it over the phone."

"That can't be good," Kurt replied. "You okay?"

"Sure ... is that the right answer?"

He smiled. "It's the expected answer. Come on, let's go inside. I'm going to call Grant and get him to find out why the president of your fan club arrived at the hospital."

Nice to have fans. Clearly I'd prefer more attractive and fewer want-to-kill-me types given a choice.

A smile jumped to my lips without much effort. Kurt and I wandered arm-in-arm into the hotel lobby. No rush. We took the stairs instead of the elevator. I couldn't help but wonder what I was going to find every time elevator doors opened; I was pretty sure Kurt felt the same way. A madman had left photographs in an elevator when we were in New Zealand, which weren't horrific in themselves but they lead to some horrible discoveries. Life is a wonderful thing: Mine is ever so colorful most of the time. Elevators, like Post-it notes, became something to avoid where possible.

I felt an immediate sense of security inside the hotel room.

Kurt made coffee. He made surprisingly good coffee. Out of my team only Sam could do better.

I made a quick call to Carla.

"Mom!"

"Carla!"

Kurt looked over and grinned at my exclamation. He called out, "Hey, kid."

"Tell Doc I said 'hi' back."

I did. "Having fun? Being good?"

"It's awesome here! It would've been gay at home."

Delightful. "You're having a good time?"

"I so am! Will you be away long?"

"Are you asking because you miss me, or because you don't want me to come back too soon? By the way, if you didn't want me to come home, that would be totally gay."

She huffed, laughed, and then replied, "That's not fair. It's a trick question."

I laughed. No flies on my kid. "I'm glad you're having fun and it's not gay. I'll be home once we've solved this case."

"Is it interesting?"

"Yeah, it really is. I kinda thought it'd be gay, but no, it's interesting."

Carla's laughter tinkled. "Did you want to talk to Rowan?"

"Nah, he's gay." I could scarcely contain my amusement. "Tell him I'll call later, I'm working right now."

"Okay, gonna tell him you said he was gay too."

I could imagine her poking her tongue out at the phone.

"Awesome, I shall continue mocking you later. Love you."

"Love you too, Mom."

I dropped my cell phone onto the couch and watched it bounce once. A tiny vibration moved outward from the impact zone.

Kurt sat opposite me on the other couch. "Gay? Rowan is gay?"

I cleared my throat. "Not that kind of gay. Was mocking the child. She's *forever* saying *everything* is *gay*," I replied, doing my best teenage impersonation.

"A lot of homosexuality going on in her life or is she really happy?"

"Neither. Teenagers!" I rolled my eyes. "If they don't like something or it's boring, or stupid ... now it is gay."

"Ah, I see."

"English is evolving or maybe devolving? Gay has gone from happy to homosexual to boring. No wonder it is such a hard language to learn."

"Talk to me about the six?"

"All the deaths so far have involved the number six. And I found another one, from six months ago."

"Do you think that's the first?"

"It could be. I have the file," I told him and hoisted myself off the couch to get the file from my bag. I dropped it onto Kurt's lap and waited for him to read it.

Ten minutes later he put down the file next to him.

"This could be the first."

"That's what I thought."

"So tell me more about the 'six' connections."

"Today is the sixteenth: Someone is going to die tonight. What's more, the only day where someone didn't die on the sixth, sixteenth, or twenty-sixth, was a Saturday."

"The sixth day of the week," Kurt said.

And on the seventh he rests.

"We need to go back over the rosters for the past several months and look at corresponding dates," Kurt said.

"Yes." I had a horrible feeling we'd find more deaths.

"We also need to find out what is so important about the number six."

I nodded. "I have a woman I'd like to interview out in Mauryville; the daughter of Mrs. Abernathy. She might be able to tell us more. Kevin said she's a nurse."

Kurt picked up the file and looked for next-of-kin information. "Husband is down in here. No mention of a daughter but a familiar sounding address. I dated a girl called Dionne. She wasn't an Abernathy though."

"I wrote down her name in my notebook. Talking to her might be a good idea."

If she was there when her mother was taken into the emergency room she may have seen something or heard something that could help. It's amazing how much people remember if they're asked. It's all about triggering the right memories.

"When do you want to do that?"

"Soon as possible." Anxiety had begun to mount. I shoved it down hard.

"Let's wait for Lee," Kurt suggested.

Good thinking. Especially with Arbab in the area.

Meanwhile we could eat and stay nice and safe within the hotel walls. Or – I watched Kurt unfold papers – we could work on finding the connection to the sixes.

We each had a laptop, it was time to fire them up and get down to the nitty-gritty investigating phase. I started by running the Abernathy's daughter, Dionne Bailey, through our system. She was new to town, in that she'd recently returned and the killings started not long after she arrived. Seemed reasonable to check her out. I also put Katrina in the system, more for kicks than thinking she was a genuine suspect. I had the feeling when talking to her that she wasn't the brightest. Scheming? Oh, hell, yes. But still not the sharpest tool in the shed. There was still a lurking sense of familiarity every time I thought about Katrina.

Kurt hunted for dates on the rosters and cross-referenced everyone working those days to time frames and compiled a list of potential suspects.

There was a hit for Abernathy's daughter.

"Kurt, the Bailey woman." I swiveled my laptop to face him.

He read the screen, looked at the driver's license photograph, and then leaned back, like he was trying to get away from the picture. He knew her.

"College or high school?" I said, turning the laptop back around. That'll be why he thought her address was familiar.

A small smile twitched in the corner of his mouth. "Dionne Simonson. High school."

"Why the different name?"

"Her mother had been married before."

"You were quite the player weren't you?"

The small twitch became a full blown grin. "As tempting as it is to dispute that, I think you've already made up your mind. Dionne Simonson and I dated for three months in our junior year."

"Three? Wow, that's damn near married at high school."

He nodded. "Everyone thought we would get married."

"And?"

"And nothing really, summer came along. The big wide world beckoned."

"And your whoring reached knew dizzying heights."

He laughed. "You do know that Grant was the manwhore, as you so delightfully put it and not me ..."

"Really?" News to me.

"Oh yeah. He was screwing anything with a pulse – at least I presume they all had a pulse. I was the fall guy."

"Fall guy?"

He needed a fall guy?

"Thing with Grant was that he was often in relationships, and ..."

"A cheating-bastard-man-whore?"

"Yeah, that about sums it up."

"And he gave you a hard time because ..." I was thinking about the Mrs. Henderson thing, then I got it. "Because it was so far from the truth, it was funny."

He smiled.

I added Grant's wife, Kim Neal, to the list of possible suspects. After all he'd no doubt been cheating on her; maybe he even still played the field. Leopards don't change their spots.

It was difficult to remember what it was I missed from small town living. Everyone knew everyone else's business and had no qualms about sharing it around. The price you pay to belong to a community. Nothing's perfect. I lived in a quiet street in Oakton, my neighbors knew me by sight, but I didn't socialize with them. My house blew up. I lived in Mauryville, knew all my neighbors, and I did socialize with them. My house blew up.

A beep from my laptop required attention.

A Messenger window opened and sat there ready. I stole a furtive glance at Kurt. He seemed engrossed in whatever he was doing on his laptop. I typed into the window.

Otherwisecat: *Hello*

Galileo: *Hey, Babe, Lexington?"*

Otherwisecat: *New case.*

Galileo: *It's dangerous.*

Otherwisecat: *Yep. Now tell me how and why you were in New Zealand ten years ago as an FBI agent when you weren't FBI then.*

Galileo: *It's not important. You are in danger. Go back to DC.*

Otherwisecat: *You died with secrets.*

A blue pop-up flickered on the bottom right of my screen. It said Galileo appears to be offline. Typical. Kurt looked at me. I smiled.

"What's up?"

"Nothing," I replied, closing the messenger window. "Nothing at all."

I talk to dead people. Perhaps it was time to call in a priest.

"We have five nurses who had access to some of the dead patients."

He'd been working. Impressive.

"Five and others – that's not as definitive as it could be."

"No, it's not. It's the patients dying on different wards that are causing the issue. That, and so far there is no one person with contact at the appropriate time to all of them."

I closed my eyes. "What if it's not a nurse?"

"I'm listening."

"Visitors are probably out as visiting times don't extend into the wee small hours. Apart from nurses, who can move around a hospital without attracting attention?"

"Doctors, radiologists. Maybe a therapist of some sort."

"How much therapy goes on between two and six a.m.?"

"Good point."

"How many of those patients would've required x-rays between two and six a.m.?"

"Doctor then?"

"How many doctors work in the hospital?"

Kurt picked up his phone, and then put it down. "Not a question I want to ask Grant."

Yeah, not now he's been ratcheted up the suspect list. But I knew how to find out. Katrina.

"Check the hospital website. If that doesn't tell us, I'll take Katrina a coffee. Pretty sure I can get her to dish dirt on docs."

"Good thinking."

The thought of a doctor killing people seemed so much worse than the notion that a nurse was responsible. I checked my watch. It was midafternoon. We had until two in the morning to find the killer or figure out how to protect the patients currently in the hospital.

"We need to go back to the hospital, Kurt. We have to look through every current patient file. We need to know who the target is."

"And Arbab was last seen entering the hospital. That is not happening."

"There is no other way." I gave him a long look which met with his disapproving arched eyebrow. "Did you ask Grant about Arbab?"

He shook his head. "I won't. He knows too much already."

Too much about me.

"There is no way around this. We need to be inside the hospital. There is a life in danger."

"Fifty-one files, not counting anyone admitted today for observation."

"Yes, but the common denominator is bad behavior. We only need flip to the nurses' ER notes and see the comments."

His head nodded as he thought about it. "We need to get you into Grant's office, so no one else sees you. I can get the files."

"Let's do a drive-by and see if the silver car is still there," I said, jumping to my feet. Holster. I picked up my holster from the nightstand and clipped it to my belt. It was good to put my gun back where it belonged. Heat or no heat, I pulled a lightweight jacket on to conceal my gun from prying eyes. My fingers fondled my badge. Instead of clipping it to my belt, I pushed it into my jeans' pocket. If I had to, I could clip it on later. "I'm ready."

Kurt was already waiting by the door, carrying both laptops stowed in their cases. "Me too."

Ten minutes later we drove through the hospital parking lot and around the surrounding streets. There was no sign of the silver Galant. I breathed a sigh of relief.

Kurt looked relieved.

We left the laptops in the trunk of the car. Accessible should we need them, but neither of us wanted to carry them around. Off we scurried into the hospital and through the corridors to Grant's office. Kurt knocked once. Grant's voice called out, "Come in."

Kurt opened the door.

My heart pounded a jumpy rhythm and I felt sick to my stomach. Grant was alone. He even seemed pleased to see us.

"The love birds. What can I do for you?"

"A few things need checking," Kurt said as we sat in the chairs we'd used earlier.

"I saw your note," Grant said to me and pointed to the large 'six' on his whiteboard. "Mean something?"

"It may do."

"What do you need?"

"Access to hospital records, current ones," Kurt said.

"All right. I'll give you my pass codes to the system. You can access it remotely from your laptops." Grant typed displaying some impressive speed. When he finished he said, "I sent you an email with a link to the system and my pass code, it's valid for today. We change our codes every twenty-four hours."

"Thank you."

"No problem. I want to catch this person, Kurt, before

anyone else dies."

"So do we."

Kurt took my hand. "Come on."

We could access everything ourselves from the safety of our hotel room. No need to hang around. Except I wanted to see Katrina.

I smiled at Grant and went with Kurt. In the corridor I told him I wanted to get coffee and take some to Katrina. Not only did I want to know how many doctors were in the hospital, but she might have seen Arbab. I just hadn't yet figured out how to broach that subject. It'd come to me.

We bought coffee and chocolate muffins, then went into the emergency room and found Katrina about to leave for the day.

Kurt muttered something about wanting to check on a patient from earlier. Kissed me on the top of the head and vanished into the rooms beyond the front desk.

"Let's not waste these," I said, handing Katrina a coffee and a muffin.

"Thank you," she said, peeling the cling film from the muffin. "Been such a busy day. Half the town has been through those doors today."

"Do you get many tourists down here?" She gave me an odd look. I shrugged. "You mentioned half the town had been in. I wondered if this was a tourist destination."

"We get a few – had a funny one this afternoon. A man from somewhere in the ..." She looked lost. "I don't know where he was from but he spoke funny, like those terrorists on the TV."

"How exciting. Who was he?" I sipped my coffee.

"I don't know. He wanted to see a doctor then settled on finding the accounting department."

"Sick?"

"No, looking for someone I think. A friend. Some girl he met a long time ago."

Oh crap. "Was his friend a doctor?"

"I don't think so. I think she was a patient here once."

"Wow."

"I couldn't help him, everyone was busy. I pointed him in the direction of accounting and off he went."

Great. So he knew I'd been treated at Stonewall Jackson in the past. How was he getting his information? And what was he doing in accounting?

Kurt popped back in. "Time to go, honey. Dinner plans, remember?"

"Oh that's right," I stood up. "Sorry. I forgot we had plans tonight."

"That's all right. I'm off now anyway."

Kurt escorted me out, one arm wrapped around my waist. I whispered in his ear as we walked, "Arbab was looking for someone who was treated here once."

"How would he know that?"

"I have no idea. How does he know I used to live out in Mauryville?"

"Good point."

I wanted to run away and hide. The minute the electronic doors opened showing our car sitting across the blacktop, I wanted to run to it. There was a great deal of control exhibited on my part, and it was due in no small part to Kurt's firm grip. Maybe he sensed my desire to run away.

"He also wanted to talk to someone in accounting."

Kurt ushered me into the car then climbed in himself.

"Arbab isn't an idiot," Kurt said, turning the key in the ignition. "There is no record of you ever being treated at Stonewall Jackson, but he believes you were. The one place that will have records is the billing department. Someone has to pay."

That was not good news until I gave it more thought. Even if he found the record of payment, the address shown would be Mauryville, maybe.

"How much could he find out?"

Kurt grinned. "As it happens, nothing. There is no patient record for you, nor is there a billing record."

"How so?"

"Caine paid the bill for a Jane Doe, unknown age, and unknown address, using a Federal Bureau of Investigation credit card. Not even the date matches your admission or discharge."

I leaned back and smiled.

Don't underestimate the FBI.

Chapter Twenty
Runaway

A poem revolved through my mind. I knew it by heart.
Line by line I watched the words form. A hand I knew
painted them, with soft strokes from a sable brush on a
huge pale-blue canvas. The black letters faded to gray as
the paint on the brush needed replenishing.

Incorporeal you.
Bending time to catch a glimpse
of the realm in which you exist,
standing before a rift in time
watching, as our worlds combine,
swirling together that which was lost.
Faces tumbling in the mist.
Unsure of reality –
obsessed by insanity.
Slipping through a crack
into a sphere I can't explain.
A place where I am whole again.
Hearing your voice,
seeing your smile,
torn by forces unseen.
Plunged into a disturbing dream.
Standing alone before a fissure in time
wishing our worlds could forever entwine.
Unsure of reality –
Gripped by insanity.

The last of the words dripped off the bottom of the canvas and formed a red cap on the ground under the easel. Missing Mac wasn't going to help me figure out how Arbab was tracking me. Thoughts whirled. Or was it? He was tracking me now, but a me that existed a long time ago. He was visiting places where once I had been, and now am again.

It was all too freaky: No one could've foreseen this trip to Lexington, certainly not someone stepping out of my distant past and coming from Saudi Arabia. And anyway – I sensed the voice of reason entering the room – that didn't explain why he was in Roanoke, killing a random Conway.

Roanoke. I couldn't think of a time I was there for anything more than a brief visit. It didn't make sense like the other sightings. Part of me knew none of it made sense, but that wasn't the part that spoke to Mac on a regular basis. I see dead people. I speak to dead people. Not people exactly, but Mac. It's not like everyone who'd ever died comes back to visit. Just Mac and sometimes Mom. I refused to allow the faces of dead crime victims I'd helped swim into focus. Mac and occasional visits from Mom were enough.

"Conway, you with me?"

My eyes flashed up to find Kurt crouched in front of me.

"Sure, why?"

"You've been staring at something over there." He pointed to the easel. "For almost an hour."

"The easel?"

"No, the nothing. There is nothing there."

I looked at the easel and watched it dissolved into a puddle of pale blue on the carpet. Black words swirled on the blue, like ripples on a still lake. The puddle grew smaller and disappeared. Taking Mac's red baseball cap with them.

"Nothing." I shrugged.

"What did you see?"

"A canvas with a poem painted on it."

"Coffee?" Kurt asked and stood up.

"Sure, coffee would be great."

I was waiting for him to get freaky over the easel thing. When he didn't, I followed him to the kitchenette and changed the subject.

"How is Arbab following me?"

"I don't know."

"It's like he's going back in time and following a trail left during ..."

He set down the cup he was holding and turned to face me. "You're talking about the Son of Shakespeare, aren't you?"

"How insane does that make me?"

"Off the charts. Or it would be, if I hadn't had a similar thought."

"How is this happening?"

Kurt's eyes met mine. "I don't know. But I bet it's an interesting explanation."

"The odd place out is Roanoke. But DC, my home –

which was Mac's house – visiting my old property in Mauryville and visiting Stonewall Jackson hospital … they are all places I was during the Shakespeare case." It was conceivable that killing the first Conway woman in DC could've just been due to me being FBI, and a total case of mistaken identity. The woman in Alexandria upped the ante somewhat; I had been there. I stayed in a hotel there during the Son of Shakespeare case. But the explosion at home, didn't that mean he'd found me? And the other DC death made some sense if he thought I lived in DC. But like the Roanoke death it was not somewhere I'd been. I had no ties to northeast DC at all.

"Where could he go next?"

"I need the original case file."

My laptop was sitting on the floor by the couch. I fired it up and logged into the FBI system. Accessing old case files was easy: Everything was digital now and there was also hard copy stored in a giant secure records room. I skimmed the front page of the file. There was a log, stating who had opened it and when. It was last opened a month ago by Special Agent Timothy Stenton.

"Interesting," I said. "Someone accessed the file."

Kurt looked at the screen. "Have another look." He pointed to a comment at the bottom of the page. "They're using it at the Academy as a training case."

I laughed. I couldn't help it. I'd delivered a few talks on the case at the Academy over the years, more as a warning of how things can go wrong from the perspective of an agent who was the intended victim of a very clever killer.

"They're teaching with that case, that's awesome. Let's hope the baby agents learn something."

I scrolled through the pages, looking for the timeline I knew was there. It was there and if this guy had access to this case, it wasn't good.

"We went from the hospital back up to Fairfax, to Mac's parents' home, then to Richmond – to my father's and to the hospital. It ended there."

Kurt's hand rested in my shoulder. "I know, I remember."

"If he's following this case, trying to find me—"

"This is his starting point. A high profile case that had you as the intended victim. Everywhere you went is a place that holds more discoverable knowledge for him."

I picked up my phone and called Caine.

"It's me. This is going to sound peculiar but I need you to do something for me."

"Go ahead." His voice never flinched. Caine was well used to me and peculiar things.

"We think ..." Because it's not as insane if two of us think it. "I think Arbab could be heading back to Fairfax to the Connelly's old house." Maybe.

"Good luck to him," Caine growled. "They bulldozed that place two years ago."

"I know, but he doesn't."

"I'll have agents waiting, if that's where he's heading we'll grab him." Caine grumbled to himself. "I'll send a black-and-white to the Connelly's place just in case he comes up with a current address. This idiot seems to be resourceful."

"Let Noel know and tell him I'll be in touch soon."

I hung up. I'd had little to do with the Connellys since I'd adopted Carla. The judge who granted the adoption also issued a protection order stating that Mac's older brother, Eddie Connelly, was not allowed anywhere near Carla. That made a difficult situation all the more treacherous. I adore Mac's father, Bob. He and my father work for my Foundation. The Butterfly Foundation that Mac and I founded to help the kids of mentally ill parents. Carla was one of those kids. Mac and I were survivors of mental mothers.

Mac's mother was not someone I wanted around my child. The protection order against Eddie pissed her off, and she stormed out of my life, throwing nastiness and hateful accusations as she went. I saw Bob at the Foundation whenever I could. The others I did not miss. I knew enough about Eddie Connelly to know that given the chance, he'd rat me out like the scumbag bastard he truly was. Hence the situation with the Connellys was tricky: Trying to sneak past Beatrice and Eddie but still let Bob into my life was akin to walking through a minefield.

Kurt was still scrolling through the old case file. "Ellie, how much of this case was in the news?"

"Shit, I remember seeing news footage of our house on the BBC the night we left for Washington. But I don't know how much else was broadcast." My memory was foggy when it came to media surrounding the case. A newspaper. "There was a letter to a newspaper from The Son of Shakespeare. We were back in Lexington when I saw that, I think."

"Did he mention he knew where you were?" Kurt searched for attached media references. "Never mind, he didn't."

"There was a story on the six o'clock news about the body found in a dumpster in Richmond," I said. "I was linked in that story because she was my best friend, way back when—"

"No, I'm looking for any public references to Mac's parents' home, or any other places you may have gone."

"He referenced them in a poem, I think. But it wasn't made public. None of the poems were."

"You sure?"

"Uh huh." I nodded.

"Then what's this?" Kurt opened an attachment. It was a PDF containing all the sick little Post-it poems written by the killer, Charles Boyd, aka Son of Shakespeare aka Jack Griffin.

"They're evidence … why would they be in a PDF?"

"Because someone created it as a teaching tool."

"How many times has it been downloaded?"

"Over a hundred."

"Can we trace each download?"

"There is a log – all downloads were from the Academy at Quantico."

"Downloaded, and it's possible they were printed and ended up in agents' notes. So what happens to notes once you finish at the academy?" I knew what I did with mine, I kept them. They burned in the explosions along with my house in Mauryville.

"I still have mine," Kurt said.

"I would've if they hadn't burned. So people keep them, like they do their sweats."

"And someone may have taken, read, or copied, someone else's notes." He followed his thought with some other notions. "Sharing an apartment or something. A roommate finds them or a party attendee. My point is, no one would think of them as being sensitive, they were used to teach a class."

"That's true. But the notes wouldn't make any sense to anyone who wasn't involved in the investigation, or didn't know anything about it."

"People remember things and all it takes is the right key word to bring that memory out."

Scary thought.

"Six months ago I was linked to Rowan by a reporter during our sojourn in New Zealand. Then I was linked again at an award ceremony. It's possible Arbab recognized me on one of those occasions. So, let's see who downloaded this file and the PDF in the last six months."

"Notice how often six comes up?"

"Yep. Beginning to really dislike that number."

"Me too." Kurt pulled up a list of people who had shown interest in the case file and downloaded the PDF. There were twenty names.

"I'll email the list to Sam. Perhaps he can get to all of

them and ask the right questions."

A heavy knock shook the door in the frame.

Kurt set the laptop on the coffee table and drew his weapon. I moved to the door, Glock in hand. A quick look through the peephole revealed Lee.

I nodded to Kurt then turned the handle and pulled the door inward.

Lee stepped in wearing a grin a mile wide.

"I smell coffee," he said, shutting the door behind him.

Kurt and I holstered our weapons.

He and Kurt did some fancy handshake thing I'd seen Sam and Mac do in happier days. Guess the whole team adopted it. Except me.

Lee smiled at me and gave me an affectionate pat on the back. "Not going as well as you thought?" he commented, pouring a coffee.

"Let's just say there is so much going on that it's way more interesting than it ought to be," I replied. "Glad you're here."

"Ellie, it's good to be here."

"We have some trouble," I said with a slight confessional tone, and headed back over to the couch and my laptop. "And apparently you do as well?"

"You want me to enlighten you on the extent of the trouble?" he replied, following with a coffee.

"Please do."

"I did some snooping into the plumber who visited your place the day of the explosions. He works for a company called Empire Plumbing. After some digging I discovered Empire Plumbing, which is owned by Central Holdings LLC in Fairfax."

The sick feeling was back with a vengeance.

"Central Holdings?"

"Yes." He pulled out his notebook. "Chief Executive Officer is Abbudin Nader."

That I knew. We'd already come across a car owned by Central Holdings. Arbab had been in it.

"Interesting," I said.

"The plumber's name is Christopher Fitzgerald or so says his driver's license – thing is I thought it was a funny name for him to have, it didn't fit his middle-eastern look. Bit too Irish."

"And his real identity?"

"Facial recognition software is the new god. He is a young man by the name of Abdul-Bari Bin Qasim Sabbagh."

"Interesting name."

"There is more. Your unwanted admirer. His full name is Habib Bin Faisal Bin Abdul-Malik Arbab."

I knew that already. He is the son of Sheik Faisal Bin Abdul-Malik Arbab.

"And your point?"

"When I started looking into Arbab's whereabouts, it red-flagged a bunch of agencies. Everyone wants him."

"Where is his daddy these days?"

"Saudi, refusing to have anything to do with his son. It was reported that Arbab attempted to kill his father a few years ago. Habib Bin Faisal Bin Abdul-Malik Arbab is on the run."

"He's not so much running as enjoying a killing spree. We know where he is, just haven't caught up with him yet."

Lee smiled. "Takes more than a terrorist to throw you off your game, don't it, Ellie?"

"I think it might."

That's my answer and I'm sticking to it. No need for Lee to worry. I can handle this. He's just a man with an ax to grind. I've met plenty of them. My fingers sought the scar around my throat. I still had a head.

"Shall I tell you about the little plumber boy?"

"Please do," I replied, leaning back on the couch and getting comfy. I felt safer with Lee and Kurt in the room.

"He's been working for Abbudin Nader's plumbing business as a legitimate plumber for about three years. So far, just two houses have blown up after a plumbing visit from him."

Just two.

"Nice."

"The first was a house in Herndon that belonged to a former CIA operative."

"How the hell would someone get an address like that?"

"See, this is where it gets really good." Lee sipped his coffee for a moment. "Plumber boy was mainly employed to search records. A painstaking and laborious job that involved searching for things like property tax records for names requested by Mr. Nader."

Kurt groaned. "Oh, fucking hell. That's how he's getting addresses."

I felt my eyes grow wider. Kurt rarely swore.

Lee faltered a little after Kurt's outburst, and then recovered. "Yep. Hours, days, weeks, spent searching individual property tax records looking for names and addresses. I've been over some myself just to see how mind-numbing it is. You can't search by name in most counties, so it has to be done by address, and if you have no clue, it's a case of picking a street and going house by house, then moving on to the next one."

"Fuck-a-doodle-do, no wonder this guy blew up my house. I'd wanna blow something up too, after spending hours upon hours searching boring databases."

Lee flashed his teeth. "Wonder if he was smart enough to use the old Control-F command, or if he scrolled through every single page."

"Even so, it would be boring, doing Control-F, and having to type in names in the search box on every single page of street names. Hell, it'd drive me to murder."

"But how'd he get the names?" Kurt asked.

"Television, newspapers, gossip magazines," Lee replied.

Sure that'd work for my name – but an ex-CIA operative? I don't think so.

"Or from an unsuspecting innocent source, like an FNG. Especially one that graduated in the last six months," Kurt added. "But again, that would only work for someone who was FBI, not so much an ex-CIA operative."

Lee's smile froze. "Say what, about a fuc'n ... what?"

"New guy, you know newly-minted agent ..." Kurt said, rolling his eyes.

"There's an FNG at the office, lending a hand."

The term FNG bought a smile to my lips; Fucking New Guy was not something we heard much in Delta. But Lee's comment about how there was one in the Delta office was the magic that removed my smile.

"Sam's there, right?" I said.

"In and out, mostly out, chasing boxes of ass."

"So – who is in?"

"Sandra," Lee replied. He was already calling her on his cell phone. "Hey, Sandra, where are you?"

I motioned to him to put it on speaker. A spilt second later her voice rose from the phone on the table. "Bullpen. Problem?"

"Go to my office and shut the door," I told her.

"All right, Ellie." We heard her walking, opening the door, the phone being placed on my desk and the door closing. "I'm here."

"Good. Where's the FNG?"

"Going through files sitting at the spare desk in the pen. What's going on?"

Kurt spoke, "Conway's getting jumpy. We want you to keep a close eye in the FNG."

"What in particular am I looking for?"

"An unnatural interest in anything to do with me," I said. "Accessing any of my old cases, or asking questions about my whereabouts."

"Are you serious? You three think someone on the inside is spreading the joy?"

I liked Sandra. She fitted this team like a well-worn glove.

"Yep, spreading the joy."

Spreading the joy all over the state. Little bloodied bodies of joy. Nope. Wrong bad guy: that'd be the one sending parcels of people all over the state. Arbab is more thrashing about trying to flush me out.

"I'll watch him."

"Thanks, Sandra. Dinner at my place once we're all back in DC."

"Of course, the grand housewarming," she replied. "I'll do dessert. The men can handle the garlic bread and booze."

Kurt and Lee protested with loud grumbles of indignation but we all knew that was about all they could handle.

"Take care."

Lee hung up.

I stretched out my legs and hit Kurt's by accident.

"Sorry," I said as he moved to avoid me.

"No, you're not, but it's okay." Thoughtfulness came over him. "FNG in the bullpen. A pivotal case involving all of us used as a training case. An exploded house. A terrorist killing Conways to flush out our Conway. Boxes of ass. A killer in a hospital." He smiled. "But I'm forgetting the best bit, my pretend-wife talks to dead men."

I kicked him. He winced.

When it was all laid out like that, it sounded quite ridiculous.

I grabbed my phone and called Comms. Within seconds I was patched through to Roanoke Police Department.

"It's SSA Conway. Who's in charge of the Conway strangling?"

"That would be Jeff Dingle, ma'am."

"Can you put me through, please?"

"Putting you through now, ma'am."

The phone rang. A deep male voice answered. "Jeff Dingle."

"Jeff, SSA Ellie Conway from DC."

"Any relation to the Conway I have on my case book?"

"Nope, but I have some questions."

"Go ahead. I heard there were three others up north."

"There are. Did Ms. Conway live in Roanoke long?"

"No." Pages moved. "She moved here six months ago from Lexington."

"Thank you, that's very helpful."

"Is this something to do with the case up north?"

"I'm not sure."

I hung up. I am sure.

Lee and Kurt were sitting in silence waiting.

"She was from Lexington and moved six months ago."

"There goes that number again," Kurt whispered.

"He thought it was you," Lee said. "This brings me to the wannabe sniper who took out the tweaker on your front lawn."

I'd forgotten about him.

"What about him?"

"The connection isn't to the boxes of ass. It was you he was after."

I felt so much better knowing that. Really I did.

"He's connected to Arbab?"

Lee nodded. "When he didn't get you, the plumber was sent in."

"Hang on, the shooter at the 7-Eleven – do we know if he was sent after me or if that was a fluke?"

"We know it wasn't the same shooter. Unless the guy we got at your place was a reincarnation of the other dude."

I smiled. Yeah, an instant reincarnation.

"For argument's sake let's say the Blake Lane shooter was hired to take me out. Is he connected to Arbab? Or connected to the boxes of ass? Or do we have an unknown situation?"

Lee's eye brows rose. "You worried?"

"No, we'll figure it out." I lied a hundred times a week to all manner of people. My thoughts turned to what he'd said earlier. "But Arbab has killed since trying to take me out at home, so he can't have been sure the address was mine?"

"That's what I thought too. He seems intent on ridding the world of as many Conway women as possible."

"Yep, that's a real possibility, but as much as I want my charming wannabe killer caught, we have to stop the hospital killer before someone dies tonight." Part of me was wondering if it was 'killers' and not 'killer.'

"Priorities, Chicky. You are ours."

I could see how my being alive could be a priority for my team and to the FBI; a lot of money went into training us all. "I saw Arbab at Stonewall Jackson Hospital today. He could still be around. The receptionist told me he came looking for a patient. He's following a trail we left a few years ago now. Sooner or later that trail is going to intersect with my actual life. It fuc'n almost did today." I took a breath. "That would not be good. I've requested help. There should be an extradition team here now."

Lee didn't even blink at the mention of extradition. "We're not going after Arbab?"

"Nope. Not right now anyway."

"Meanwhile, someone is killing patients," Kurt reminded us.

"Refocus this party and let's get something in place to protect patients," I said. Time was marching on and we had to figure this out before two in the morning. "Kurt, we can access all the hospital records, yes?"

"Yes." He fired up his laptop and used the link and password provided by Grant.

"Can we search key words? If so, look for 'uncooperative' and similar descriptions."

"On it, Ellie," he said, tapping on the keys. "I'm cross-referencing to show anyone about to be discharged. They're the most at risk."

My head was beginning to ache. Maybe my brain would implode and save Arbab the trouble of killing me. I just loved being the focus of a lunatic bent on revenge; knowing it may be several lunatics really upped the joy factor. Despite knowing I needed to let go of the Arbab situation I found the practice very difficult.

Knowing someone wants you dead is one thing. Knowing it's only a matter of time before he stumbles upon you is another.

It was painfully obvious that I needed a way to put this to rest and concentrate. I knew what I had to do. I had to call Jonathon Tierney for an update.

"I'll be right back," I said and took my phone and the room key. Both men looked up. Both wore grim expressions. "I'll just be in the corridor. While I'm gone, find out where Robin Conway is from. I doubt it's Deanwood, where she was killed."

It was easy to see their protests. They were written all over their very expressive faces. I ignored them and left.

The minute I stepped into the hallway I felt vulnerable. Absurd. I'd let Arbab rattle me. Jonathon answered the phone on the first ring; there were no security measures to go through this time. That told me he had my cell phone number added to the safe list. This was serious shit.

"You got him yet?"

"No."

"He was in Lexington today, at Stonewall Jackson Hospital. You might want to pass that on."

"You can do it. I'm going to give you liaison ability."

"Is that wise?"

"Yes. You're on the ground and have the most at stake. I've texted you the phone number and name for the team leader."

My phone buzzed alerting me to the text message.

"All right. I'll talk to him."

I hung up and read the text. I was to call Tim Cosgrove. How fitting that the man who returned Arbab to his father in the first place be the one who brings him in again. This was going to be an interesting phone call.

Being in the hallway started to feel more insecure than it had before. I opted to go back into the room and use the bedroom. It was weird not talking in front of Kurt and Lee, but they weren't involved in this part of my life. It was my former life, but I wasn't a pop star formerly known as Squiggle. I was an FBI agent, seconded to a CIA task force, who was once known as Demelza.

Steadying my nerves, I pressed the numbers in with care and hit talk. Sixteen rings later, the phone was answered. I didn't recognize the voice but it had been a very long time.

"Is this Tim Cosgrove?"

"Yes."

"Jonathon Tierney gave me your number."

"For?"

"An extension of Operation Kiwi."

He exhaled audibly. "Where are you?"

"In Lexington. You?"

"Also in Lexington."

"Arbab was here today, at the hospital."

"You know this?"

"Yes, I saw him."

"Who are you?"

"A deceased friend."

There was noise in the background. The sound of weapons being stripped and cleaned; I could almost smell the gun oil.

"Demelza," he said without a trace of doubt. "I'll come to you, where?"

I gave him the hotel address and told him our room number. I also mentioned we'd be heading for the hospital later on, as there was something there we needed to deal with.

I'd made a decision while talking to Tim and it changed everything.

"I think I know where he'll be, or where he'll go. You might want to stick close. Time to flush out this prick," I said.

"Remember we can't take him in public. The way this works ... hell, you know how this works."

"Yeah, I do."

"We have a small hitch – there is a current BOLO because he is a person of interest in an NCIS case. We don't want NCIS getting wind of his whereabouts – it'll be harder to extract him from custody."

"Then you do need me to flush him out. LEOs will report sightings to NCIS."

"The thing working in our favor is his last sighting. According to NCIS, this was in northern Virginia. No one's looking in Lexington."

Except us. We're looking.

Tim assured me he'd be at my door in minutes. Guess that meant the rendition team was staying in our hotel. Made me feel a tad safer.

Things were not looking good for what was supposed to be a restful day spent trying to find the hospital killer. It felt better once I was back in the same room as my team. Kurt and Lee looked over at me and watched as I sat down on the sofa.

"Anything on Robin Conway?" I said.

"She's from Richmond, moved to the Deanwood area last year," Lee said.

"Just like the Roanoke woman moved from Lexington … now they make more sense." It wasn't immensely helpful sense, but it was keeping to the places within that old case file. "We need to flush out Arbab," I said, bracing myself for the onslaught I felt sure would follow.

"You're sure?" Kurt replied. His calmness blanketed the room.

"I can't think of another way to stop any more deaths."

"There has to be." His voice was quiet. "This is unacceptable."

"The cavalry is coming. It's the best way. We think the fucktard is still in Lexington. I think he's frequenting my old haunts. Let me find him. We'll finish this then get back to stopping the hospital killer." I sounded a helluva lot cockier than I felt. "There is an extradition team meeting us here. It's not like we're taking on a terrorist alone."

I slipped in the rendition thing and waited for the explosion.

"The risk is unacceptable, Ellie," Kurt said.

I couldn't believe neither of them was going to comment on the rendition team.

"No, what *is* unacceptable is the needless death of innocent women and he won't stop until we stop him." Or he gets me.

"There has to be another way to flush him out."

"Yeah, well, I don't see Christopher Chance walking in anytime soon with another plan," I said aloud without thinking, and with a heavier sigh than I intended. It was too late to check myself. The words were out there being assimilated by Lee and Kurt.

"You read *Human Target* comics?" The incredulousness in Lee's voice tumbled across the carpet and writhed at my feet.

I smiled, squishing the words under my right foot. "No, I watch the Fox version of *Human Target*. You know the one with Mark Valley as Christopher Chance?"

It still grated on me that the powers that be shit-canned the series after only two seasons. It was awesome. Pure action and great entertainment.

Kurt looked over, bemused. Lee nodded and grinned. "I never knew you were a fan."

"There's a lot you don't know. Even after all these years."

"It's you, Chicky. You're the legal equivalent to Christopher Chance, and we're right here beside you."

For a moment I was stumped. Lee and Kurt were about as far from Guerrero or Winston as it was possible to get. Physically speaking. Although I saw some definite shared personality traits with each character. It seemed smart to keep that to myself.

"I'm the bait. I can't be the bait and Christopher Chance." There was this hidden romantic side to me that hoped for a Christopher Chance rescue though, and I intended it to stay hidden. "Let's do this thing. Parade me around in public and draw out our terrorist."

"I'm not liking it," Lee muttered.

"Me neither." I hoped like hell the rendition team was paying attention. My death wish ended when I became a parent. I noted Lee hadn't moved. Nor had I. We were in no rush to engage a killer. I looked at him and saw his cheeky smile. "What?"

"Guess I never figured you'd go for a blond."

"Pardon?"

"Rowan and now Mark Valley."

I rolled my eyes skyward. "Thought we'd moved on ..."

"Nope." He settled back. "Here's the rub, Chicky: You didn't want to be with someone like us." He paused, pointing from me to himself. "Understandable that you wouldn't want to date anyone in our line of work again. But here you are dropping Christopher Chance into the conversation and going all doe-eyed over Mark Valley."

"I was not," I huffed. Ridiculous. "And anyway Valley is an actor. He can hardly be called one of us!"

"Really? An actor? That's all? You know I served in the

Gulf War, yeah?"

"Yeah." I didn't like where this was going all of a sudden.

"Let's just say he wasn't always an actor. Unless all actors go through West Point but that seems a little extreme."

And my bubble burst into shiny droplets of water.

"No way!"

No way was I prepared to accept he was a soldier who served in the Gulf.

"Sorry, Chicky. The man knows his way around a weapon or two."

"And your point is?"

"You protest too much. You're not anti-LEO. You're scared."

Scared. I don't fuc'n think so. I addressed his LEO comment and left the rest alone.

"Christopher Chance is not a LEO. I believe he described himself as a death-retardant specialist. He's a mercenary."

Kurt laughed.

Lee explained, "And Mark Valley was a soldier and that makes him one of the good guys who can handle a weapon and himself in any given situation."

"But he ain't a LEO."

He smiled. "You got me."

I suspected he had a point he wanted to make with all this and it wasn't just to stall the inevitable. "And your well-hidden agenda here is?"

"Rowan's a helluva guy, no doubt about it. But he doesn't make you feel safe."

News flash: No one makes me feel safe anymore.

"Did you forget I am quite capable of defending myself and my family?"

"No, Chicky, I did not." His eyes met mine. He and Kurt were there the day I put a bullet in Abbasi's head after he abducted Carla. "I'm just saying you want more and Rowan can't give it. He doesn't know what we know. He doesn't see what we see. His world is that of a gilded lily."

Poetic.

"If he's so shit at real life, why did I leave my daughter with him? And why did I deem him to be the safest person for her to be with?" Even as the words left my mouth I could hear my brain reminding me about Rowan's bodyguards. Lee's smile faded a little.

Kurt gave a light cough. I glared at him. Just because he was there watching me talk to the bodyguard doesn't mean he can get involved now.

Lee's smile reestablished itself on his face. "You let her go with Jed. I doubt you'd have done it if Rowan's bodyguards were anything less than ex-SEAL. Face it, Chicky. As good as he is, he's not the physical security-providing type and that irks you. Deep down, you miss it."

He'd checked up on Jed. Why that surprised me I did not know. I wanted to refute his comments and shoot him down in flames but he was right. Damn Lee and his knowing me better than I know myself. I needed an out.

A smile crept over my face.

"So, you gonna hook me up with your buddy Mark, then?"

Lee tipped his head back and roared with laughter. "Chicky, if I thought for one second you were serious, I'd do it."

Who says I'm not? I should've known by the comfortable way he held a weapon on *Human Target* that it wasn't all acting. I could do worse than date someone like him.

Enough already. I glanced at my watch.

"Lee, vests?"

He lifted a black bag and set it on the table. Lee handed out three vests. I took mine into the bedroom. It was necessary for me to wear the vest under my shirt. Walking around in a bullet-proof vest that bore a big yellow 'F.B.I' on the back wasn't very conducive to covert anything.

My phone buzzed. A text from Cosgrove. They were outside the room.

"Come on – let's do this thing. We have a specialist team at our door." I stood up while reaching for the gun on the side table. I slid the Glock into my holster and pulled on my jacket. "You got spare mags?"

Lee nodded.

I rotated my stiff shoulder and took two full magazines from the side table. They slotted into pouches on my belt. Time to go be a target. Not just any old target, but the very one Arbab wanted. All thoughts of family were locked in a safe box within my mind. My focus shifted to the task at hand. I added wireless microphones and re-ceivers. Lee and I pushed the receivers into our ears and checked they were working.

I fought the urge to growl, "Come get some." I left the semi-sanctuary of the hotel room. In truth, I was feeling mighty vulnerable and not at all sure that this was the best course of action. Christopher Chance hadn't shown up. But Tim Cosgrove and five other men had. For some reason I expected to see uniforms but they were all in jeans and shirts. No obvious signs of weapons or who they really were.

"Demelza." Tim's voice was quiet and serious. "It's been a long time."

"Yes," I said. "It has."

I did a quick introduction. Everyone shook hands.

"I need you to draw Arbab out, to get his attention, and for you to draw him away from any public areas. If possible," Tim said.

Sure, no problem.

"He wants me, so, that shouldn't be too difficult."

"We don't want to remove him in front of civilians. It could get messy. Attention is not our friend."

"Fair enough."

"Vest?" Tim said.

I smiled. "Yes, we're all wearing vests."

Lee told them which communication frequency we were using. It would be easier if they could hear us, but only use our channel in an emergency. Too many voices in one's head caused confusion. The team was to follow without raising suspicion.

Lee and I slid our right palms together, catching fingertips. "Alert and safe," I said to him.

He nodded. "Alert and safe."

Together we walked down the hallway to the elevator and the end of all sanctuary. The sliding door from the hotel opened onto the parking lot. Bright sun made me squint, despite my dark glasses.

From within my ear I heard Kurt pick up our frequency, his voice was soft and low. "Okay kids, alert and safe."

A wave of panic hit me. I breathed through it and kept walking to Lee's car. I knew that Kurt would follow within a few minutes, never letting us get out of range. Somewhere around me were snipers and specialists sent by Tierney and lead by Tim. I couldn't see them but I felt them.

I slid into the passenger seat, thankful I wasn't driving. The car dipped to the left as Lee sank into the driver's seat.

Kurt's voice flowed as he typed, "I'm getting hits back from the BOLO I put out on his car."

That is why my team is so awesome. He put out a Be On the Lookout on a car, not a person. NCIS don't know about the car. They're looking for a person.

"The car was last seen entering the Interscape Café parking lot. A police officer watched the driver leave his vehicle and enter the café."

"Great," I said. "Can't someone just pop a cap in his ass and get this over with?"

"Interscape Café ... his car is still in the parking lot."
He typed some more. "We have eyes on the driver using a
computer."

"Eyes?"

"Police cruiser spotted the car and one of the officers
went in for a coffee. He observed the driver of the car sitting at one of the computers. He reported he appears to
be waiting for his coffee. Commented that he looked of
Arab descent."

Excellent.

"On our way."

"Cruiser is leaving the area."

Ten minutes later we pulled into the tree-lined parking
lot. I surveyed cars as I'd done once upon a time before.
Lee parked away from other patrons. It was all so familiar
I wanted to scream. My past was rising up and trying to
choke me. Memories of Mac filled the scene.

It took only one cleansing breath to convince myself
that I had this covered. Not only was I wearing a vest under my button-down shirt but I had my big girl panties
on, kickass cowboy boots, and my Glock 17. I got this.
Once more with conviction. I freaking *got* this.

"Going in," I whispered.

I didn't mean to whisper; my voice failed me. Maybe I
didn't have it. Lee and I stepped out of the car. I stood by
the trunk: it took everything I had to keep out the past
and the memories that seeped from the brick building in
front of me.

Lee grinned and nudged me with his elbow. "We've

been here before, Chicky. Remember the rainbow peo-ple?"

With that the horror subsided and a memory of a wasted Mac appeared. "Damn, he was hilarious," I replied and sauntered into the coffee shop like there was nothing wrong. We joked around at the counter while ordering, which afforded me a chance to scan the room for Arbab. I spotted him on a computer in a corner, facing the screen. With a slight incline of my head I pointed him out to Lee.

He smiled at the barista, "We'll be over there?" Lee's hand waved toward a booth near the computer and Arbab.

I spoke to Kurt, "Ten people not including staff or Arbab."

He replied, "Make sure he sees you."

"There are only ten people in here," I said.

"Ten people is ten people too many. Make sure he sees you. We need him to see you and follow when you leave."

From nowhere a questioning female voice called out, "Rylee?" I turned to see Grant's wife coming toward us.

I glued a smile to my face and replied, "Hi, Kim."

Kurt spoke in my ear, "Not good, get rid of her."

Pretty sure I didn't eat a bowl of stupid for breakfast.

"Rylee, wanna sit with me?" She came to a stop in front of me. Her eyes moved to Lee. "Unless of course you have company."

Lee's eyebrows rose. "We're old friends," he said. His voiced dripped with honey. "Now is not a good time, gorgeous. I'm having a crisis."

Did I detect a slight lisp? I found myself fighting not to laugh.

Kurt whispered inside my head, "Now I've heard everything."

Kim's face lit up. Guess she liked being called gorgeous by a big ol' gay Lee. "Oh, I'm sorry." She touched Lee's arm.

"I'll see you later with Kurt, no doubt," I said. My intention was to hurry her along.

"Of course, 'bye now." She turned to Lee. "Hope you resolve your crisis."

"I'm with my bestie and Rylee is an expert in crisis control," he oozed.

There was definitely a lisp. I bit my lip hard. "Crisis?" I hissed as we made our way to the booth. "And it appeared to be some kind of homosexual crisis at that."

Arbab had not looked up. You'd think people talking would attract his attention. We sat. He never moved his eyes from the screen in front of him. To get his attention I'd probably have to tap him on the shoulder and ask about his father.

"Is this not a crisis?" There was no trace of his earlier lisp.

I smiled. "Think it could be."

Kurt was chuckling in my ear. Lee was trying hard not to smile.

"Give me a minute, but watch me," I said. "I'm going to the bathroom."

To reach the ladies' room I had to walk past Arbab. I was hoping he'd look up as I moved by him.

Bring it on.

I trotted past his table and went to the ladies' room. A few minutes and the beginning of a potentially disastrous headache later I was leaning on the door frame to the bathroom, hoping I could suck it up and make it back to our table.

The whole sixteen paces I had to walk to get to the table were excruciating.

Every step sent shards of pain through my left temple. I was way beyond 'mild headache' and free-falling into 'serious pain' territory. This is where a normal person would mention something to their co-worker the doctor, especially when it would just take a whisper.

Normal was a sticking point. I have never said I was normal and just couldn't make myself fit in the little boxes other people seemed to like so much. It's a personality flaw. I'm working on it. The pain suddenly increased. I saw Lee move his feet so I could get past. I misjudged, stood on one, fell over his legs, and landed with an unceremonious thump on the table. Lee's hand shot out and grabbed my arm, stopping me before I fell off the table and onto the floor.

"Okay?"

"Sure."

A dark gray hole swam where Lee's face should've been. I was screwed. Bile rose. As I tried to stand the floor fell away.

I heard Lee's voice followed by Kurt's.

Falling.

Damn, that didn't go as well as it could have.

Free falling. Gray became fuzzy black. Sharp spikey pain drove through my skull. Like someone was battering railroad spikes into me with a sledge hammer. The last clear thought that formed was of Arbab: surely he couldn't ignore the spectacle I'd made of myself.

Everything swirled into nothing. The last thing I saw was Kurt's face coming from beside me. It was all lost. Nothing left but blinding pain.

Chapter Twenty-One
Thorn In My Side

I didn't need to open my eyes to know where I was. The noise. The light filtering through my closed eyelids. The familiar smell of disinfectant.

The smell. I rolled sideways and vomited. Holy crap. Half my head tried to explode. My right eye refused to open. My left was reluctant. I lay back, the pain jolted off to the right and lodged behind my eye. I was in hospital: the least they could do was give me some decent drugs.

The hand that touched my shoulder felt familiar. His cologne was warm. Without warning I vomited again.

"I'll get you something to stop that," Kurt said. "I wanted to run some tests before I gave you anything."

My throat felt dry.

He held a cup of cool water for me to sip.

"Tests?"

"Don't want you stroking on me."

For a split second I imagined my face half-frozen and words that wouldn't come. Me neither.

"Migraine?"

"Yes. Lay back, try to relax. I'll get you Demerol and Phenergan."

"Nice mix."

"Stop the vomiting, stop the pain, keep you manageable," he replied with a smile. "I forgot how combative you can be." He moved away, but the room wasn't empty.

I figured Lee was there.

Whispered voices. Whispered voices? Voices?

"Lee?"

"Chicky." A chair scrapped against the ground and a shadow fell. "Here. What do you need?"

"A new head." Pain shot outward from behind my eyeball. "Who else?"

I gave up trying to open either eye.

"Tim Cosgrove, ma'am." Another chair moved, grating on my every nerve.

Ma'am.

"I hate ma'am."

"Pardon, ma'am? I didn't catch that."

"Call me ..." My name was gone. I tried again. "Call me ..." There was nothing there. Who the fuck was I?

Lee spoke, "Rylee Henderson."

No, that doesn't sound right.

Kurt came back and cleared the room. He jabbed a needle into my hip and gave me another drink of water.

"Kurt, who am I?"

"What?"

"Who am I?"

"You know who I am, but not your own name?"

I could hear concern but not see it. My eyes refused all instructions from me; one opened but couldn't process information. There was something very wrong.

"You are a doctor." There was more. In my mind, a manila folder opened. I read the contents of the first page. Kurt was an FBI Supervisory Special Agent with

Delta A. "FBI."

"Good. Who was in the room before?"

"Lee ..." I waited, hoping another folder would materialize and show me who Lee was. I knew he was a friend. He called me Chicky. That felt okay. No folder appeared. "I don't know ..."

"You will." Kurt's voice changed, he must've looked away. "Lee, did she hit her head?"

"No, I stopped her head before it hit the table."

"One hundred percent sure?"

"Yes."

"The migraine is messing with your memory, Rylee. SA Lee Davenport was in the room," Kurt said.

SA, Special Agent, FBI. Even with a befuddled mind I could see a correlation. Two FBI agents. Who was the third?

"Who is the other man Tim? Who the fuck am I?"

"Cosgrove. He's a specialist with the CIA." He brushed hair off my face. "You are my wife."

Somewhere something clanged into place. I had another drink. It all made sense. I could feel the wedding ring on my finger. Then without warning it felt wrong, very wrong. Deep in the murk the wedding ring on my finger caused everything to spiral out of control. Nothing being as it seemed overwhelmed me. The drugs?

Within my mind terror lurked. My name didn't make sense, yet Chicky did. I needed to see. But my eyes would not open.

"I can't open my eyes."

"Get some sleep. You'll feel better when you wake up."

"I'll try."

I had no idea how much time passed. A drugged daze clouded everything, including the passage of time with a happy coating of 'who-gives-a-fuck'. Everything that felt so confusing became unimportant. Then it all made sense. I'd been flashy-thinged, *Men in Black* style. Because that was the only logical explanation for why I couldn't remember things. Kay or Jay had flashy-thinged me. Any minute I expected to see Kay talking to a pug dog and a man rip off his skin to reveal a giant cockroach. The *Men in Black* theme song filled my head.

There was no way of knowing if I slept or if I was in a zombie-like state of unconsciousness. At some stage the song stopped. The voices in my head were soft, deep, and male. Not intrusive yet but I knew they were there. There was a certain comfort in hearing the voices. No words, just the intonation of men talking. Somewhere deep in the dark a woman's voice called out. Mom? No, it couldn't be Mom, she was dead. That I knew for sure.

The voice called again. "Rylee?" A name that didn't fit me. I ignored it. It came back again. Closer, more insistent. Someone yelled out.

"Rylee!"

A lot of noise followed, more people rushed into the room. Someone rubbed my sternum. The back of the bed dropped flat.

"She's coding." Two words and I felt Kurt's stress level sky-rocket.

Too much was happening near me and I couldn't stop or process any of it. Then the dark came. The welcome sleep.

No noise.

Soothing.

Dark.

Chapter Twenty-Two
Stairway To Heaven

My eyes wanted to open but I couldn't control them. I knew I should talk but nothing happened. A mask was over my mouth and nose. I felt air rush into me. My eyes pinged open and rolled back in my head. Surely that's not good?

Stunned, I watched from the ceiling as Kurt and two nurses worked on me. Me. It was beyond bizarre. I wanted to yell at them, to tell them I could see and I was right here. No matter what I said, my body lay there, unresponsive. I watched Kurt charge the defibrillator and shock me twice. One nurse forced air into my lungs via an Ambu Bag, the other did compressions. That was going to hurt later.

A nurse spoke, "Could be the Demerol causing this."

Kurt called for Narcan. I watched him inject it into a vein on my arm. "Let's hope it's not too late, if it is."

I couldn't see Lee or Tim. Then the coolest thing happened.

I poked my head out through the wall and found them both. Lee was leaning on the wall outside my room. He looked upset; he held his phone in his hands, just staring at the blank screen. Tim was pacing back and forth. As he moved away I saw a Sig Sauer on his right hip and noticed another in the waistband of his jeans. From the holster placement I could tell he was comfortable firing with either hand.

Back in the room they were still working on my lifeless body.

I turned my head and saw Mac next to me. He slung his arm around my shoulders and kissed me. "You can't be here, babe. It's not your time. Go back." He had something in his hand. He showed me.

A candy bar. Not just any candy bar. It was a 3 Musketeers candy bar. My chocolate snack of choice.

"I want to be with you." It's all I've ever wanted and now I am. I'm not going anywhere.

Kurt said, "Clear." Sweat beaded in the worry lines on his forehead. His voice had an edge I'd never heard before. "Come on, you're not trying."

I watched as he shocked my rag-doll body again. Mac threw the candy at Kurt. It hit his boot and bounced off. His eyes flicked to the floor and his reaction was immediate. Kurt ordered glucagon and injected it straight into a vein on my right arm.

"Go back, Carla needs you." Mac pushed me gently.

Carla? Who?

"I want to stay."

He kissed me. "It's time to go. They need you back now."

Kurt looked up at the clock on the wall. "We're running out of time." He looked down at me. I just lay there staring as the nurse continued compressions and the other nurse kept forcing air into my lungs. He dipped his face close to my ear and whispered, "Come on, Conway, you can do this."

Something tugged at me.

"Hey, that was cool, Mac. Kurt whispered in my ear and I heard it way up here." My incorporeal hand brushed my ear. "I felt it too."

A force I couldn't see dragged on my legs. Weight. That's what I felt. Weights making me sink. It took great concentration to stay with Mac. When I looked at my body, my eyes were shut. Maybe Kurt shut them.

Mac took my hand and pulled me down to my body. He pushed me on top of myself. There was no way to stop it. I melted in. With one last kiss he faded away.

A beep came from the machine next to me. Then another. Then another. Within seconds the beeping was regular and strong. My chest hurt as I breathed in. I wanted to cough but figured that'd be an adventure in pain.

I opened my eyes. Kurt was standing right by me. He pulled a new gown over the one he'd cut off me. He had to unplug the tubing in my left arm from the IV pump to get the gown on my arm. He reconnected the tube, reset the pump, and fastened the gown behind my neck.

"Thank you," I said. My voice was croaky, my throat dry. He lifted the back of the bed up about forty-five degrees, and gave me a sip of water. Then indicated I should lean forward a little, he fastened the rest of the ties and helped me sit back.

"Can't have you exposed, with Lee and Tim about to come in."

"Not for that, for bringing me back."

"That's my job."

"You seemed pretty determined to bring me back."

"Can you imagine having to face Caine, Sam, and Lee, if I couldn't bring you back?"

"The candy bar was cool."

He looked at me. "Candy bar?"

"Mac threw a candy bar, it hit your foot ... then you asked for glucagon?"

Kurt looked under the bed, then bent down and picked up a candy bar. "It did hit my foot. I thought it fell from the bed. How did you know?"

"I was with Mac and saw him throw it."

"You're spooky."

"All for one and one for all."

Kurt turned the bar over in his hand revealing the shiny red and blue logo; he held it up so I could see it too. "3 Musketeers."

Then I remembered. Caine, our SAC, Sam, and Lee, worked with me. I am SSA Ellie Conway, and it still sounded like a ship. There was a moment of pure relief as my name settled and felt right. Until then I'd envisaged my life being like *Fifty First Dates* and I didn't want to be Lucy, living the same day over and over again. Never being able to move forward or remember anything of that day.

"I'm FBI."

He smiled. "You are. But while you are here, you are Rylee Henderson."

"What happened?"

"I don't know for sure. You were sleeping, and then you crashed. It could have been a reaction to the drug I gave you for the pain, but I doubt it. You've had Demerol for migraines in the past. It's not something you've ever had a problem with. But I gave you Narcan in case it was the Demerol. It did nothing, so it wasn't Demerol that caused the crash in your vitals. The only other sensible cause was extremely low blood sugar, and that was evident by the way you came back after the glucagon. Low blood sugar is new for you."

"I remember bits and pieces. Someone was in here before; it wasn't you, Lee or Tim. Who was it?"

"A nurse came in and did routine obs. Temp, etc."

"What time is it now?"

"Two fifty-five in the morning." The penny dropped or the candy bar did. "Fuck." Kurt unplugged the pump. "We almost lost you," he said as he removed the needle from my arm and applied pressure to the tiny hole left behind.

"What?"

"I think someone administered insulin," Kurt said.

I was a victim of the hospital killer.

"The nurse."

"That's how the killer is killing. No wonder there wasn't an obvious cause of death."

Kurt yelled for Lee.

Lee burst through the door followed by Tim.

"Someone tried to kill her. That nurse who came in

just before she crashed … either of you get a good look at her? I'll recognize her again."

Tim nodded. "I did."

"Find her." He leveled a hard stare at both of them. "Lock this place down. I think she administered insulin while she was in here. You're looking for a small syringe – it takes two mils to kill a normal adult, more for a diabetic."

"We're looking for a two-mil syringe?" Lee asked. "Have to ask – Chicky is anything but *normal*."

"Thanks," I grumbled.

"I mean that in a good way," Lee said.

"In *this* case she's *normal*," Kurt said.

Lee and Tim left.

"Was I that much of a pain in the ass in the ER?"

"Not really, you get nasty though." He rubbed his jaw. "You have a decent left hook by the way. You didn't like me applying an icepack to your left hand."

That explained why my fingers felt stiff; I smacked Kurt. I am such a charming woman.

"What does my chart say?"

"I don't know. I only have the med chart in here."

"If Mac hadn't been here, I'd be dead," I said. It was the truth as I saw it, not a reflection on Kurt's ability.

"I would've figured it out."

"Okay, I'd be a vegetable that breathes."

"I would've figured it out. Low blood sugar was next on my list."

"I'd hate to be trapped in a vegetative stasis." I'd soon-

273

er die than not live.

"Chicky Babe, I would've figured it out."

A smile reached across my lips. First ever Chicky Babe from Kurt. He would've figured it out.

"It's easier to talk to dead people when you are dead people."

"I'm glad you came back. Don't know if I could handle being haunted by you."

"Doc, do I have clothes?" I tried sitting forward but it hurt like hell. Bruised ribs at the very least.

"Yes." He walked across the room and picked a bag up from a chair then put it back down. "First though, I think you should eat. I don't want a repeat of that whole flatline shit you pulled."

"Vending machine, I don't want to eat anything prepared here. Someone might not be happy I'm alive."

Sooner or later people need to stop trying to kill me. Maybe I need to stop pissing them off.

He nodded. "I'll help you get dressed soon. I cannot leave you, okay?"

"I figured as much."

"How do you feel?" Kurt appeared curious but not in a medical way. "You sound okay, in fact better than I would expect from most people who'd been through what you just survived."

"I'm not most people."

"Don't I know it," Kurt said with a smile.

"I don't feel any worse than after a migraine. Tired, a little disjointed mentally – things aren't as clear as maybe they should be."

"You should be under observation for at least twelve hours in a hospital."

I choose to ignore that comment.

"Who admitted me?"

"Grant signed the forms."

"I have records here ... do you have them? If someone accessed them they'll know who I am."

"Chicky, I have your records. Before we left DC I had a duplicate set made." From the table behind him he picked up a thick file and placed it in my hands. "It's all here, your exciting list of head and brain traumas, the migraines, everything."

"The reconstruction to my shoulder? The dates?"

"No one but Grant has seen this file. No one."

I closed my eyes and welcomed sleep, but it resisted. Thoughts of hospital records would not leave my consciousness. My eyes opened again. Kurt was watching me.

"Welcome back."

Had I slept?

"What's the time?"

"Almost four."

My thoughts about records became vocal.

"My records, the ones that are kept in this hospital. I used to live here. They have records."

"There are none. When you were admitted with a fractured skull and broken arm after being drugged by Charles Boyd, all records were removed from this facility. Caine insisted. That's how I had them in Richmond when

I took over your care."

"There is nothing here?"

"Nothing in the records department. There may be records on the computer system but they won't marry up to anything official in the records room."

Kurt showed me the thick file in his hands.

I looked at the name. Rylee Gabrielle Henderson.

"When did you come up with that?"

My eyes closed again before I heard his reply.

The door flew open, jolting me from sleep. Lee pushed a woman into the room.

"This is her," he growled at Kurt.

"Yeah." He looked at the woman who glared back at him. "You're not a nurse." I had no clue how he could tell, everyone wore the same color scrubs. Pale green. She looked like a nurse. Small, pretty, with her blonde hair pulled back into a pony tail. Stethoscope around her neck. A photo identity tag hung from a pocket.

"Kurt Henderson," she said, her voice devoid of emotion.

"Do I know you?" Kurt said.

"Once."

Kurt shook his head, he couldn't remember the woman.

"What is it you want with me, Doctor Henderson?"

"You can start by explaining the insulin you injected into the port on my wife's drip."

She almost scoffed, but thought better of it and tried for a more appalled reaction. "I'm a doctor. By definition

I can do no harm. And you accuse me of attempted murder?"

Above everyone floating on the ceiling, Mac attracted my attention. He waved and pointed at the woman. Then held up two fingers.

"Why is the number six so important?" I said.

She turned her head and focused on me. "Excuse me?"

Tim barreled in and closed the door. He threw a banana at me. "Eat."

"Thanks." I guess.

"Now."

I didn't know him well enough to know quite how to read him but I sensed trouble, so I ate the banana. He stood by the door, hands behind his back. He reminded me a bit of Lee, as he stood at parade rest.

Lee didn't react at all. He was focused on the female doctor. That meant he trusted Tim. Good to know. I had a feeling I was supposed to know who Tim was. Another elusive memory wiped by the flashy thing.

"Six," I said once I'd finished the banana. "Why six?"

She didn't answer. Lee kicked her foot.

"Answer the question."

Kurt had his laptop open, running searches on hospital files and records.

"I have patients who need me," she said.

Lee reached over and removed her hospital identity card. "Doctor, you are not leaving this room until you answer the questions."

"Why did you pose as a nurse?" Kurt asked. "When you

came in, you did the nurses' duties and wore your top out over your pants."

Oh, that's how he knew; some kind of doctor/nurse code that meant doctors tucked in their scrubs and nurses didn't.

"Where is the syringe?"

She shook her head. "I don't know what you are talking about. I did not come into this room. I've been up on the ICU all night. A patient of mine coded earlier this evening."

Really? So did I.

Kurt looked at Lee as if to say, where did you find her? He replied, "She was sitting outside the ICU having a coffee."

Lee passed the credentials to Kurt. "Run them. If she used the elevator or opened any doors it'll show on the record for her swipe card."

Kurt did. The record showed she hadn't left the ICU floor.

"Search her," he said.

Lee found nothing in her pockets and Kurt looked at Tim.

"Tim, go back to where you found her and search trash receptacles. She may have ditched another identity card." Tim hurried away after whispering something to Lee first. I saw Lee nod and move back to Tim's position by the door. He handed over guard duty. He must know something.

Kurt perched himself next to me on the bed and

checked all records from all the doors that had swipe-card entry. Doctor Sandy Richards swiped out of the ICU, seconds before a nurse accessed the elevator from emergency and exited at the ICU floor. Five minutes later the same nurse went back down and then swiped into the ER, from the staff entrance.

"We need to find a nurse who works in the ER. Her name is Annabelle Richards."

The doctor stiffened.

"Your sister?" Kurt asked.

"No," she replied. "I don't have a sister."

"A happy coincidence that you have the same surname and look very similar?"

"I'm not one for coincidences," I said, watching the laptop screen with Kurt. My head was starting to hurt again. It wasn't bad but I could tell the Demerol was wearing off. "Kurt," I whispered. "I need more ..."

"Okay," he whispered back. "Hang in there."

"Even Tylenol will help. I need to stop it before it gets real bad again."

Kurt stood up, leaving the laptop on the bed with me. He walked over to Lee and spoke quietly. Lee nodded and stepped out the door.

"What's wrong?" Richards asked me.

"Nothing," I said.

"If you need help, tell me, I'm a doctor."

I pressed my fingers to my right temple.

"One who tried to kill me."

"I. Did. Not. Try. To. Kill. You."

"You're right. For a little while there you succeeded."

Lee came back in with Grant. They conversed by the door, then Grant left. Kurt gave me three white pills to take in a tiny clear plastic cup. "Tylenol," he said.

I swallowed them.

In my hand he placed another tiny clear plastic cup containing two tiny white pills. "Codeine, take them."

I did. I knew that combination would knock the migraine back to a dull drone. Kurt had given me something similar on our visit to New Zealand last winter.

Tim reappeared with another woman. His hand was wrapped around her upper arm and she was swearing up a storm.

Nice.

"What the fuck is that bitch doing in here?" squawked the nurse, glaring at Sandy and trying to wriggle from Tim's grip.

Lovely.

"Annabelle Richards?" Kurt asked.

"Yes. So?"

"Why were you on the ICU floor," Kurt said while checking the time, "at two forty-five this morning?"

"Visiting," she snapped.

"For God's sake, Annabelle, what is it you've done?" Sandy said. It felt like she was trying to defer the blame.

"Did you visit Doctor Richards?" Kurt asked.

Annabelle shook her head.

"What were you doing on the ICU floor?"

"I have a friend who works in the ICU. Our shifts

matched up and I went to see if he wanted coffee."

"Name."

"It doesn't matter. He's not important."

"Name."

Sandy spoke up. "Tonight we only have one male in the ICU. A nurse. Bruno Sonnenberg."

Kurt looked at Tim.

Sandy interrupted before he could speak. "If you are going to bring him in, we need to get someone up there to cover for us. We have patients."

"I know," Kurt replied. "What I'm going to do is send Lee up to the ICU to have a chat with Bruno."

Lee left. He knew what to do.

It was time for me to be me. Luckily my brain was co-operating. It takes more than a little Tylenol and codeine to impair my thought processes. Great, I knew how my body handled drugs but not who Tim was. Stupid brain.

"One of you needs to tell me who came into this room tonight. And now. Because I'm tired. Dead tired. It's been a long day. And my friend over there is getting plain pissy." I smiled at Tim who fondled the gun on his hip and kept watch over the door.

Sandy said, "I haven't left the ICU floor all night." She shot a nasty look at the other woman.

"What the hell is the relationship between you two?" I asked. They looked so alike they could've been sisters. I was pretty sure they were sisters. "Can we get personnel files on these two?"

"Yes," Kurt said. "I'm searching them now."

Both women looked uncomfortable. As they should. Considering one of them tried to kill me, I thought I was doing a marvelous job of maintaining my composure.

"Speak. Cough it up. Tell me what the freaking deal with six is." Right then I saw it. A glimpse of something in Annabelle's eye. It was enough. "Six," I repeated. It flashed again.

That's why Mac held up two fingers when he saw the first woman. Two of them. They were doing it together. The thought flapped about inside my head for a few seconds before I let it out.

"You did it together."

A rapid movement caught my eye. Mac was back. Grinning and giving me the thumbs up.

Dead men don't lie.

"Annabelle went up to the ICU with a list of patients from the ER; they chose the victim together. Sandy gave her the insulin already drawn up into a syringe. And she went back into the ICU, leaving Annabelle to do the deed."

Lee came back in.

"Bruno has been seeing Annabelle for about seven months. He did not see her tonight. They've been flat out upstairs and he hasn't had a break."

"Bruno is your alibi? For those nights when you're seen going into places you shouldn't be?" I said to Annabelle. I had a feeling he didn't always work in the ICU.

"Look at this," Kurt said, showing me the screen. "Personnel files. I found the six."

I read the page he had open. It was sad.

"You want to tell us your version of what happened to your son?" I asked Sandy. "Because right now things are looking grim for you and your sister."

She turned to her sister. The open hostility we'd witnessed earlier melted away.

"They deserved to die. People like that, making a fuss, pulling everyone's attention away from those who really need it," Sandy said. A single tear trickled down her face. "He was six years old and should not have died. But she came in, that old woman, kicking and screaming and causing a fuss. Everyone rushed to calm her down ... and he died, alone. Six years old."

Annabelle took over as Sandy broke down. "He was little and so scared, and he never cried. Not once. We were both on duty that day. Sandy was upstairs. I was in the ER. Aaron came in by ambulance from school. He'd fallen and hit his head on a concrete step." Annabelle's voice crumbled. "He shouldn't have died. But no one was watching him. He tried to get off the gurney and fell."

I looked at Kurt. We both knew what happened when Aaron fell. He hit his head again – a fatal blow.

"And tragic as this is, you think that justifies killing innocent people?" I couldn't help myself. "A doctor and a nurse, trusted health professionals, killing people who behave like a lot of injured and sick people do. Yes, in a perfect world the sick would have more grace, but often they don't. You took an oath to do no harm!"

Lee cuffed them both, called the local police, and escorted the women out to wait for their ride.

Kurt phoned Grant. He looked like shit when he came in. He looked as though he hadn't left the hospital in at least twenty hours.

"You got them?" he asked.

"Yeah, a doctor from the ICU and a nurse from the ER ... sisters."

"Annabelle and Sandy." Grant ran his hands through his hair. "Crap. Ah, Jesus. It never occurred to me that a doctor would—"

"Did you know about her son?"

"Of course. We all did. It happened here. It was tragic," he said, his voice ringing with sorrow.

"It was the trigger," Kurt told him. "Local police can handle the arrest and the paperwork. We'll give them copies of everything we've discovered. As soon as Rylee is well enough, we'll head back to Washington."

"I can't thank you enough for coming down," Grant shook his hand, and then turned to me. "I'm sorry you risked your life here tonight."

"I'm not. We got them. Your patients are safe. You might want to implement some damage control with the media though."

"Yeah," Grant said with a small laugh. "This will be quite a circus. Don't suppose you two want to stay and help?"

"No, thanks," I replied. I was beginning to feel desperate to get home; then I remembered it blew up and my new house wasn't ready yet. Knowing my house blew up and that I was building a new house seemed like quite an achievement considering my patchy memory. Home was out of the question, but even a hotel in Washington felt safer and more like home than Lexington did now.

Grant left. I think he was going home. He looked like he needed to.

I closed my eyes and hoped to wake up and find it was all a nightmare. When I woke I realized it was real. I'd died and come back. That was impressive. My eyes sought out the clock above the door. It was nearly five-thirty.

Tim and Kurt were in the room discussing how safe it was for me to stay in the hospital. Tim declared it foolish considering Arbab had witnessed my collapse in the In-terscape Café and had more than likely followed us to the hotel and hospital. The plan *was* to get him to follow me but not to another place full of civilians.

Felt strange that he hadn't made his move yet. Chances are he was hoping I was already dead, I imagine he saw the commotion my coding caused. Tim was still talking.

"There will be media crawling all over this hospital by morning. We need to leave," Tim said. "Is it safe to move her?"

"She needs observation – I'm a doctor, she'll be fine."

"Good to know."

"Let's get ready to move out," Kurt said. Tim was sent to stand guard outside the door. Moving hurt. I felt like I'd been hit by a train. I stood with one hand on the bed trying to steady myself as Kurt took my clothes from the bag and helped me dress. It didn't feel weird. The man had saved my life, with a bit of help from Mac. I could cope with him seeing me almost naked and helping me dress. Anyway, he was my husband. A smile reached over and poked Kurt.

"You okay?" he said, helping me put my boots on.

"Yeah. Ribs are killing me."

Kurt laughed.

As I stamped my foot into the second boot, I sucked up the shock waves that vibrated through my bruised ribs.

"Moving you out of hospital right now goes against every medical bone in my body. But it's not the first time we've had to move you for your own safety ..."

"You told Tim I'd be fine."

"You will be. You're the toughest person I've ever met. You will be fine."

"Tough? Me?"

"Okay, bad choice of words. Resilient is probably more accurate."

Bon Jovi's 'Bounce' filled my head. It's true I've been knocked down a few times, and I've even been counted out, yet here I am. Guess that's resilience.

The door flew open. I jumped.

Chapter Twenty-Three
We All Sleep Alone

Gun fire erupted in the corridor. Lee slammed the door shut and ducked down.

Tim and I made eye contact, he threw me a Sig. I caught it in my right hand, dropped the magazine into my left hand, checked it was full, and slid it home.

Another burst of fire came from the hall beyond our door. A weird, disjointed, out-of-body type thing happened. I watched everyone and could analyze the situation but felt nothing. Nothing. It was like being on autopilot.

There was one way in and one way out of the room. Tim had a Bluetooth flashing in his ear; he spoke while maneuvering into a better position to cover the door. Kurt and Lee tipped the bed. Not an easy thing to do. Hospital beds are heavy and stable. They rammed it against the door to create a barricade and cover. Two small nightstands provided the only other cover. Besides them there were four chairs and some medical equipment. The bathroom to the right would provide some shelter.

I sat on one of the chairs against an external wall. Internal walls are notoriously flimsy. The external walls of this hospital were brick. No 9mm round was going to pass through brick and mortar. There was no way I was about to consider that 9mm rounds weren't being used.

Breathing as deep as I could, I ran through a check list in my mind. Something which takes milliseconds, but feels like forever.

Focus.

I tuned into Tim.

He was communicating with his team who were already stationed in various parts of the hospital. His team. They must've been in place the whole time, waiting for Arbab to show himself. Then I remembered I had a team. Kurt, Sam, Lee, they were my team. A sense of relief came upon me as I realized I knew what I was doing. I may have been flashy-thinged but it didn't erase all my memory and training.

Gun fire preceded screaming. Hysteria. Panic. Running feet. Fast moving gurneys. Chaos. The purpose of opening fire was to cause chaos. Terror.

Duh! That's why they are terrorists.

"Tim."

He looked at me quickly, and then returned his attention to the door as pounding feet ran by.

"Demelza," he whispered. "You ready for this?"

"Nah, I've changed my mind."

"Demelza?" he whispered.

"Let's not play this game. Let's walk out, get shot, and die."

"Your death is not an option," he replied with a thick undertone of calm.

Truth is I was confused. He called me Demelza. Lee called me Chicky. I thought I was Ellie and Kurt said I was his wife, Rylee. It wasn't all falling into place. Parts of the puzzle were free form and the corners were shaky.

Glass sprayed into the room. The small window in the door shattered. A bullet lodged in the wall a half foot from my head. Kurt grabbed my arm and pulled me to the floor. I gasped as pain wracked my rib cage. Tim and Lee shook small sparkling chunks of glass from their hair. Tinkling pieces dropped all over the floor. Light caught some of the broken safety glass on its smashed edges, sprinkling tiny rainbows across the skirting near the bathroom door.

Pretty.

Another bullet lodged in the wall. I looked over. I was sitting there moments ago. Lee returned fire, even though he couldn't see the shooter.

Wasting ammunition and giving away his location. He knew better than that.

Tim adjusted his position near the broken window, using what looked like a dental mirror. He rotated the mirror to scan the hallway then, without warning, he dropped to the floor behind the bed. Bullets flew.

He used hand signals and told Lee where he'd seen the shooter. Watching them triggered a flood of memories. I saw Tim taking Arbab away in Wellington, New Zealand. Everything slid sideways and Lee was laughing at Mac in an internet cafe in Lexington. Rapid momentum leapfrogged me forward eighteen months: Lee crouched next to me on the ground watching paramedic's work on Mac. With a slow fade-out the scene changed again. We were in New Zealand, Lee was mobbed by screaming Grange fans at Christchurch Airport and I was trying not to laugh. A venetian blind effect transformed the airport scene into an interview room. A kid, Joey, was telling me how his friend Carla had disappeared and he thought she'd been abducted.

The kid grabbed my arm; he was panicking and wanting me to find Carla. It was like I was there all over again.

A wave of holy hell crashed over me. I could feel the color drain from my face as the tide receded. I clung to a sketchy image of Carla, as if it were my life preserver. I had to find her. But I couldn't remember who she was. I knew she was important. The words that spoke of a relationship surfaced. How I introduced her to others. "This is my daughter Carla."

I had to remember Carla. Remember how it felt to know her, to spend time with her. It didn't seem to matter how hard I tried, nothing came. Yet, I could remember searching for her once before.

Except this time I'm the lost one and I don't think shooting anyone in the head will make this all right.

Life faded out. Or maybe it was me that faded out of life.

With an almighty crash it came back. Lee tapped me on the shoulder. I jumped.

"Chicky, we're out of here."

Blood dripped down his face.

"You're bleeding."

"I know."

"Kurt can—"

"Chicky, we're going now. Tim is waiting. Let's do this."

He hooked his hand under my armpit and lifted me up. It hurt, but not as much as standing by myself.

My foot hit something solid yet not hard as I tried to walk. Panic wormed its way up my body.

Tim was calling us.

I hit something else with my other foot.

"Doc?"

"Come on, Chicky, let's get out of here."

Chapter Twenty-Four
It's All Coming Back To Me Now

There was a definite chill in the air as we climbed out of cars in the hotel parking lot. I don't think I spoke after leaving the hospital.

Words didn't hold enough meaning. I had no idea what happened in the hospital. Lee was still dripping blood. I motioned for him to wait then went back into the car and grabbed the first aid kit from under the seat. In the cool pre-dawn I unzipped the field kit and took a thick, sterile wound dressing. I ripped one packet open, tore medical tape from the roll, and stuck the dressing to Lee's forehead.

"Thanks," he said, touching the tape with his fingertips to seal the edges.

"You're welcome." I stuffed the field kit under my arm and closed the car door.

Lee escorted me into the back entrance of the hotel. There was no one around. We hurried down a wide hallway and into the elevator. This time I didn't care what potential hell could be waiting. I was in no shape to tackle the stairs and wanted to get to my room as fast as possible.

Ragtag is the best description of how we appeared. Behind us I heard footsteps and ignored them. I figured it was Tim and his team coming back. Lee asked for my key card. I slapped my pockets and came up empty. Cologne I knew wafted in the air. An arm snaked between us and swiped a card.

My head turned in time to see Doc turn the door handle. I reached out and touched him, expecting my hand to hit the door and not warm flesh.

"I thought ..."

"Wasn't me on the floor," he whispered. "I was tending to a wounded nurse."

I could only remember my boot hitting something that felt like a person. I had no visual to accompany the feeling. "Who was it?"

"I don't know. Someone who was in the wrong place at the wrong time." Kurt held the door. "Inside."

I followed him in the door. Lee closed it behind us. Everything was a mess. The coffee table was tipped over, cups spilled over the carpet. Files lay in a muddle and my laptop was upside down on the floor.

"What the hell happened here?"

Lee filled the coffee maker. Without looking up he said, "Looks like a natural disaster. But in fact it was you. We bought you back here before going to the hospital."

Oh.

Doc stood the table back on its legs and picked up the cups. He turned my laptop over and placed it on the sofa.

My phone rang. The noise came from under a sofa cushion. I fished the phone out and answered it.

"Take care. We're leaving with the target plus one." Tim's voice.

"What happened?"

"The target followed you and was in the hospital the whole time we were – what you did worked, we got him. He's not talking now. It'll be awhile until we know all the details."

Not talking but not dead. A distant memory surfaced of removing someone from one country and taking them shrouded in secrecy into another. The target was heavily sedated for the entire trip. Sedated, stripped, given an enema, put in an adult diaper and overalls, and then de-livered unconscious to a final destination. Arbab was heading to a black site. He wouldn't be coming back. I love extraordinary renditions.

"Thank you."

"Just returning a favor," he said. "Turn on the news." And hung up.

Who was that masked man? A horse whinnied. Away in the distance I heard the words 'Hi ho Silver! Away!'

I dropped my phone onto the sofa. "Tim said to turn on the news. Seems we have two fewer problems. Hospi-tal killer is behind bars, and Arbab is in the process of be-ing removed from the United States."

Kurt and Lee grinned.

"Coffee is almost ready," Lee said.

Kurt switched on the television while I tried to sit without hurting my ribs any more than I already had. There was no waiting to see what Tim meant. A red ban-ner trailed across the bottom of the screen announcing breaking news in Lexington. Moments later a stern-faced newsreader filled the screen, Doug someone or other.

With careful enunciation he told his listeners of the drama which had unfolded at Stonewall Jackson Hospital in the early hours of the morning.

"A doctor and her sister were arrested for killing patients and their last victim was Rylee Henderson, wife of Supervisory Special Agent Kurt Henderson, a doctor in the FBI." He went on to say Rylee was admitted suffering from a severe migraine.

I breathed a sigh of relief. No mention that Rylee was me.

The newsreader stopped talking and then said, "New information has just come to light. Rylee Henderson was in fact Supervisory Special Agent Gabrielle Conway, working under cover with SSA Henderson. Conway was ill and receiving medical care when the killer struck without warning."

Numbness spread to my limbs from my very core. Lee set a coffee on the table in front of me. "Okay?"

I nodded and kept watching.

"Conway has reportedly had a bad week, with her death prematurely announced in Washington several days ago, followed by the explosions that destroyed her home. She's probably best known as the 'poet with a gun' and for the creation of the Butterfly Foundation with her deceased husband Special Agent Cormac Connelly. Conway's work with 'at risk' children of mentally-ill parents hit the headlines when her poetry book became a bestseller."

Every phone in the room rang.

Over the noise I heard the newsreader still talking. "Conway was linked to rocker Rowan Grange. She is survived by her father, brother, and daughter, Carla."

For the second time in a week my death was announced on television. This time I knew we needed to leave it be. If I rode in hollering about not being dead, Arbab's friends may hear of it. Arbab had always struck me as someone who would shoot his mouth off at the drop of a hat; I didn't for one second think he hadn't told others what he was planning on doing in the USA. Hollering about my non-dead status might also trigger someone else from my past to surface. I'm very good at pissing people off and often they're not the forgiving type. I'm sure Tim and his team didn't want to stage another rescue anytime soon. It needed to blow over by itself.

I wanted to lean back but it hurt. I gritted my teeth and did it anyway. Phones still rang. No one moved to answer them.

Everyone stared in silence at the television.

It was me who broke first. "I have a daughter?"

Probably not what either of them wanted to hear.

Kurt turned off the TV, moved my coffee cup, and sat on the table in front of me.

"It will come back, Ellie. Your memory will come back."

Until then, I didn't know it was missing.

"I remember a kid calling me mom in a graveyard, and how relieved I was she was okay."

"It will come back."

"That was her? My daughter?"

"Yes."

"Something I did must've put her in danger. She's probably better off without me."

I jumped as Lee hit the wall with a closed fist. He didn't so much dent the wall as punch a hole right through to the bedroom.

The ringing stopped for about five seconds then started up again.

Kurt reached for my phone first, he read the display. "You need to take this, it's Rowan."

"Rowan?"

Who the hell is Rowan?

"Grange."

Oh bullshit!

"Just because the TV said I was linked to Rowan Grange ... which must be crap. Hello, they don't have a great track record where truth is concerned! You don't have to fuck with me!"

He tried to thrust the phone into my hand. I wouldn't take it.

"Answer it."

He turned the phone so I could see the name and photo of the person calling. Maybe he had a point. Mac laughed in my mind and responded with, "Maybe's ass."

If I didn't know Rowan Grange, why would I have his picture on my phone, flashing at me along with his name?

I hang out with jokers, was the lone answer I could

come up with while the phone rang or, more accurately, sang. One of Rowan's best-known stadium rock numbers.

"Everything's gone pear-shaped and you think now is the best time to screw with me?" I snarled. "Death wish, much?"

"Answer it," Kurt said, keeping his tone even yet insistent.

I took the phone and pressed talk. "Hello?"

"Ellie, you okay?"

Whoever it was sounded like Rowan Grange.

"I am," I replied, trying very hard to keep suspicion from my voice.

"You don't sound it."

"I'm fine."

He started talking but nothing he told me would gel into anything resembling parts of my life. I tried hard to remember why Rowan Grange would be calling me. There had to be something there. Katrina. The conversation I had with her meandered through my consciousness as Rowan told me how he'd spent the night. I sensed he was trying to get a handle on what was happening with me and I didn't know what to tell him.

Everything Katrina said scrolled by; I paused the conversation at the part where she said I looked like the woman who was dating Rowan Grange.

If I am, then that would be why he called. It seemed reasonable that I should say something girlfriendish. Yet a large chunk of me was going totally fan-girl over having Rowan call me and I couldn't concentrate. Oh. My. God.

He's Rowan Grange!

Time to stop him talking.

"Rowan?"

"Yes?"

"I'm fine. Can I call you later?" My heart pounded, I totally blew him off. Guess that doesn't happen to people like him very often.

"Can I talk to Kurt or Lee?"

"Sure." I handed the phone to Kurt who stood up and moved away speaking in hushed tones.

"It's rude to talk about someone when they're in the room," I said.

Kurt smiled and carried on. I heard him explain to Rowan that I'd had a migraine, there was an incident in the hospital, and there were some lasting effects to my memory. He didn't go into detail. Just as well. I wasn't sure how a person would respond if they were told their significant other had no memory of them. I wasn't sure how being Rowan Grange's significant other sat with me. I put it in the surreal basket along with motherhood.

Lee passed me his phone. "Here, it's Caine, and Sam is on Kurt's phone for you."

"Awesome."

I spoke briefly to Caine, then Sam. Kurt gave me my phone after he'd hung up and it rang again. He reached into my lap and picked it up. Kurt answered it then handed it to me, saying, "Jonathon Tierney."

I had a very brief conversation with Tierney – long enough to assure him the team he'd sent were on their way to their destination. Which he already knew; Jonathon for all his cold exterior and aloof mannerisms was checking on me, not the rendition team. It struck me as odd that I had a vivid memory of working with the bird-eyed, beak-nosed man all those years ago, yet recent life seemed foreign.

The minute I hung up the phone rang again. Singing in my hand. I looked at the display. One word: Dad.

I answered it.

"Kid, you okay?"

"I'm fine."

"The correct response is yeah, I'm okay or sure. It's never fine. Where's Lee?"

"He's here. Do you want to talk to him?"

"Yes, please."

Why is everyone calling me when they keep asking to talk to Lee or Kurt?

I yelled at Lee, "Incoming." The phone flew through the air. He caught it and lowered himself onto the other sofa.

"Simon, she's okay. There was an incident. We're charging two women with attempted murder of a federal agent." He stopped talking for a second then said, "Yes, she did code, but Kurt brought her back."

I couldn't hear my father's response but I expected it to be measured and calm. Throughout the conversation I tried to picture my father in my head. When I succeeded, I attempted the exercise with my brother, Aidan. It wasn't easy. There was something blocking him from being a whole person to me. I let my broken mind drift. Bam! There he was, a scared little kid being beaten by our Mom. I could see it all happening. Stepping in front of her as she raised the electric cord, it came down on my back. Aidan screamed. I pushed him away, yelled at him to run. Then he was an adult sitting on the front porch of my house in Mauryville. The image I had of him faded in and out, it just wouldn't stick.

I moved on to trying to visualize Rowan in my house with me. All the time there was a figure hovering about me, one I didn't need to imagine. Mac.

My eyes closed. It was time to go back to see what I was missing. I started with the memory I'd found earlier. The graveyard with Kurt, Sam, Lee, and Carla. If I could imagine Carla as a real person, maybe I could see her and remember life with her and the Rowan thing would just fit into place.

Remote feelings followed disjointed images. Nothing involving a teenage girl would cement. I let my mind wander back. Why were Kurt, Sam, and Lee so clear, but Dad, Carla, Rowan, and my brother, Aidan, so difficult to grasp hold of? Part of me expected to see Will Smith waltz in the door and zap me with the flashy thing again. Pretty sure they're supposed to erase all memory not just bits and pieces.

I whistled out air and opened my eyes.

"Your coffee is going cold," Lee said. He was slouched on the sofa, legs stretched out, one hand holding a cell phone and the other tapping on his coffee cup.

"Where's Sam?"

"Washington."

"Why isn't he here?"

"He's working on a case." A smile crossed Lee's lips.

"It's amusing in some way?"

"Yeah, someone is sending boxes of meat to people ... you've had three boxes of ass yourself."

"Boxes of ass."

Bingo. Something came back.

"Earlier this week – the delivery guy was shot, we captured the shooter."

"Yep."

There was a feeling of needing to regurgitate everything I could recall before it evaporated or became buried again. "I picked ... Carla up from Dad's and took her to a hotel. People were being killed. Conways. The next day I found out Arbab was in the country."

Carla was just a name. I found out about Arbab but couldn't remember who told me. Why couldn't I remember? Man, the whole forgetting shit was getting old. With a swift kick my cup flew from the table and smashed against the wall by the television.

Lee leaped to his feet.

"What the hell was that for?" Kurt asked, gawping at the cold coffee running down the wall.

"Why can't I remember?" I snarled and struggled to my feet. "Why can't I?"

Lee took a dish towel and started to wipe the wall.

Kurt sighed. "Come on, let's see if we can figure this

out," he said to me. My feet didn't walk, even though I told them to. "Ellie?"

Waves of anger rolled through me.

"What the fuck is wrong with me?"

His tone changed. He turned special agent on me. "Conway, sit back down."

Swarming crazy thoughts of never filling in the gaps flooded over everything. Kurt took my hand. I slapped it away. My wrist twisted behind my back, in two strides the side of my face was pressed against a wall. I kicked backwards hoping to connect with his shins. Kurt's grip tightened, he bent my wrist further. His object was instant submission and he achieved it.

"Hit me once, shame on you ... hit me twice, shame on me," Kurt whispered in my ear.

"Everything okay over there?" Lee asked.

I couldn't see him, but I knew one word from me and Kurt would be on his ass. How could I know that and not remember my kid? She was just a name. I needed more than a name.

"We're good," Kurt replied. "Aren't we, Conway?"

"Yeah, fuc'n awesome."

Kurt released his grip a little. I pushed back, twisted, and pulled my arm free. I couldn't even feel my ribs anymore. Blind rage flowed in my veins. My right fist connected with the side of Kurt's face. My left hit him under the jaw. I connected with his face again with my right fist and the next thing I knew I was on the ground with Kurt straddling me. He had my arms pinned to the ground above my head. I bucked, getting my feet flat on the ground. His face was three inches above mine. "Stop!"

"Get off me."

"Calm the fuck down."

"Get off!"

"No."

Energy sparked. His eyes grew dark. His tongue flicked over his lips. Things stirred within me. "Doc, I ..."

"Yeah, Conway," his voice matched mine. Quiet. Husky. Unsteady.

So close.

He rolled off me and lay on the floor. Lee looked down at me.

"You two kids had enough now?" he asked, reaching out for my hand to help me up.

I hurt. Maybe there was something I could say but I didn't know what, so I said nothing. Phones were still ringing. I took myself into the bedroom and crawled across the bed, burying my face in a pillow and stretching out. The best I could hope for was suffocation. All I could see was Kurt's face above mine. His darkening eyes. Heat from his body burning.

I tightened my grip on the pillow, pulling it harder over my head.

Chapter Twenty-Five
Start Me Up

I smelled coffee. When I opened my eyes Kurt was there holding a cup. He sported a decent bruise on his right cheek. It matched his left side, color-wise, but the bruising was more compacted and defined on the right. Purple and blue spread out along his jawline on the left, almost making it to his cheek bone.

"You look like shit," I said as a smile broke free.

"You hit like a girl," he replied, grimacing as he tried to smile.

The knuckles of both my hands ached. I glanced at the backs of my hands. Red grazes and patchy bruising across my knuckles. Looked like I'd been in a bar fight.

"Where's Lee?" I shuffled up until I was sitting. My ribs complained loudly causing me to wince. That was when I noticed a blanket over me. One of them must've come in while I was smothering myself.

"He's calling people back and dealing with the fallout from the hospital," Kurt replied. He sat on the edge of the bed and passed me the coffee. "How you feeling?"

"Confused." I didn't want to say what was playing on my mind when I fell asleep. As I sipped the coffee I noted something was missing. "Do I smoke?"

"You used to. When I first met you, you were a smoker."

"I'm not now?"

"No."

Odd, I feel like I am.

"I want a cigarette."

"Okay. Lee smokes, I'll get you one."

He left the room, leaving me feeling I was in a foreign land. Kurt came back with a burning cigarette in his mouth and an ashtray in his hand. He handed the smoke to me. The most natural thing in the world was holding that cigarette between my index and middle finger of my left hand. Coffee in my right, ashtray balanced on my knee.

It felt right.

I took a big drag on the cigarette, tasting the chemicals and tobacco as the warm smoke rush into my lungs. My head spun. Dizzy beyond belief. I couldn't stop the spinning. Kurt's hand held my wrist. His grip loosened and he removed the cigarette stubbing it out in the ashtray. He took my coffee cup too.

My lungs went into a spasm. Coughing made me more lightheaded and hurt my ribs. A laughing shadow fell across me.

Lee.

"Chicky, you quit a long time ago," he said, openly amused as I coughed until my head spun again.

Kurt passed me my coffee. "Have a drink."

I did. The taste in my mouth was disgusting. I was no smoker. I swallowed more coffee.

"I don't smoke." But the act of smoking reminded me of something. "Rowan does?"

They both nodded.

"Sam does?"

Again they nodded.

It felt like progress, but if everything was going to take such extreme measures I may not survive to see my memory return.

"I have an idea," Kurt said. "It's time we left Lexington, but before we go, let's take a trip out to your old home."

"Really?"

It sounded great. Going home. That's gotta be the right thing to do. "Okay, sounds good."

"Road trip," Lee said with a grin. "I've never been out to your place in Mauryville."

"Should be interesting all round then," I replied. "I'll have a shower, and then we can go."

"I'll get our gear packed from the living room," Lee said and ambled from the room.

Kurt didn't move.

I avoided eye contact while I tried to get a handle on what was happening. Throwing Kurt on the bed and screwing his brains out or inviting him into the shower were the first things that occurred to me and nothing anywhere indicated that would be wrong, except the tiny, waving red flag in a far corner of my mind. I was supposed to be dating someone. Even the television said so.

Lee bounced back into the room. "Chicky, Sam called. Another box arrived for you, this time it was sent to work."

"Yay, me and the mystery packages."

"You are one popular chick."

"Tell him we'll be in Washington late tomorrow. Can he handle it until then?"

"He can."

Lee left.

Kurt smiled. "You sounded like you again."

I shook my head. "Anything with Sam and Lee feels okay. Like I know where I am with them. History, it's … safe."

Kurt nodded. "And me?"

My eyes met his and a blast of honesty followed. "I remember every time our paths crossed. There is this overriding mystification surrounding you and me. We're a team, we work well together, and we mesh. I trust you with my life and the lives of the rest of my team. But there is something else happening and I don't know if it's real."

His eyes never left mine. "You mean this?" He pointed between us.

"Yeah," I said. "Is it?"

"It's always been there."

"Did we ever …?"

"Act on it?"

I nodded.

"No. Been friends, been colleagues. Relied on each other, taken care of each other, and no, we've never acted on it."

"Why?"

"You had Mac, and then you married him. After his

death, you shut down. You needed friends, not someone hitting on you. Then I joined your team and you met Rowan."

"You dated though?"

It occurred to me that if I hadn't forgotten some significant things this may never have been aired, or maybe I knew this and had forgotten. The jury was out as to whether that was good or bad. So far it didn't feel like I was destroying team relationships.

"I dated briefly over the last few years. Don't think women liked the competition, not just with my job. One look at you and they spiraled into insecurity."

"Because of me?" It seemed ridiculous. Me? I'm a freaking wreck.

"Because they couldn't compete with you. If we're being totally honest here ...?"

"We are."

"You're a threat. I have a hard time concentrating on anyone else when you are around. Women pick up on that sort of thing."

I knew I was smiling. It was funny. Me. I was a threat. How the hell does that work? Laughter bubbled up.

"What's so funny?"

Words choked me as laughter became hysteria. I couldn't breathe. My ribs hurt. Nothing would stop the crazy laughter. Everything was funny. Strong hands grabbed my shoulders and pulled me forward. Arms wrapped around me. Laughter dissolved into tears. At first they were tears from too much laughing but they became gut-wrenching sobs. I was all over the place and nothing made much sense.

Kurt held me. I knew it was him. I wanted it to be him. My life flashed before my eyes. How did I miss this? Kurt spoke but it wasn't to me. Lee must've come to see what was going on. Kurt's shoulder was saturated with tears.

Time stood still.

Strangled sobs replaced all-out bawling and I started to feel better.

"Hey, okay?" Kurt whispered, holding me close.

"Yeah." Everything paused while those dreaded words formed. "I'm sorry."

"For what?"

"For this ... for the bruises on your face ... for being a major pain in the ass ... for your wet shirt."

I took a breath. Damn it hurt.

"I'm sorry for everything I've put you through."

"Ellie," his breath felt hot in my ear, "I could've walked away anytime. My choice was to stay." He pulled tissues from a box and crammed them into my hand. I wiped my dripping nose. So attractive.

"Why didn't you?" As I said it I realized it was one of those questions you should never ask unless you were ready for the answer. I wasn't ready for anything, except a straitjacket.

"This is where I belong."

"Some kind of evil penance for being bad in a former life?" Maybe he was into self-flagellation. He'd swapped the whip for life near me.

"Maybe."

"Thank you."

"You're welcome." He held me at arm's length and smiled at me. "You want to have that shower?"

I nodded. My head hurt, my ribs ached, but on the plus side my heart felt lighter. I needed help in the shower, or at least with my clothes.

"I don't think I can ..."

"It's okay. I'm here."

And that made it all right. God, my life was a mess. Pear-shaped didn't quite cover it now.

A quote popped into my head.

The most merciful thing in the world, I think, is the inability of the human mind to correlate all its contents. H. P. Lovecraft (1890 - 1937), *The Call of Cthulhu.*

All I needed now was a song. What would top this off perfectly? Matchbox Twenty exploded from within. 'Unwell'. I couldn't guarantee the sentiment was true. I may very well be crazy.

Okay, I don't make friends with the shadows on the wall, but a ghost in the mirror, or a ghost in a Messenger window, and I'm all over it.

Chapter Twenty-Six
Heaven Can Wait

Kurt drove his car. Lee followed us in his. Our black SUV convoy headed out of Lexington. I watched the scenery, enjoying a sense of the familiar the closer we got to Mauryville.

I asked Kurt to stop outside the bookstore on Main Street. Lee pulled in behind us. I stepped out of the car and stood in front of the store. Suddenly I was bombarded by images. A woman with wild blonde hair smiling and talking, hands animated. My best friend Holly. I saw her serving a customer, then pouring coffee for a uniformed police officer.

I opened the door and an old-fashioned bell jangled. Standing in the store the world flickered. Time slipped backward and stopped.

***

Eyes bored through the glass and into my back as I grinned at Holly who stood behind the polished wooden counter.

"All day?" I asked, indicating the man outside.

"Yes. The last five hours."

That did make it all day, so far.

"No Kevin?"

"No."

"What about the other fine, brave officers who protect

and serve?"

She raised an eyebrow. "Cops crawl all over this store grabbing free coffee and eating cookies every day ... but today ..."

I smiled. We didn't have the biggest police presence. Kevin plus six full-time officers and two part-timers made up the entire Mauryville police department with backup provided by the state police out of Lexington.

"Typical. Where are they all?"

"There was some problem out at Parker's Apiary – so I think they all went."

The lure of free honey perhaps, or it was a slow morning and no one wanted to sit on a speed trap.

"Staties?"

She shook her head furiously. "They'll think I'm the crazy book lady, I don't want state police coming out to a 'some guy parked in front of my store' call."

That was something I could understand.

I took my badge from my jacket pocket and clipped it to my belt, then adjusted my jacket to reveal a mere hint of the Glock on my hip.

"Okay. I'll go have a word."

She smiled. "I'll get you some coffee."

I looked over my shoulder at her as I walked to the door. "You do know this is kinda overkill, right? And Kevin may even be pissed about me interfering in his town."

We tossed our heads back and snorted with laughter.

***

Lee touched my shoulder.

"What's happening?" he asked. "What can you see?"

"I don't know yet. But I remember being here, maybe five years ago. Holly owned the store. Someone was parked outside, creeping her out. So she called me." I didn't know if Lee knew Holly. "Do you know Holly?"

"Yes."

I turned and looked out the window. "I know when it was. I was on my way home from Richmond. We'd been working on a serial rapist case, and I'd spent a day with mom and dad."

Another episode of the residual memory swallowed me.

***

The bell above the door jangled as I let myself out. The man watched me approach him. I rapped on the window and indicated he should wind it down.

"Good morning, sir. Can I help you with anything?" I leaned in and scanned the interior of the car then took a sneaky deep breath. Just in case he'd been smoking dope or something.

I smelled something but it wasn't dope; it was failure in his personal hygiene. He was overweight, smelly, and the experience was extremely unpleasant.

His mouth turned up at the edges, more a sneer than a smile.

"No. I am resting."

"Hard day, sir?"

"Long drive."

"And your name is?

His eyes traveled slowly down my body lingering where they shouldn't and stopping abruptly at my belt. I felt violated. He oozed creep.

"I have done nothing to interest a special agent."

So he could read, or he at least recognized the shield.

"How about I decide that? Your name, sir?"

I noticed the beads of sweat building on his forehead. The weather was mild but not warm enough to cause perspiration like that. Maybe there was an underlying medical condition or he was nervous.

"You may hand over your license and registration."

His hand fingered the key in the ignition.

"Time for me to move on," he said with a hint of confidence.

***

I knew I was in the store with Kurt and Lee, that I wasn't in my own past. What I could not understand was how I could smell the horrid troll outside Holly's book store when he was a memory.

"What can you see?" Kurt asked.

"Me, well, not me, because I am me. But I'm talking to someone outside the store."

"Are you okay?"

"Yes." The truth. I am okay. The man outside the store is the past, it's already happened. It doesn't matter what he does, I've already survived it.

I let the scene envelop me.

***

"Take the key out of the ignition and step out of the the car." I swung his door open. "Now."

"Don't you think you're overreacting?" His tone was borderline smarmy, but his eyes portrayed an aversion to authority. Maybe he had trouble with women.

"Out," I replied, reaching in and removing his keys. "And then you can give me the relevant paper work, can't you?"

He struggled to get his backside off the seat. I bit my lip in an effort to stop a growing smirk. Anyone who can't get in and out of a car, has no business driving it. The leather squeaked under sufferance as he pried his large denim-clad ass from the seat. After about two minutes of huffing and puffing he stood on the sidewalk.

Standing in his shabby clothing, he was an unattractive short man. His stomach protruded well past his belt and cast a shadow over his filthy, shoeless feet. He was a good four inches shorter than me and proceeded to puff himself up – in an attempt to look impressive?

I looked at the car, a 2006 red Corvette bearing Virginia tags.

Mid-life crisis or stolen?

I pulled my notebook from my back pocket and wrote down the tag number and a description of the car.

"License?"

He reached a fat-fingered hand around his boundless

hip.

"Be very careful," I cautioned.

The hand came up empty. He shrugged. "My wallet must have fallen out in the car."

I considered it was likely after witnessing the effort involved in hoisting his bulky frame out of the seat. And I might look, but not yet. And not with his piggy, washed-out blue eyes looking me up and down. I felt dirty and sick.

"What's your name?"

"Robert Saville," he articulated with slow precision.

He said it as though it should mean something, but it didn't ring any bells for me. I wrote it down.

"Date of birth?"

"September twenty-ninth, nineteen hundred and fifty-five."

So, he said everything with deliberation, like it was important. It was a weird way to say the date.

"And you are in Mauryville for what reason?"

He shuffled his hideous feet, inching closer to me. A frightening grin spread across his face revealing several missing teeth. Stale tobacco mingled with his offensive body odor and made me feel nauseous. My eyes flicked to the store window and met Holly's horrified stare.

Now I could really see why Holly was antsy about his continued presence outside her store.

"I didn't know a person had to have a reason to visit this delightful town."

Yeah, but we're particular about what lurks on our

pristine streets. Bare-footed, toothless, sleazy trolls are not welcome.

***

I leaned my head on the store window. Proving I was in the store and not in the past. A moment of reality was a welcome relief.

"How you doing?" Kurt said.

"Doing all right," I replied. "How you doing?" Everyone's got their cross to bear, having one foot in the past, and not being able to remember everything about my present, is mine. But this revisiting of the past must have a purpose.

"I'd be a liar if I said this situation wasn't a concern."

A smile crossed my lips. "I want you to promise me something."

His eyes narrowed as he glanced at me then back to the road. "What?"

"Promise first."

"I promise," he said. His voice was tight in his throat.

"If at any point you lose me again ... if I go down longer than my brain can survive intact ... do not resuscitate me."

Kurt slammed me against the wall next to the window, his arm across my throat. His eyes darkened. If looks could kill, I'd be dead.

He hit his head on the wall a few times then looked at me again.

"Who the fuck are you?"

I shrugged. "According to who?"

"Okay, fair comment. But, the Ellie I know, the woman who fought so hard to get where she is today. is not a quitter. She doesn't quit anything."

"I quit smoking."

His head hit the wall again. I fought to keep my smile inside.

"If anything happens to you, I am disregarding that promise. Just so you know." He checked out the window then let me go.

Within minutes I was back in the past and very much alive.

***

"And why are you in our town?" I asked, hooking pleasant into my voice and hoping it stuck.

"I'm passing through and stopped to rest."

"Passing through to where? What is it way out here that interests you, Mr. Saville?"

Color rose in his cheeks. His mouth opened and closed. His fingers fumbled near his shirt pocket. Luckily for him, I could see the pack of cigarettes.

He pulled the pack from his pocket and placed a cigarette in his mouth. The pack went back into his pocket and he gave me an expectant look.

I wasn't about to light his smoke for him.

"Where was it again, that you were going?"

He removed the cigarette and began patting his pockets.

"Just passing through."

"To where?" I found my patience gone.

"I was looking for highway sixty-four."

"Guess you missed all those signposts announcing the correct exits on your way here then."

He continued patting his pockets and now added grunting noises to the experience. He was sounding very much like a rutting pig.

Nasty.

I pulled my cell phone from my pocket. "I'd like you to stay where you are," I told him and then I moved away toward the door of the bookstore. Standing half inside the store doorway gave me some privacy. He was so busy trying to find a lighter he wasn't even looking my way.

I called Comms and spouted everything I'd written down at the lucky person manning the desk.

In under a minute I had confirmation that Saville owned the car. It had been reported as a suspicious vehicle twenty-four hours earlier in Lexington. He was also wanted for questioning regarding an indecent assault in Lexington. There was a report of a handgun in the vehicle.

"This is a current case?"

"Yes, Agent."

"I have eyes on Saville. Can you send a picture of Saville to my cell phone please?"

"Sending the photograph now. Do you need assistance, Agent?"

"Yes, ma'am, I do. At twenty-one Main Street, Mauryville in Rockbridge County."

"We'll send the nearest state police unit."

"Thank you."

I hung up. Holly waited for me to speak. I looked at her.

"Go inside. The car was red-flagged by Comms and he may have a gun. Staties are on the way."

***

A hand touched my arm. I followed the hand to a familiar muscular arm. Lee spoke, "Ellie, you still with us?"

"Sure. Who was Robert Saville?" I looked into his eyes. "It seems important, who was he?"

"The name doesn't ring a bell. I'll look it up."

I watched him climb back into his car and lift his laptop from the passenger seat.

Kurt moved closer, he followed my gaze out the door but I don't think he could see the red Corvette parked by Lee's car.

A woman's voice startled me and I looked at the counter, a dark-haired older lady stood by the till. "Can I help you?"

Not Holly.

"I-I used to live out here. My friend owned this store."

"I see. I've only been here a year. A caretaker of sorts. I manage the store for Holly Conway; she moved north with her husband."

I looked at Kurt and whispered, "Conway?"

"Holly married your brother."

"Okay, got it." I had no fuc'n clue. I thought the memory of Holly was because she was my friend, I had no idea it had anything to do with Aidan. How come I could remember Aidan and not Holly? Damn you, Will Smith. And your flashy thing.

"Aidan?"

"Unless you have another brother."

"I don't think so."

"Good answer. You want to go outside?" Kurt suggested.

I nodded.

Lee called me over to his car.

"Holly made a complaint about him. You called state police in for backup. Saville was implicated in the disappearance of his twelve-year-old daughter. The daughter was Holly's best friend. The child went missing from Richmond and he turned up in front of Holly's store, fourteen years later."

"He's linked to something else," I said. "There is another reason he was here." I leaned against the hood of Lee's car and thought about the name.

"There is another case number attached to this file; it's classified," Lee said. "I can get Caine to open it for me."

Kurt stopped him. "Let Ellie bring it back. If that case has something to do with Saville and the missing kid, then she should be able to recall details. We'll contact Caine later if we need to and then you can verify what she remembers."

I didn't even care that Kurt was talking about me like I

wasn't there. I could see the red Corvette and a fat troll of a man, but no one else could. On some level, the whole past coming back thing freaked me out.

A smattering of honesty fell from my lips, "Kurt. This is getting worse. It's like I'm living in two worlds. This one where I can see you and Lee, and I know there isn't a red Corvette parked on the street here." I was talking too fast. "And another, back in time, when Holly worked here and Mac and I were still net buddies."

He was looking at me as if I had sprouted horns. It was conceivable that my head would spin and green vomit would spray across the street. Either I was possessed or insane. Neither option thrilled me. Kurt's hand took my arm.

I felt his fingers close around my upper arm, therefore I was still real.

"This could be what needs to happen. Maybe your mind is going back to fill in the gaps from where it felt most comfortable."

I grinned. "Do I look like a rose garden?"

"You want an answer?"

"No, but stop piling on the shit – you'll bury me." I realized then I was still breathing, and I felt better. Like maybe it would work out. No contradictory comment from Mac's ghost followed. "Promise you'll bring me back if the past tries to keep me?"

"Now that's a promise I will keep," Kurt said with his hand on his heart. "I promise I will bring you back."

There was no way for me to figure out how he would

accomplish that; I just had to trust him. The past was about to swallow me again as everything shimmered like a heat wave on the road.

***

The state police were on their way. My phone buzzed. I checked the display and opened the message. A photograph of Robert Saville. Mr. Saville looked much different once. He was thinner and younger. From the photo it looked as though they were a rough seven or so years from then to now. Still, it was the same man.

I looked at the picture on my phone again and wondered what happened to cause him to become the disheveled blob of a creature on the sidewalk, fumbling for a lighter.

The man looked over at me.

I smiled.

He took that as an opening and shuffled forward. I held up my hand.

"Stop right there. Go back and wait where I told you."

I walked toward him speaking. "Your car was reported as a suspicious vehicle in the vicinity of an indecent assault. Do you know why Lexington Police want to talk to you?"

"Really?" he replied, his eyes darted toward the car.

"That's what I'm asking. Why?"

Before he realized what was happening I grabbed his wrist, turned him to face my car and pushed him down on the hood.

"Spread your hands and feet. Do not move. I'm going to frisk you for a weapon. This is for my safety, sir."

He started to complain. I reminded him not to move.

"Do you have any weapons on you, sir? Knives, guns, sharp implements?"

"I do not."

With quick but firm hands, I checked his pockets and searched him. It was unpleasant. No weapon. He enjoyed the process entirely too much.

Bile rose in my throat.

I tossed up whether to hook the disposable cuffs from my belt and cuff him. He was still leaning over my car. I asked him to stand up straight. His jeans tented in the front.

He really was enjoying the process way too much. I indicated that he should walk back toward the building.

"I'd like you to sit against the wall there," I said, pointing.

"Am I under arrest?" he asked, with a glazed look in his eyes.

"Not yet. I am waiting for a colleague to arrive; until then you will do as I ask."

I hoped my tone implied he would do well to not tempt me.

My decision to wait for backup before searching the car was determined by his reaction to the pat-down search. I didn't want to be the object of any more of his perverted thoughts.

Holly attracted my attention by holding up a cup of

coffee. I smiled and joined her in the doorway.

"Who is he?" Holly asked, passing me the cup.

"Robert Saville," I replied. "The car was reportedly seen in the vicinity of an indecent assault in Lexington. The person who called it in said the driver had a handgun on the front seat."

Holly sipped her coffee. Half a cup disappeared before she spoke.

Subdued, she said, "I think I know who he is."

This was news.

"You said you didn't recognize him?"

"And I don't. His name, I recognize his name."

"This is where you fill me in."

"When we lived in Richmond as a kid – I would've been twelve – the kid across the road went missing. She was my best friend. Her father's name was Bob Saville. He disappeared a few months later."

"Did the kid ever turn up?"

She shook her head. "I remember we couldn't even walk to school by ourselves after that. No one played in the street anymore."

"Did they have other children?"

"An older boy I think. I can't really remember. Dad moved us out here within the year."

"What was your friend's name?"

"Leticia. Do you think he's dangerous?"

"I don't know. So Leticia would've been born in seventy-eight, like you?"

Holly nodded. "Now what?" she said.

"I want the state police here when I search the car."

Holly leaned over a stand and peered through a window. "He can afford a brand new Corvette but not shoes or decent clothes?"

"Do you want to talk to him?"

She shook her head in horror.

Interesting. This much *interesting* blew my idea of going home for a break, to re-charge my batteries, right out of the water. I knew I needed a change of scenery and some rest after three weeks working on a horrendous serial rape case, but I couldn't very well ignore the Saville thing. Even though I wasn't even sure what the Saville thing was, it felt wrong.

A police car bearing the state seal cruised past, made a U-turn, and came back. I waved from within the store. Two officers responded in kind. I ducked out the door and closed in on Robert Saville. Still sitting where I left him. The tent receded under the shadow of his stomach. A shudder of revulsion ran through me.

"Why are you outside *this* store?"

He took his time dragging his eyes upward from the spot on the sidewalk he'd fixated on. His gaze lingered on my body unnecessarily.

"I wanted to see Holly."

A shiver ran up my spine. So he did know Holly.

"Why?"

"For old time's sake," he replied.

I heard the even footsteps of the police officers as they walked toward me.

"Agent Conway?"

"Yes," I said, looking into the smiling faces of Greg and Chris Mitchell.

Double trouble. The only identical twins I knew in law enforcement.

Imagine my surprise finding them partnered together.

I couldn't tell them apart, not having spent enough time with either to figure out the quirks.

"Mr. Saville is passing through and has been parked up in front of Holly's book store for five hours. During that time he stayed in his vehicle and stared in the window, causing distress to the owner of the store." One of them scribbled in a notebook. "He's wanted for questioning by Lexington PD."

I took them both aside, out of earshot. "This guy's a perv. I was waiting for you to search the vehicle. The pat-down search earlier excited him way too much; I didn't want him coming up behind me while I was bending over in that car."

"Poor choice of words!"

I stifled the desire to laugh.

"Just search the car and find out what this person wants here in Mauryville, will ya?" I asked with a grin only they could see. "And how about name tags with your first names on them?"

"Yes, ma'am," they replied, grinning back at me.

The one on the left spoke, "I'm Chris."

I shook Chris's hand.

"Ellie."

I turned to Greg. When I shook his hand I found the point of difference I needed. Greg had a scar across the back of his right hand.

"Let's get this over with," Greg said. "You want to wait with Mr. Saville or in Holly's store?"

"Store," I replied and headed indoors.

Five minutes later Greg came in and handed me a gun. "A Berretta M9," he said.

"Indeedy," I replied.

"We'll hold him here; Lexington can come out and talk to him. By the way, he says it's not his and he didn't put it in the car."

He could say the earth was flat, but frankly, I wouldn't believe him.

"Can you deal with the weapon? We should trace its origin. His being here is no coincidence. Get as much information as you can and include his destination."

"Do you want to do this?" Greg asked.

I shook my head. "I can't. Holly and I are too close. I don't want to jeopardize anything that comes from this interview, down the line."

***

And just like that I was back standing on the street with Kurt. No Corvette. No Saville. No haunted past. And yet nothing felt real.

I was taking so many breaks from reality I doubted it would ever feel real.

"Home, I need to go home," I said. The road disappeared in the distance and I knew that down it was my home. The place where I used to live.

"Okay," Kurt replied. He ushered me into his car. The road was familiar, yet not. As we drove I realized what I saw may not be what everyone else could see. Then the sense of going home took over.

Kurt pulled into a long driveway. Trees lined the drive that curved around in front of a house. My house. I climbed from the car and headed around to the backdoor.

Behind me, I heard Lee asking where I was going. But I felt if I stopped to explain it, everything would disappear. I'd see what they saw, a burned out shell, not what I needed to see. I opened the backdoor and followed my usual path through the house to my bedroom upstairs.

***

The radio in my room was on. There was debate about a spate of bombings that cut a slice through Virginia. They were making assumptions that the bombings were linked to appearances by author Michaela Kennedy. I'd heard the buzz about the week's unexpected explosions before heading home from Richmond.

I rolled over, tugged the covers over my head, and repeated the words 'not my problem' until I fell asleep.

My phone vibrated on the nightstand, buzzing like a demented blowfly until I flipped it open and read the screen.

"Withheld number," I muttered and snapped it shut. I checked the time: Half past ten. The phone vibrated in my fingers. The same withheld number message appeared. A few moments later a message icon popped up. New voicemail.

Curiosity won out.

I clicked the icon and waited for the automated voice to finish. "You have one new message. Message received at 10.32 a.m. To hear the new message press one—"

I pressed one and picked up a pen from the nightstand. No paper.

"First new message." A female voice followed the automation. "Agent Conway this is Director O'Hare."

I gulped. The director was calling me?

"I believe you are at your home in Mauryville and would appreciate your help at my country house. Please call me back."

I wrote the number on my hand. For a few minutes I stared at the phone.

There was no imagining why the director of the FBI would call me at all or in what possible way I could help her. Terrible things crawled into my mind, worse things than the senseless explosive attacks across the state. I ran downstairs with the phone in my hand. I filled the coffee maker and switched it on. I was going to need coffee, no matter what happened.

On the way back to my room I made the call. Noticing, as I pressed the numbers, her phone number spelled her first name, Caitlin. Clever.

My heart pounded as I waited through shrill ring after shrill ring.

"O'Hare."

"Ma'am, Agent Conway here."

"Thank you for your prompt call back, Agent. Sorry to intrude on your personal time like this."

I didn't have a speech prepared for if the director called, so I stumbled over my words and managed, "How can I help?"

"I'd like you to go out to my home. We have a guest staying. Our guest may be missing."

"Ma'am?"

And she picks me?

"Ellie, you're the only agent I know of living out in Mauryville," she said and gave me her address. Which I already knew. "It's more of a neighbor thing. Low key."

"Yes, ma'am."

"Less ma'am, more Cait, just like at the summer festival and the town barbecue."

We are neighbors. She lived twenty minutes due west of my address and we socialized in town just like normal people. I'd been very careful never to let on that I knew the director in a social context. She rose to where she is today by sheer guts and determination, and I intended to do the same.

"You will be assisting my brother."

That added a different dimension. I'd met Sean O'Hare once before. His reputation went before him. He was ex-CIA and now a security expert. We often used his company to secure crime scenes because his was the best.

"He knows I'm coming?"

The last thing I wanted was to walk in on Sean O'Hare under stress and suffer his wrath, which was legendary.

"He'll be expecting you."

"Good to know. I'll be there in about thirty minutes."

"Thank you, Ellie." She sounded relieved; I hadn't expected that.

I hung up, leaped off the bed, and hurried to my closet picking up discarded clothes as I went. Almost everything I'd gathered ended in the laundry hamper except for my jeans. Amazing. That left my bedroom fairly tidy. I'd promised myself I'd do a few things while I was home this time. I sidestepped a two-foot tall stack of books, waiting for a home in the large bookcase that took up half my bedroom wall, to get to my closet.

In my closet, I found a long-sleeved dark gray tee shirt, then hooked out underwear from a drawer and spun into the bathroom. Within five minutes, I was wiping condensation from the mirror and wishing I'd turned the fan on before showering.

The mirror fogged again as I brushed my hair. I didn't have time to blow it dry, so I slipped a hair tie onto my wrist for later. I could blast the heat in the car and that would dry most of my hair on the trip.

I choose a tailored jacket and pulled it on. I picked up my hip holster from my dresser and snapped it onto my belt. My gun was still in it. I keep them like that, ready to go. I plunged my badge and keys into one jacket pocket and my cell phone into another.

The smell of fresh coffee wafted up the stairs.

I filled a travel mug with coffee and turned off the coffee maker. From the kitchen cabinet I took a large scoop of chicken feed. With the mug in one hand and scoop in the other I negotiated the backdoor, even managing to lock it behind me. On the grass outside the back door I scattered the feed then dropped the scoop on the porch steps.

Abigail the bantam hen stalked over the grass, clucking and pecking.

"See ya, Abigail," I called out as I shut the car door.

She didn't hear and didn't care. And she was low maintenance. That's why I liked having a chicken as a pet.

***

I stood in the middle of the burned and broken shell of my home. Charred wood fell around me. I'd disturbed the delicate balance. It took me a few seconds to understand where I was and why. The blackened house I stood in used to be my home. Knowing my home was almost totally destroyed by an explosion didn't stop me seeing what was once there.

Kurt was yelling at me.

"Ellie get out of there!"

"I'm coming." I picked my way through the rubble. It still smelled like fire. A large hunk of something fell, just missing me. I moved faster. Dust from falling timber billowed over me.

I emerged into daylight wiping soot from my hands onto my jeans and found two relieved-looking men.

"Did you at least make some progress?" Kurt said, brushing dust from my shoulders with his hands.

"Yes, we need to go to O'Hare's place."

Mouths opened and closed. Lee's mouth flapped like a goldfish. Kurt found his voice first.

"O'Hare lives in Washington."

I shook my head. "She has a country place down there." I pointed toward the mountains.

"You can remember that?"

"Yes. I helped her with something. It feels like I will find out what when we get there."

"All right," Kurt replied.

He turned to Lee and maybe thought I couldn't hear him. "Let her follow this. She's bringing back her memory piece by piece, and we need her back."

"This is stuff before my time. This feels like it's back just after she did all that secret squirrel stuff with the CIA."

"Maybe it is. She says it was five years ago. That puts it midway between then and now."

I shut the car door and waited. Kurt slammed his a few seconds later and smiled at me.

"You feel okay?"

"Yep." No. Not at all. Not even near. I looked at a phone number written on my hand and wondered how it got there. I knew it was one I'd called before and then I remembered the phone message. It was the director's phone number. If it was on my hand now, did that mean I was bringing the past into the present? It seemed smart to keep that little bit of lunacy to myself.

We headed off, the road familiar. Lulled by this, the past sprang to life all around me.

***

The drive was quiet with only two other vehicles on the road, and I knew both the drivers. We waved as we passed each other.

I finished the last mouthful of coffee just before O'Hare's driveway. The gates were shut.

So I drove past a few hundred yards and then doubled back, checking there were no cars parked anywhere nearby. It was too far from town for anyone to be out here on foot. Horse was an option but I didn't see any horses tied on the roadside.

I pulled up the driveway, wound down my window, and pressed a button on the gate intercom.

A male voice answered, "Yes."

"Agent Conway to see Sean O'Hare."

"Buzzing you in, Agent."

There were perimeter cameras. The gate opened inward and I inched the car forward. Once clear the gates began to shut. I waited, watching in the rearview mirror.

Just in case someone tried to slip in behind me.

I continued down the long tree-lined driveway. To my right I glimpsed a horse and foal in a field. On the left, open pasture lead to thick woods. The driveway swept past stables then forked. An impressive house loomed on the left as the driveway continued on to the right.

I glimpsed another large house some distance away and through trees. I chose the closest house. I parked by a four-car garage and walked back to the house. Another camera caught my eye. It tracked my movements.

I knocked on the back door. I certainly wasn't going to use the front door of the house. 'Stately' best described it. I was more hired help; I chose the door that seemed more appropriate.

A tall dark-haired man, with steel-gray eyes, opened the door. Sean.

I showed him my badge and announced myself.

"Come on in, Ellie. It's good to see you again."

He extended his hand. We shook.

I wondered if he did remember me, or if he was just being polite.

"Cait ... Sorry. Director O'Hare mentioned a guest and a possible missing person."

Sean laughed. "Call her Cait ... much nicer than what I call her. And that is the situation."

We stood in a spacious farmhouse-style kitchen. Dominating the room was a large pine dining table with ten chairs spaced around it. A set of french doors opened off the far end of the room. Another door, this time solid, opened off the right-hand side, next to what appeared to be a walk-in pantry.

Sean opened the doors and invited me into the living room. It was hard not to smile. I was in Cait O'Hare's living room. Most people didn't get past her outer office. I felt special.

I could see a computer screen and the view from about six security cameras on it.

I turned to Sean. "What is it you need from me?"

"I have a missing guest and she needs finding."

"Have local and state police been—"

"That can't happen."

"Can't?"

"Won't," he said. "I need your help in locating her."

"Okay." Weird. But okay. "Her?"

"Our guest."

I watched his eyes as he thought.

"Is?" I asked. "I need to know who I'm looking for and the sooner we get on with the search the better."

"Michaela Kennedy."

"The author?"

He nodded.

A *New York Times* bestselling author was missing. How embarrassing. Guess if something blows up we'll know she's close. I slipped into work mode.

"For how long?"

"Three hours at the most."

"Where was she last seen?"

"Going upstairs to bed last night."

"Any chance she could be missing longer than three hours?"

Sean shook his head. "No. The house is alarmed and the grounds monitored by heat-tracking security cameras."

"And?"

"I set the system last night, to record from eleven p.m. to seven-thirty a.m."

"There was no warning alarm? The cameras recorded without a hitch, and the guest is gone?"

"Yes."

I ran through a list of customary and obvious questions, getting the answers I expected. Except for the last one: she was missing and without her cell phone. Who leaves their cell behind these days? I mean, really? Unless of course coverage was shit, which was a possibility.

It was shaping up to be quite a mystery. That made two mysteries in quiet little Mauryville within twenty-four hours. Unbelievably strange.

"Can I see her room, please?"

"Sure."

Sean motioned for me to follow him. We entered a wide hallway and proceeded to the end. A staircase led to the upstairs bedrooms.

I talked to Sean as I looked around the room, accidentally kicking something on the floor near the bed. Kneeling down, I lifted the valance and spotted a book quite a way under Ms. Kennedy's bed. I stretched my arm out and hooked it closer with a finger. Once I had it in the light I could tell it was a leather-bound journal.

I opened to the first page and realized it was for notes, not a personal diary. It must have fallen from the nightstand, prior to connecting with my booted foot.

"Was Ms. Kennedy working on a new book?"

"I expect so," Sean said.

I flipped through the journal, scanning pages looking for a hint as to her movements. Or maybe something that indicated she knew about the bombs? In the middle of the book I came across two names. Robert and Leticia Saville.

"Did you hear about the stranger in town yesterday?"

He shook his head.

"Something I should know?"

"Could be. A man named Robert Saville parked in front of the book store for five hours."

"Must really like books."

"Never got out of his car."

He looked over at me, curiosity brimming. I ignored the look and asked, "Your guest writes fiction, yes? Must really like books."

"Touché."

"Looks like she was doing some research into the Leticia Saville kidnapping, back in nineteen ninety-one." I paused to gauge his reaction.

If smoke could've poured from his ears ...

"I take it Leticia is related to Robert Saville?" He exhibited great control as he spoke. "And this Robert Saville was in Mauryville yesterday?"

"Yes to both questions."

This was not good.

"Did the FBI investigate the kidnapping?" Sean asked.

"More than likely; it was sixteen years ago in Richmond; wouldn't be hard to check. It'll be on the computer system."

He pulled his cell phone from his pocket. I carried on. The journal didn't have much by way of current information, just some questions regarding the case. It seemed Michaela found the father's subsequent disappearance peculiar. She also queried where the mother was and why she wasn't a prominent figure in the media during the event. I heard Sean talking.

"Cait, do you remember the Saville kidnapping back in ...?" He looked at me.

"Nineteen ninety-one," I replied as I turned a page.

"Nineteen ninety-one," he repeated into the phone.

Several pages later I found a list of questions and I interrupted Sean. "She was going to interview him."

He nodded and hung up.

"Cait was part of the team that worked that case; it was early in her career. She never spoke of it to Michaela."

"No recent questions then?"

"No."

"Did Cait say who she thought was responsible for the missing kid?"

"She remembers the father was the main suspect, but they never had a strong enough case to arrest him."

I sat on the edge of the bed and thought aloud with the help of my notebook, "Saville arrives in town and parks outside Holly's store for five hours. Holly feels insecure. Local police all busy. She calls me. I discover his car was seen in the vicinity of an indecent assault. There was a report of a handgun in the vehicle. He's a person of interest. Holly was his missing daughter's best friend. State police arrive to back me up. They find the alleged stolen gun and take over questioning Robert Saville. The next day Michaela Kennedy goes missing." I picked up her notebook and turned to the page after the questions. I read the page then handed the book to Sean. "I think she met him somewhere this morning."

There was a date, today's date, and it was circled.

Sean didn't look surprised. He might not have been, but I was.

Saville could have picked her up early this morning out on the road. Michaela would have known when the alarm and cameras were off.

"Still want me here?" Instead of a missing person there was an author meeting someone to conduct an interview. It was looking like I could get on home and organize my books.

"Why did she leave her notebook here? Wouldn't she need the questions? Seems like she went to a lot of trouble thinking them through," Sean replied. "Why leave her phone?"

"Good question. Maybe she has another notebook that she takes to interviews. Something more like a stenographers note pad, or I dunno, just not that one."

He nodded turning the leather-bound journal over in his hands. "That would make sense, this looks like it's special and she wouldn't risk losing it."

I pointed to the inscription inside the front over. It was from Cait for a birthday.

"She will probably come back under her own steam

once she has finished her interview," I offered with a confidence I didn't feel. "She could've forgotten her phone."

Sean smiled. "Good try. Let's go." He stood by the open bedroom door. "We need to find her."

***

Noises from around me demolished my past. This was my life now, a collection of fleeting scenes and disjointed feelings. I needed concrete. I needed memories. I needed to remember what makes me me. I needed to get back to the memory, to find what it was that was so important.

"Ellie!"

I jumped. My eyes focused on a man in front of me. Sean O'Hare.

"Sorry. I startled you?"

Before replying my eyes shifted left then right. I was standing on the back porch of a house that felt moderately familiar. I flicked my eyes up to find Sean's steel-gray eyes looking down at me. "Ellie, I didn't expect to see you out here."

"Didn't expect to see you, either." He was in the memory that enveloped everything. But I last saw him in New Zealand; he and his wife had moved to Christchurch. "Vacation?"

"Yes," he said smiling. "And you?"

"Lost."

His eyes clouded, puzzled. He looked beyond me.

"Kurt, Lee, just like old times," Sean said, confusion evident in his voice. "Come on in."

He ushered us through the door and into the warm and light kitchen I remembered. Sean pointed to the pine table and chairs in the middle of the room. "Have a seat."

Lee sat next to me. Kurt at the end. Sean opposite me.

"Physically lost?" Sean asked.

"No," I said. "I know where I am." That much I was sure of. "I've misplaced some memories."

Imagine if we could just plug in a flash drive and replace the missing files. Imagine if inside our heads there was a little pop-up reminder to back up the day's events. How does a person back up their memories? Write it down like in *Fifty First Dates*? Maybe I should get a notebook and document everything. I don't want to be that woman. I want a USB port in my brain so I can plug in a flash drive and retrieve memories in an instant.

"Misplaced?"

I looked at Kurt for help and he took over. "Ellie has lost some memory. I believe it will return. I think what we're seeing, and what she's experiencing, is stress-related amnesia. She's forgotten those emotionally closest to her. Those she feels compelled to protect."

It sounded so simple, ridiculous even, when Doc said it.

Sean nodded.

"There was an episode in the hospital. Ellie was admitted for a severe migraine and fell prey to a killer. We lost her for a few minutes. So far, the effect of both the migraine and the incident leading to her momentary death is a little more missing memory."

Sean looked back at me. "How did you end up here?"

"I wanted to go home. It triggered a series of memories, Robert Saville and his missing daughter, and Michaela."

"That was not a good time for any of us," Sean said.

"Any chance one of you will fill us in?" Lee said.

Sean smiled. "Cait and I have a younger sister, Michaela Kennedy. For security reasons the relationship between ourselves and Michaela has never been publicized."

Lee and Kurt looked at each other.

"Michaela Kennedy the thriller author?" Kurt asked.

Sean nodded.

Kurt appeared thoughtful. Lee's face showed he knew what was significant about Michaela Kennedy and Mauryville.

"She was abducted from here?" Lee said.

Sean and I both nodded.

I heard Sean talking, telling them about the case, but I couldn't stay focused to hear what he said.

When his voice stopped I asked Lee what I'd missed.

"Sean is filling us in on the Saville connection," Lee said. "How you doing?"

"Hanging in there. Watching it all happen again. Except it's like it's happening for the first time."

A sense of desperation fell over me. What if I was insane? My worst fears realized. I could be my mother.

"I don't get how this will bring back my life, but I can't stop it happening."

"Chicky, would it help if you told us exactly what you saw?"

"It would help if I could take you with me."

Sean was leaning back in his chair.

"I think I'm supposed to find Leticia Saville. Help me, Sean." They were my words but they were foreign. I was the person who didn't ask for help. My words hung like neon signs hung from the kitchen roof and swayed from side to side.

"Leticia Saville? The missing child?"

"Yes."

"Really? After all this time?"

"Yeah."

"You know this?"

"Everything that happened when Saville turned up in Mauryville is happening again. I can see it unfolding all around me. I'm slipping in and out of the past. Just moments ago I was in Michaela's bedroom, upstairs here, with you. Reading her journal." I paused and imagined them conspiring to have me tossed in the nearest psych unit forever. "We didn't follow it far enough. Leticia is close. I know it."

"We weren't looking for Leticia. We were looking for Mikki. Can you skip forward?"

I shook my head. "I've tried that. It needs to be linear."

The past surrounded me with its familiar smells and sounds. There was something comforting about knowing how it all unfolded.

***

346

Sean handed me the journal and pointed to something. A chemical formula. It was fascinating because I recognized it. She had written the molecular formula for cyclonite, better known as RDX, in her notebook. Nothing else, just the formula scrawled across the middle of a page, two blank pages after the questions for Saville. We really did need to find her.

"You know the media is talking about the bombs and saying they're linked to Kennedy's appearances?" I gave him back the book.

"Yes. She has nothing to do with the bombings." He was adamant. "Nothing."

"What was the explosive used, do you know?"

He shook his head.

I knew. There was a discussion about the explosive while I was in the Richmond field office yesterday morning.

"C4."

"Which is RDX, mixed with a plasticizer, plastic binder and a marker," Sean said.

"Why would Kennedy have the chemical formula for the main ingredient of C4 in her notebook?"

"Research?"

He had me there. Could well be research. She was a thriller writer. Yet it seemed strange to me, not that it was written in her notebook but how it was written, like it meant something, but she didn't know yet what it meant. Maybe it was an idea she'd had.

I walked down the stairs ahead of Sean. My mind was

running scenarios so fast I couldn't keep up.

At the bottom of the stairs, I pulled out my phone. I called my Supervisory Special Agent and walked into Cait's kitchen to talk to him in private.

"Caine, can you look up Robert Saville in the system and tell me if he resides in Richmond and his line of work?"

I read his DOB from my notebook.

He didn't question why I wanted to know and within six seconds had an answer for me. He did reside in Richmond, also owned residential properties in six other cities in Virginia.

His employment record was interesting. His last known job was sixteen years before, as an electrician.

"Do any of those cities correspond to recent bombings?" I couldn't very well ask if Michaela Kennedy had visited recently, we don't have that kind of information in our system.

Big brother is good, but not that good.

Five cities including Richmond met the criteria. That left two cities. I couldn't decide if the coincidence was growing or there was something more to it. I needed to know if Kennedy visited all the cities and what the connection between her and Saville was. Really was. Not the supposed interview it appeared on the surface.

I thanked Caine and snapped my phone shut. Sean was standing behind me, I could hear him breathing. I turned and smiled. Not wanting to discuss my phone call I launched into a tirade of questions, "Where do you want to start? Have you searched the grounds?" They seemed extensive and he was alone, so perhaps he'd been waiting for me, although I doubted he was the sit and wait type. "And the woods? What about the other house I saw when I arrived?"

I slipped my phone into my pocket and wondered how much he'd heard. I didn't want it in my hand drawing his questions back to me.

He grinned. "Take a breath," Sean said. "I've had a quick look around the properties. Checked the horses were still here and cars weren't missing, that kind of thing."

I took a breath and exhaled slowly, re-focusing my attention on the possibilities ahead of us. "She could've gone anywhere with Saville," I stated. "Assuming she is with him."

I never did find out if the state police gleaned travel information from him or if the Lexington Police came out to talk to him.

"Let me make a call to the state police."

Sean shook his head.

"No police."

"My call will be expected. I handed Saville over to the staties yesterday. So it's follow-up."

I whipped out my phone and called before he could argue. Once through I asked for Greg or Chris. Greg announced himself over the phone.

"Hey, Greg, it's Ellie. What happened with Saville yesterday?"

"Oh, hey, Ellie. We sent the gun to the lab." I could hear paper moving about and tapping on a key board. "We questioned him for a few hours. Lexington PD came out and did the same. They have his contact details and told him not to leave the state. They had nothing to connect him to the assault, except a sighting of his car. He's denying the gun. We charged him with secreting a firearm. With no outstanding warrants, or previous convictions, he was freed without bail and ordered to appear in Lexington District Court. Saville stayed at the Maury River Motel last night. He was moving on this morning. Heading back to Richmond he said."

"Thanks, Greg. Do you know if he is still at the motel?" I figured that was pushing the general enquiry but had to try.

"We checked him in and he checked out this morning. Everything all right?"

"Yep, everything's great. Thank you. I wanted to make sure he was on his way out of the area."

"I checked and he's gone, paid his bill, and left at nine forty-five."

"Thanks Greg. Take care now."

I hung up.

"Nine forty-five. If he picked her up, then it was after that."

Sean frowned. "She hasn't been gone that long."

"Cait called me at ten-thirty. I presume you called her right before that."

"Yep."

"She could turn up within the next hour or so ..."

"Or not," Sean added. He slouched against the kitchen cabinets, rhythmically knocking his head against a door. "Do you want to wait?"

No, I want to go smash that fat pervert into the nearest wall and find Kennedy. He may have weaseled out of an indecency charge but I had no doubt he was guilty as sin of something.

***

I heard Sean talking to Kurt. Then Kurt replying. I didn't care that they were talking about me. I didn't care that Sean wanted to bring Rowan and Carla down to Mauryville. My phone rang, jolting me from the mess within my mind. The display said it was Rowan. I took a breath and answered it, remembering how I answered the phone when Mac rang. I figured if I was dating Rowan, I'd react in a similar way.

"Hey," I said, inserting as much bounce as the short word would allow.

"Hey, yourself. You sound good. Everything okay?"

"Absolutely." How much did I tell him about my work on a daily basis? He's not one of us. I opted for less is more. "We're following a lead."

"Any idea when you'll be home?"

"Not yet, a few days maybe. Do you need me home?"

Do we share a home? No. that doesn't feel right. Frequent guest felt about right.

"Carla is missing you."

I didn't know what to say. She hadn't even figured in my consciousness all day. A pang of guilt hit me. She's a kid. My kid. She misses her mom. I had to react.

"Put her on the phone. That'll help."

I spoke to Carla. Each word she said I wanted so much to be something that triggered a memory. I wanted to remember what it was like to be her mom. She sounded like such an awesome person. When I said goodbye a thought cemented.

"Guys – I can't remember being Carla's mom, but there's something wrong with me. Leticia's mother must have felt the loss of her child and conversely, Leticia would have missed her mother. Why did her mother give up?"

I knew I had a child and I was fighting tooth and nail to remember her. It went against everything I knew to be true for a mother to give up.

"Because she thought Leticia was dead," Lee said. "She moved into the grief phase. I can't think of another reason for a mother to give up."

Kurt nodded. Sean chewed the inside of his cheek and watched me.

"Why?"

"Police and FBI don't give up on kids. Why would the mother?"

Lee rocked back on his chair. "Someone gave her cause to believe her daughter was dead."

"And she didn't want justice?" I replied.

"That person might have convinced her she'd lose

everything."

"Her husband."

From my first look at the case I'd believed that Robert Saville was responsible for the disappearance of his daughter. I'd also suspected abuse. A new thought manifested.

"Saville abducted his own daughter. She got away." I leaned against the wall. "The very first thing I would do if I was a kid ..." I stopped.

Because the very first thing I would've done was run as far away as I could, because my dad was at sea, and my mom was a lunatic. But this kid's mom wasn't. Her dad was nut job. "She would've found a way to call her mom."

There was a collective sigh.

"That's why the mother moved on. She knew where Leticia was," Kurt said. "And no one picked this up?"

I shook my head.

I remembered looking into the case, but it was a cursory glance, for information and background on the father. He was the only suspect. No one had enough evidence to pin it on him. Police ended up thinking he'd killed the girl. But no evidence meant they couldn't touch him.

The new thoughts regarding Leticia didn't stop the past from sucking me back in. Next thing I knew I was climbing out of a car with Sean and we were still trying to find Saville.

***

Sean and I approached the manager's office at the motel after scanning the parking lots outside the rooms. No red Corvette.

Sean had a photo of Michaela. "Have you seen this woman?" he said to the grouchy-looking old man at the desk.

"No."

"How about this man?" I showed him a picture of Saville. It was his driver's license picture and nothing like his current state. "Imagine him looking homeless, toothless and driving a red Corvette."

The old man's craggy face cracked into a gummy grin. "Self-important son of a gun he was too."

Sounded like him.

"He gone?"

"I hope so," he replied. "He left about nine forty-five."

"Direction?"

"West."

"Thank you."

"He did something, didn't he? Looked like he'd done something."

Looked like he spent too much time with his hands in his own pants to me.

"Just want to talk to him, that's all," I said and slipped my card onto his desk. "If you see him or that red car, gimme a call."

He pocketed the card.

We headed west. A red Corvette was going to stick out on the road, especially out here, where there's little traffic and what traffic there is tends to be large four-wheel-drives or pick-up trucks.

Twenty minutes with no sign of anyone else.

A telling hunch formed in my gut. I turned the car around and headed back. I knew a few places along the river. Old cabins. There were numerous old hunting lodges and fishing cabins scattered along the wooded banks of the Maury River. A few in particular held promise. I parked on the roadside in the general vicinity of a cabin I remembered seeing on my many walks.

"Down here," I told Sean.

A derelict cabin loomed as we walked in from the road. I motioned to Sean to go right. I took the left. There was no sign of a car and nothing to indicate one had been in there over the last few months.

With the Glock in my right hand and my badge clipped to my belt, I approached the small porch and the door. One grimy window next to the door afforded me nothing but my own reflection.

I knocked.

"FBI. Open up."

No answer. I rolled my eyes. Like I expected one.

Another knock.

The door remained closed and there was no movement inside.

My hand grasped the doorknob and turned. Not locked. With a creak and a grind the door opened.

Light streamed in upon an undisturbed dust-laden scene. The past revisited. I stepped into the mustiness, trying not to send dust clouds into the air or destroy the natural balance.

"Hello!"

The dust lay silent.

No one had been there. A yellow curled newspaper lay on a small table. The date was July fourth nineteen seventy-eight. I followed my own footprints out and shut the door.

Sean was waiting.

"Next one, "I said. " It's a quarter mile away."

We climbed into the car and I drove on, pulling up short of an overgrown track.

The first thing I noticed was a broken branch and bent grass.

Someone had been there. Maybe someone out walking a dog. I spotted dog prints in the soft dirt to one side of the track. The branch was broken at people height.

I pointed it out to Sean. "Looks fresh."

We scoured the ground for footprints. And found a partial heel print some way in from the broken branch. No dog paws that far in.

"He could still be here," Sean muttered.

"Or it could be some horny teenagers," I replied. Options. Let's not close our minds to our options.

Sean drew his Sig. I had my gun in my hand. We stuck to the edges of the path, avoiding branches that would crack and give us away and also avoiding the looser stones on the middle of the track.

Quiet footsteps. Slow measured approach. Conservative breathing.

No sign of a car.

A bird flapped and flew across in front of me, startled by our approach. A chain reaction ensued. Birds all over the area took flight. I could only hope that any occupants of the cabin were unaware.

This time we scouted the entire building together. One door and windows just on the door side, facing the river. Or it would be if the trees and shrubs hadn't become overgrown. We crept along, keeping off the old porch that ran the length of the cabin. Sean made the approach, I covered him. He peered in a window and held one finger up to me.

I took a breath, adjusted my grip, and moved up beside him.

Sean knocked.

"FBI!" he called then looked at me real quick and whispered, "I can't say that."

"I won't tell."

I reached past him and knocked myself.

"FBI – open up." My voice was quite loud but I wasn't prepared to shout.

There was an answering thud.

Sean tried the door. Locked.

Not a good sign.

He took a step back and kicked, aiming for the wood next to the lock. The door splintered and his foot shot right through. I grabbed his arm as his balance failed, letting him lean on me while he extracted his foot. No one opened fire. Lucky.

With Sean free, I slipped in front of him and opened the door.

Daylight burst in. The place was a mess. Upended table, broken chairs. Against the far wall a bed. Tied to it was a woman. Bound and gagged. Sean ran over to the woman, holstering his weapon.

I swept the entire room, not wanting to be taken by surprise. The chances of there being anyone else were slim; if Saville was still there he would've used the opportunity Sean gave him to take us out.

I took off outside and made sure no one had come back.

Once I was satisfied the area was clear, I went back in. Sean had untied the woman and removed the tape from her mouth. She didn't look anything like Michaela Kennedy.

I waited for an explanation.

"My name is Fran Hutchings," she said, her voice dusty.

She looked about twenty.

"How did you get out here?"

"A man picked me up – I was hitching."

She knew she shouldn't have been, so there was no need for me to say anything.

"He bought me here. Said he'd be back, had something else to take care of."

"When was that?"

"This morning, just after ten."

"You're local?"

She shook her head. "I was staying with a friend from college and we had a fight, and I stormed off saying I was going home."

"Where's home?"

Sean was beginning to get antsy. I shot him a look that said 'wait.'

"Virginia Beach."

"That's a long walk. Describe the man to me."

She described Saville right down to his self-important air, poor hygiene, scruffy clothes, and unpleasant disposition. I couldn't believe anyone would get in his car willingly.

"You think I'm stupid don't you?" Fran said, her voice cracking as tears fell.

"No. I think you were angry and your judgment was affected by your desire to go home."

"I could've been killed—"

"You were lucky; I doubt you'll hitchhike again." I patted her shoulder. "We all make mistakes. Lesson learned?"

She nodded.

I called local police and had a brief conversation with Kevin. He told me he would send a car to the address I gave him. The problem we now faced was what to do with the girl. Taking her would be a mistake, but leaving her would also be a mistake.

After a brief moment of thought I called Kevin again and told him we were moving on, that his patrol car needed to look out for us. There was a small amount of resistance but I sweet-talked him around to my way of thinking. I hung up and turned to Sean.

"We're moving Sean. Can you head back up to the car and get the crime scene tape from the trunk?"

He nodded. I tossed him the keys; he snatched them from mid-air and took off at a run.

"What about me?" Fran asked.

"I'm taking you with us. Local police will meet us as soon as they can and then you'll go with them."

"Thank you," she said. From the floor by the rickety old bed she picked up a book.

"Is that yours?"

She shook her head. "He threw it at me and told me to read it." She smiled. "Don't know how he expected me to turn the pages with my hands tied. I think he's a fan of the author or something."

Yeah, but he's not very smart.

"Did you try to read it?"

"Nope, it bounced off my leg and landed there on the floor. I couldn't reach it. Just wanted to see what it was." She turned the book over in her hand.

A small chill ran through me when I saw the cover. *Deadman Walking* by Michaela Kennedy.

Sean came back with the tape. I took the book and thrust it at him. "He's a fan."

His eyes hardened. "I'll run tape around the shack," he said, handing the book back to me.

"I'll take Fran up to the car." As I motioned for her to leave, I whispered to Sean, "Any stalker-related behavior directed toward Michaela that you want to tell me about?"

"I wasn't aware of any stalkers." His jaw squared. I don't think his little sister was telling him everything. This made me wonder why. Walking up to the car, I considered why Michaela would withhold information about a possible stalker. It was possible she didn't know herself, or she thought she could handle it. Or she didn't want her big brother and big sister overreacting. Would I tell anyone if I were her and my brother was ex-CIA and my sister the director of the FBI? Um, no. It was a pride thing.

Fran and I waited in the car for Sean. As soon as he jumped in we took off for the next cabin. I hoped we'd meet a police car on the five-minute drive but alas we did not. Another decision needed making. Leave her in the car or take her along?

Sean and I walked ahead of Fran. We'd asked that she stay behind us, far enough that she could turn and run if need be.

We approached the old cabin with as much stealth as possible, sticking once again to the grassed verges and off the gravel that would crunch and give us away.

I checked on Fran's position every few seconds.

Once the cabin came into view I stopped her and showed her a sturdy tree to wait beside with instructions to run if there was gunfire or yelling. The car was unlocked, which felt risky – anyone could get in, but I needed Fran to be able to run back and lock herself in, just in case.

"I'll be okay," she assured me.

I ran to catch up with Sean.

"Let's do this thing," I said, pulling my Glock from its snug holster and adjusting my grip. I motioned to Sean to skirt around the cabin, giving it as wide a berth as possible. I could see a door and several grimy windows at the front. I presumed it was the front. If the woods weren't so dense the windows would look out over the river. There seemed to be no path or break in the vegetation on that side, making access to the river difficult.

Difficult but not impossible.

Sean appeared at the far edge of the cabin. He signaled to tell me there were no other doors, just one small window at the back. Fortunately for us. He also signed that he'd heard a voice. He indicated it was a male voice by pointing to himself.

Time to make our move. We both had cover, so our positions seemed optimal. Approaching the door from the side, and keeping back from the window, I knocked on the wooden exterior and called out. "FBI! Come out with your hands above your head."

Listening for voices and movement I heard a muffled male voice. I bashed on the side of the cabin again. Music.

With my sleeve I wiped some of the grime from the window, clearing just a small spot and not well enough for me to see anything. Music and a soft male voice over the top.

A radio.

I reached out and turned the door handle. A gun shot erupted behind us. Instinctively I ducked. The door swung open. In the filtered sunlight I saw a transistor radio sitting on a bed. From the corner of my eye I saw Sean run past me heading for the road. I gave the cabin a quick look. Someone had been there, but there was no sign of Michaela.

Sean hollered, "Ellie!"

I turned and ran. As I ran up the cutting that led to the road I saw the rolling lights of a police car. I was almost at our car before I saw Sean on the ground with Fran. She was sprawled face-down on the gravel. Looked like she'd been running away. Sean looked at me.

"Single shot to the back of the head," he said.

Two police officers clambered from the car on the road.

"Back of the head," I repeated glancing over my shoulder. "Shooter could still be here somewhere."

Pfft. A tuft of grass parted. *Pfft.* I dropped and rolled to the side of the cutting. Sean followed me.

Sean yelled out to the police, "Shooter!"

They disappeared from view. I could hear their radios. My eyes scanned the bushes, flicking back to the lifeless body on the gravel every few seconds. I watched the pattern created by bullets hitting the sand and stones. My eyes tracked back. I knew who we were after. He was too fat and out of shape to climb. Being in a tree was out of the question but I knew he was high.

"Sean, the roof."

He nodded. I pushed myself backwards on my stomach, sliding into the underbrush until I found a small area to turn. Staying low to keep any silhouette to a minimum, I crept, slithered, and crawled back to the cabin. From under the low bushes I could see the cabin. I heard another gunshot and focused on the most probable area of the roof. Someone returned fire, the bullet lodged in the wooden exterior of the cabin. Another gunshot. This time I saw the muzzle flash and I knew where he was. A movement in front of me caught my eye. I trained my Glock on the leaf that moved. It moved again. This time the leaves parted revealing Sean's face. We made eye contact. I pointed up with my left hand. He nodded and disappeared into the woods.

Time to move. Another shot rang out. Another clear muzzle flash. The police officers were pinned down. Sean and I had to take out the shooter. I scooted to the back of the cabin and discovered a ladder.

I figured if I took it, he'd be screwed; eventually he'd run out of ammo but meanwhile he might get another lucky shot and kill a cop. Sean appeared beside me.

We whispered in tones so quiet we were almost reading each other's minds. "I'll go up," I said.

"No," he said.

"He thinks we're out front, pinned down."

Before he could reply, I checked my magazine then eased up the ladder. Sean could either follow me, or grab my leg and pull me back. The later would be dangerous and alert the shooter.

One rung from the top I popped up my head for a look. Fat dude at twelve o'clock, lying prone. Thoughts collided. I could shoot him outright or risk arresting him.

Arrest. We still didn't have Michaela.

I pulled myself onto the roof as quietly as I could. When I stepped forward, the roof creaked. He tried to turn his head but was cast like a beached whale. Not feeling overly confident about the state of the rusty tin roof I moved with care. Sean's weight hit the roof behind me and I felt the whole structure dip.

"Put down the weapon," I called. Standing, I could see the dead body, police car and our car, but not the cops. The man tried to roll and bring up his gun. "Don't be a dick, put it down!"

"Bitch!" he replied, still struggling to roll but was trapped by his bulk resting on his elbows.

I was right behind him. I kicked the stock of the rifle he clutched. He lost his grip on the rifle and it slipped forward and fell to the ground below. His hand dangled after it, fat fingers wobbling.

"You are under arrest," I said. I reached over, grabbed his dangling arm and twisted it behind his back, forcing his face into the roof. It was harder reaching his other arm, his body had collapsed on it. Cuffing him wasn't easy. Just being near him was vomit- inducing.

"He's all yours," I said to Sean, who was watching with amusement. "How d'you want to get him down?"

"Toss him over," Sean replied.

"Might kill him."

"He's well padded." Sean shrugged. "Might bounce?"

"He might."

Saville squirmed causing his fat to wobble. "You can't do that – you're a fed. You can't treat prisoner like that."

God, how I hated his oily voice.

"Wrong. He's not, I am." I walked back to the ladder. "See ya down there then."

A sickening thud beat me down. It was followed by another thud, this time controlled and agile sounding.

As I rounded the corner I saw Sean standing over Saville. I could hear music and it made me smile. It'd be hard not to smile at *Sesame Street*. The Muppets were singing 'Cabin in the Woods.' They were right, there was a monster and I bet he did stand by the window. But now he lay on the ground trembling.

"Did he fall?" I asked.

"Yeah, rolled right off. Clumsy."

Two cops ran toward us. For a moment all I could hear was Tom Petty and the Heartbreakers singing 'Cabin Down Below.' Not a song I expected, but the message was clear. The thought of Saville wanting to love anyone in a cabin triggered my gag reflex.

Two songs about cabins in succession. That meant something.

"You okay?" one called to Sean.

"Yeah, prisoner fell off the roof," Sean said as they stopped in front of us in a cloud of dust.

"Unfortunate," the cop replied.

"Very," I said. "Have you called this in? We're going to

need a crime scene unit out here."

"We made the call when we saw you two on the roof."

The other cop picked up the rifle. "Where'd he get a rifle?"

"From one of his cabins," I replied. "What we didn't know, folks, is that Saville has cabins out here. It's where he brings his victims."

"Cabins?" the cop said. I love it when I have to explain my ability to glean information from thin air.

"I reckon so. He may own one but I suspect he rents another one or two seasonally."

"That makes sense," Sean said, unwittingly rescuing me from having to confess to weirdness via songs. He poked Saville with the toe of his boot. "Where is Kennedy?"

Saville groaned and farted.

Oh, man. I pulled my shirt neck over my mouth and nose. My eyes stung.

Sean stepped back. Both cops turned away gasping.

"You want to puke?" Sean said, glancing at me.

"I might," I replied, my voice muffled by my shirt. "I'll be over there." I moved back to where the cops were. Fresh air.

A few minutes later Sean joined us. He was an unusual shade of green.

"I wouldn't put him in the car," he said to the officers. "That weren't no fart."

"Do we know where Kennedy is?" I said.

"Follow me," Sean replied. I followed him back to the

cabin door and inside. He moved the bed aside and re-vealed a trap door.

"This is the cabin he owns," I muttered as Sean opened the trap door.

"Mikki?" he called.

We heard nothing. Sean descended first. Seemed fair: I took the roof, he can do the dark dingy hole under the cabin. The first thing I noticed about the dank space was the stale air, laced with fat-man body odor. I could almost make out my hand in front of my face. I knew I was still behind Sean because I felt the heat radiating from his body. There was a sharp noise, a flame flickered. Sean's Zippo lit the area. We could see a steel-framed bed and a shape tied to it. Other than the bed there was nothing much in the room. Sean handed me the lighter and hurried to the immobile figure. I saw a sofa, on it a book. I picked up the book and flipped through it; the zippo light gave just enough of a glow to make out the faces on the pages. A year book. I put it back where I found it.

"Mikki?" Sean said. He'd untied her wrists and ankles. She wasn't moving.

"Sean?" I said, moving closer with the light. "She okay?"

He took the tape off her mouth. His fingers searched for a pulse.

"She's alive," he said. "Only just."

"Let's get her out of here."

He fumbled in his pocket and produced a small red case. He broke the top off a small vial, injected a clear solution from the syringe then swirled the vial to mix the components.

"What is it?"

Sean drew the liquid back into the syringe and expelled air bubbles. "Glucagon," he replied pulling up Michaela's clothing to expose her stomach. He injected the solution. "And now we wait."

***

I wasn't holding a lighter. When I looked at my hand I was holding a pen. Sean was watching me, as were Kurt and Lee. They all looked like I'd been talking. I felt like a freak and had no idea what, if anything, I had been saying. I rolled the pen between my thumb and forefinger. God, it's weird how my mind works. I could've sworn I was holding a syringe.

"Where were you?" Sean said.

"Under the cabin," I replied.

"With Mikki?"

"Yeah, with Mikki. We got her."

Sean smiled. "Yes, we did. Now think – what was it that made you think of Saville's daughter?"

"There was a book." My mind conjured the book again but this time I knew I was still sitting at Sean's kitchen table. It was pretty cool to be able to flip through a book I'd seen in the past without having it physically in my hands. I turned the pages of the book, a high school year book. I recognized three people I previously did not know. Grant, Kurt, and Katrina. Katrina's picture was circled.

The feeling at the time was that she was going to be Saville's next victim and we caught Saville just in time. Now I knew she wasn't just another victim.

I looked at Kurt. "Katrina is Leticia Saville."

His eyes widened. "Did Saville know she was in Lexington?"

"I doubt he did early on, but he had the year book, so I think he figured it out."

"Was she a victim of child abuse at her father's hand, or was he going to abduct her, like Mikki?"

Well, being a victim of child abuse would explain her slutty behavior in high school. He wasn't going to abduct her like Mikki, but he wanted something.

"We'd have to ask her. But I think her childhood was destroyed by him. I also think the mother knew where she was, and that her adoptive parents knew the whole story."

Sean was catching up, or remembering everything around his sister's disappearance. "And Mikki – she started asking questions. If she'd figured it out that Leticia was in Lexington, Saville would've gone to prison, just not for murder."

"Yeah. There she was asking questions of the man who'd been stalking her – which she was clueless about by the way. Well, not clueless. She knew she had a stalker just not that it was crazy dangerous Saville. He must've just about messed himself when she contacted him, after all the bombings and so forth."

As soon as the words left my mouth I realized how true they were. That was a smell I'd never forget.

"Now what?" Lee asked.

"We go talk to Katrina and slap a nice big 'case closed' stamp on a cold case."

Sean rocked back in his chair. "What I don't get is why he stopped outside Holly's book store for hours."

"He was chickenshit," I said. "I think he stumbled upon the year book in one of the rented cabins, and saw the kid he thought was his. Remembered Holly moved out here with her folks and wanted to confirm that Katrina was Leticia. He didn't have the balls to ask Holly, and then I came along and ruined his day." I thought about it. Holly never knew. She had no idea her former best friend was even in the area.

I rotated my shoulders. My right shoulder was stiffening up.

"Shall we go prove this?" I said to Kurt.

"I think a wee chat with Katrina is in order," he replied, standing up. "Just out of interest, Sean, your sister was okay?"

"Yeah, she was unconscious."

"Unconscious?"

"Michaela is hypoglycemic. When we found her, her blood sugar level was so low she was almost in a coma," Sean said.

"Did you know that, Ellie?" Kurt asked.

"Yeah, but not until after Sean administered Glucagon from an emergency kit he carried."

I looked at the ballpoint pen in my hand. Something more akin to an EpiPen needed to be developed, for hypoglycemia – would be so much easier.

"Quite a coincidence that you almost died due to low blood sugar this morning, don't you think?"

The smile that settled on my lips was real. "There are no coincidences."

We left Sean to whatever he'd been doing before we interrupted his day with our problems and headed back to Lexington. My guess was he was going to go call both his sisters.

Sometimes remembering the past helps us to appreciate what we have now.

As Lee pulled the car into the hospital parking lot I spoke, "Kurt, am I insane?"

He replied fast, "No, you're mentally hilarious."

Lee chuckled. "Dang, you got that right."

"I suppose that's a medical term?"

"Of course," Kurt replied opening the car door for me. "Come on; let's go prove your theory."

They never ceased to amaze me. I have some weird brain episode, go back in time, can't remember important stuff from yesterday – yet somehow come back with information on a cold case – and my team is right there, prepared to prove I am right. Go Delta! I must've done something right some time to warrant this much faith.

I grabbed Lee's arm stopping him in his tracks. "I may not say this often enough, but you guys rock. You are why Delta A is the best investigative team in the FBI."

"Chicky," Lee crooned. "It's good to be appreciated."

Chapter Twenty-Seven
Gotta Have A Reason

Back in Lexington recent events were no clearer in my mind but I had a damn fine handle on the past. I was sure I had the events correct surrounding Katrina/Leticia, but even so, I knew explaining how I knew would make things way too interesting and just a tad unbelievable.

Katrina was at her desk in the ER reception. She smiled as we approached her.

"Can you get someone to cover the desk?" I said.

She nodded and called out to another woman. The woman took over and Katrina came out from the protective shell that was the reception.

"What are you two doing back here?" she said. Then saw Lee and stopped in her tracks. He has that effect on women. I counted slowly in my head to three and *bam*! "Oh My God! Tony Sharron, from Grange?"

Lee flinched as he replied, "No. SA Lee Davenport from the FBI."

Katrina paled.

"We need to have a word," Kurt said. "Somewhere quiet. How about Grant's office?"

"Sure, I suppose. He's probably in it."

Kurt led the way. Katrina made attempts at small talk but I was tapped out and Lee was still sulking from the Tony Sharron comment. It'd been quite a while since anyone had mistaken him for Sharron. I noted he still didn't find it funny. Kurt left us outside the office while he went in and spoke to Grant. A few seconds later Grant opened the door and ushered us in.

Grant addressed Katrina, "If you would like me to stay I will."

She frowned. "What is this about?"

Kurt spoke, "Have a seat, Katrina. Grant's just leaving." He opened the door and ushered him out. "I'll call you back in if required."

Kurt and Lee perched on the edge of Grant's desk. I sat next to Katrina on the chairs in front of the desk. Katrina's nervousness was obvious. Time to put her out of her misery.

"Katrina, we found evidence."

No, we didn't, this is a total hunch. I pulled my fancy pen that doubled as a digital recording device from my pocket and turned it on; I placed it on the small table between us. I spoke clearly, stating the time, date and who was present in the room. Then carried on with the questions to Katrina. "We uncovered some old information that suggests you are Leticia Saville, a missing person."

I had my fingers crossed.

The color drained from her face.

Well whaddya know? I'm right.

"Leticia Saville," she repeated. "Well now ... I haven't heard that name in a very long time."

"Could you tell us how you went from being Leticia to Katrina, from Richmond to Lexington?"

Panic flashed in her eyes.

"Am I in trouble? Will I go to jail?"

"No. We're not looking to bring charges against you. I just want to close the case," I replied.

Kurt gave her a glass of water and she started to talk. "I ran away from my father."

"From your father?"

"Yes."

"Please state your father's name for the record."

"Robert Saville. One night, while mom was out, he came into my room and tried to make me do things to him. I was twelve. He went on and on about how he was going to educate me in the ways of being a woman. How I was a whore and needed educating."

"Then?"

"I hit him and screamed at him. He tried to pull off my pajama pants. I kicked him in the head. And told him I would tell mom and that she would believe me. He got mad. He held a cloth over my face. When I woke up I was in the back of the car, it was really dark. I didn't know where I was. He wasn't there." She sipped the water. "I got out of the car and ran. I didn't know where I was running to, I just didn't want to be near him ever again."

"And then?"

"I kept running, keeping off the road, in case he was coming for me. I passed houses but didn't stop. At a gas station I used the bathroom and the phone. I'm pretty sure no one saw me. I called Mom. I told her everything. She told me to hide somewhere and she'd find me."

I knew the mother knew more than anyone thought.

"Mom came. There was a woman in Lexington she went to school with. They were sorority sisters. She and her husband agreed to help. My name was changed. I had a new social security number and a new life. Mom visited a lot once the fuss died down."

"It never occurred to anyone to tell police?" Color me silly, but it would've been so much easier than changing an identity.

"I asked once, when I was older. Mom said Saville was a lying scumbag, but one who led a charmed life. Everyone believed him, they always had. She didn't see how what he'd done to me would make any difference. Nothing seemed to make any difference and she couldn't risk me being back in that situation."

I've met people like that. People who appear to blind authorities to their true selves and leave regular folk, who can see through the bullshit; dumbfounded as to how it keeps happening.

"Where's your mom?"

"She died three years ago."

"And your adoptive family?"

"They raised me, I call them Mom and Dad. Dad is in a care facility for Alzheimer's, and Mom, she's a nurse there. Are they going to be in trouble?"

I shook my head. "I have no interest in destroying the lives of people who saved you. All I want to do is close the case."

"Do I have to use Leticia as my name now?"

"No."

"What about my husband?"

"He doesn't know?"

She shook her head.

"Secrets have a way of unfolding, Katrina. You might want to let him in on this one."

"It won't be in the newspaper though?"

"If it is, it won't be any of my doing. I'm going back to Washington, DC, and I'm closing the case. There will be no press announcement."

"Thank you."

"One more thing. You had an older brother?"

"I did. Adam was four years older than me."

"Where is he now?"

"He died in a car crash in Los Angeles eight years ago. Adam left for college about a year after I disappeared. I never knew where he was. I assumed he thought I was dead."

"I'm sorry."

Sadness enveloped Katrina. "He was in all my happy childhood memories."

I was glad she had some happy childhood memories. I turned the pen recorder off. We were done.

She smiled but it wasn't the lighthearted smile she'd had when we first met.

"You are that woman?"

Kurt interceded, "She's definitely that woman."

"No, Kurt, I mean, she's the FBI agent dating Rowan Grange?"

Kurt grinned. "She's a busy woman. Married to me and

dating Rowan."

"You know, I believed you two were married. You look good together."

And that was my cue to leave. I didn't need anything else confusing my missing memories.

Chapter Twenty-Eight
Strangers In The Wind

We were at a cafe, about halfway to Washington, DC, having something to eat when my phone rang. I looked at the display. Rowan's smiling face. I had a quick flash of a concert, police, and a feeling of utter horror. Not what I expected.

"Hi." I kept it light.

"You doing all right, honey?"

Yeah, sure, just wish I knew you from Adam.

"Sure, I'm ..." What'd Dad say, oh, that's right. "I'm okay."

"Sean O'Hare called me and suggested I bring Carla down."

So everyone has Rowan's number?

"Don't worry about it. We're heading home now. Just wrapped up a case."

"You're sure?"

"Absolutely."

"Where's home, baby?"

Okay, that's tricksy.

Events prior to Lexington emerged. My house exploded, but Kurt picked me up from the Marriott at Metro Center.

"The Marriott."

"Good guess. You could go to your dad's and we'll meet you there."

"Dad's sure?"

"Ellie?"

"Okay. Dad's."

I hung up. Kurt and Lee waited with about as much patience as a couple of starving lions.

"Do we know where my dad lives?"

"Yes, we do," Lee replied. "Had more than one bar-beque at Simon's."

Interesting.

"Do I know your parents?" They evidently knew mine. I looked at Kurt. "Well, not yours, they're dead."

Lee and Kurt grinned. "Somethings haven't changed. You're still as tactful as ever," Kurt said.

I brushed it off.

"Lee, do I know your parents?"

"No, Ellie, you do not. They moved outta state a few years ago."

"Florida?" Never could see the attraction of Florida to old folk.

He shook his head. "Santa Barbara, California. Mom took a job with the Justice Department there."

So his parents aren't retirement age. That's quite a move. I looked at Lee and had a feeling I should know what his mother does.

"She's a judge, Ellie."

"I knew that, didn't I?"

"Yes, you did. Only because I told you when Mom took the job in California."

"What about Sam's?"

"Yes, we've met them. When Sam was stabbed. His parents came up from North Carolina."

"And everyone knows my dad?"

"Simon? Hell yes."

"Elaborate on that."

"He runs the Butterfly Foundation with Mac's dad, Bob. We're all involved Ellie."

Great.

"Seems my life is an open book."

"Only to us, Conway. Only to us," Kurt replied.

"Good to know."

We left the café; Kurt drove me, Lee followed behind in his car.

I closed my eyes and hoped my missing memory pieces would return before we were home. I wanted to recognize my child and my boyfriend. I wanted to remember my dad properly. The smell of pancakes washed over me. As clear as day I saw myself in my kitchen making pancakes. Breakfast. I placed plates in front of Carla and Lee. Lee?

My eyes opened, I picked up my phone and called him.

"Lee, why did you have breakfast with me and Carla the other day?"

"I came by early to tell you about your death."

I blew out a sigh of relief. Lee laughed.

"I thought something was going on."

"I guess to a person who has memory issues, a family breakfast scene with big ol' me in it would be disconcerting."

"Shit, Lee, over the last twenty-four hours I've had

three, no four names. Been hunted. Been murdered. Been shot at and met my secret past. Discovered I'm dating Rowan Grange. Have a daughter. Found out Kurt loves me." Kurt made choking sounds. "Oh, and solved a cold case on an ancient memory. Really, Lee, making you breakfast is just par for the course."

"Whoa there, Ellie ... Kurt does what?"

I hung up on Lee and stole a sideways glance at Kurt. He was a little flushed looking.

"I'm sorry, it just slipped out."

"Don't worry about it. I doubt it was that big a secret." His hands gripped the steering wheel so hard his knuckles were white.

"Liar."

Chapter Twenty-Nine
All I Want From You

As ridiculous as it felt I still couldn't get it together and remember life with Rowan. We walked around my father's back yard in the dark. The edges of the garden beds were glowing with solar-powered lights. The whole area had the feel and appearance of a fairy garden. There was peace. Quiet. Cool. Peaceful.

I knew Carla was watching from within the conservatory. Sitting in the dark, looking out the large windows, hoping everything would go back to normal. I thanked the stars above that I remembered her. I remembered everything about my daughter, right down to how messy her room was and her favorite nail polish color and brand. It didn't take long for Carla to come back. Joey too was fairly quick. I liked Joey. He was Carla's most consistent best friend. Being a girl she seemed to have endless best friends.

Rowan touched my hand.

"Penny for them?"

I smiled. "I think these are worth all the gold in Fort Knox."

"Must be good thoughts."

"Uh huh. Was thinking about Carla."

He nodded. "Fort Knox."

I saw the dark outline of the garden seat and opted to sit. Rowan sat next to me. He exuded patience.

"Why don't I remember us?"

"You're the only one who can answer that."

I considered his response for a few minutes.

"Does it bother you?"

"Yes."

That seemed an excellent response. "Why?"

"Because ..." he faltered and tried again. "Because I like you. We're good together."

"We're so different."

"Not so much. Yes, we have remarkably different occupations but we share the same level of passion for those occupations."

"And that makes us not so different?"

"Yes, it does. We're similar, Ellie."

"What did we do together?"

He smiled. It felt like the first time I had witnessed such a warming event.

"We went out to dinner, away for weekends, hung out at your place, took in the occasional movie, spent lots of time with Carla, and we laughed. We laughed a lot."

"We didn't live together?"

The smile was back.

"No."

I sensed something, like maybe he wanted to and I didn't.

"Why not?"

"Your choice. I accept it."

"But why? It sounds like we were very happy, so why not live together? I gave a reason?"

"You were trying to provide a stable environment for Carla. My lifestyle is about as unpredictable as yours. It makes sense."

"Okay." That did make sense. I was juggling a demanding vocation, parenthood, and a rock star. Awesome. I rock!

Rowan's hand took mine. I watched in the semi-dark as our fingers entwined.

"How close are we?"

"I thought very. You don't tell me much about your work."

I heard it. The phrase I used and recognized from my recent past. I grabbed it with enthusiasm. "You're not one of us. My work makes you sick."

His smile creased the skin around his eyes. "In my defense I have not actually been sick. But you are right, I am not one of you. I don't see what you do on a daily basis. I don't know how you deal with the things you see, and still carry on."

I took a breath as a memory crept in. A memory of twinkling flatware and red roses.

"It was sunny and warm, we had lunch alone. In a hotel room. Red roses, champagne." I looked at him for confirmation. His eyes met mine but he said nothing. Another scene swamped me, one that felt earlier than the red roses and sunshine. I wished I could forget some things forever. To have the ability to choose what memories I retained would be awesome.

Rowan interrupted my musings. "You remember?"

"I remember how sick you looked when I told you about the kid who had been kidnapped, drugged, and raped. I remember we were in Christchurch, New Zealand, and that you took me to the Casino for dinner."

"You remember," he repeated, throwing an arm around my shoulders and hugging me to him. I slid my arm around his waist and hugged back. The smell of his cologne triggered a host of memories, including a good number of very personal ones that I would never speak of.

"Darlin', you're hanging on awful tight – and I'm not complaining, just want to make sure you're okay?"

"I'm okay."

Everything I always knew flew through the air and landed tidily. No more jumbled mess and missing pieces. All the corners were in place and the memories stabilized.

"Ellie, are you back?"

"You smoke Winstons and we wrote a few songs together."

"Welcome back."

"What were you doing in Japan?"

"Promo for the new album."

"What's it called?"

"*Poetic Explosion.*"

"Poetic Explosion?"

"Uh huh."

"Why?"

"It's how it is. One minute you're traipsing along and suddenly you meet this girl who writes poetry and it all changes."

Seriously? Come on.

"Me?"

"Yes."

I could hear the women screaming. "The whole album?"

"The album is a story."

"Mine?" I remembered him writing when we finally put the Abbasi brothers where they belonged. I was talking, he was writing. I closed my eyes for a minute and remembered a few long nights we'd spent since. Throwing lines back and forth. I could already feel the hatred when they figured out who the record was about.

"Yes, you helped. Why is it I think you don't quite remember everything?"

"I knew about this?"

"You have co-writing credit on four of the songs."

Yep, that qualifies as forgotten information.

"Okay."

"Where to now?"

I didn't know if he meant that minute or the future or what. A few frozen seconds later I went with my gut. I know this man. Flashes of life with him glued everything together. And still I could make no sense of him being with me.

"I don't want to sound weird ..." My words were silenced by out-and-out laughter. I waited for him to stop. "I don't get it."

"You don't want to sound weird? Really? You don't get

it?"

"Not that. Jeez – I know why that was funny. I don't get you and me."

He frowned and choked back his amusement. "Elaborate."

"You're this huge rock star women fawn all over, people clamor to be near. Christ, I've seen the behavior around you. People can't do enough for you." He nodded.

What else could he do? It was all true.

"Why haven't you ditched me for one of those women?"

"What makes you think I like the attention?"

We both laughed.

Hello, rock star, attention seeker extraordinaire.

"Seriously. I ignore you for days on end, disappear with little or no warning, and ask enormous favors when it comes to my child and as far as I can tell I appear to carry on as if you don't exist – most of the time."

"It's *all* the time. I'm treated very badly," he replied with a smile that melted my underwear. "I've dated women who hang on my every word and refuse to have an opinion that I didn't give them. Then years ago in a DC hotel I saw you."

"But—"

He held a finger to my lips.

"I saw you. In those twenty seconds you said more with your eyes and body language than anyone I'd ever met."

"God, you talk shit."

"Eric Clapton is God. I'm just Rowan," he replied.

"You still talk shit."

"The heart wants what the heart wants."

I could see I was getting nowhere.

"Is this life?"

"Yeah, Ellie, this is life."

"And we're okay?"

"We're okay."

I believed him.

"I have one more investigation to complete and then I'm taking some time off."

"You wanna come on tour?"

I grinned. "Not even a little bit. I remember the last concert I went to. I remember Christchurch."

It was right there in front of me and I couldn't look away. I couldn't un-remember it. The noise, the crowd, and Sam yelling in my ear. The metallic smell of blood mixed with the acrid smell of exploded flesh. I could cope with never having to smell that combination again. I wanted to forget but the memory was stuck. Maybe remembering things like that had the potential to save lives.

"Christchurch was hell. I don't ever want to go back to that."

Rowan nodded. His day-old beard growth caught my hair.

"One day I'll get you to a gig."

"One day."

Pigs might fly.

Chapter Thirty
Five Minutes From America

With my left hand holding the doorknob, I leaned my head against the cool wood and rapped with the knuckles of my right hand.

It felt like I'd been there for the longest time when the door handle turned beneath my hand. I let go and steadied myself as the door slowly moved away from me.

"Chicky Babe," Sam said, still half asleep. "S'up?"

"Gerrard has a lead from the lawyer dude. I'm going with him."

"Lawyer's dead. Arbab probably killed him," Sam replied rubbing his face.

"We expect that to be the case, but a body would remove all doubt. Arbab had friends – the plumber Abdul-Bari Bin Qasim Sabbagh and the research assistant – we thought they were the same person but Gerrard thinks they're not. It's possible whoever has turned up is linked to Arbab."

"Yeah." I could see his brain switching on. "Who is he after?"

"Ben Fisher."

"I'll run him and let you know if I find anything. Where you heading?"

"West Virginia."

"He's taking you over the state line."

"I'm over twenty-one."

Sam grinned. "What do you want Delta to do?"

"Find the corpses that belong to the meat packs. I keep hearing Elvis every time I think about those boxes. He's singing 'Return to Sender.' It's making me edgy. I'm thinking this whole thing with the meat has something to do with the mail service."

"Hot damn. Elvis is never wrong. I'll get onto to it and see if they have any interesting threats on their books."

"Keep me posted." I said.

Sam grinned back, "I'll keep you posted about the Postal Service and hope no one's gone postal."

"Damn that was bad!"

Postal workers were prone to going postal and whether the USPS approves of the term 'going postal' or not it exists for a reason. Hell, Wikipedia even has a list of notable postal shootings. It's not a new phenomenon. "Gerrard is waiting downstairs."

"Yeah, it was bad, might have some truth to it though." Sam checked his watch. "It's almost five a.m. Early start. Where's Carla?"

"I wasn't asleep so may as well be working. Carla is with Rowan at Dad's."

He nodded.

"Drive safe."

"Sleep well.'"

I was at the end of the hallway before I heard his door click shut. When I got in the car my phone rang. Sam.

"Yep?"

"You came out here to see me instead of calling."

"I was in the neighborhood."

"Take two." He paused. "S'up, Chicky?"

"I was in the neighborhood."

I heard so clearly the 'Neighborhood' song from *Sesame Street* that I was sure Sam and Noel heard it too.

"Sam, it's cool."

I just needed him to lay eyes on me. So someone who wasn't with me in Lexington knew I was okay and not flipping in any shape or form.

"Get Delta fired up over the meat packs. I'll see you in a few."

"All right, Chicky." He didn't sound convinced. "You're okay?"

"I'm awesome."

"Go team."

He hung up.

Apart from a private concert that comprised Elvis singing 'Wooden Heart', 'Return to Sender', 'It's Now or Never', and 'Promised Land', I had brief appearances by The Eagles with 'Love Will Keep Us Alive', and Bread singing 'Baby I'm a Want You.' And just when I thought it was over, Kevin Costner and Modern West tossed a little fun into the mix by playing 'All I Want from You.' It was an uneventful trip.

I kept my musical interludes to myself, mainly because I had no idea what to do with the songs. I got the whole 'Return to Sender' thing, but was clueless to make sense of the rest. We crossed the state line. I saw a sign saying 'Welcome to West Virginia'. The jokes I'd heard as a kid came flooding back.

Welcome to West Virginia, set your clock back thirty-five years. West Virginia invented the toothbrush; if anyone else had, it'd be a teethbrush.

West Virginia where a bug zapper and a six pack is Friday night entertainment. I'm not as politically correct as I should be. One day those thoughts are going to pop right out my mouth.

Gerrard broke my contemplations wide open.

"I'll get us a room at this motel. It'll do as our base while we look for Fisher."

I looked around. We were on the outskirts of a town. It didn't look very big, or very inviting.

"Doesn't look like there are too many places for a person to go here." I scanned the street. "Is this the main street?"

"Looks that way."

"Where are we?"

"Inwood."

He closed the car door and walked over the cracked blacktop to the building marked reception.

A sign proclaiming the Oasis Motel had a vacancy blinked too fast. Maybe it was getting ready to expire. Minutes later Gerrard was back and in the car.

"They have one room, upstairs. Parking over there." He pointed to a drab two-story cinder block building. I counted eight rooms at the bottom and another eight on top. Concrete stairs were stuck at each end of the top floor. "Unit thirteen," Gerrard said.

"Didn't think motels and hotels had thirteens."

"Maybe they didn't play *Psycho* up here," he offered. Gerrard parked in the spot designated to unit thirteen.

"I feel better already," I replied, unfastening my seat belt and exiting the car.

We took our bags from the trunk and climbed the steep stairs.

Thirteen was possibly the most depressing room I'd ever entered. There was no joy in knowing we'd be sleeping there. Bags stowed and facilities checked out, we left to try to find Ben Fisher.

From what Noel had discovered, Fisher was a researcher, one of the people responsible for the kidnapping and subsequent murder of Gabrielle Conway, the wife of a naval lawyer. He was a hands-on type researcher. He also found evidence to suggest Fisher hired the shooter who opened fire on me at the Blake Lane 7-Eleven. They were known associates. More evidence came forth during Gerrard's investigation than the police had discovered. The Blake Lane shooter was an ex-marine sniper, Jim Sanderson. He'd been working as a gun for hire since leaving the marines in 2006. Extensive Intel on all Conway women in the DC area meant Sanderson didn't pick his spot across from the 7-Eleven by accident. They knew I'd either stop there or drive by there at some stage during the early evening.

I fancied laying my hands on Fisher, preferably with fingers interlocked around his scrawny neck. We didn't know if he had killed Greer Conway, Robin Conway, or

Gillian Conway, but if I had to guess I'd say he at least provided information that led to the murders.

Our first port of call was the local convenience store. We flashed badges and photographs. Both drew blank stares. This wasn't doing much to improve my childhood opinion of the state.

Moving on.

The same exciting welcome was offered up at the drug store, pet store, book store, and diner. I noted we'd passed three churches. Three within a mile, all on the main road. Our next stop was a bar. The owner had a more novel approach to our questions. They kicked us out. Something about not serving pigs. Not very Christian. My guess was we intimidated him with our surprising number of teeth and sweet smelling breath.

The second bar was a mite friendlier. We were allowed to tip the pole dancer; for every tip the owner allowed us to show our photo to another patron. I suspected the pole dancer was the owner's nana. In a dark corner I noticed a youngish woman. She wasn't anyone's grandma. While Noel was otherwise occupied with the geriatric pole dancer and patrons at the bar, I wandered over.

"Hey," I said, showing her my badge. "Can you I ask you a few questions?"

"Whatever," she replied, shrugging.

I laid pictures on the table. She recognized a picture all right, but not Fisher. She recognized the murder victim, Gabrielle Conway.

"I saw her at the motel on the edge of town."

"Oasis?"

"Yeah."

Our motel.

"It was over a week ago."

"Was she with anyone?" I handed her a twenty.

She palmed the cash. "Two men, one Arab, and one scrawny white boy."

"You didn't recognize the scrawny white boy?"

She sneered. "I don't get out much on account of my aversion to daylight."

Oh, how interesting.

"You saw her though?" I tapped the picture of Gabrielle.

"Sure, it was night time."

"You positive it was her?"

"Yeah. I was visiting a *friend* at the motel. I saw her, and two men, but never saw the white one's face."

Got it now: Her friend's name was John.

"She seem happy?"

"Not really. But ya gotta look at it in context. If I was staying at the Oasis I wouldn't be all giggly either."

Fair enough. I was so looking forward to nightfall; if this is what comes out during the day, nighttime should be a real treat.

"You think the white boy could still be there?"

"Maybe. He didn't look like he had much going for him."

Judgmental or maybe just realistic.

"Thank you," I replied, sliding another twenty to her.

"Thank you," she said, stuffing the money into her ample bosom. I felt it was quite safe there.

We walked back to the motel. Each of us searching for reasons not to go back just yet. We resorted to window shopping at the local pawn shop.

We decided to eat in the diner before going back. It seemed smart to stop in at the motel reception and ask if anyone knew Ben Fisher. His name drew familiar blank stares. I showed his picture and that of Gabrielle Conway.

"Her," the woman said. "She stayed here for four days."

"Really?"

"Maybe."

"Did she or didn't she?"

"She paid for four nights up front."

"How?"

"Cash."

"She sign in?"

"She was with an Arab."

I pulled my phone and flicked through some pictures until I found one of Arbab and one of his buddy. "Him or him?" I asked, showing her.

"The second one."

"Thank you."

"Is Ben Fisher staying here?" I scrolled back and showed her the photos again. Showing her a picture of Fisher.

"Oh, the skinny boy. It might have been him with the Arab. I couldn't be sure."

I wasn't in the mood to pay out.

"Okay, thanks."

We walked away leaving her a tad dumbstruck. As we climbed the steep stairs Noel asked about the photos of Arbab on my phone.

I had no escape.

It seemed smarter to wait until we were in the room before I explained my interesting past to him.

"I did my homework." I just tossed it out there hoping he'd leave it.

"Nice try."

"I know people."

"Yeah, me too, and they tell me you have a classified past."

It was hard not to smile. "Hidden depths."

"We need to talk," Noel said as he swung open our motel door and ushered me in.

I let out a long sigh. As I breathed in, I smelled something I hadn't noticed earlier. A waft of Axe body spray. It floated down beside the bed toward the bathroom. It wasn't Noel. He didn't wear Axe. Axe was more a younger man's smell. Joey wore it. The brand was aimed at men from eighteen to twenty-four, the marinating age group who haven't yet learned that less is more. I dismissed it as some previous guest's residue.

"My past no longer has relevance in your case. Fisher is not connected to my past – he is solely someone of interest to you."

"I don't know that for sure. How can you?"

Another sigh escaped.

I sat on the edge of the bed and prepared myself to tell him about Arbab and New Zealand, and his rendition.

"This stays between us. You cannot include any of this information in your investigation."

"Any other conditions you'd like to impose?"

"You do realize if I tell you – I have to kill you?"

"Always the wiseass."

"All right, listen up I will say this once only." I stretched my legs out then pulled them up under me. "A long time ago, I was seconded to a special joint task force – I went in as a deep-cover operative. No one in the task force knew who I really was. It looked like someone within the force was playing for both teams."

"You were a mole?"

"I was."

"Dangerous."

"Very."

"It appeared that my partner was killed by the terrorists we were trying to find. I spent a few weeks trying to locate the camp. Never found it. My guide was not very helpful. About six weeks after I returned home, Tierney called me to his office. My guide had triggered several flags and was in New Zealand. I left at once to assist in the rendition." I took a breath. "Ameer was found in an apartment with another man, Arbab. I sent Arbab back to his father in Saudi – in disgrace. This action alone saved his miserable life. There was an explosion, but not before I saw Dion Edwards' face at the door of the apartment.

He was my former partner, believed killed, and now obviously working for a terror organization. I was *killed* in the explosion along with four Americans and Ameer. We believe Dion Edwards survived."

"He's on the FBI most wanted list, also on our top ten terror watch list."

"Yes, he is."

"Arbab came after you?"

"Yes. He may have seen someone who looked a bit like the woman he knew as Demelza in some trashy magazine in the last six months, which may have sparked his interest." My phone went and I welcomed the interruption. Noel was still trying to digest my confession.

"Yo, Chicky."

"Sam, whatcha got?"

"A crime scene. Could be connected to the boxes of ass."

"Yes!" I realized I was possibly overly exuberant in my response.

Noel's phone buzzed like a dying blowfly.

He checked the displayed number before answering it. After about twenty seconds he hung up and stood up.

"There's been activity on Fisher's bank account in Maryland."

"He's not here."

He nodded. We started packing up our stuff. Maryland was our next stop. I hoped the motels, wherever we ended up, were better.

It seemed that Conway was held at the motel before

her death. Why, was the mystery. Why take her out of state and hold her for days? Why not just kill her?

"What room was Conway held in?"

Noel shrugged and hoisted his bag over his shoulder. "I don't know."

"Perhaps we should know." I took my bag and headed for the door. I grabbed the handle and swung open the door. On the other side of the room I heard a faint pop.

"Noel!" I hollered, diving down the stairs, as the windows above me blew out, sending shards of glass all over the blacktop and vehicles below. I was against the building, as glass rained down followed by pieces of concrete, wooden frames and cloth. A piece of fabric sailed by me. Curtain. It was curtain. Flames touched the railing above, reaching out like tentacles from the building.

"Noel!" I yelled. Under the roar of fire, and ringing in my ears from the explosion, I heard a croak.

"El!"

I flew down the last few stairs and around the corner. A hand grabbed my foot from under the stairs.

Noel.

"How bad are you hurt?" I asked, looking down at him. He was sitting in an awkward position. The weak light from the ancient motel sign caused the glass shards over the ground to sparkle, but didn't give me enough light to see by. I pulled a small flashlight from my belt and shone it on Noel. Blood dripped down his face and one arm. The other arm was cradled against his body.

He grinned. "I dove over the banister; think I did my

shoulder in."

"Better than landing on your head," I replied, taking my phone and calling emergency service.

My bag was on the stairs. I pulled it through and opened it up; with the torch in my mouth I searched for a first aid kit. I took wound pads and tape – checked for glass in the large cut on his arm, then wrapped it as tight as I could. His head proved more difficult. A piece of glass was sticking out of his scalp.

"You have glass in your head, I can't take it out. We'll let the ER handle that. How does your shoulder feel?"

"I'll live."

"Good to know." I kicked glass away and sat on the ground in front of him. "Want to hazard a guess as to who blew up the room?"

"Fisher. The little fuck must've gotten wind we were here. That means someone told him."

I thought about the people we'd spoken to. The motel owner was last, probably not her. Could have been the ho; easy money.

With a *whoosh* a piece of wood fell, it smacked into the ground and sent splinters flying. People spilled out from the other motel rooms.

"He knew we were here. I doubt anyone ordered this. Arbab and his friend are en route to a black site; they're not talking to anyone now."

"Fisher probably doesn't know that. Looking to score points."

I lifted my phone and called Comms. Someone used

his bank account but I doubted it was him. I put a BOLO out without knowing what kind of vehicle he was driving. My money was on some kind of pick-up truck.

"How old is Fisher?"

"Twenty-five," Noel replied. "Why?"

"When we got back to the room I got a whiff of Axe deodorant. I hadn't noticed it when we dropped our bags off earlier."

"Next time you smell something, tell me."

Sirens wound up the road. Before long I could see flashing lights; minutes later paramedics and police ran toward the building. More sirens, then fire fighters and hoses appeared.

It was bright lights, smoke, and chaos all the way.

"SSA Conway!" Someone was calling me.

"Under here," I hollered back.

A police officer and a paramedic appeared by my legs. The paramedic called for help to move Noel to an ambulance right away.

The police officer tapped my arm as I watched Noel being lifted onto a gurney.

"Agent Conway?"

"Yes." I turned to face him.

"Anyone else in there?"

"No."

"Do you know what happened?"

I fought swirling fog to focus on his words and reply. If the ground would just stay still it would be easier. Then I noticed I could feel my back. It's not something you feel, usually. A dull fuzz was spreading from the side of my head. I pushed my hair back, trying to tuck it behind my ears. It was wet. My hands gathered my hair together, searching the length for the hair tie I thought was there. Nothing but wet hair.

I looked down, avoiding looking at my hands.

"Did you see a hair tie anywhere?"

"Agent?"

I remembered what he asked me. "I heard a quiet pop when I opened the door – next thing I knew I was half-way down the stairs being pelted by falling debris."

Falling debris and explosions were a recurring theme in my life. You'd think I'd be used to it. The ground swayed.

"Are you hurt?"

"No," I replied, fighting harder to stay in the present.

"Ma'am there is a *lot* of blood on you." He grabbed my arm and yelled for help.

"I'm fi ..."

The last thing that went through my mind was Kurt's name.

Chapter Thirty-One
Palisades

A familiar smell told me I was safe and that I was awake. My sense of smell doesn't work during deep sleep, yet I can recognize a scent I've smelled once on the wind when I'm awake. Beeping came from somewhere beside my head. Unobtrusive footsteps crossed the floor. A hand touched my shoulder.

"Welcome back," Kurt said. "Open your eyes for me."

"Not if you're going to shine your evil little light in them," I replied, staring into his blue eyes as they peered into mine. I tried to sit up.

Hands pushed my shoulders back onto the bed.

"Stay put."

"Where's Noel?" I looked around the room. There was no one else but us.

"He's in surgery," Kurt replied.

"Shouldn't you be doing that?"

He smiled. "He's in good hands."

"Why does he need surgery?"

"To remove some large pieces of glass embedded in his skull and to reconstruct his shoulder. That was some blast."

Thank God he landed on his shoulder and not his head.

"Will Noel be okay?"

"I think so – he's going to be off work for a few weeks."

It was time to ask for a damage report on me.

"And I'm here because ...?"

"You don't know?" He frowned. "What's your name?"

Had I felt more like me, I would've had some fun with that, despite his worried expression. Just this once I let him get away without my smart mouth getting involved.

"I am Supervisory Special Agent Gabrielle Conway, El-lie."

"Yes, you are." He seemed relieved, and I couldn't blame him. Recent events being what they were.

"So?"

"Some pieces of glass were removed from your back and you had a large gash in the back of your head."

I didn't remember anything hitting me.

"Go figure," I replied.

"They tell me the last thing you said was my name."

"Don't go reading anything into that," I replied. "You're a doctor. I wasn't feeling great."

He smiled. "Whatever you say, Conway."

A song started. The volume built and built until I was sure Kurt could hear it too. 'Palisades.' I really had to stop the crazy association between Kurt and Kevin Costner. One thing was true. Kurt couldn't scale my palisades, and he couldn't take down my walls. Not unless I let him and I wasn't about to do that. No sir, I was not.

He was taking my blood pressure with a small frown creasing his brow. I could still hear the song and had to fight to stop from singing along.

"You lost a lot of blood," Kurt said, taking the cuff off

my arm.

That accounted for me asking for him then; nothing silly about that.

"Concussion?"

"Doesn't appear to be." He sat on the edge of the bed. "But with your track record I'm erring on the side of caution."

Smart man. Especially with the live concert in my head, but I wasn't about to tell him about that.

"We still in West Virginia?"

"No. You missed the excitement of the medevac."

"Medevac," I repeated.

That had a strong military sound to it.

"So where are we?"

"NNMC."

"Navy hospital ... we are in Maryland?"

"We are. In Bethesda."

"I'm not navy."

"No, but Noel is. We had one helicopter and a choice to make. He's sicker than you, it was an easy call."

"Is my dad here?"

"And Carla," he replied. "They'd like to see you."

"We have a crime scene ..."

"I know." He looked away for a minute and studied the monitors that beeped in the background. "I'll give you a half hour before I start unplugging you. Then we'll talk about the crime scene."

"Okay," I said. "Can I sit up?"

Kurt stood up and passed me the control for the bed.

"Go for it."

He moved the pillows and rearranged them so I was comfortable then opened the door.

I went to scratch my head and felt something rough under my fingertips above my right ear. I followed the roughness around the back of my head. It seemed huge. I traced the edges and realized it was a bandage and it circled my head.

"Kurt? This is a big bandage."

"Yes."

And the vainest of all thoughts jumped from my mouth in utter horror. "Do I still have hair?"

He grinned. "You have hair. Minus a three by one inch area from above your right ear and around the back of your head. It's okay. I was careful."

"Great."

"I was careful; your hair will cover the section I had to shave. I went underneath. But maybe don't tie your hair back for a few weeks."

"Thank you."

It seemed stupid that my biggest concern was a shaved head. Noel was in surgery. It could've been so much worse.

"Mom!" Carla squawked rushing through the door and bounding toward me. She pulled up short and approached with sudden caution. "Can I hug you?"

I held my arms out. "Of course." I couldn't understand why she didn't throw herself at me like she usually did. Maybe I looked really terrible. With my arms wrapped around my daughter I looked at Kurt, hoping my eyes conveyed my question.

He shook his head a little. I saw my dad out of the corner of my eye. He waved.

"Carla, sit with me," I said, encouraging her to let me go.

She sat on the edge of the bed. I moved over. So far so good.

"Okay, kid?" Dad asked leaning in to kiss my cheek.

"I'm okay."

After an hour of convincing my family I was okay and that it was Noel everyone should be worried about, Kurt unplugged the equipment attached to me. The beeping and the tubes vanished. Dad and Carla disappeared.

It was time to get back to work and visit the crime scene. My team was waiting.

Chapter Thirty-Two
I Get A Rush

"A blood bath." I let air escape my lungs in a slow, controlled exhale.

"Literally," Sam replied, leaning next to me against the cold wall. Beads of moisture clung to his upper lip. The air was cool and he was sweating.

"It's just gross," I replied.

"The hearts bobbing on top in the tub were an interesting touch," Sam muttered wiping a hand over his face.

"If by 'interesting' you mean fuc'n creepy, then yes, they were."

We waited outside, our breath visible with every exhale. Lee was next door interviewing the neighbor who called the police. Kurt was inside the house with the medical examiner.

Five adults lived in the house, all were missing. We had a lot of missing people all of a sudden or, more accurately, we suspected there were a lot of missing people, related to our case.

"Are these related to our boxes of ass?" Sam asked.

"I have a feeling they are." My mind wandered to the tattoos I'd seen. "Sam, we ever hear back from biometrics?"

"We did, but the three tattoos that they did match belonged to live people who weren't missing half their ass."

That's the thing, tattoos aren't always as unique as

you'd think.

"That's good for them, not so good for us."

"They'll keep the photographs in the data base until someone comes up with an ID. Photos are being added all the time, we might get lucky."

I saw Lee hustling across the frozen driveway. He waved. The medical examiner and Kurt called out to us from the front doorstep. We all huddled for the sharing of information.

The ME went first, "Five adult human hearts. The blood is also human."

"That's not good," I said. "I hoped they were pigs' hearts or something." Even so I had a feeling they belonged to the missing occupants. I looked at Kurt hoping he had some answers.

"Not a lot, Conway, but we'll run DNA and try for a match from our previous body parts. And one interesting thing: All five worked for the USPS."

"Postal workers," I echoed. Boxes of ass in the mail and now dead postal workers. My eyes flicked to Lee. "Bingo! There's the link."

His brow furrowed. "Link. Only you could look so pleased over mailed boxes and postal workers. If that's the link then I don't get it."

A song drifted into my ears on the breeze. Elvis doing it again with 'Return to Sender.' I knew it was the link.

"Elvis is never wrong."

"Ellie, one day he just might be," Lee replied.

"Not today."

"You need to give me more."

"What? Elvis isn't enough?"

"Chicky babe, he's more than enough for me," Sam said with a wide grin.

I laughed. For me too.

"For whatever reason, postal workers are the target of a killer, and certain people are receiving their body pieces via supposed mail ..." I said. "Why?"

Kurt had a contribution, "What do the recipients have in common?"

"The packages actually turned up," I said, unimpressed and somewhat sarcastically.

"And you say it like that because you have had bad experiences with missing mail?" he asked.

I smiled. "You know I have. Shit, if a fed can't get her mail then who the hell can?"

Sam and Lee high-fived Kurt as he said, "Try that then."

While they were busy patting each other on the back for their brilliance, I was thinking about how anyone outside my circle would know I was pissed at the mail service. My phone buzzed. I checked it quickly.

A twitter update: *joanneJ @EllieConwaySA this isn't a mail service this is torture #wheresmymail*

The penny dropped followed by a roll of quarters. Holy shitballs.

"Twitter. The killer is using Twitter," I announced and typed a private reply on my phone to *@joanneJ* saying she needed to check my profile and call the phone number immediately.

"The killer is doing what?" Kurt asked.

"Using Twitter, the killer is following hash tags. Someone just tweeted me using the hash tag *#wheresmymail*, but we've used more than just one hash tag to talk about our mail issues."

"And it's possible to follow them?"

"Yeah, you click on the hash tag and it brings up a list of all references to it. Or use Tweet Chat, which enables you to follow hash tags."

My phone rang. I looked at the screen and saw it was the office. "Yep."

"We have a call for you from a Joanne J."

"Start a trace and put her through."

Two seconds later a confused woman spoke, "Hello?"

"Joanne, it's Special Agent Conway here, from Twitter. We have a little problem with the hash tags we've been using."

"Have I done something wrong?"

"Absolutely not. I'm going to ask for your address and you should know we're tracing this call; it's for your protection."

"Can I verify who you are?"

"Of course," I replied, hoping my brain would kick in and come up with some smartassed way to do this via cell phone. "When I hang up I want you to call the number back and ask for Caine Grafton, Special Agent in Charge. He will verify who I am. I'm going to snap a picture of myself holding my credentials right now and send it to you. You can ask Caine for a photo of the credentials on file."

"I never would've thought of that," she replied.

"Hanging up now."

Me neither, until just then.

I took a photo with my camera, holding my ID by my face. Seconds later the picture was sent to Joanne's cell phone.

Caine called me within moments.

"I've spoken to Joanne from Twitter. There are two agents on their way to her home."

"Thanks."

"No good can come of social networking," Caine growled.

"I'm pretty sure you said the same thing about electricity."

He harrumphed. I hung up.

The ME had excused himself.

"Okay, so we have five hearts," I said. "Where are the bodies?"

"Moving five bodies is not easy," Kurt added.

"We're looking for a truck of some kind," I said. "Sam, Lee, go door-to-door and ask neighbors about vehicles in the street over the last few days."

"On it, Chicky Babe," Sam said. He and Lee took opposite sides of the street and started knocking on doors.

Kurt and I looked at each other. "You think the other bodies will all be USPS workers too?" I asked.

"It's possible."

I groaned as I said, "Time to get the USPIS involved."

"We know anyone over there?" Kurt asked.

I shrugged. "If we did, I would've been asking for an investigation into my missing mail."

"Chances are someone has noticed missing employees and the USPIS is already involved. They investigate violent crimes against employees of the Postal Service."

I heard another groan and realized it was from me. "Are we going to have a jurisdictional tug of war over this?"

"I hope not," Kurt replied.

"Me too. The last thing I want is a lecture on how the special agents of the USPIS are the oldest law enforcement agency within the US, and how they've been using 'Special Agent' since eighteen-oh-one."

It was tricky keeping the condescension from my voice. Some agencies are just not fun to work with, or rather, some agents. I shouldn't lump all the USPIS agents in the same bag. Not their fault I once came across a rather boring, lacking-in-humor special agent with the Postal Service.

"Aren't you a mine of information?" Kurt said. I was impressed with the way he kept the sarcasm to a minimum.

"Be prepared."

"Didn't know you were a scout," he said.

"And I didn't know you were such a smartass. Life's a learning curve." I smiled. Things were moving and reshuffling within my internal filing system. "Moving right along. We need to find the bodies. I need a computer. I'm going to the office."

I waved to Sam and Lee as I drove out of the street. Kurt was riding shotgun. I reached forward and flicked on the radio. The Clash's 'Bank Robber' filled the car. Bizarre. The song caused more reshuffling.

I don't think I spoke during the drive. I parked in my space and headed for the stairs, running two at a time up to my floor, with Kurt hot on my heels. I held the fire door for him, letting it go as he reached his hand out to take the weight. Sandra called out as I passed her; I waved as I hurried into my office. On the desk was the pile of files from earlier in the week. I flipped through them. The bank robbery case file was missing. I turned on my computer. Not a problem, I had an electronic version. As the computer powered up I remembered where the file was. With legal: I'd closed the case. Legal were building their case against Madeline and Howard White. I scrolled the information on my screen while Kurt planted himself in a chair in front of me.

"What are you looking for?"

"An answer," I replied. I stopped scrolling. It wasn't there. So I pulled out my notebook and went back over the notes from earlier in the week. I found the information I needed. I had written the name of the bank employee who had gone home sick the day of the robbery. Having not needed to run her through our system in the initial investigation because it wasn't anything to do with her, I now needed to run her name.

"Who are you looking for?" Kurt asked.

"Marjorie Smith."

"Why?"

I chewed my lip as her driver's license popped up on the screen. I jotted down her address and phone number. I did a fast search for any other information. Six months ago her sister committed suicide. The sister, Luella Smith, was a postal worker and there was a report from the United States Postal Service regarding her suicide; she drowned.

"Road trip," I said jumping up from my desk.

"Why this woman?" Kurt said, following me.

"I don't know. All I know is The Clash song came on the radio and I need to talk to Marjorie."

He strode along beside me. I could feel his mind working and trying to catch up with my thinking.

"I'm not following," he said holding the stairwell door open for me.

I talked as we descended into the underground parking, "When I was investigating the string of bank robberies I heard that Clash song, 'Bank Robber,' in my head; also Marjorie Smith's name came up. She has worked for the bank for twenty-one years. She had nothing to do with the bank robberies."

"None the wiser here!"

"Her sister killed herself six months ago – she was a postal worker."

We reached my car. Kurt held his hand out for the keys. I threw them to him; it was easier to let him drive than argue. Considering what I'd just told him about knowing there was a connection because a song played.

"Where to?"

I read out the address of the bank. "Let's try her at work first."

She wasn't at work so we headed over to her home. Kurt did a drive-by. There was a car in the driveway. We parked down the street and walked back.

I knocked on the door.

Muffled footsteps sounded then stopped.

I knocked again.

The footsteps grew louder.

The door opened revealing a tallish woman in her early forties. She looked fit, calm, and was well dressed in tidy jeans and a smart shirt.

"Can I help you?" she asked.

I pulled my badge.

"I'm Supervisory Special Agent Conway; this is Supervisory Special Agent Henderson."

"Is this about the bank robbery?"

"No," I replied. "Can we come in?"

She stood aside letting us pass then directed us to the living room. There was nothing to indicate anything amiss in the house or with her. That bothered me. Could it be that my missing memory incident and sudden death had messed up my psycho-prophetic talent?

Mac's voice overrode my doubts, "Trust your gut."

Upon the mantelpiece I saw a picture of two women. One I recognized as Marjorie; the other looked like her.

Same height, same coloring, same eyes. Their mouths were a little different. Her sister's mouth was quite hard looking. Straight, not a happy mouth.

"Is that your sister?" I said, pointing to the picture.

"Yes," she replied. "Have a seat." She indicated the sofa.

Kurt and I sat down. Marjorie sat opposite us.

"I'd like to ask you about your sister." My eyes never left her face as I watched for anything that resembled nerves.

"Why?"

"Because we think her death may be tied into other postal worker deaths."

Her mouth flicked up in one corner. I almost missed it as it was so quick.

"My sister drowned. I don't see how that could relate to any other deaths."

"Was it accidental?"

"I would've said so, but they told me it was suicide."

"What was behind your sister's suicide?"

"I told all this to the investigators from the postal service." She seemed a little annoyed.

"They investigated her death?"

"Yes, they did, but it was too late. They should have investigated all the complaints she'd made while she was alive."

"Complaints?"

"My sister worked for the USPS for twenty years. She loved her job."

"What complaints did she make?"

"She had to deal with dogs, abusive people, and people blaming her for missing mail."

Kurt gave my foot a discreet tap. I moved my head in a tiny acknowledgement.

"Excuse me," he said, rising to his feet with his cell phone in his hand. "Just need to take this."

"It didn't ring," Marjorie stated.

"Silent," Kurt replied and let himself out the front door.

His phone never rang, silent or otherwise; he'd gone to call in back up and to get Sandra to run a comprehensive report on both sisters. I was sure he also called USPIS.

I turned my attention back to Marjorie as Elvis sang 'Return to Sender.' If that wasn't confirmation I don't know what was.

"Did your sister use Twitter?"

She nodded. "We both did."

I couldn't help but find her a little too accommodating. If she was killing people and sending them to me and others, I would have expected a little more in the way of disturbing mannerisms when confronted with the FBI.

"She died six months ago?"

"Yes, Agent, she did."

"That must have been awful for you. I'm very sorry for your loss."

At that moment I heard Dire Straits. I listened, not recognizing the opening bars of the song at all. It all became clear. I was hearing 'Private Investigations.'

"Marjorie, have you hired a private investigator over the last six months?"

"No."

Her head didn't agree. I detected a subtle nod. As if she wasn't sure.

A private investigator would have been able to supply her with the addresses she needed to have the boxes delivered, and maybe even supply the addresses of victims.

"You're sure about that? Because I can check," I said.

I turned my head so I could see Kurt through the window; he was on the phone.

"I haven't," she said with more conviction.

All that did was make Mark Knopfler sing louder. He was pretty sure she'd hired a private investigator.

I heard the front door open and then shut. Kurt came back in. He looked like he knew something.

"Marjorie, do you know Danny Diamond?" he asked, sitting back down next to me.

Her cheeks flushed. "No."

"He knows you and he told a colleague of ours that you owe him five hundred dollars for services rendered."

"I don't owe him anything. I don't know him." She was flustered.

I love how people jump into denial mode, as if that makes it all better. We have evidence that you did something, but hey, you can just deny it. We'll believe ya!

"You never hired Danny Diamond from the Diamond Detective Agency to locate people for you?"

"No."

"I knew Danny had limited morals but I never thought he was liar," Kurt muttered so Marjorie could just hear him. "Seems he found some of his missing morals when the newspapers reported boxes of meat being delivered to various people."

"I don't know what you mean," she whispered.

"Maybe you don't," he replied. "After all he was hired by Luella Smith, not Marjorie."

Oh now that's cold, setting up Marjorie by using her dead sister. I was mightily impressed with Kurt.

"Hang on. You telling me Luella set this up before she checked out? That she put everything in place ahead of time?" I asked.

He nodded. "It's looking like that."

Smart. I think I would've liked this Luella chick. I wasn't so fond of her sister though; she was hiding something. I didn't believe for one second she knew nothing.

"When was Danny hired?"

"Six weeks before her reported death. All the arrangements were in place. He was paid up front."

"So maybe, Marjorie, you should tell us what you did with the information that Danny provided."

"Envelopes came addressed to me. I had instructions to forward them to a post office box."

Ironic.

"Box number?"

She handed me a slip of paper from her refrigerator door. "Thanks."

"What name?" Kurt asked.

"Fred Kensington."

"Thanks."

We had a name and a P.O. Box. So far we had more than the USPIS. I wasn't planning on sharing. From what Marjorie told us, the mail service had their chance and opted to do nothing. Inter-agency cooperation was flying out the window.

"Don't leave town, Marjorie," I said and turned to leave. "If you think of anything else, call me." I handed her my card.

I caught up to Kurt. We headed to the post office where the box was held and flashed badges at the woman behind the desk.

"We need to know who pays for this box," I said, sliding the piece of paper to her. She punched a few keys on her computer.

"Fred Kensington," she said.

"Does he have an address?"

She looked at me with bloodshot eyes. "One second."

The woman printed out a copy of the post office box authorization.

"Thanks. How does he pay?"

"He doesn't. The box was pre-paid for a year by a woman, I think it was a woman. It's a funny name for a man."

"Yeah, but so is Marian," I replied.

She smiled. "How many people would've taken John Wayne seriously as Marian?"

"Very few. Do you have a record of the payment?"

I passed the authorization to Kurt who called Sandra at the office and had her run both the name and the address.

"Yes. Credit card." She printed the credit card details and gave them to me. Luella paid in advance. Nice. She was one vengeful about-to-be-dead person. Perhaps she missed her calling in life. She should have been a project manager of some sort, or maybe an independent contractor. My mind took off on a tangent imagining Luella as a hit woman until Kurt nudged me.

"Thank you," I said to the smiling woman with tired eyes.

Kurt was still talking on his phone as we left. I used mine to call Sam and Lee.

"Stand by, we might need back up."

Kurt hung up and opened the car door for me.

"Where too?" I asked. "Lee and Sam are waiting."

"The address was a baseball field. Sandra turned up a current on his driver's license." He took my phone from my hand and spoke to Sam and Lee. "Meet us outside Marjorie's house."

He read them the address then handed me back the phone. I had the feeling he was starting to read my mind.

"Sam, I want you and Lee to talk to the neighbors on either side of Marjorie's house before we get there. Find out how often the new neighbor across the road visits her," I said.

"On it, Chicky Babe."

I hung up. Kurt was looking at me with that bemused

expression he wore so often.

"You really do scare me. You haven't seen this yet."

Kurt showed me the photo Sandra had sent. Fred was the spitting image of Marjorie – except he was male.

"And we thought she knew nothing. Brother?"

He shook his head. "Oh no, way more complicated than that. I think it's Luella."

"But she's dead," I replied.

"No body. There was never a body."

"She killed herself." I was having trouble keeping up which wasn't usual for me.

"She drowned in the Potomac. Her body has yet to surface," Kurt said. "There was a suicide note, but no body."

"That wasn't in the report I saw, from USPIS." My eyes rolled skyward at the lack of information in the report they filed.

"No, it wasn't."

"Incompetent much?"

"That's what I was thinking. But how much does Marjorie know?"

"They're siblings who were, it seems, close. She knows her sister is alive."

We detoured a little on the drive over to the house, giving Sam and Lee time to talk to the neighbors. I enjoyed the coffee break.

Kurt pulled up short of the driveway. The same car was still there. I saw Sam and Lee were parked a few houses away, on the other side of the road. Sam gave a slight wave. I reached around and took my vest from the back seat. We were looking for someone who'd been hunting and chopping up people; it was doubtful she would take too kindly to our arrival. From our car I could see Lee and Sam put on their vests. I grabbed Kurt's and handed it to him.

"Bullets are bad for the constitution."

He grinned and put it on.

"You think Fred/Luella is here?" Kurt asked, fastening the Velcro side and shoulder of his vest.

"No idea. Hell, I thought she was dead. Am I the person to ask?"

"We all thought she was dead. But you, I don't think you really did."

Lee tapped on my window.

"What did you find?" I asked as he pulled his notebook out.

"There is a neighbor across the street who is a frequent visitor to Marjorie's. Dinner every Sunday, from what the neighbors have said. They've never been seen out together. But one neighbor reports seeing the man entering the garage late at night. He moved into the house across the road almost a year ago."

"Fascinating. And he has a name?"

"Fred, that's all they knew."

"Awesome," I said with a smile.

"Is Fred home?"

"We scouted around the house, lots of raised gardens out back, but no sign of life. Neighbors say he works during the day, but don't know where."

"Good."

"We rolling?"

"Oh, yeah."

I took four radios from the glove compartment and handed them out.

I switched mine to channel six and depressed the squawk button. "Delta A for Comms. Over"

There was a slight crackle. "Comms for Delta A. Go ahead. Over."

"Delta A going into an address. Arrange a warrant." I relayed the address to Comms. "We're active on channel six. Over"

"Understood Delta A. We're monitoring your frequency. Over."

I clipped the radio to my belt. Everyone else switched to channel six and did the same.

"Lee and Sam, take the back. Kurt and I will go in the front."

We stood by our car and heard the doors lock automatically. For a moment there was just us, shoulder to shoulder in our circle. We took a collective breath, touched hands and it was on. Lee and Sam broke away and headed silently up the driveway, separating to take different directions around the house. Kurt and I walked purposefully to the front door. Weapons in hands.

I knocked. Kurt watched for signs of life.

Marjorie opened the door. She seemed surprised. She would be more surprised when Sam and Lee stormed in the back.

"Come outside, ma'am," I said taking hold of her arm. I led her away from the door. "I'm sorry," I said and searched her for weapons. I handcuffed her and sat her on the grass in front of the house. She was involved somehow, I just didn't know to what extent and that meant she was a potential assailant. Better to be safe than dead.

Kurt was just inside the doorway. He signaled it was clear. I joined him. We cleared the living room, dining room, and kitchen. Sam's voice bellowed into the hallway beyond the kitchen. "FBI!"

I answered, so he knew where we were. Death by friendly fire would suck out loud.

A large cupboard in the hallway drew my attention. I opened the door. It was a linen closet. A linen closet with nothing on the floor. There was a big gap under the shelves, big enough to sit in. Big enough to conceal something like a trap door.

Sam and Lee moved to secure the bedrooms while we inspected the odd closet.

"Down here, Ellie," Lee called. "Back bedroom."

I motioned to Kurt to stay where he was and to watch the closet. I ran to Lee.

"What is it?"

He was standing in front of a bedroom closet. "Check it out. There is something under this house."

I peered inside and saw another big clear gap in a closet. This time I could see a trap door.

"The one in the hall has carpet in it. This must be the

one they or she uses; the other one may be an emergency exit."

"Going down?"

Not keen.

"One sec, watch that." I pointed to the closet.

I ran back to Kurt.

"Looks like there is a basement room, accessible from the closet, here and in the back room; I think that was Luella's room."

"Dangerous going in there. Could be booby-trapped. Plus, if she's down there she's not going to be happy to see us."

"Camera, we need a fiber-optic camera."

"SWAT."

I used my radio. "Delta A for Comms. Send SWAT to our location. Tell them to bring a warrant. Over."

"Comms for Delta A, understood. SWAT dispatched."

Every radio crackled at once as a message came over for all of us. "SWAT for Delta A. Ten minutes out. Over."

I smiled at Kurt.

He nudged me. "What is it with you and men with big guns?"

"It fills me with joy watching them storm buildings." I shrugged. "It's a girl thing and maybe a gay guy thing too."

Kurt reached into the back of the closet and ripped the carpet back. It was too easy. Hadn't even been secured. Underneath was a trapdoor.

"You think there any other exits or entrances?" he

asked.

"Garage maybe. Stay here."

I left the house to have a quick word with Marjorie. "Where do the trapdoors in the bedroom closet and the linen closet go too?"

"I don't know what you are talking about," she said. It was the most unconvincing lie I'd ever heard.

"How long have you lived in this house?"

"Since Luella died."

"You didn't share the house before then?"

"No."

I brought up an image of her bank file in my mind. This was a new address.

"Is the house as it was when your sister died?"

"Yes."

"Is there anything you would like to tell me?"

"I don't think so."

"Anything unusual happen in the house?"

It was like pulling teeth. I knew she knew something.

"Once," she said. "Once I put a box of soaps in the linen closet, on the floor. When I got home the next day the box was on a shelf."

"You're sure?"

"Yes."

"Have you ever put anything on the floor since?"

"No."

I left her on the grass and headed to the garage. At the door I turned and called out. "Why don't you put your car in the garage?"

"Because Luella's is already there."

Seemed like she was trying too hard to know nothing. I opened the side door and felt for a light switch. No car. A big empty space where a car should be, but no car. The room hummed.

Down the sides of the garage were chest freezers. They lined both sides. I counted five on each side. At the end of the garage was a small room. I opened the door and found a stainless steel room, complete with stainless steel counter and a sluice. It was immaculate without reeking of bleach. I detected a faint scent. Pine disinfectant.

"Kurt. Go for Ellie. Over."

"Go Ellie. Over."

"Garage is lined with freezers, found a steel-lined room. Over."

"What's in the freezers? Over."

"Looking now. Over."

I shut the door to the creepy sluice room and opened the lid of the first freezer.

"Packages of meat. Over."

"Swap places. Over."

I closed the lid and left the garage. I passed Marjorie.

"You all right, Agent?" she called after me. "You don't look well."

She had to know. The electric bill alone would've hinted at something untoward going on. I ignored her and hurried to Kurt.

"You going to puke?" he asked.

"I might," I replied, taking a breath and sliding down

the wall. "Ten freezers, chest variety. This could be the cold storage we were looking for."

"I'm going to look," he said and hurried away.

I watched him go. From the end of the hallway Sam spoke, "You think the other woman knows?"

"I don't see how she can't," I replied. "She said Luella's car was in the garage. It ain't."

"Freezers suck power," he said.

I nodded. "You'd think she'd notice a high electric bill." My mind started working on why she wouldn't notice. Surely the bills were paid by her?

Her sister was a planner.

"Sam, can you watch this closet? I have an idea."

"Sure," he replied, jogging down the hallway. I slipped out the front door and joined Marjorie on the lawn.

As I glanced up, I saw the SWAT truck and two black SUVs arrive. I waved. A hand waved back.

"Marjorie, who pays the taxes and bills related to the property?"

"An accountant," she replied.

"Do you ever see utility bills?"

She shook her head.

Luella had tried hard to give her sister complete deniability. Maybe if the bank robbery hadn't landed on my desk, no one would've figured this out.

"Why did you say Luella's car was in the garage?"

"Because it is. I looked there when I first came to the house." Panic edged into her voice for the first time. "Her car was there."

I was about to ask her why she hadn't sold the car but I still had Mac's truck and someone could easily ask the same of me. It's not always that easy walking away from the dead.

Two armed men approached us.

"Hey, Conway," the tallest one said, a wide grin plastered across his face, the warrant in his hand.

"Jefferies," I replied, then looked at his partner. "Andrews."

"What have we got?"

"Hidden basement room with access via two closets. No visual. Got your fancy fiber optic camera about?"

"We'll go have a looksee," Andrews said. He touched his throat as he spoke again, "Ready the camera, need to get eyes under this house." He headed back to the truck.

"Who is down there?" Jefferies asked.

"No visual, so no way to know for sure, but could be our target. A woman wanted for at least fifteen murders."

Marjorie gasped.

I ignored her.

"Who is on site?"

"Delta A," I replied. "Sam and Lee. Kurt is in the garage."

"Come with me," Jefferies said, indicating I should follow him. We walked toward the house. Kurt's voice came over the radio on my belt.

"Calling in the crime scene unit. Over."

"Is this it?" I knew he knew what I meant.

"Yes. We have bodies, we have the room used to

butcher them."

"How did she transport them? Over."

"I have no fuc'n clue, yet. Over."

There was a bang as a door shut on the truck. I turned to see. A perimeter was being set up. Marjorie was staring at something across the road. My heart did a sickening thump. A glint from a window. I pushed Jefferies hard knocking him sideways. "Gun!" I yelled.

Another glint from the same window in the house across the street and then shattering glass. "House straight across the street. Front window."

The SWAT team on the ground moved fast, taking up covered positions. Another shot rang out. A piece of dirt kicked up near Marjorie. Terror smeared across her face. Two seconds later the look became permanent. Marjorie slumped sideways as brain and blood sprayed across the grass around her.

"Conway?" Jefferies called.

"Let's get out of here," I replied and wiped residual splatter off my face. I jumped to my feet and ran for the house, making it inside the open front door just as a bullet hit the door frame. Jefferies bolted in after me and slammed the door shut. We heard the wood splinter as bullets hit it.

"Keep down," Jefferies said as we moved around the corner of the hallway by the closet with Sam.

Kurt was still in the garage and I didn't want him coming out to see what was going on. I hit the squawk button on my radio. "Kurt, gunshots. Stay where you are. Over."

"I heard. Everyone okay? Over."

"Marjorie's dead. We're okay. Over."

"What's going on?" Sam asked. "Hey, Jeff."

Jefferies did the man eyebrow-face-lift thing in lieu of speaking. He was listening to his team outside via his ear piece.

I spoke to Sam, "Someone opened fire from the house across the street."

"Guess now we know where the tunnel goes," he said.

I nodded.

Sam continued, "If the person is shooting out front, we could get in underneath them and take them by surprise."

"We cannot assume this person hasn't set traps."

More gunfire. Sam nodded.

Jefferies turned and disappeared out through the kitchen door.

"Looks like Luella, or Fred, was visiting her sister when we arrived, which is why there was no one home when you checked the house across the street," I said.

Seconds later Jefferies was back, with Andrews and two cases, one long and silver and one that looked like a drill case. It was a drill case.

Andrews drilled a small hole near the trap door and poked his handy camera in a cable down it.

"No traps on the door."

He pulled the camera out and hurried down to Lee. Minutes later he called back. "This one has an explosive device set on it."

"So it's the hallway one we use," I called back. "Could

be her escape route."

Andrews returned and said, "Going in there is a suicide mission. You've got a shooter who doesn't care and has nothing to lose."

He was right. Luella had already shot her sister. She'd killed at least fifteen other people. She didn't care.

You can't reason with someone who doesn't care.

"Take her," I said to Andrews and Jefferies. "No negotiation. She's already shooting at us. Toss a flash bang and get her attention then storm that house. Or get a sniper into position and remove her from the equation."

Jefferies smiled. "You want to call this?" He pretended to take his throat mic off and hand it to me.

"No, you're the SWAT man – go do your thing."

"When are you going to apply for SWAT?"

I smiled back. "How about never?"

Mac's voice filled my head. He was so clear and loud I thought for sure everyone could hear him. "Never say never, Ellie."

He was right. Never was a very long time. Nothing is impossible and anything can happen.

Jefferies spoke to his team and ordered his snipers into position.

"You can shoot as good as any of my snipers," he said.

"Yeah, but that's just me having fun."

Sometimes when there wasn't much happening, I enjoyed going out to Quantico and playing sniper with Jefferies' SWAT team.

"Chicken?"

I laughed at him. "Go do what you do and don't get dead."

Andrews and Jefferies left the house.

I sat on the floor with Sam. Lee had moved out to the hallway. His trapdoor seemed less of a breach risk than ours. Lee sat at the end of the hall. He'd pulled shut the door to another bedroom. The hallway was the safest place to be with the doors shut.

Kurt spoke to us every now and then over the radio. He was alone in the garage counting body parts. I was so grateful it wasn't me trapped in there.

My phone rang; I pulled it from my pocket and saw the display. Carla.

"Hey, kiddo. You all right?"

"Watching the news. I can see your car."

All black SUVs look the same.

"Really? My car? Imagine that."

"Mom!" Exasperation resounded in her voice. "Why are there SWAT guys by your car?"

"Trying to get the person we're after. It's okay. We're inside another house. Quite safe."

She sighed. "Grandpa said you'd be okay."

"He was right."

"Will you be home soon?"

"Soon."

She hung up. Today Carla seemed older than fourteen. No squealing. No shrieking. No giggling. It occurred to me that I was responsible for taking the fun out of her day. I felt like shit.

Leaning back on the wall I listened to the noises coming from outside. Gunshots. Then voices. Then more gunshots. The shooter was still shooting. Why couldn't Jefferies' snipers get a clear shot and end this? My eyes drifted to the trapdoor. It'd be so easy. She's busy shooting. She can't be in two places at once. I shook my head hoping the thoughts would fall out. It's not that I couldn't do it; it's that it would be very irresponsible of me to put me and my team in that sort of danger.

I hated sitting.

Waiting.

Listening.

Gunshots.

I picked up my radio. "Delta A go for Comms. What channel for SWAT Team Three? Over."

"Comms go for Delta A. Team three are using secure channel. Over."

"Patch me in. Over."

"Yes, ma'am, understood. Over."

I waited for a second and then we heard the chatter from SWAT come over my radio. I listened for a lull in the talk. "SWAT three. Go for Delta A. Over."

"Delta A. Go for SWAT Three. Over."

"You want help? Over."

"What did you have in mind? Over."

"Gimme a rifle."

"Done. Over."

"Bring the rifle to the back of the house. I'm going up on the roof. Over."

I beamed at Sam and Lee. "I'm heading out."

They both gave me looks of horror. I silenced them with one of my own. It was different from the stinkeye my team received when they screwed up. This was 'shut up, I know what I'm doing', not 'do it again and I'll shoot you myself.'

I bounded out the back door. I could just see a green leg on the roof of the garage. There was a sniper up there. Sam appeared behind me. "You need a leg up?"

Andrews came around the corner in a hail of bullets.

"What is she shooting?" I asked.

"Something that has full auto. Could be an M16; she's a shit shot but everyone gets lucky once in a while."

"If that's the case she got damn lucky when she took out her sister."

I figured she was blind firing.

Andrews handed me a rifle with a sniper scope. "There's no wind."

"Good."

I'm a crap shot in the wind. I smiled and looked down at the M40A3 I cradled in my arms.

"Suits you," he said. "Keep a low profile. We don't want her getting lucky again."

"Ladder?" Sam asked glancing around.

"Don't need one," I replied. "Gimme a hand."

He cupped his hands and bent down. I slung the rifle over my shoulder using the sling attached to it, and put one foot in Sam's hands.

"Up you go," he said standing up. I grabbed the guttering. It was just sturdy enough for me to use. I pulled myself up onto the roof and scurried away keeping my profile low. Creeping higher as I moved. At the peak I peered down. Perfect.

I lay down and adjusted the scope until I had a clear view. I could feel my heart beating as I concentrated on breathing. Slow, steady breathing. Calm thoughts. My angle was better than the garage roof. The shooter was sitting back in the room. Didn't look as though she was aiming. She must have been closer to the window when she picked off her sister. I aimed at her head. When her head filled my scope, I whispered into the microphone.

"I have the shot."

My order came back, "Fire when ready."

I held my breath and squeezed the trigger. She fired another round before mine hit her. I watched through the scope and saw her jerk backwards, the gun falling to the floor.

I scanned the rooms I could see for any other signs of life. None.

"Target neutralized."

The SWAT ground team moved in to clear the house. I was buzzing. The adrenaline rush was unbelievable. All the training I'd been doing over at Quantico had paid off.

I slid backward, dragging the rifle with me. I turned at the edge of the roof by the guttering and handed the rifle down to Sam. He gave it to Andrews.

"Move, I'm jumping," I said.

They moved aside. I jumped and rolled onto the grass.

Standing up I brushed myself off and rotated my shoulders. I had a burning question.

"Why was no one on the roof?" I asked Andrews.

"It was the best place for you," he said.

"Come again?"

"Our men were on the garage, the roof next door, and the rooftops on either side. This roof was for you."

"And you knew I was going to ask for a rifle?"

"Conway, we can read you like a book."

Sam laughed. "They were taking bets to see if you'd go down the tunnel or just ask for a rifle."

Andrews smiled. "Once upon a time she would've hit that tunnel." He turned to me and extended his hand. "Now you've grown some and are less impatient. We'd have you in SWAT Three any day." We shook hands.

"One day I might just ask."

I hadn't been working on my rifle skills just because it's fun. Weekends spent in Quantico training were designed to increase my chances of survival in sticky situations and therefore increase my team's chances of survival. I did devote more time to using assault weapons like the M16 and SG 550 than working on sniper skills with a M40A3, because breaching rooms and clearing buildings was way more fun than lying in one position for hours, waiting for the ultimate shot.

A girl has to have some fun. And with that Cyndi Lauper bounced into my mind singing her heart out, 'Girls just want to have fun.' There was no hiding the smile on my face. She was right. Girls do want to have fun.

I did my best not to sing along.

Chapter Thirty-Three
Destination Anywhere

It took most of the afternoon and all the next day to finish the mountain of paperwork associated with the four crazy cases we had worked. I didn't consider the cold case to be one of the crazy four; that was a whole new level of insane and just didn't fit anywhere, plus I was only signing off on the case file. No charges would be brought.

If it hadn't been for the bank robbery it would've taken us a lot longer to end the killing spree of postal workers. The numbers on the boxes all came back as employee numbers. A dead woman had been traveling the eastern seaboard killing her colleagues. For someone who loved the service but hated the public, she sure had a funny way of showing it. We never did establish how much Marjorie knew, but it seemed feasible that she knew a lot, and maybe even helped her sister with the bodies. The sister, using her alternate identity as a man, had rented the house across the road a year before. The tunnel system and everything was carefully excavated well before her supposed death. The neighbors all loved the multitude of raised flower beds. Good use of the large amount of dirt he-she pulled out from under the houses.

After that messy case, and the sisters who were killing in Stonewall Jackson Hospital down in Lexington, I was glad I didn't have a sister. I was equally glad to have my memory back and intact. Most of it. I didn't know what I didn't know, so for all I knew, I could have had it all back.

Mac's voice popped into my head, "If you don't miss anything, it wasn't worth missing."

"Maybe," I whispered. "Maybe."

"Maybe's ass," Mac said. It was so clear I could've sworn he was in the room.

I closed the last manila folder in front of me and added it to the pile ready to go to legal.

My cell phone rang. I didn't recognize the number.

The minute I answered I knew the voice on the other end. NCIS Special Agent Adam Cohen.

"Conway, Agent Gerrard wanted us to fill you in."

"Agent Cohen. How is he?"

"Recovering," he said. "We found Fisher's body in a dumpster."

"Interesting."

"Baltimore PD found him. He was the victim of a mugging that ended in murder."

"You're kidding!"

"Karma is a bitch."

There was a smile on my face. Karma is indeed a bitch and a welcome one.

"Any word on the body of your missing lawyer?"

"No, nothing yet."

Crap.

That meant they'd keep looking. I hoped Tierney could keep a lid on my involvement with Arbab in the light of ongoing NCIS investigation. I knew how persistent they were. What was I thinking? No one got past Tierney's blocks, dead ends, and concocted cover stories.

"Good luck. How long before you'll have the boss back on deck?"

"He's out for a few months."

"Take care, I'll be in touch with Agent Gerrard at some stage."

I hung up.

Outside my office FBI life carried on. Phones rang constantly. From under my desk I took a cardboard box, opened the top drawer in my desk, and removed personal items. My spare hand gun, spare holster, several packets of gum, photographs, notebooks, and some girly stuff. I put the box under my desk and headed off to Caine's office.

He called me in after one knock.

I sat in the chair in front of his desk.

"Busy week," he rumbled, spinning his laptop to show me the case logs.

"Yep."

"Good work." He leaned back in his chair, thoughtfulness rippling across his craggy face. "You thinking of leaving us for SWAT?"

No matter how hard I tried, I could not stop the smile.

"No."

"Sure?"

"Absolutely. Why?"

He passed me a folder. "Have a look."

I opened it and read the letter inside. Nice.

My head shook. I remembered the buzz I felt taking

that shot. "Good to know Jeffries thinks I can do it."

"You ready?"

Deep breath. "Yes."

"You want me to be there?"

A smile spread. "No, they'll think something bad has happened. Let me do it."

We both stood. Caine walked me to the door; instead of shaking my hand he pulled me close and hugged me hard.

"I'll see you Sunday night at Simon's for dinner."

I shut the door as I left.

Two minutes later I was in my own office again. I picked up the phone and called Lee.

"Hey, grab Kurt and Sam and come on in here."

They all strolled through the door seconds after I hung up the phone.

I rocked back in my desk chair and looked at Kurt, Lee, and Sam. "Sit down."

They pulled chairs closer to my desk and sat. "I'm taking some leave."

"Leave?" Sam asked.

"Three months."

"That's quite a chunk," he said, crossing his legs.

"I need it."

"You'll be back?" Lee didn't disguise the moment of panic in his voice that sent sparks of confusion to his eyes.

I smiled. "Of course and I'm just a phone call away." I took a breath. "We're still a team." Because we were a team they deserved an explanation. "Between terrorists, bank robbers, a serial killer, a hospital killer, a cold case, and memory loss, I need some breathing space."

I need some mental health time.

"Meanwhile, we'll keep the Delta A fire burning," Kurt said. "Weekly dinners are still on."

Lee nodded, "You and Carla will still be there, right?"

"Of course. I'll even take my turn."

I stood up and closed my laptop. I picked up the box from the floor and set it on my desk. They watched in silence while I put my laptop in the box.

"See you all on Sunday at Dad's."

One by one they stood and came over to my desk and hugged me.

Sam's arms damn near swallowed me. "Toughest week in a long time, Chicky babe. See you Sunday."

"Yes, you will."

He let me go and grinned. "I will."

Lee elbowed his way in. "It's not going to be the same around here," he said smiling.

"I should hope not."

He gave me a hug. "Sunday."

"Sunday."

Kurt was last. Lee and Sam waited by the door.

Kurt's voice almost became lost in my hair as he wrapped his arms around me; it was no effort to hug him back.

"You've been hit in the head more times than Kevin Costner in *Dances with Wolves* and you scare the shit out of me." He squeezed me hard and then pulled back. "Thank God you are just as resilient. Sunday."

"Sunday." I smiled. "I have to go." I extracted myself from his embrace hoping I was the only one who knew how reluctant an extraction it was. Modern West were singing, 'Indian Summer.' The song was a perfect fit and scared the hell out of me.

"Hang on a minute. I have something for you," Kurt said.

I saw Sam pass him a gift bag.

"This is for you, from us." Kurt placed the bag in my hands. "Open it."

I peered inside, and removed yellow tissue paper. Underneath the tissue was a yellow band. I lifted it out.

"Silicone band?" I said. Not seeing the relevance.

There was no writing on it. Kurt took it from me and pulled it apart.

"A USB drive?" I said, as he clipped it around my wrist.

"Sixteen gig of memory. I thought if you wore a flash drive it would stop you running into a burning building any time soon."

I looked at the band on my wrist and smiled. "The first thing I'm going to do is transfer everything from Mac's flash drives to this. Thank you."

I took the box from my desk and walked past my team. From the corner of my eye I caught a movement. I turned, ready to drop the box and draw my Glock. All three men followed my gaze. The shadow of a butterfly floated across the back wall of my office then paused before breaking into a million small silver butterflies. The swarm twisted across the room, out the door, and into the hallway.

"Ellie?" Kurt spoke first. "What was it?"

"The ghost of a butterfly," I replied walking out the door before anyone of them could raise a comment.

Rowan was waiting out in the bullpen with Sandra.

"Ready?" he said, walking over to me and taking the box from my arms.

"Yeah, let's go."

Let's go before I stay, or before I say something that jeopardizes the team dynamic.

Modern West was interrupted when a deep voice inside my head announced, "Elvis has left the building."

We are able to find everything in our memory, which is like a dispensary or chemical laboratory in which chance steers our hand sometimes to a soothing drug and sometimes to a dangerous poison.

Marcel Proust

About the author:

Cat Connor is a prolific crime thriller author hailing from New Zealand. Her expertise in the genre is reflected in her engaging and suspenseful narratives, which have garnered a loyal following. Her work is known for its intricate plots, dynamic characters, and relentless pace, keeping readers on the edge of their seats until the very end. She has authored multiple books, including the popular "Byte" series, which follows the exploits of an FBI unit that investigates serial crime.

Cat's passion for crime and espionage is evident in her writing, as she strives to create a world that is both authentic and thrilling. Her meticulous attention to detail and extensive research have won her critical acclaim and accolades from readers and peers alike. In addition to writing, Cat enjoys speaking on topics related to writing and publishing. Her talks are known for their candidness, humour, and practical advice. With her unique blend of talent, expertise, and passion, Cat Connor has established herself as one of the most exciting and accomplished authors in the crime thriller genre.

Her other passions include music, reading, tequila, red wine, coffee, and chocolate. When she's not writing she can be found binge watching TV shows and spending time with her much adored animals; Diesel the mastador, Patrick the tuxedo cat, Dallas the tortie Birman, and Jimmy the thug.

You can follow and contact Cat at the following places:

Website: www.catconnor.com
Twitter: @catconnor
Facebook: @cat.connor
Instagram: @catconnorauthor
Bluesky: @catconnor.bsky.social
Threads: @catconnorauthor

Also by Cat Connor:

If I were a carpenter - SSA Kurt Henderson's story (novella)

Array - a collection of short bytes

www.ingramcontent.com/pod-product-compliance
Lightning Source LLC
Chambersburg PA
CBHW030748030726
47497CB00001B/195